THE BLOOD
OF PATRIOTS
AND
TRAITORS

ALSO BY JAMES A. SCOTT

The Iran Contradictions
The President's Dossier

THE BLOOD OF PATRIOTS AND TRAITORS

A MAX GELLER SPY THRILLER

JAMES A. SCOTT

OCEANVIEW PUBLISHING

SARASOTA, FLORIDA

ISBN 978-1-60809-526-1

Published in the United States of America by Oceanview Publishing

Sarasota, Florida

www.oceanviewpub.com

10 9 8 7 6 5 4 3 2 1

PRINTED IN THE UNITED STATES OF AMERICA

"[T]he tree of liberty must be refreshed from time to time with the blood of patriots [and] tyrants."
—*Thomas Jefferson*

Jefferson's observation was the inspiration for this novel.

FOREWORD

READERS MAY APPRECIATE the predictive nature of this novel knowing that I began researching and writing it in September of 2019, approximately thirty months before Russia invaded Ukraine. My writing continued through the fall of 2021. During that period, the USA-NATO relationship was in question. At issue was whether or not the United States would help defend European nations that might come under attack, as required by Article 5 of the North Atlantic Treaty. In part, Article 5 states: ". . . an armed attack against one or more of the [NATO nations] in Europe or North America shall be considered an attack against all [and triggers] collective self-defense . . ."

I completed *The Blood of Patriots and Traitors* manuscript on October 18, 2021, approximately four months before Ukraine was invaded. That horrific event and those portrayed in this novel were not difficult to imagine. In his April 2005 address to the Russian people, Vladimir Putin said, "The breakup of the Soviet Union was the greatest geopolitical tragedy of the 20th century." Nine years later, when Russia invaded and occupied the Crimea, John Bolton, a future National Security Advisor to the White House, quoted Putin's 2005 lament and added, "It's clear [Putin] wants to re-establish Russian hegemony within the space of the former Soviet Union. Ukraine is the biggest prize. That's what he's after. The [recent] occupation of the Crimea is a step in that direction."

To quote the late Dr. Maya Angelou, "When people show you who they are, believe them the first time."

CAST OF CHARACTERS

Maxwell Geller—Former CIA officer, in Moscow and at CIA headquarters.

Vanessa Blake—CIA officer, Max's significant other from his past.

Prescott Hamilton (a.k.a. Rodney)—CIA officer, Max's former boss.

Jill Rucker—CIA officer, Max's former associate.

Eva Soriano—CIA officer, Rodney's deputy.

Sherri Layton—Max's friend, former CIA officer, now CEO of a security consulting firm.

Tony Davila (a.k.a. Tony-D)—Former U.S. Special Forces soldier, now engaged in private and governmental security projects. He is one of Sherri's *go-to* guys for difficult projects.

Alexi Petrov—Lieutenant Colonel (Promotable), Russian Army. RAMPART is his CIA code name. Olga Petrovna is his wife.

Konstantine Zabluda—Lieutenant Colonel, Russian Army, former assassin with Russian military intelligence, detailed to domestic counterintelligence with the Federal Security Service (FSB).

Ipatiev—Russian Army major, was deputy to Lieutenant Colonel Zabluda when they were in the field as assassins.

General Orlov—Zabluda's supervisor at the FSB.

Sergei Golovkin—An intelligence analyst with the FSB and Petrov's friend. CRYSTAL is his CIA code name, recruited by Max.

Colonel Burke—Army attaché at the U.S. Embassy in Moscow.

Boris Kuzmick—An FSB sergeant. Yulia Kuzmickova is his wife. They helped Max during a previous visit to Moscow.

Ted Walldrum—President of the United States.

General Douglas McClure—U.S. Army, Chairman of the Joint Chiefs of Staff.

The CIA director is unnamed to add mystery to her persona.

THE BLOOD OF PATRIOTS

OF PATRIOTS

AND

TRAITORS

CHAPTER 1

Thursday morning, January 2020
Bondi Beach, Sydney, Australia

I SAW HIM coming from way down the beach. I reached into the folds of my towel and thumbed the safety off my Colt .45. It's a big gun. When you point it at 'em, they pay attention. When you shoot 'em, they go down and they don't get up.

Next to me, Vanessa was lying facedown on the blanket. With my left hand, I gently squeezed her tanned thigh just below her skimpy, yellow bikini bottom.

"Van!"

She sat up with a start, responding to the urgency in my voice. "What?"

"A hundred yards at our ten o'clock. The suit walking in the surf, carrying his shoes."

Van shaded her eyes against the morning sun. "What's he doing on the beach in a suit?"

"Exactly."

Her instincts were sharp. Van stood, stretched, and used the opportunity to check our backs. She warned, "Another suit at your five o'clock, seventy yards out, headed this way."

"Go to the car. There's a gun in the glove compartment. Use it for your protection. I can handle these two. If there's any trouble, drive yourself to the consulate."

Van put on her sunglasses and big straw hat, and sauntered across the sand toward the carpark on the rise behind the beach.

British intelligence hoods—MI6—wanted to question me about a London burglary, a couple of blown operations, and a warehouse massacre. The Russians wanted me for bank robbery, murder, and skyjacking. With all those angry spies after me, I should have made myself harder to find. But everybody needs a relaxing day at the beach once in a while, and Thursday was mine—until the suits showed up.

As I turned to watch Van's shapely figure move toward the parking lot, I stole a glance at the suit coming from my right rear. He had shoes in his left hand, and his eyes were locked on me. He stopped, removed his coat, draped it over his shoulder, and held it there with his right hand. I glanced at the guy walking in the surf. He had removed his coat, too. Obviously, they had been warned about me. Both were signaling they weren't armed and their hands were full. That was the signal they were sending, but it didn't mean they weren't armed.

I stood and walked in Van's tracks back to the lifeguard tower, so that both suits had to approach me from my front. A couple of surfboards were propped against the two-by-four latticework that supported the tower. I stood with my back to them, in case there was a sniper somewhere behind me. The long beach towel draped over my shoulder hung down far enough to cover my right hand and the .45.

The two suits came together a few feet in front of me. The one I had spotted first wore a blue-and-white-striped seersucker suit. The other man wore a tan tropical worsted.

The tan suit said, "We come in peace."

"Lucky for you." I moved the towel a little so they could see my gun.

They smiled.

"It doesn't take two of you to declare peace. Which one is the spokesman?"

The tan suit lifted his loafers.

I turned to the seersucker suit. "Go down to the water's edge and stay there."

"As you wish." He turned and headed for the surf, swinging his shoes.

I asked the tan suit, "What do you want?"

"Max Geller."

"You've got him. Who are you and why do you want me?"

"We're from the Company. Rodney sent us. He needs you to come back for a job."

I laughed. It wasn't a nice laugh. "Maybe he shouldn't have fired me. Screw him."

"Rodney warned us you'd say something like that."

"If Rodney knows me so damned well, you wouldn't be here. I've got money in the bank, the woman I love on a beach in Australia, and the wound in my back where Rodney stuck his bureaucratic knife. Why in hell would I ever go back to the CIA?"

"Rodney hoped you'd do it for your country. There's a Russian in Moscow with information vital to our national security. He wants to defect and he wants you to bring him over. He won't trust anyone else."

"He's one smart Russian. I wouldn't trust you either, and I don't trust this defector. He could be a dangle to lure me back to Moscow. I'm a wanted man there."

"Yeah, we heard you robbed a bank in Moscow. Is that true?"

"Yes."

"Man, that was some serious badass. How much did you get?"

"Enough evidence of corruption to ruin careers in Washington." True. "And ten million dollars." Not directly from the robbery, but it doesn't hurt to feed my legend.

He whistled in admiration. "Did you keep it?"

"Every penny." Minus taxes.

When the moment of awe passed, tan suit remembered his errand. "Well, we don't believe the Russians are setting a trap for you. One of our Moscow assets vouched for the defector."

"I don't care if Mother Teresa vouched for him, I'm not going back to Russia."

The tan suit smirked. "Rodney said you'd probably say that, too. If you did, he wanted me to tell you that he'll be forced to go to Plan B, and you won't like it."

"What the hell is Plan B?"

"Ask your girlfriend, Vanessa . . . next time you see her."

My first emotion was concern for Vanessa. Before I could wrestle with the sinister possibilities of Rodney's Plan B, survival instincts in my reptilian brain went on alert. The trigger was two other men carrying beach gear approaching us from the direction of the surf. They were wearing ensembles right out of the *Are You Kidding Me? Beachwear Catalog*: sunglasses, gold chains, and crotch-grabbing swim trunks. Their outlandish flowery shirts were open, exposing chests that were hairy, beefy, and white, white like this was their first day at the beach since birth. They were striding toward us with a little too much purpose.

They must have seen my attention shift to them, but for sure they knew the game was up when I said to tan suit, "Get down, now!" and he dove sideways, landing facedown in the sand. The two hairy guys dropped the beach junk—blankets, towels, umbrella, cooler—and out came the guns.

It was easy to decide who to shoot first, the guy with the sawed-off shotgun. I had to put him down for good. If he got off a blast, that might be the end for me. Even as I fired two shots at the place where his heart was supposed to be, I knew it was one bullet too many. His partner was going to get off one—maybe two—shots at me, before I could even look at him. I dove to my left so I wouldn't land on my shooting arm. When I landed, he had me covered, and smiled.

A hole the size of a golf ball appeared in his chest. He screamed and did a moonwalk backwards and collapsed in front of a third man who had dropped to his knees in the sand. The kneeler was unmoved by this little display of mayhem. He was holding his pistol in both hands and aiming at me.

Before either of us could shoot, his head exploded. It was obvious that I had a friendly shooter somewhere behind me—maybe it was Van shooting from our car. But with a Glock at that range? No way. The two Agency suits had vanished into the panicked, scattering sunbathers. I raced across the sand and up the steps to the parking lot.

When I got to my rental, Van was gone, the driver's door was ajar, key in the ignition. Panicked, I scanned the street. No sign of her. My spare gun was still in the glove box. There was a note under the windshield wiper, driver's side. It read, "Go home and wait." Unsigned. The note was typed, which meant that Rodney had anticipated my refusal to go back to Moscow, or not. It could have been left by friends of the shooters who died on the beach. I started to sweat as a wave of concern and fear washed over me.

On the beach below, there was pandemonium. Women were screaming. Gawkers had formed a wide circle around the three dead bodies. Of course, tens of cell phone cams were recording the scene as visions of viral internet mayhem danced in the sick minds of the photographers. The cops were a wailing siren away. I had to be gone when they arrived.

I drove to the apartment I had rented for our week of sun and sand. Van wasn't there. I couldn't call the police. I would have to admit I was at the beach. If Rodney had Van, I wasn't worried. She worked for the Agency. On the other hand, if she had been taken by friends of the men who had just tried to kill me, they would use her to get to me. That meant they would be showing up at the apartment soon. I got out of my swim trunks and into jeans and a polo shirt. With a shot of scotch and a couple of spare clips for my .45, I settled down to wait.

Whoever had taken Vanessa let me stew until early afternoon before I heard a key in the lock. To my great relief, she entered the apartment. I wrapped my arms around her. "Are you okay?"

"I'm fine." Van didn't look distressed; she looked pleased. "I knew you were worried, Max. They wouldn't let me call. Sorry."

I didn't care. I was relieved that she was with me and safe. "What happened?"

"When I went to the car, a couple of people from my office scooped me up and took me to Rodney."

"Did you see what happened on the beach after you left me?'

She was concerned. "No. What happened?"

"Tell you later. Where's Rodney?"

"In a house nearby. He wants to see you. The car that brought me here is waiting for you."

"What did Rodney say to you?"

"He offered me a new assignment."

I got an uneasy feeling. "Can you tell me about it?"

"Rodney wanted me to tell you. He's sending me to Moscow to plan the exfiltration of an important defector."

"Son-of-a-bitch! That's his Plan B!"

Van looked puzzled. "What are you talking about?"

"The suits on the beach this morning, they said Rodney wanted me to bring out the defector. When I refused, they told me to ask you about Plan B. Rodney's using you to blackmail me into doing the job."

Van pushed me away. "No!"

"Yes! The defector asked for me."

She got defensive. "Well . . . you refused, and Rodney asked me. I'm going to do it."

"Van, listen to me. Moscow is the toughest operational environment in the world for a spy. Before the CIA sends people to Russia, they get months of training specifically for that assignment."

"I know that. Rodney's going to give me a crash course in Moscow tradecraft."

"*Crash* is the right word."

Her lips went thin and her hands went to her hips.

I needed a more persuasive argument. "Let's assume you attended the yearlong Moscow prep course—you didn't. Let's assume you speak fluent Russian—you don't. And suppose you have trusted Moscow contacts—you have none—who can verify the existence of this defector. Let's assume you have all these tools. What happens when you go to meet this defector and he turns out to be a squad of FSB thugs? What happens then?"

After a thoughtful pause, Van said, "I'm not you. They'll harass me and expel me from the country."

"No! That's not what happens. They saw us together in Australia. They know you're important to me. So, they have a bargaining chip. They'll throw you into a cell at Lubyanka. Then, they'll call Langley and offer to trade you—a serving CIA officer—for me—a disgraced former employee, wanted in Russia for murder and bank robbery. That," I pointed my finger at her, "is a five-minute-decision meeting on the Seventh Floor, and I'm on my way to Moscow in handcuffs and leg irons."

There are times when people see only what they want. That was Vanessa's time. "What if the defector is real? Getting him out is a career-maker, if I pull it off. I want my shot. You took yours. You got rich. Don't deny me mine."

"Okay. I get it; you want your shot, but in an op like this, you plan for the worst case. Worst Case 1: You go to Moscow. It's a trap for me. You become an embarrassment to the Agency and it's a black mark on your career. I get traded for you and executed after a show trial.

"Worst Case 2. I go to Moscow and it's a trap. They have me. I get executed after a show trial. I leave you enough money so you can have any life you want. Your career is intact. You get another shot at that career-maker, if you still want it."

She went defensive. "What about the best case, if I go to Moscow?"

"If you go to Moscow, I have to gamble my freedom that you're right and there is a real defector. I'm not willing to make that bet."

Van folded her arms across her chest and glared at me. I had seen that stance and look before. She was through listening. I went to see Rodney.

CHAPTER 2

Three months earlier, October 2019
Moscow's Defense Military Management Center, the Russian Pentagon

WHEN LIEUTENANT COLONEL Alexi Petrov left the top-secret briefing, he knew he had to defect.

Key military commanders involved in the operation were present in the auditorium. The Minister of Defense spoke to them from a ceiling-high screen at the front of the room. In front of the screen, generals and admirals sat at a circular table—the inner circle—in high-backed, white captain's chairs, their computers arrayed before them. Further away from the screen, three ascending sections of seats, separated by two aisles, rose from the floor to the back of the room in movie theater configuration, each row higher than the preceding one. These seats were filled by the staff officers of the brass down front. From the screen, the minister told them how, in a year, they would change the world. Petrov's thoughts turned to Putin, the ego behind this plan. It occurred to him that those who didn't fight wars never tired of starting them.

The auditorium was air-conditioned, but Petrov was on fire and perspiring. When the briefing was over, he zombie-walked through the security checkpoints and out of the building. On the steps, he leaned against the wall and coaxed a cigarette from the pack with shaking hands. He lit it, inhaled deeply, and let the cool air wash over him. With luck, none of the two thousand cameras in and around the complex would record his apparent distress and trigger an inquiry.

Petrov pushed himself off the wall and straightened his spine, as a squad of four black-clad security guards passed in the street that separated the building from the high spiked fence that circled the complex. He tried to appear in control, but fear clawed at his gut and depression had seized his mind, blotting out all but images of the dead. Petrov wanted to scream and run. Colonels do not run screaming through military compounds, if they want to remain colonels . . . and free. He had to see Sergei. Who else would talk to a suicidal army officer and not report him to the security services?

*   *   *

The next morning, Petrov watched from across the street as Sergei Golovkin exited the school where he deposited his daughter each morning, before walking to the corner café for coffee. When Sergei was settled with coffee and a newspaper, Petrov approached his table.

Looking up, Sergei said, "Alexi!" He rose with a smile and gave his friend a bear hug and aimed two cheek kisses that intentionally missed their marks. "Sit with me. How are things on our invincible general staff?"

"Hell."

"It's better than eating sand in Syria. Two more years on the staff and you can retire."

"I won't be in Moscow for two more years. Can we talk in your car?"

When they were seated in the car, Sergei asked, "What's wrong?"

"I'm to be promoted and they've ordered me to take a brigade . . . into combat."

"They're sending you back to Syria?"

"No. They're opening a new front. That's all I can say."

"Oh, Alexi . . ." Sergei gave his friend a sorrowful look.

Petrov looked away and shook his head. "Chechnya, Crimea, Syria," he turned back to his friend, "I can't wade in any more blood, Sergei. Before I let them send me into combat again, I would—"

"Don't say it," warned Sergei. "Don't even think about harming yourself again. Next time, I may not be there to stop you. Think of your family."

"I think of my family all the time. I think about killing them, too."

His voice tense with concern, Sergei said, "You need to get help. Talk to a professional about those feelings."

"Where would I get this help, from our patriotic psychiatrists, trained to think that citizens who disagree with the state are crazy?" Petrov chuckled grimly. "The irony is their diagnosis would be correct in my case."

"Then, get away from the pressure of the job. Retire."

"And live on a lieutenant colonel's pension . . . the way Olga spends money?"

"Retire and take the bank job Olga's father offered you in Cyprus."

Petrov sighed. "It's just another government job, with duties related to the security services. I might as well be working at the ministry."

"The Cyprus climate is mild and the salary generous. You and Olga can maintain your lifestyle. What more do you want?"

"I want to be free of this government."

Sergei exhaled heavily. "We're Russian, my friend. We were not meant to be free."

Petrov looked forlorn.

Sergei said, "There must be someone in Moscow who can help you."

"There is. That's why I'm here." Petrov leaned into his companion. "You are my best friend. I love you. You know my secrets. I would never reveal yours. Do you believe me?"

Sergei said a wary, "Yes . . . of course."

"I hope so, because I know one of your secrets. Last December, I had that nightmare again. I needed to talk. I came here to catch you before you went to work. I saw you sitting in this car, talking to a man. Days later, I saw his face on television. They said he was Maxwell Geller, a CIA agent who robbed a bank and killed several employees."

"Alexi—"

Petrov raised his palm. "You don't owe me an explanation, Sergei. I assume it was FSB-CIA business and none of mine. All I want from you is the name of a CIA contact. I want to defect. I have to get out of Russia. I can't go into combat again. I can't!"

After a pause, Sergei said, "This is a very dangerous time to contact the CIA. I wouldn't trust anyone at their Moscow Station. Anything you tell them could end up on Ted Walldrum's desk in the White House, along with your name. If it gets back to the Kremlin, you won't have to fantasize about killing yourself. The state will do it for you."

"You are dealing with the CIA. Don't you have that same worry?"

"Yes, but I made my commitment long before the current Washington leadership came to power. Either the CIA can protect my identity or it can't. It's out of my hands."

"How do you live with that threat?"

"I assume that I'm already a dead man. I just keep trying to fool myself and everyone around me that I'm not. I wake up. I kiss my wife. I hug my child. I carry on . . . and watch for signs that the FSB is onto me. It's stressful. I haven't contacted the CIA for months."

"What about Maxwell Geller? You talked to him. You trusted him."

"I knew Max years ago when he was stationed in Moscow. When you saw us talking last year, he was no longer with the CIA. They fired him for saying unkind things about his president. That should be a lesson to you."

"Do you still trust him?"

"Yes."

"I want him to get me out. How can I contact him?"

"I have no idea. Last year, he came out of nowhere to question me about a couple of murders and Ted Walldrum's alleged activities with prostitutes at the Riga-Ritz. That was our only conversation. I never saw him again. I don't know when he came to Moscow. I wouldn't have known when he left, had he not robbed the bank and hijacked a plane to France. When I heard of him again, one of our front companies in Panama had paid him five million dollars for a video that would have implicated the SVR"—the Russian foreign intelligence service—"in wet work."

Petrov was animated. "This man has courage, Sergei. I want him to get me out. There must be some way to contact him. Think."

Sergei sipped his cold coffee and searched his memory. "There was an American woman in Moscow with Max, Sherri Layton. She owns a private security firm outside of Washington, D.C. Layton might know where Max is, but how would you contact her? Even if you could, I doubt she would put you in touch with him, and Max would have to be insane to return to Moscow."

CHAPTER 3

Days later, November 2019
FSB Headquarters on Lubyanka Square, Moscow

Lieutenant Colonel Konstantine Zabluda accompanied Colonel Dragonov to General Orlov's office. FSB headquarters was a new posting for both men and this was their first meeting with the general.

The general asked, "What progress have you made on the surveillance of the suspected traitor, Sergei Golovkin?"

While Dragonov, the senior of the two, took the lead and droned on, giving details of surveillance schedules, and the placement of microphones and cameras, Zabluda examined the simplicity of the general's office. It contained little of the usual memorabilia of a senior officer's career. There were only three photographs. One was the obligatory official portrait of the Russian Federation president hanging behind the general's no-frills desk. The second was a recent picture of the general and his extended family on the credenza behind the desk. Beside it stood a decades-old, framed photograph of the current Russian president in his KGB uniform, taken at the Brandenburg Gate in Berlin. Standing next to the president was a younger version of the general seated before Zabluda. The general-to-be was in the uniform of a KGB lieutenant. *This man has no need for the trappings of power*, Zabluda thought. *He is wired directly into the power source.*

Dragonov was saying, "During the period we have been surveilling Sergei Golovkin, he has taken no questionable actions and made no suspicious contacts."

The general said, "Let me see the contact list."

Dragonov handed it over and waited while the general scanned it.

"Zabluda, you're my army expert on this project," said the general. "Who is this Lieutenant Colonel Petrov? He met with Golovkin last week?"

"Sir, Petrov and Golovkin have been friends since childhood. They grew up together, attended the same university, and joined the army together. Golovkin went into military intelligence. Later, he was recruited by the FSB. Petrov joined the tank troops."

"What is Petrov's job?"

"He's a war plans officer on the general staff."

Eager not to be left out, Dragonov said, "As a precaution, I think we should alert the GRU"—military intelligence— "that Petrov is meeting with the traitor, Sergei Golovkin."

"*Suspected* traitor," corrected the general. "And why don't we take out a television ad that Golovkin is under suspicion. Then, we could sit on our hands for years while our suspect breaks contact with his CIA handler and goes underground . . . *if* he is a traitor and *if* there is a CIA handler."

General Orlov gave Dragonov a chilling glare. "It was rash decisions that cost you your command in St. Petersburg. Only the intervention of the deputy director saved you from a harsh fate. You need to be less impulsive and more circumspect, Dragonov. Lose another American spy and that fate may find you."

Zabluda allowed himself a brief smile.

The general continued to address Dragonov. "The next time Petrov meets Golovkin, put a team on the colonel. Let's see who he talks to after he meets with our suspect. That's all."

Dragonov saluted and shot an envious look at Zabluda on the way out.

When he had gone, General Orlov turned to Zabluda. "Tell me about Petrov. What sort of officer is he?"

"Very heroic on the battlefield and highly competent on the general staff. A hard worker and a hard drinker, according to my sources."

The general sat back. "Vodka problems?"

"No."

"Married?"

"With two grown children, girl and boy. University graduates. Both are FSB officers."

"Mistresses?"

"No, sir."

"How would you characterize the key element of his personality?"

"Aggressive. He produces results regardless of obstacles."

With sarcasm, the general observed, "A genuine hero of the Russian Federation. Our Colonel Petrov is an aggressive tank troops commander, hard fighter, hard drinker, and handsome. Tell me, Zabluda, what do you think are the chances of finding that combination of traits in one man . . . and no mistress?"

"I'll look again, sir."

The general grunted. "Build a dossier on this *hero*. Be discreet. Incorporate the results of Dragonov's surveillance."

The general looked toward the window and paused before he spoke. "Be wary of Dragonov, Zabluda. The man is ambitious, arrogant, and a fool with a powerful patron. In my experience, those are the ingredients of an incompetence time bomb. The only questions are, 'When will it explode?' and 'Who will be caught in the blast radius?' You've been singed once. Make sure you're not at ground zero the next time."

The general left his chair, went to the window, and looked out, hands clasped behind him. He turned and gave Zabluda a hard look. "You found my warning to Dragonov amusing?"

Zabluda immediately regretted the smile.

"The same admonition applies to you. Both of you are here on probation. Both of you bungled the surveillance of Maxwell Geller when he illegally entered Russia last December. Your job was to find him, kill him, kill his Russian informants, and destroy the evidence he collected on the American president. You failed. To put the icing on your fiasco, you stole—attempted to steal—money we used to lure Geller into your trap. Those circumstances would have been a death sentence for most men. Do you know why you are still alive?"

Zabluda replied, "No doubt because the evidence Geller collected has disappeared."

"No," said the general. "You're alive because our president prevented your execution."

Zabluda was shocked. He knew someone had intervened, but Putin? "Why did he do it?"

"The president was impressed that you killed the traitor Bogdanovich and his MI6 protectors in the heart of London last year, and for uncovering the spy, Kulik, in our London embassy. He forgave you your larcenous tendencies and for letting Geller get away with the evidence he collected. Lucky for you, that evidence hasn't surfaced. Why do you think that is, Zabluda?"

"Maybe Geller is using it to blackmail his president."

"Maybe? I don't like *maybes*. This is an intelligence organization. You are paid to bring me facts. Let me give you two. One, if the evidence Geller collected is used to remove the President of the United States from office, you are a dead man. Two, if you and that fool Dragonov make a cockup of the Sergei Golovkin investigation, both of you are dead men. Those are not *maybes*."

The general continued. "The president was impressed with you. I am not impressed by a thief who couldn't keep what he stole or an assassin who, with all the resources of the Moscow security services at his disposal, couldn't find Maxwell Geller before he robbed a bank and hijacked a plane to make his escape. The president can afford to be forgiving. I cannot. So, you had better impress me with the Golovkin investigation."

General Orlov returned to his desk. "I don't approve of what you were doing with your revenge unit. I think killing old spies and traitors is not a deterrent to treason. Do you know why, Zabluda?"

"No, sir."

"You're a combat veteran. Have you ever fought men who were outnumbered and knew they were going to die?"

"I have, many times."

"How would you characterize their mindset in those circumstances? Were they inclined to give up or . . . ?"

"They tried to kill as many of us as they could before we killed them."

"In other words, they were dead men, they knew it, and their goal was to cause as much damage as possible before the reckoning."

"Yes, sir."

"So it is with traitors. I have studied them. Most don't become traitors for money or for a flat near London's nightlife or a condominium in some Washington bedroom community. They become traitors for ideological reasons. They betray us because they despise our system of government, a colossus so vast they have little chance of changing it. They know this, but like your outnumbered and outgunned former adversaries, they try to do as much damage as possible before they die. Aside from the ill will of other nations, nothing is to be gained by pursuing these traitors once they have fled Russian soil, because killing them will never deter like-minded men. I have so advised the president. Obviously, he does not agree with me. So, here you are."

"Sir, I don't understand why I'm here. If you disagree with what I do, how can you certify me for return to those duties?"

"You're not here for me to re-certify you as an assassin. The president is well aware of your talents in that department. You're here for me to determine if you are anything more than a blunt instrument. Evidently, the president hopes you have something to contribute to Mother Russia other than the dead bodies of old traitors. So, you had better show me something, Zabluda, and I am not easily impressed."

CHAPTER 4

Thursday afternoon, January 2020
Sydney, Australia

VANESSA WAS ANGRY because I didn't want her going to Moscow to bring out the damned defector. She didn't care that the defector story might be a fabrication to trap me.

The car Rodney sent Vanessa home in after she disappeared from Bondi Beach was waiting downstairs. It took me to a small house on a quiet street, not far from the St. Anne Catholic Church. A taciturn, middle-aged Hispanic woman I knew as Eva Soriano opened the door before I could ring the bell. She wore a black pantsuit and white blouse, and her thick black hair in a French roll. The last time I had seen her swarthy face and penetrating dark eyes was in another safe-house with Rodney. He was trying to decide whether to shoot me or let me live with the political secret of the century in my head. I never knew whether Eva was Rodney's gofer, guard, or mistress. Maybe all three.

Eva directed me to a first-floor sitting room. "Wait in there. Rodney's on a call."

"Where's the bathroom?" I asked.

It was down the hall, past a couple of doors.

On my way back, one of those doors was open and Jill Rucker was leaning against the frame giving me a clinical appraisal. "Long time, no see, Max."

"It hasn't been long enough." Jill had tried to shoot me two years ago. "Why are you here?"

She smiled. "I just came along to see how the other half lives . . . now that you've got all that money. It didn't help you this morning, though. I hear you almost got your ass shot off on Bondi Beach and your girlfriend had to save you." Over her shoulder, I could see a table draped with a sheet. It was covered with the disassembled components of an AMXC sniper rifle, scope, and silencer. There was a cleaning kit on the floor.

Eva came at us with a stern look. "Play nice, children. We all have to share the sandbox." To me, she said, "Rodney's ready for you."

Eva led me upstairs to a room where Rodney was sipping tea and looking at a televised soccer match. Even in casual attire—linen pants, polo shirt, and polished penny loafers—he looked as though he had just been released from the care of his valet. Eva turned off the TV and closed the door as she left the room.

Cup and saucer in one hand, Rodney stood and offered his other for a shake. I declined. "No thanks. I don't want to catch anything."

He shrugged. "Same old insolent Max. It's comforting to know that some people don't change. Thank you for coming. Tea or scotch?"

"Screw the pleasantries. You aren't really going to send Vanessa to Moscow, are you?"

Carefully, Rodney placed his cup and saucer on the small table beside his chair, sat down, and laced his fingers across his stomach. "Since you don't want to go, I propose to send the person closest to you. As a bonus, she wants the job. We'll get word to our would-be defector that Vanessa is your capable colleague and lover. He can take her or rot in Moscow. What do you think he'll do?"

"I think you're using Vanessa to force me to bring out your defector. Why me?"

"Because the defector asked for you, by name. He won't deal with our guys at Moscow Station. All I want you to do is go to Moscow, contact our defector—by the way, his codename is RAMPART—and assess the situation. When it's safe to travel, notify Moscow Station. Our guys will do the rest. Don't tell RAMPART that Moscow Station is involved. He might balk. Tell him it's your guys, your plan, and you will be overseeing the execution of it."

"Who is this defector and why did he ask for me?"

"His name is Alexi Petrov. He's a war plans officer at the Russian Defense Ministry. He wants you because CRYSTAL recommended you as being trustworthy."

CRYSTAL was the CIA codename for Sergei Golovkin, a Russian asset I recruited years ago when I worked out of our embassy in Moscow. I met Sergei again, two years ago, during my ill-fated trip to Russia. He was helpful, but wary of our Moscow Station staff.

I said, "If your defector really wants to get out of Russia, he'll talk to whoever's driving the bus. Send somebody from Moscow Station to make contact with the guy."

"We've done that. RAMPART didn't respond. He will not talk to anyone but you."

"How does . . . RAMPART know what I look like? Send in a ringer from Moscow Station and tell him to pretend he's me."

"RAMPART knows what you look like because your face was on every Russian newspaper and TV screen after your Moscow bank shootout."

I couldn't see a way out of this mess. If I had to go in, I needed all the facts. "Did somebody from Moscow Station ask CRYSTAL if he vouched for the defector and recommended me?"

"The defector said CRYSTAL vouched for him. Unfortunately, CRYSTAL—like the rest of our Moscow assets—has gone dark.

They won't accept meetings and they're not clearing messages from their dead drops."

"Why?"

"The FSB has stepped up its counterintelligence activities. Either they suspect some of our assets or there is some other reason for their increased diligence. The other problem could be our president. Considering that he and Putin are chums, our Russian assets may be afraid their names could appear in Walldrum's daily intelligence briefing and end up on Putin's desk." Rodney made a face like he'd gotten a whiff of an unpleasant odor. "We haven't gotten a decent piece of intelligence out of Moscow since you and Jill Rucker brought us the keys to the Russian money laundering operation in Panama and that other material we agreed never to discuss."

"If RAMPART won't talk to the CIA, how did you get the word that he wants me?"

"RAMPART knows our military attaché in Moscow, a Colonel Burke, U.S. Army. They were posted in Egypt at the same time a few years ago. RAMPART attended a welcoming reception for Burke when he arrived in Moscow a couple of months ago. During the festivities, RAMPART slipped Burke a thumb drive containing some classified documents and a request for your services."

"Addressed to the CIA?"

"Addressed to your friend and our former CIA colleague Sherri Layton, asking her to contact you. Burke brought the thumb drive and request to us." Rodney gave me a suspicious look. "How do you suppose RAMPART got Ms. Layton's name and the fact that she lives in Northern Virginia?"

I shrugged. "The Russians do have an intelligence service. They probably discovered that Sherri and I dated before she left the Agency." They also knew that Sherri and Jill were with me in 2018 when I went to Russia and got the goods on President Walldrum. That was the material we agreed never to discuss—the material that Rodney and company buried, and then fired me.

"Can I see the note?" I asked

Rodney smiled. "No. It contains classified information."

The more I heard, the less I was inclined to go back to Moscow. "So, all you know about RAMPART is that he told you he works in the Russian Defense Ministry and wants to defect?"

"We know enough."

"I don't. What I *do* know is you don't want me anywhere near the Agency, after what happened to that material we agreed never to discuss. I know too much. So, tell me why this Russian is important enough for you to drag me into an Agency operation. What bait did RAMPART dangle to get you that desperate?"

Rodney was slow to answer. He looked away, probably trying to decide how much—or which lie—to tell me. Finally, he said, "I'm afraid you're not cleared for that either."

I was angry when I got there. Rodney's razzle-dazzle didn't improve my mood. "This story is bullshit. How do I know—how do you know—it isn't a trap to lure me back to Moscow so the Russians can put me on trial and execute me?"

"We've considered that possibility . . . and discarded it."

"I'll bet you have, just like you discarded me and the evidence of Walldrum's Moscow connections before you fired me." There, I had said what I had promised never to say. Rodney bristled and I didn't care. I wanted to get under his skin. "Come to think of it, if I shot you right now, nobody would have to go to Moscow for your defector."

As soon as I spoke the words, Eva opened the door without knocking. She held a gun next to her thigh and glared at me as she asked Rodney, "Is there a problem?" The implication being if there was a problem, it was going to be mine.

"It's all right, Eva," Rodney assured her.

She asked, "What do you want to do with him?"

"Send him to Moscow. Give us a moment, please . . . and take his gun with you."

Eva relieved me of my .45 and departed. This time, she didn't close the door.

Rodney took his favorite .32 automatic from beneath the chair cushion and held it in his lap. He studied me briefly and made a decision. "As bait, RAMPART gave us Russian defense policy papers and parts of the Russian war plan for Syria. Satisfied?"

"I'd be satisfied if he'd given you *our* war plan for Syria. Do we have one?"

That cut too close to the bone for Rodney to appreciate my humor. He gave me a bored look. "Who's going to Moscow, you or Vanessa?"

I was sure Rodney wasn't going to shoot me unless I attacked him. I was equally sure he would send Vanessa to Moscow just to spite me. He was holding the trump cards. I conceded.

"I'll go, but I'm a wanted criminal in Russia. How do I get in and out?"

"I have a rather ingenious plan to get you in." That meant it was his plan. "You're going to become a Russian. You'll have to go to Germany for prep and be launched from there."

"That's the only good news I've heard today, but why Germany."

"First, some background." Rodney loved to share background. It displayed his superior knowledge. "Last summer, in Berlin, a former Chechen troop commander was killed by a Russian assassin. The Germans captured the shooter."

"Was he a member of Putin's revenge squad, Zabluda's outfit?"

"Yes, but Zabluda is off the grid, thanks to you." Rodney inclined his head to one side. "Tell me, how did you get the Russians to sideline Zabluda and pay you all that money?"

"I had a good lawyer and a piece of damning evidence: Zabluda on video, killing people. The Russians had to pay or go to court and watch their wet work aired in public."

"You're a ruthless character, Max."

I agreed. "What's the plan to get me, RAMPART, and his wife out of Moscow?"

"A diplomatic flight straight to the States. When you're ready to exfiltrate, call Colonel Burke at our embassy. He'll pick you up and smuggle you onto the plane."

"Why is the Army involved?"

"RAMPART knows Burke. We want RAMPART to feel comfortable."

"What's the back-up plan for moving RAMPART, if there's a problem with the flight?"

"Moscow Station is working on that."

"This op has been in the works for a couple of months, and there's no back-up plan?"

"I told you, we're working on it."

"No, you're not. You're putting all your money on the diplomatic flight because you want to get this guy out of Russia fast. What's the problem, Rodney? Are you afraid he'll change his mind? Or does he have some hot intel you need right now?"

Rodney didn't answer.

A plan that depends on everything going smoothly is a plan to fail. Things can go wrong and often do. When that happens, you need a back-up plan. Survival in Russia can depend on following the unofficial guidance in a collection of one-liners for Western spies called Moscow Rules. My own contribution to that collection is a line delivered by Robert De Niro's character in the movie, *Ronin*: "I don't walk into any place I don't know how to walk out of."

I told Rodney, "I'm not going back to Moscow with only one way out. I don't want to be standing on some street corner, holding a Russian defector's hand, waiting for a taxi that never comes. And remember, RAMPART could be bait to trap me. So, here's my back-up plan. When I get to Moscow, I want a car on the Platnaya Parkovka parking lot at Leningradsky Train Station. Something powerful, black, and official-looking, but not ostentatious. Keys in a magnetic box in the right rear wheel, ten thousand euros and ten thousand rubles concealed in the rear-door panels, along with travel documents for me, RAMPART, and his wife. Make RAMPART an FSB lieutenant colonel and me a low-level FSB driver.

"In the trunk, I want three days' rations of water and MREs"— meals, ready to eat—"for three people, an FSB uniform for me, and two license plate changes, with matching registration papers. Throw in a couple of AK-47s and four loaded banana clips."

Rodney snorted. "How about some hand grenades and an anti-tank weapon?"

"How about a *yes* or a *no*?"

Rodney said a reluctant, "Yes. Moscow Station will have the car in place when you arrive."

"When I get to Moscow, I'll check. If the car's there, I'll make contact with RAMPART. If not, game over, and I'll get out of Moscow as best I can."

"Fair enough, but I think you are overreacting."

"Think what you want. You won't be there."

"It would be best to move RAMPART on a Friday or Saturday. That way, he won't be missed at work until Monday."

"What's the schedule for the diplomatic flight?"

"Moscow Station will have it on alert from next Friday evening until Monday morning. That should give you adequate flexibility. I hope those arrangements meet with your approval. We tried to think of everything."

"Everything except the part where some beat cop recognizes me, and I get thrown into Lubyanka prison."

Rodney's smile melted. "I suppose that's where the AKs come into play."

Somewhere in the house, a telephone rang. I heard the floor creek as Eva left her post outside the door, presumably to answer it.

Rodney asked, "Did you follow the news of the Berlin assassination, or were you too busy wallowing in gaudy luxuries with your fellow *nouveau riche*?"

I didn't like his smug tone. So, I gave him the needle. "When you have millions tucked away, like I do, no news is good news." I knew he resented the fact that the guy he fired on a trumped-up charge used the opportunity to make a fortune.

Rodney continued, "Even if you had been following the news, you wouldn't have known that the Russian spotter for the Berlin hit got away."

I had followed the story. "There was no mention of a spotter in the news."

"That was as planned. We—and the Germans—wanted the Russians to think we weren't aware of the spotter. He's an element of an emerging *modus operandi* for Russian hit squads in Western countries. The Russians have compartmented these operations. Russian foreign intelligence locates the target. A spotter goes in to establish the target's behavior pattern. An assassin—or team of assassins—will come in and execute the hit. Immediately after, the assassins leave the country, usually flying to Russia on Aeroflot. Sometimes the spotter departs with the assassins; sometimes he moves to the next target. After the Chechen hit in Berlin, the spotter went to Heidelberg, Germany, your old stomping ground. That's where you're going. The spotter is your target and your ticket to Russia. I have a team in Heidelberg working out the details. They will brief you when you arrive."

Eva entered the room, ignored me, and whispered in Rodney's ear.

Rodney looked up at her with concern. "When is it going to happen?"

Eva whispered to him again.

"Mr. Geller's transportation?" asked Rodney.

"I've adjusted it to the new schedule."

Rodney said a firm, "Thank you," Eva's cue to leave. This time, she closed the door.

Rodney looked worried. "The timetable for your trip to Moscow has accelerated. You'll need to leave for Germany immediately. Eva has your tickets and a new passport. I can have a car take you to your apartment to pack, but I'm afraid a long goodbye with Vanessa won't be possible."

I didn't want a goodbye with Vanessa, long or short. She would be angry that I was going to Moscow, not her. Saying goodbye would only intensify her anger at a stolen career opportunity.

I told Rodney, "I don't want to explain this to Vanessa. I'll leave that to you. Can you have someone turn in my rental car and close out my apartment?"

"Of course."

"Is this a paid mission or straight up blackmail, with Vanessa as hostage?"

"Eva has a contract for your signature. Time to go."

As I walked to the door, Rodney added, "Considering the circumstances of your departure from the Agency, I understand that you don't trust me. Believe me when I tell you getting RAMPART out is much more important than any unpleasantness in our relationship. I wouldn't have dragged you away from your new life to quarterback a run-of-the-mill defection."

"Save the pep talk, Rodney. The only reason I'm going to Moscow is so that Vanessa doesn't have to. I don't care if RAMPART promised you Putin's schedule for world conquest." I could have left it there, but being manipulated galled me. I wanted him to sweat while I was in Moscow. "You know what I'm thinking?"

"Do tell. I flunked mind reading."

"I'm thinking about the last time you sent me to Russia. I bribed and shot my way from St. Petersburg to Moscow and brought you enough evidence to bury Ted Walldrum. You buried the evidence instead and fired me, and Walldrum is still in the White House."

"That wasn't my call."

"You agreed with it. Now, I'm the only one outside of government who knows what you all did and why. That must keep your little circle of Washington conspirators awake at night. And here you are again, selling me a ticket to Russia and some fairy tale about a defector."

"This is different, Max."

"Is it? If the Russians had caught me two years ago, they'd have buried me and the evidence I collected, saving you the trouble of doing it for them. That would have been a win-win. If this defector story is a lure so the Russians can catch me, it's the win-win you didn't get two years ago. The Russians get their justice. You and the bureaucrats who buried the Walldrum evidence get to stop worrying about who I might tell. I'll check out this RAMPART character, but if he uses the letters *F*, *S*, and *B* in the same sentence I'll kill him. Then, I'm coming for you."

CHAPTER 5

THE CAR THAT took me to Sydney's airport was an upgrade from the one that brought me to Rodney. It was a heavy Mercedes with a thick plexiglass privacy petition separating Eva and me in the back from George, the driver, and Jill, riding shotgun. George spoke not at all and was built like he spent his days in the prison weight room, while doing ten-to-twenty . . . and he looked like he had already done a "dime"—ten years, in underworld lingo.

Rodney sent Eva with me on the pretext of discussing the terms of my temporary employment contract and travel arrangements. I was given no excuse for Jill. I assumed the real reason for their presence was to keep me from bailing out, kidnapping Vanessa, and disappearing into the comfort of my substantial bank balance. I had considered that. This seemed to be one more instance of Rodney being a step ahead of me. Was it better to have him ahead or behind? Neither gave me comfort.

I reviewed my contract, signed two copies, and gave one to Eva. She gave me an envelope for my copy that already had my Australian post box address printed on it.

"You can mail that when you get to the airport. I don't think you want it in your pocket when you pass through Russian immigration."

"Maybe you can tell me how I'm supposed to get past Russian immigration."

"As Rodney told you, you're going to assume the identity of a Russian assassin."

"How am I supposed to do that?"

"You'll get the details in Heidelberg. The concept is simple." She raised her chin and looked down her nose. "Of course, the success of the deception depends on your skills."

This witch was just as snotty as Rodney. No wonder they got along so well.

She continued. "I understand you have a sharp wit. Maybe you'll enjoy a little spy joke from Rodney. One spy asks the other, 'How do you steal a Russian assassin's identity?' The other spy says, 'First, find a Russian assassin . . . and kill it. The rest is easy.'" She turned away from me with a satisfied smile.

"I wasn't aware that Rodney had a sense of humor."

"You don't know him as well as I do."

"I'm sure I don't."

She gave me a nasty look. The atmosphere got frosty and the conversation scarce. When we started seeing airport signs, Eva said, "We'll be flying business class. Our itinerary is from here to Frankfurt with a brief layover in Singapore. I—"

"Excuse me. Did you say *we*?"

"Yes. My job is to get you safely to Heidelberg."

"I know the way to Heidelberg, Eva. I don't need a babysitter to get me there."

"With MI6 and the Russians looking for you, you might want to reconsider your needs."

Eva handed me a passport. "For purposes of your safe travel to Germany, you're Albert John West. Remember the name and answer to it, if addressed."

I flipped to the picture page and memorized the particulars of my new ID.

As I moved to put the passport into my pocket, Eva snatched it. "I'll need this to arrange special treatment for us."

I would definitely surrender my passport for special treatment . . . as long as it wasn't in a small room with large, inquisitive men.

George parked the car and the four of us walked to the terminal. We found seats in a quiet restaurant corner and Eva left me in the tender care of George and Jill.

Jill scanned the passing crowd and announced, "You were predictable. With millions in the bank and no job, any intelligence officer with a brain knew you were coming here to chase after little Miss Iowa State Dairy Tits. The Russians aren't stupid."

"Why is it," I asked, "that on the few occasions we have spoken of the women in my life, you have had something nasty to say about them? Are you jealous?"

Jill took her eyes off the crowd long enough to give me an exaggerated look of incredulity. "You're kidding, right?" She turned back to assassin-spotting. "I just hate to see you chasing women who are not your type."

"And what is my type?"

"Midwest is your type, but definitely not Iowa. You would be at home with someone more sophisticated, like someone from Chicago."

"Aren't you from Chicago?"

Before we could finish that conversation, Eva appeared and gave George a nod.

He uttered his first and last words, "Safe trip, Eva."

That triggered a thought. "Speaking of safety, Eva, how are you going to defend me if the Russians walk in here and start shooting or try to kill me on the plane?'

"We're armed."

"That's comforting." Sarcasm. "How are you getting your guns past security?"

"Jill and I have credentials as law enforcement officers. We're extraditing you to Germany and on to the States."

I laughed. "When do you cuff me and put the trench coat over my wrists?"

"That's not necessary. You're a nonviolent criminal, an embezzler, returning to testify against your accomplices. That's why you need the protection of U.S. marshals, Jill and me."

"You're kidding." Her look said she wasn't. "Was this embezzler story Rodney's idea?"

"The U.S. marshal idea was Rodney's. The embezzler idea was mine." I detected some self-satisfaction in that revelation. Turning serious, Eva said, "From here on, I'll keep eyes on your back and sides. You watch your front. I hear you did a good job of that on the beach this morning."

"I had a gun this morning. What do I use if I see a threat, offensive language?"

"I have a snub-nosed .38 in my boot. I'll give it to you after we clear security."

This was getting serious. "Do you know something I don't?"

"Yes. The RAMPART operation falls apart without you."

"Just because he asked for me?"

"No. There are other considerations that—"

Before Eva could finish, a cop-looking guy in a suit approached us. The cop asked, "Marshal Novak?"

"Yes?" replied Eva.

"I'm Officer Watson, your escort."

Eva asked to see his ID. He checked the credentials of Eva and Jill. Satisfied, Watson took our passports and tickets from Eva and led us to the front of the aircrew line. A security officer gave us the fish-eye before validating our tickets. I went through the metal detector. Eva and Jill didn't. Watson led us upstairs to a conference room in the business class lounge. He gave Eva the key and told her to leave it at the desk when we left for the departure gate. Since we weren't in a secure room, I decided to wait to resume the conversation about my special place in the RAMPART operation.

We hit the buffet. I hit the bar. Eva watched me with a disapproving eye. Jill sipped sparkling water. After the meal, they accompanied me while I shopped for a change of clothes, some toiletries, and an overnight bag to carry them. I also purchased a coat under which to hide the gun Eva promised me. It's nice to have lots of money.

Our flight departed Sydney at 5 p.m. Business class was comfortable, and I felt safe. My protection detail took their duties seriously. Jill reserved the single window seat, last row, my side of the aircraft. She could observe anyone entering the business class cabin or approaching my seat from front or rear. Eva and I sat five rows ahead in two center aisle seats. During the flight, Eva and Jill changed seats periodically. The bodyguard sitting next to me slept. The bodyguard at the rear of the cabin kept watch. Sounds extreme, but there are a lot of dead people who underestimated Russian ingenuity when it comes to killing.

When the plane reached cruising altitude, Eva conducted a reconnaissance of the passengers around us. Satisfied, she turned to me. "What's going on with you and Jill? At the safehouse, you were clawing at each other like a pair of alley cats."

"Jill usually wears a headscarf. Have you seen the scar it covers?"

"I have."

"I gave her that scar. We were on a mission. We had an operational dispute. She tried to shoot me . . . twice. I hit her with a lamp. She hasn't forgiven me; I haven't forgiven her."

Eva leaned close to me. "In spite of all the scratching, Jill may have forgiven you. She took out the two Russians who tried to kill you on Bondi Beach. She's one helluva good shot."

Eva slipped me the .38. "Did you really rob a bank in Moscow?"

"I did."

"Why?"

"Two reasons. The first one I can't tell you about. The second was to get ten million dollars." The first reason was true. The second was . . . well, that's the Max Geller legend.

Smiling, Eva said, "Mad Max Geller. Is that why the Agency fired you?"

"Yes." More legend, but Eva wasn't cleared for the truth.

That was the end of the chitchat. Eva slid her gun into her lap, covered it with a newspaper, and pretended to read, while watching every passenger and staff member who approached us.

Business class was quiet, too quiet, and there was too much time and solitude to think. Anger, fear, and regret fought to dominate my emotions. Looking back on the past few hours, I was angry. Angry with Rodney and the CIA for sending me back to Moscow. Angry with Vanessa for not appreciating the sacrifice I was making to save her from failure or worse. Angry with this faceless Russian in Moscow who wanted only me to bring him over.

And there was fear. Not the paralyzing kind that renders you immobile in the face of danger. My fear came from a clear-eyed assessment of what the FSB would do if they caught me on Russian soil. Hell, they had tried to kill me on Australian soil.

Fear dissolved into regret. Some about the people Jill and I had killed to get out of Russia last time. Some deserved it; some didn't. All were human beings.

I regretted my broken promises to Omega, the Moscow anti-government group that had risked their lives to give me evidence that

Ted Walldrum, President of the United States, was in the grip of the Kremlin. Everything they gave me had gone into a bureaucratic black hole in Washington. Most of all, I wondered if I had misled Yulia's FSB boyfriend, who had secretly filmed Ted Walldrum with prostitutes and entrusted the photographs to me. All he wanted in return for himself, Yulia, and their baby was to get out of Russia and live normal lives. That didn't happen. The photographs—key to their freedom—had become just one more bit of stuffing for the black hole.

Those dark thoughts were interrupted by our stopover in Singapore. It was long enough to rent hotel rooms, conveniently located inside the secure area, but too short to get rested. We took connecting rooms. Mine was sandwiched between my two bodyguards.

My concern for Yulia and her family kept me from resting. I knocked and pushed open the door to Jill's room. She was in her travelling blouse and pants sitting at the room's only table. On it, her service weapon lay beside two glasses and two miniatures of scotch. Jill gave me a seductive smile.

In a throaty voice, she said, "I thought you'd never open that door. C'mon in and sit." The invitation was just campy enough to let me know she was interested in company, not romance, a subtle distinction that a less sensitive man might have missed.

She poured and said, "I swept the room for bugs. We can talk. I'm sure you want to know what I've been up to since our last meeting in the executioner's cellar."

"Absolutely not," but I couldn't suppress a smile.

Jill threw her head back and let out a high-pitched cackle, exposing a great set of teeth, including upper canines that were both sinister and sexy.

I sipped scotch and began the conversation I came to have. "How come you're working for Rodney? I thought you were going back to counterintelligence."

"I wanted to. Somebody thought Rodney should keep an eye on me for a while. They probably wanted to be sure I would keep quiet about our Bonnie and Clyde act in Moscow."

I added, "And St. Petersburg and London."

Jill said a quiet, "Wow. What were we thinking?"

"Survival."

I asked, "Since you're working Russia with Rodney, would you know if Moscow Station brought out an FSB defector since we were there?"

Jill hesitated. I'm sure she was considering how much to tell me about her work. After all, I was *persona non grata* at the Agency . . . unless they wanted to use me to bring RAMPART out.

After a sip of scotch, she said, "I might know if they had brought out someone, but I wouldn't tell you. I will tell you they didn't. Why are you asking?"

"When we were in Moscow, do you remember the woman pushing the baby carriage in Gorky Park. A man joined us—"

Jill finished my sentence. "The FSB guy who gave you dirty pictures of our president."

I must have looked surprised.

Jill shrugged. "At the time, you wouldn't tell me what you were up to. I read your after-action report to Rodney. The woman pushing the carriage, Yulia, was a maid at the hotel where our future-and-current president did the nasty. The FSB guy, who wouldn't give you his name, was her boyfriend. His job was to photograph the dastardly deed so the Russians could blackmail Walldrum. Your report didn't say how you convinced him to give up those photos. What's that story?"

"In return for the Walldrum photographs, he wanted the CIA to help him defect. I wasn't with the Agency and couldn't guarantee that. So, I put seventy thousand Swiss francs in a Geneva bank account for him."

"That wouldn't have done him any good unless he could get out of Russia."

"He had a ticket: photographs and names of Americans who had been compromised in sexual encounters by the FSB. I told him to shop his album to Moscow Station in return for a way out."

Jill leaned her head over the chairback, looked at the ceiling, and said, "Oh, Jesus."

"What?"

"The FSB guy's name is Boris Kuzmick. He did make the offer to Moscow Station. The Langley assessment was that Kuzmick was part of a Russian disinformation campaign to discredit our agents and diplomats."

"Was Rodney involved in that assessment?"

"He led it."

"Then it was a cover-up. Rodney must have guessed that Kuzmick was my source for the compromising photographs of Walldrum. If Kuzmick defected and was interrogated, a lot of people would find out that the Walldrum photographs had been buried, too many people to keep quiet. That's why Rodney didn't bring Kuzmick out. Bastard!"

I went back to my room. Jill closed the door behind me, but didn't lock it. Was that a challenge or a test? I was in no mood for either. I felt sorry for Kuzmick and Yulia, and their baby. They were going to rot in Russia because some people in Washington were worried about their careers. I took my sorrow to the liquor cabinet and my body to the bed. I dozed off just in time to wake up for the next leg of our flight to Frankfurt.

CHAPTER 6

THE FLIGHT FROM Singapore to Frankfurt, Germany, took over thirteen hours. That was a long time, even in business class, where the food and entertainment were excellent, and my seat converted to a bed. Rodney had pushed me out of Australia so fast, I hadn't had time to think through the details of getting out of Moscow, if it was a trap, or if things got screwed up. On the plane, I had plenty of time to consider that possibility. I needed to adjust my Plan B.

It's one thing to make a dash for a friendly border with Russia in a well-provisioned getaway car. That's the easy part. The hard part is getting past customs authorities on both sides of the border you're trying to cross. For that, I might need the cavalry.

Our plane arrived in Frankfurt on Friday afternoon. We took adjoining—not connecting—rooms at the airport's Sheraton hotel. I set my alarm for midnight and took a long nap.

When my alarm sounded, I slipped out of the hotel, went to the airport, and used a public phone to call the States. It was a little after 6 p.m. East Coast time, and I gambled that Sherri Layton, my favorite CEO, was still in the office. If Rodney's diplomatic flight didn't work out, I was going to need Sherri's help. She had CIA and Russia experience, and access to a talented pool of brains and muscle, the cavalry.

Sherri was a single mom when we started out together at the Agency. We dated briefly, until the father of her child reentered her life, crippled her financially, and disappeared. Just when Sherri's career was taking off, her income needs caused her to leave the Agency and enter the more lucrative world of private security. Over the years since she left, I had steered Agency jobs to her company, and we had worked together on a few. Our romantic relationship was dead, but mutual respect and trust were alive.

Her voice was music to my ears when she said, "This is Sherri."

"Max, here."

She laughed, a warm, old-friend laugh. "I thought you had dropped off the earth."

"I tried. My former employer forced me back into the arena."

"Doing what?" There was concern in her voice.

"In 2018, do you remember that thing you said let's never do again?"

"Like it was yesterday."

"Let's do it again."

She hesitated. "Which destination, first, second, or third?" She was asking me if I had to return to England, Russia, or Panama.

"The second one."

Brief silence. "That's suicide for you and bad for me. I won't go back." The silence was longer this time. "Why are you doing this?"

"My employer has a hostage. Either I go or the hostage has to." Sherri knew that Vanessa was the only hostage who could make me go back to Russia.

I kept talking, hoping to persuade her. "I don't need you with me. I have a front door out. I need a back door, if the thing goes sideways."

"What thing are we talking about?"

"I have to escort a package?"

"There had better be gold bars in it."

"More like the crown jewels."

Sherri sighed. "What do you need?"

"A six-man heavy metal band, with instruments—" badasses with guns. "It'd be like old times, if you could lead it. Fun."

"Fun . . . like with two guys holding guns to your head and Tony-D climbing down the elevator shaft to save you, while I watched on your body cam monitors?"

I said a cheerful, "Yeah, just like that."

"When does this *fun* begin?"

"As soon as you can get into position, like, now."

"Jeez, Max, you used to plan ahead. I have a shop to run." Pause. "How long?"

"Four days, maybe. Two weeks, max. You hired a manager. Let him run the shop."

She ignored my suggestion. "Who's paying the bills, you or our former employer?"

"I am. Same rate as last time."

"Where is this back door?"

"Three possibles. One, Zilupe, Latvia. Two, Lake Pskov, Estonian side. Number three is my preference—Vaalimaa, Finland."

"The checkpoint at the Zsar Outlet Village?"

Russia hands like Sherri know this checkpoint is an easy way out, especially on weekends, provided your papers are good forgeries. Lots of Russians cross there to shop at the Village.

Sherri asked, "What's the stationing plan?"

"One team at the outlet. Put two in southern Estonia so they can support me at Lake Pskov or a northern Latvia crossing. I'll send coordinates for my exact crossing, if my front door doesn't work."

"Communications?"

"Sat phone, primary; cell, alternate."

Sherri suggested, "IR beacons might help us locate you."

Infrared beacons would definitely be helpful for a night crossing.

I waited while Sherri thought through the op.

She said, "I'll have to bring the band over from the States. Transportation?"

"Whatever it takes, just get there. See you when I see you."

"Let's hope the front door works and you won't see me. Be careful, Max."

I went back to the hotel and to bed. I slept well. My revised Plan B was in place.

The next morning, Saturday, I had lunch with my bodyguards at the hotel. Afterwards, Eva rented a car and we began the fifty-five-mile drive south to Heidelberg.

Starting the conversation, Eva told me, "Rodney said you know Heidelberg well."

"I went to high school there," I said, with fond memories. "My parents were colonels, assigned to the Army headquarters."

"What's it like? Jill and I may get in a little sightseeing after you're off to Russia."

"It's got a fairytale castle, a six-hundred-year-old university, lots of good restaurants, and a river runs through it. Small, intimate, and close enough to whatever you want to be close to."

"Lots of tourists?"

"Over a million visitors a year, but they pretty much confine their activities to the waterfront and the area around a one-mile pedestrian zone called the Hauptstrasse. The castle anchors the east end, and the Bismarkplatz—a transportation and shopping hub—anchors the west end."

Eva got to the punch line. "Right now, there are three tourists in the city who didn't come for the sights. They're Russian assassins stalking another Chechen freedom fighter, and they—like all of the Kremlin's hit men in Europe—have probably been told to be on the lookout for you."

"Is that what you were talking about at the airport when Watson interrupted us?"

"Hit men are only part of it. When we got the RAMPART mission, a task force was assembled to find a way to get you into Russia. The task force recommended that you go in with the ID of a Russian in the Kremlin's database."

"It doesn't matter whose ID I'm carrying if their facial recognition program flags me."

"Right. That led us to search our database for a Russian spy working without diplomatic cover, who resembled you. Enter Georgy Vasiliev. You two could be brothers. We found him in Berlin, spotting for the hit man who killed that Chechen last summer."

"Vasiliev is in Heidelberg?"

"Yes. He's the guy whose face and ID are going to get you into Russia, with a little help from Langley Tech Services. That's not my department. They'll explain it to you when we arrive. The bottom line is if anything happens to you, months of planning go down the drain. That's a problem because whatever RAMPART promised Langley is time-sensitive.

"What did he promise Langley?"

"Above my pay grade, but it caused a stir. It was agreed you were the one to bring him over."

"Because he asked for me?"

"And because you're good. I'm not blowing smoke up your shorts. That was the consensus."

"What about the phone call you got in Australia to move up the timetable for this op?"

"No details were discussed. They wanted you on the next flight to Germany."

I told Eva, "Rodney is having Moscow Station pre-position a getaway car for me in case his brilliant exit plan doesn't work. I need a few items added to the equipment in the trunk. Add two infrared beacons and two phones: one sat, one cell, both with encryption apps."

"Who are you going to signal with beacons?"

I lied. "I'll use them to throw off anyone looking for me with night vision equipment."

Eva gave me a *Do you think I'm stupid?* look, but she moved on to the next issue. "Moscow Station isn't going to leave encrypted phones in a parked car for the Russians to find."

"They can use commercial encryption apps. It's my ass on the line. If I don't get what I need to survive, I'll abort the mission and get out of Russia the best way I can."

"You've already given Rodney that ultimatum. He won't like it repeated."

"Then, tell him its blackmail. He seems to like that." I was getting angry again.

We drove the rest of the way in silence, with Eva snatching glances at the rearview mirror and Jill riding the back seat, with an Uzi on her lap. Maybe I wasn't taking the Russian threat—or the MI6 threat—seriously enough.

CHAPTER 7

WHEN WE ARRIVED in Heidelberg, Eva dropped Jill and me at our destination and drove off to find a parking space on the narrow street. The destination was an apartment building on the Panoramastrasse, a high-rent street, on a ridge with a sweeping view to the west that gave the street its name. The building was a white structure, four stories high, with an apartment on either side of the center stairwell. The quality of safehouses had apparently improved since my departure from the Agency.

Jill let us into the building and the second-floor apartment with her own keys. I followed her down the hall to the living room where I came face-to-face with two men and a woman.

Jill announced, "Max, this is everybody. Everybody, this is Max. He's the reason we're here, but he's not with the Agency anymore and he has no clearance. So, don't use your real names and don't tell him shit."

Jill was joking, of course. I knew everyone. Jim was a disguise specialist from Tech Services. The woman, Allison, was a polygraph examiner—lie detector operator, to the unwashed. She was also a voice stress analyst. The third person was Seth Newman from my old office. Seth was obviously in charge of the German end of this operation. That surprised me because he had a disdain for details and an inflated opinion of himself. No matter how large or small the gathering, Seth was the only one present who thought he was the smartest person in the room.

My guess generator was telling me Seth, Eva, and Jill had been in Berlin to size up the spotter I would be impersonating. They followed him to Heidelberg to organize the setup. Seth stayed here to coordinate with the Germans. Jill and Eva had come to Australia to escort me to Heidelberg. Rodney was in the wings playing the puppet master.

In the middle of those musings and renewing acquaintances, Eva entered the apartment with her key and joined us. The group moved to a small bedroom that served as an operations center.

Seth said, "Max, we've got a tight schedule and I need to get you, Jill, and Eva up to speed before our German liaison officer comes to brief us."

Eva said, "Max has the background. Give us the current situation here."

"Right." Seth played the red dot of his laser pointer over an enlarged map of the neighborhood as he talked. "Our AO"—area of operations—"is a rectangle about eight city blocks long and two blocks wide. The long sides of the rectangle, running south to north, are Rohrbacher Strasse on the west side and Panoramastrasse on the east boundary. The northern boundary of our rectangle is Gross Michalegasse; the southern is Karlsruher Strasse. Our north and south boundary streets are two city blocks in length and connect Rohrbacher Strasse in the west to Panoramastrasse in the east."

Seth continued, "The Russians' target is a Chechen named Deni Umarov. He lives with a bodyguard and a German shepherd in a hotel on Karlsruher Strasse, on the southern border of our AO—" red pointer dot on the location. "Umarov keeps to a predictable schedule. Every morning at dawn, and every evening, ninety minutes before sundown, he and the bodyguard walk the dog." Seth traced the route with his laser. "He goes east on Karlsruher Strasse to Panoramastrasse and walks north for several blocks to this dog park."

I said, "The local name is Hundewiese. It means 'dog meadow.' I lived here, remember?"

Seth made an annoyed face and continued. "At the dog park, Umarov sits on a bench and plays throw-and-fetch with his dog for about an hour. After the dog relieves himself, they retrace their route back to the hotel. Otherwise, Umarov rarely goes out. The German authorities suggested he get rid of the dog so he can vary his schedule and keep the Russians from anticipating his movements. Umarov declined. He considers the dog an extra layer of security."

I asked, "Why is Umarov in Heidelberg?"

"He's waiting for the Germans to approve his application for political asylum. The Russian government filed a protest, claiming Umarov is a war criminal. The Germans are investigating."

"What's the Russians' beef with this Chechen?"

Seth gave me a *Why do you care?* look, but said, "He commanded troops that killed lots of Russians during their many attempts to pacify Chechnya. Can I finish the important stuff now?"

Seth moved the red dot of his pointer to the western boundary of our AO map. "Here's the Hotel Diana, on Rohrbacher Strasse. A vacationing Ukrainian couple is staying there, but they're not on vacation and not Ukrainians. They're the Russian assassins sent to take out Umarov."

"How do you know that?" I asked.

Eva answered with impatience. "We have them on video arriving in Switzerland from Russia with diplomatic passports. They're in the Agency database as members of Unit 29155."

Seth continued. "The Russians have ridden their bikes to Panoramastrasse for the past ten days. They turn south and pass Umarov and the bodyguard walking the dog north. They always pass our Chechen on the same stretch. It's a bend in the street where there are trees on the dog park side and a high wall on the other. Activity along that stretch is hidden from view, except from high windows in the houses behind the wall. This is where the Russians intend to strike."

"Good place for an ambush," I observed. "How do they get the timing so precise?"

"That's your guy, Vasiliev, the spotter," replied Seth. "He rents an apartment across the street from Umarov's hotel. Vasiliev radios the bicycle couple when Umarov leaves the hotel to walk the dog. With that information, the Russians can time their ride to pass Umarov at roughly the same spot every time. Umarov has gotten used to seeing them and discounts them as a threat."

"How do you know that the spotter is communicating with them?" *Details, Seth.*

Seth rolled his eyes, "The Germans tracked him from the Berlin hit and bugged his room."

"Did they bug the Russian assassins, too?"

"Yes. We get feed from both bugs."

Eva cautioned me, "He needs to finish this briefing tonight, Max."

Seth summarized. "In a nutshell, the Germans will take down the assassins when they move on Umarov. Max, you and Jill take down the spotter, Vasiliev, and move him to a house nearby. Jill knows where. Allison and Jim will be there to help establish your Russian ID."

"Sounds like everything is under control. Why the rush to get me here?" I asked.

"Two days ago, the Russians agreed to hit Umarov tomorrow."

The downstairs buzzer sounded.

Seth announced, "That'll be our German team commander, Oberstleutnant Hans Richter. He's here to update us on his plan to deal with the assassins."

The German was big, tall, blond, and ramrod-straight. He wore a nice suit, but this guy was built for a SWAT uniform. Seth introduced him, but not us. Richter tactfully ignored Jim and Allison. He gave Eva and Jill a nod of familiarity, appraised me, and delivered his spiel to Seth.

"My command post and a sniper team are in a house overlooking the kill zone, where the Russians plan to attack the Chechen. Also, I will have teams of men and women—disguised as dog walkers—on and near the Hundewiese. You will be at my command post. After we take down the assassins, you may give your team permission to take down the spotter. Not before."

Seth asked, "Will there be patrol cars to seal off the kill zone once the assassins move?"

"Ah, yes," said Richter, "that provision has changed. I took the decision to forego blockades around the Hundewiese. From our monitoring of their communications, we learned that when the assassins passed by the Hundewiese this morning, they became suspicious. They shared their concern with the spotter. He is planning to use a small drone to conduct a reconnaissance of the kill zone, before an attempt on the Chechen. The spotter will make the *go* or *no-go* decision, based on what the drone sees."

"Can't you jam the drone?" asked Jill.

"Jamming the drone would make them more suspicious. They will abort the mission and try later. For them, this Chechen is a target of opportunity, not one of necessity."

Eva asked, "What if one or both assassins escape?"

"That is unlikely. I have surveillance teams deployed along their escape route, all the way to the Frankfurt airport. We will take them down before they board their flight to Moscow."

"That's . . . that's . . ." I'm sure Seth wanted to say "ridiculous." Instead, he went the diplomatic route. "Why would you allow the assassins to reach the airport?"

"Because," Richter explained, "they must discard their weapons before passing through security. We can, then, apprehend them without endangering other passengers."

Eva spoke. "Excuse me, Oberstleutnant. We were given assurances that when Umarov was attacked, you would kill the assassins or capture and hold them incommunicado here in Heidelberg. Now you're telling us they could be running free from here to Frankfurt?"

Richter puffed himself up. "Regrettably, since those assurances were given, there has been an intervention by the local government. I have new orders. They are explicit: 'Conclude this operation with no civilian casualties.' Consequently, if anyone escapes the kill zone, we will take them down at the airport when they are unarmed. Likewise, there can be no shooting by your team when they take down the spotter."

Eyeing the Glock in Seth's quick draw belt holster, Richter added, "There will be no running gun battles in the streets of Heidelberg. This is not the O. K. Corral. Are there questions concerning the rules of engagement?"

There were a lot of questions, but we knew we were not going to get the answers we needed from Richter.

"Good," said Richter, to no one in particular. He told Seth, "Please be in my command post at 0-500 hours tomorrow morning. Good night and good luck tomorrow."

When our German host had gone, Eva turned to Seth. "Richter said he had agents covering the assassins' escape route all the way to the airport. What is their escape plan?"

"The Russians plan to shoot Umarov from their bicycles, continue to the next street—where Herr Richter had promised to set up a roadblock—ride west, back to Rohrbacher Strasse, catch a streetcar to the train station, take the train to Frankfurt airport, where they catch an Aeroflot flight to Russia. They've rehearsed this three times since they've been here, including taking the train to Frankfurt."

"Streetcar?" asked Eva, incredulously.

I fielded that one. "Streetcars in Heidelberg run on a predictable schedule . . . at least they did when I lived here."

Eva's black eyes were flashing lightning bolts. "Bicycles, streetcars, trains, and an airplane to Moscow? Are you shitting me? Where's the . . . the hot air balloon and the submarine? That's enough moving parts for a major screwup. If just one of those Russians gets past Richter and contacts his controller, Max is a dead man when he gets off the plane in Moscow."

"In that case," I said, "Max will not be going to Moscow."

Angrily, Eva addressed Seth. "Richter's plan is unacceptable. You need your own plan for dealing with any Russians who make it out of the kill zone. So, let's get to it."

Everyone looked at Seth who was in hostile eyelock with Eva.

She said, "Have you got a problem with my tactical assessment?"

"I've got a problem with your perception of who's in charge of this team."

"Then, you should take that up with the complaint department." Eva unholstered her cell phone and dialed a number. While it was ringing, she handed the phone to Seth. It was on speaker. The voice at the other end came out loud enough for all to hear that unmistakable drawl.

"This is Rodney."

Seth gave Eva an unkind glance and took the phone into the hall, closing the door behind him. A few minutes later, he returned and handed the phone to Eva without looking at her.

Seth addressed the group. "As of now, Eva is running the op."

All eyes shifted to her. Eva stood still, one hand on her hip, her eyes on the floor. A few moments passed before she looked up and scanned the group. "This isn't a dick-measuring contest with Seth. It's about keeping Max alive to do his job. We are not going to fail him.

"Seth, tell me everything I haven't already heard about how the Russians plan to escape after they kill Umarov."

Seth and Eva went into executive session. Jim and Allison went out for a meal. Jill and I played cards, but not strip poker, as she teasingly suggested.

After Eva's session with Seth, she and Jill took me to a rented house down the street where we would conduct the Vasiliev interrogation the next day. The place had been swept for bugs. We could talk and I had a lot of questions that needed answers before I could think about sleep. The opportunity to ask them came when Jill, Eva, and I were sitting at the kitchen table having a dinner of cold cuts, black bread, cheese, and wine.

I said to Eva, "Assuming this defection story isn't BS, how, exactly, do I get RAMPART to the diplomatic flight?"

She left us momentarily and returned with a thin folder stamped TOP SECRET SCI NOFORN for Sensitive Compartmented Information, No Foreign Nationals.

Eva said, "Your instructions and contact information for RAMPART and the embassy are in this folder. It also contains the interrogation questions for the spotter tomorrow. Memorize everything you need. Copy nothing. Take nothing from the folder. Return everything to me in the morning. Your room is the first one, top of the stairs, third floor. We start early."

That was a bit bossy, but she was the boss. I went to my room. Half an hour later, I came downstairs. Jill and Eva were drinking schnapps.

Eva gave me a hard look. Only half joking, she said, "I thought I sent you to your room."

I handed her the file. "I can see that a lot of work went into that, but I know Moscow, it's my neck, and I want to do things my way."

"Which is . . . ?"

"I am not meeting RAMPART when he gives me a signal. I'll contact him my own way at a time of my choosing. If he's bait in a trap, I won't make it easy for the Russians. And I'm not calling the embassy with coded messages to this Colonel Burke. The FSB monitors embassy phones and they have my voice print."

Eva said, "Now, we know what you're not going to do; tell us what you will do."

"If this defector is legit, I'll bring him out this coming Saturday or Sunday or next weekend. I'll call on the quarter hour, hang up, and call five minutes later. No voice communication. When Burke gets the second call, I'm ready to move. I want to be picked up at this hospital." I showed Eva the address and name I had scribbled inside her TOP SECRET SCI NOFORN folder.

"Why a hospital?" she asked.

"You can sit around for hours, look worried, and no one thinks it's unusual."

Eva and Jill nodded their approval.

I took that as a signal to expand my wish list. "Next Saturday, I want a meeting with someone from the embassy who can assure me that this magical diplomatic flight is ready to go, and that Burke will collect RAMPART, Mrs. RAMPART, and me from the hospital when I call."

"When and where do you want this meeting?" asked Eva.

"Saturday afternoon, one thirty, at the Slavyansky Bulvar Metro Station, near the Oceana Shopping Mall. I'll be waiting for the last car on the Green Line, going southeast to the Kurskaya Station. I'll have a newspaper in my right hand and a cell phone in my left."

Through a derisive chuckle, Eva said, "You love this spy shit, don't you?"

"I love staying alive. So, send me someone who won't be conspicuous enough to get us both killed. No buzz cut Marines in civvies."

* * *

Several months later, in Washington, I pieced together what happened the following morning by reading our team's written after-action report and viewing DVDs of their oral testimony.

It was just after sunup. Umarov, his dog, and a policeman standing in for his usual bodyguard approached the bend in the Panoramastrasse kill zone. The bodyguard, Umarov's first line of defense, was nearest the curb. The dog was between the bodyguard and Umarov.

The two Russian assassins rode their bikes downhill toward Umarov, the male assassin staying close to the curb, the female taking the middle of the narrow street. They were dressed in stylish biking suits.

Oberstleutnant Richter and Seth Newman were in a fourth-floor apartment that—selected for its orientation at the bend in the street— gave Richter's sniper a field of fire down the long axis of the kill zone. Richter and Newman observed the zone through binoculars, while the sniper put crosshairs on the male assassin's right shoulder and waited for him to show a gun.

Then, several events occurred in rapid succession. The Russians drew pistols. Before either could shoot, the sniper fired. His bullet hit the male assassin, lifted him, throwing him over the handlebars. He tumbled down the street several feet, bleeding and saved from a concussion by his helmet. His gun was still attached to a lanyard around his neck.

The flight of her accomplice momentarily blocked the female assassin's line of fire to Umarov. She turned her bike ninety degrees, going behind Umarov and his policeman-bodyguard, firing as she went. The sniper couldn't get a shot at her because Umarov and the bodyguard blocked his line of fire.

The bodyguard pulled his gun. The Chechen's dog didn't know him and went for his arm. Instead of dealing with assassins, the bodyguard was trying to keep an eighty-pound German shepherd from eating his forearm. *Murphy's Law: If it can go wrong, it will.*

German security officers ran from the Hundewiese, converging on the target. The female assassin emptied her pistol at Umarov and the bodyguard. Two of Richter's men ran toward her, guns drawn. They were cut down by a hail of bullets from the downed male assassin, firing from where he landed in the street. A sniper's bullet tore into the male assassin's shoulder, snapping his collarbone. He screamed and rolled toward the gutter.

The female assassin stopped her bike behind a tree, pulled the pin on a grenade, and threw it into the street in front of her downed partner. Instantly, the kill zone was obscured by billowing clouds of white smoke, taking Richter's sniper out of play. More Germans ran toward the action, guns drawn and yelling.

The female assassin dropped her pistol and snatched a PP-91 submachine gun from her backpack. From the cover of the tree, she sprayed the oncoming Germans with a fusillade of bullets.

The downed male assassin had smoke, too, but only one good hand. He held a grenade between his knees, pulled the pin, and tossed it away, obscuring the area with even more smoke.

In his command center, Richter was yelling at the sniper, "Do you have a shot?"

"*Nein!*"

Richter cursed and yelled directions into his radio for his team to converge on the Russians.

Meanwhile, the female assassin backed away from the tree she was using for cover, her movement concealed by thick smoke. She walked quickly away from the kill zone, discarding clothing as she went. First the biker's helmet, replaced by a flowered scarf. Next, the blue windbreaker, revealing a dark green waistcoat, matching the green headscarf. From her waist, she rolled down an ankle-length skirt to cover the biker's tights. When she reached her car, parked around the corner from the streetcar stop, she was unrecognizable as the bike-riding assassin. As she approached the vehicle, she popped the trunk lid with her remote. In went her weapon. Off came the cycling shoes. Out came a pair of green flats.

The transformation was complete when a German-speaker behind her asked, "Fraulein, did you drop this?"

The assassin turned. Eva was standing a few feet away, wearing a trench coat and holding an automatic with a long-barrel silencer. The assassin smiled deceptively and reached backward into the trunk for her gun. Eva shot her three times and dashed to the car, catching the Russian before she fell. Eva dumped the assassin backwards into the trunk and tossed in her silenced automatic. She took a photograph of the dead assassin and slammed the trunk lid shut, just as the streetcar for the train station glided to a stop at the bottom of the hill.

As Eva walked away from the car, I can imagine her muttering, "That's the way we do it at the O.K. Corral . . . Hans."

* * *

In Oberstleutnant Richter's command center, Seth Newman watched the chaos and made a decision. He keyed his radio and gave me the order. "Go, Max! Go, now!"

Jill and I were in Eva's rental car outside the building where Gregory Vasiliev, the Russian spotter, was staying. Jill picked the front-door lock, while I stood by with a stun gun in one hand and a silenced Glock in the other. When the lock gave, Jill pocketed her tools, pulled her stun gun, and gave me a nod. She pushed the door open. I entered, with her covering my back.

The stairs to the second floor were straight ahead. Vasiliev was coming down with a travel bag in one hand and a gun in the other.

When he saw us, he dropped his bag and raised the gun. I fired the stun gun before he could squeeze off a shot. He danced an electric jig when the volts hit him and tumbled forward down the stairs. Jill popped him with a sedative and we dragged him to the car. I rode with the Russian in the back seat. Jill drove us the short way to the house where I had spent the previous night. It was a solid, old structure at the end of Panoramastrasse.

Vasiliev was scheduled for a 10:25 p.m. Aeroflot flight to Moscow. I had just a few hours to extract enough information from him to become him, without him guessing what we were up to.

CHAPTER 8

THE CELLAR ROOM was whitewashed, rectangular, narrow, and claustrophobic, with one small window high up at ground level and blacked out. The room was also wired so everyone in the next room could hear the interrogation.

Seth and I were the interrogators. The subject was the Russian spotter, Gregory Vasiliev. I had six hours to get what I needed to know to survive my passage through Sheremetyevo Airport in Moscow and not get handed over to the FSB.

Because I resembled Vasiliev, Jim, the Langley tech, had disguised me with contacts, a brown wig, and a false moustache to deceive our subject. The morning paper and remnants of two breakfasts were on the table before Vasiliev. The aroma of sausages and coffee hung in the air. I wore different clothes than when Jill and I had taken Vasiliev down. We wanted Vasiliev to think it was the day after his takedown and he had missed his flight to Moscow.

Seth and I leaned against the wooden table with our backs to the only door. Vasiliev was in a chair facing us and very close. We watched him regain consciousness and recover from the effects of the sedative Jill had given him. He raised his chin from his chest. I followed his wary eyes as he took in his surroundings. The chair he was flex-cuffed to—wrists and ankles. Me standing in front of him holding the stun gun. Seth leaning on the table holding a pistol casually at his side. Us and the table between Vasiliev and the door. Two-thirds of the room yawned behind him. I could imagine him calculating the escape possibilities as zero. Vasiliev's eyes came to rest on us. Without a word, he examined us, from shoes to scalp. He had a good eye. In German he said, "You are not German. Who are you?"

"Friends," I answered in German.

"You are Americans," he sneered, still in German.

In English I said, "We're American friends, if you want us to be."

He glanced at the stun gun in my hand. I put it on the table and explained. "I wanted to talk to you yesterday. You were going to shoot me. Can we talk now?"

In German, he said, "I want to call the Russian consulate in Frankfurt-am-Mein."

I replied in English. "You have a Swiss passport. Why do you want to speak to Russians?"

Switching to my language, he said, "I have not good English. I want call Russian consulate."

I went behind the table, flipped opened his file, and glanced at it. "During the past year, you've lived in England, France, and Germany. You spoke the local languages in each of those countries. You can talk to us in whatever language you like. I speak Russian, English, German, and Farsi. My colleague here speaks Russian, German, English, and French. Take your pick."

Vasiliev came back in perfect English. "You obviously don't understand English or German. I told you I want to call the Russian consulate."

I sat on the table. "No one from the Russian consulate is coming to see you because you're carrying a Swiss passport and you're dead. You died in an unsuccessful attempt to assassinate a former Chechen freedom fighter. Even if you were alive and went back to Russia, you would have to explain why you bungled the hit and killed German policemen and civilians in the process. You should reconsider any Russian contacts. You have better alternatives in the West."

"I am not dead," declared Vasiliev.

"Sure, you are. It says so in the newspaper." I held a page from our phony edition of the *Frankfurter Allgemeine Zeitung* so Vasiliev could read the article. The lead announced in German, THREE ASSASSINS KILLED IN ATTEMPT ON CHECHEN REFUGEE.

"Here are your comrades." I showed him photographs of his hit team. The woman lay bloody and crumpled in the car trunk where Eva had left her. The male would-be assassin was lying faceup in the Panoramastrasse gutter where the German sniper's second bullet left him. "These are two of the dead assassins." After he glanced at the photos, I said, "You're the third."

"If you're going to kill me, do it. I will not betray my country to the CIA."

"We don't want you to betray your country. All we want you to do is tell us about your dead friends. They're dead. So, you can't betray them. You help us and we'll give you a new identity and resettle you in a place where you won't have to worry about a one-way ticket to Moscow."

"I will not help you." He said it with finality.

"That's too bad . . . for you," said Seth, the bad cop in our little play. "Because if you don't help us, you will become a very inconvenient commodity. You'll be an embarrassment to your Kremlin masters. For the German government, you would be living proof that the authorities lied about your death to help us Americans. Finally, you would be an embarrassment to us. We wouldn't have the benefit of your services to please our masters. Also, we will lose face with the Germans. We convinced them to report you as dead. In return, we guaranteed that you would disappear and not reappear, alive, to cause them a credibility problem. So, if you don't help us, the best outcome for everyone—except you—is for you to die."

I chimed in with good news. "Help us and you'll get a resettlement package in America."

Vasiliev was unmoved.

Seth gave me a *screw it* shrug and jacked a round into the chamber of his Glock.

"So, what's it going to be?" I asked. "Do you want to die for not telling us about two dead agents who bungled an assassination or do you want a nice retirement? Think about it."

Seth laid his gun on the table and began unrolling a plastic floor cover behind Vasiliev's chair. That did not escape the Russian's notice.

"Let's start with something easy," I said. "When did your hit team arrive in Heidelberg?"

Grudgingly, he asked, "Why do you want to know about them?"

We don't. We just want you to start talking so we can work you around to the questions we really want to ask. I said, "That's not how this works, Gregory. If you want the retirement package, we ask the questions, you answer them."

Vasiliev licked his lips. I saw hope in his eyes. "They arrived two weeks ago."

I asked for the date. He gave it. In my earpiece, I heard, *That's true.* The message was from Allison, operating the voice stress analysis equipment in the next room.

Since we already knew the answer, it was a test question to see if Vasiliev would start out lying to us. He passed. He knew that the only way out of the room was to answer our questions. He was probably making the mental transition from assassin to retiree and Green Card holder. Depending on whether Vasiliev wanted a quiet or noisy retirement, he was starting to imagine himself running a little shoe repair business on Main Street in Upper Horseshoe, Iowa, or leering out of his t-shirt concession at bikinis strolling along Miami Beach.

"When they arrived from Russia, through what country did they enter Western Europe?"

He hesitated before saying, "Switzerland." That was true.

"When did they arrive from Russia?"

His answer was consistent with Eva's information about them coming through Switzerland.

In my earpiece the technician said, *That was stressful for him.*

No surprise. We were getting close to Vasiliev's forbidden territory.

"Was your hit team assigned to Unit 29155?" That was a Russian military unit, Putin's revenge squad in Europe.

Vasiliev glared at me. "I will not betray secrets."

I smiled. "Unit 29155 is not a secret. We know it's an element of Russian military intelligence, the GRU. It operates under diplomatic cover out of the World Trade Organization in Geneva, Switzerland. I'm asking if your two dead assassins belonged to that unit. Did they?" It was a borderline question. If he stepped across, he was ours.

Vasiliev hesitated. "I don't know. My orders were to go to Heidelberg, find rooms for myself and the team, and scout the target. The team would contact me when they arrived." I knew that was a lie before I heard Allison say, *Probable deception*, in my earpiece.

"If that's true, Gregory, how did you know the team arrived in Geneva when they came from Moscow?" I let him think about that for a couple of beats. "This isn't going to work if you lie to us. We're being fair with you. You need to tell us the truth. They're just two dead bodies. Were they members of Unit 29155?"

"Yes."

In my earpiece: *No stress. Probably true.*

"Good," I said. "Let's go to the operation here in Heidelberg." I took him through a few hoops. When did they arrive? Where did they stay? A lot of nonsense so we could get to what I needed to know. He answered truthfully.

"Tell me about their escape plan." He did. I cross-examined him and he confirmed the details we already knew, the streetcar, the train to Frankfurt, the Aeroflot flight to Moscow.

Now for the real stuff. "What was the plan when they arrived in Moscow? Was your team to be debriefed in the airport or somewhere else?"

"Somewhere else." *No stress. Probably true.*

"Walk me through the process, from when they left the plane to debriefing."

He tensed. "They are dead. Why do you need to know this?"

"So that you don't have to kill for a living, and failure is not a death sentence. Remember our bargain, Gregory: I ask, you answer."

He sighed. "They get off the plane. They go through immigration."

"No special treatment for GRU agents?"

"They just present their passports."

"Russian passports or the phony Swiss ones?"

"Russian. Can I have some water?" The sedative probably made him thirsty.

"When we finish. What would have happened when they presented their passports?"

"Computer check."

"Would they have been flagged in the computer as GRU?"

"No." *No stress.*

Seth asked, "What about the palm and fingerprint scanner?" His tone was hostile and accusatory, as if we knew about the machine and he was angry because Vasiliev had tried to hide it from us. In fact, we didn't know if the scanner existed. That was a key piece of information I needed to keep me from getting caught in the airport.

Vasiliev admitted, "The immigration officials are testing scanners at Sheremetyevo. They select passengers at random."

I asked, "When are the selections made, before, during, or after immigration?"

"The immigration officer makes the selection during the interview." *No stress.*

"Are passports run through the scanner, too."

"Yes." *No stress.*

I feigned anger. "How could you forget the scanner? If you're not truthful with us, we'll find out and your trip to the States is off. Is that clear?"

He gave me a sullen, "Yes."

I needed to reassure him. "You're not giving us state secrets. This is just two people getting off a plane in Moscow and you're describing their walk through the terminal. Then what?"

"They go outside, get a cab, and go home."

"When would they meet their handler for the debriefing or after-action report?"

"I don't know." *High stress, probably a lie.*

"Let me ask you something you do know. When you arrived in Moscow, would you have gone through the same terminal process as the hit team?"

"Yes." *True.*

"Would you have contacted anyone by phone or in person in the terminal?"

"No." *No stress.*

"When were you supposed to meet your handler for a debriefing?"

He frowned and shifted in the chair. "Why do you want to know about me? You said you wanted to know about the others."

I reminded him, "You said you didn't know about the debriefing process for the team. It was probably the same as yours. That's why I'm asking about you." Vasiliev probably didn't believe that, but he was at another fork in the road to his future.

"So," I said, "you would have gone home directly from the airport?"

A delayed, "Yes." *True.* He added, "I would have called my superior from home and gone to the office the next day."

"To present your after-action report?"

"Yes." *True.*

"Good. I'll get you some water."

I went to the door. Eva was waiting. She gave me a cup, along with a nod of approval.

I cut the cuff from Vasiliev's wrist so he could drink. He drained the cup and asked for another.

I had his flight reservation. Misleading him, I said, "You were to fly yesterday, after the hit?"

"Yes." He bought our deception about what day it was. Good!

"Okay, we're almost finished," I told him. "Before we wrap it up, I need to ask you a few more questions. Is everything you told us true?"

Vasiliev: "Yes." Allison: *Stress, but not out of the ballpark. After all, he is being stressed.*

"Did you withhold anything about entry procedures at the Sheremetyevo Airport?"

"No. I told you everything." *Stress.*

Vasiliev gave me a *What now?* look.

I said, "I hope you were honest with us. We're going to give you a polygraph test."

Vasiliev's face hardened.

I flex-cuffed his free wrist to the chair arm. Allison came in on cue, hooked Vasiliev to the machine, and I questioned him again. When that process was completed, Seth injected Vasiliev with a cocktail of scopolamine and something from the CIA's witchcraft lab. None of the drugs or machines can tell you with a hundred percent certainty that the subject is lying or telling the truth. However, when we finished questioning Vasiliev, using different methods, all of his answers were consistent with what he told us during the voice stress analysis. The results confirmed for me that none of what we were doing was foolproof because Vasiliev had not told us the whole truth.

I was still wired into the voice stress analysis tech and the whole session was being recorded. I said to Vasiliev, "We're going to take a quick break. Don't go anywhere."

When Seth and I were in the outer room, I told him, "Go in and start rolling up the plastic. Do it slowly and follow my lead." Seth nodded and returned to the interrogation room. I poured a cup of water for Vasiliev and followed Seth. He was taking up the plastic floor covering, starting at the rear wall, rolling it toward the back of Vasiliev's chair. I could see the tension flow out of our guest. He thought he had dodged the bullet, literally.

I sat on the edge of the table and gave Vasiliev a disappointed look. I told Seth, "Stop what you're doing. Gregory has not been completely truthful with us."

The Russian's body tensed.

He had left out one detail that changed the framework of what he had told us. I had deliberately not asked about it so we would have him by the gonads.

"Vasiliev," I said, "who was in charge of your three-man hit team here in Heidelberg?"

"We worked independently. I documented the target's behavior pattern and passed the information to the others." I knew he was lying before Allison said, *Deception.*

Now, we were ready to extract a piece of vital information that might keep me alive and buy the time I needed in Moscow to reach the defector before the FSB discovered I wasn't Vasiliev.

I said, "We know you were the leader of the Heidelberg hit team."

Vasiliev said nothing.

I continued, "We monitored your communications with the shooters. You picked the day for the killing and told the shooters. You gave them the *go* signal on the day of the hit."

Vasiliev's eyes fixed on me like angry lasers.

"So, if you were the team chief, you would have reviewed the operation with your team, before you—or the entire team—met with your superior to present your after-action report. Isn't that how it was supposed to go?"

Seth abandoned the floor cover and came to my side. He took a silencer from his pocket and just stood there, the silencer in one hand and his gun in the other, looking at Vasiliev.

In a sympathetic tone, I reminded Vasiliev, "We're just talking about dead people. We're not talking state secrets." I repeated, "As team leader, isn't that the way you would have done it with your two dead shooters?"

I sensed he was struggling with himself before he said, "Yes."

I didn't need a voice stress analysis to know that answer was true.

"Okay, let's go back. If the shooters had returned to Moscow, when would they have reported in and to whom?"

"They were to leave a message on my home phone, telling me they had arrived." *True.*

"What was the next step, exactly?"

"When I got home, I would check the message and call them to arrange a meeting for the three of us." *True.*

"When and where was the meeting to be held?" He told me. It was irrelevant.

"When were you to report that you had returned to Moscow, before or after the meeting with your team?"

"Before. I was to call my superior at GRU headquarters and give him a coded message notifying him that the team had returned." *True.* The answer to that question was super relevant. It told me how much time I had before someone at GRU headquarters asked, "Where is Vasiliev? Didn't his flight come in last night?"

I asked more irrelevant questions and got back to the information I wanted. "When would you have reported the mission was a failure?"

"As soon as I landed, and I would be summoned to headquarters immediately." *True.*

That was not good for me. I needed time in Moscow to contact RAMPART.

"If shooters are injured when they arrive in Moscow, where do they go for treatment?"

Vasiliev said there was a special GRU clinic. He gave me the address.

I gave Seth a nod. He pocketed his silencer and began rolling up the floor covering.

I went into the next room to call Langley. Eva was already on the phone, verifying the existence and address of the GRU clinic. She listened, smiled, and gave me a thumbs-up. The clinic might be useful as a distraction if I needed one.

Over the speakers, we could hear the conversation between Vasiliev and Seth. Vasiliev asked, "What will happen to me now?"

"You'll go to Washington. The CIA will debrief you—" Seth stopped in mid-sentence.

Vasiliev protested, "The other one"—referring to me—"said I would not have to give up state secrets!"

Seth didn't answer. He realized he had made a big mistake. Now, Vasiliev knew he was not getting a free ride into retirement for telling me about airplane debarkation procedures in Moscow. Even from the next room, I could sense the heavy silence between the two men. Damage had been done, but not on my end. Vasiliev was someone else's problem now.

Eva grimaced at Seth's mistake and asked, "Got everything you need from Vasiliev?"

I had.

She checked the time. "You've got a plane to catch and lots more prep before you do. Jim and Jill are waiting for you and Vasiliev upstairs. Grab yourself a snack from the sideboard before you go up. The next phase is going to take a while. I'll give Seth a hand with Vasiliev."

Allison was packing up her equipment. I stashed my pistol and stun gun in my overnight bag, and headed for the food and drink sideboard. There was a half-filled coffee carafe warming on the hot plate. I filled my cup with the good German brew and sat down with a couple of sandwiches.

They came out of the interrogation room in single file, Seth leading, Eva trailing, Vasiliev in between, wrists flex-cuffed in front of him. He didn't look happy. I watched him, memorizing his gait so I could emulate it. Vasiliev's eyes locked onto the digital wall clock showing the day and time, 5:47 p.m. At that moment, he knew we were scamming him about the time of day and the date. His plane wasn't going to leave for five hours.

As Vasiliev came abreast of the hot plate on his left, he wheeled in that direction and threw a vicious elbow that caught Eva in the forehead and dropped her. The Russian spun back to his right, grabbing the handle of the carafe. Seth turned toward him just in time to catch a face full of hot coffee. He screamed and covered his face. Vasiliev dropped the carafe, snatched Seth's gun from its holster, and turned to shoot Eva. Lying on her back, Eva fired first, putting two bullets in Vasiliev's chest. My hand was still in my gun bag. Upstairs, Jill heard the shots and ran down, gun in hand, but the shooting was over. Both of us watched a lump forming on Eva's forehead as we helped her to her feet.

Allison had rushed to Seth and administered first aid. "Should we call an ambulance?"

"No!" replied Eva. "Take him to the hospital . . . and get that damned holster off his belt first." She glanced at Vasiliev. "It's too late for him." To me and Jill she said, "Get the plastic and wrap him up before he bleeds out."

I got the plastic floor cover. Jill helped Eva and me wrap Vasiliev's body and we dragged it back into the interrogation room. Eva sat on the floor with her back against the whitewashed wall. She held her head, stared at our gristly package, and sighed.

"Are you okay?" I asked.

Her head snapped up, eyes flashing. "I killed two people today! What do you think!"

"They were bad people, Eva. Forgive yourself."

More flashing eyes. "You're the worst damned amateur psychiatrist I know. You need to stick to spying and leave head shrinking to professionals." With a little less heat, she added, "I don't feel bad because I killed them. I feel bad that I had to kill them because other people fucked up. Richter, with his 'All possibilities are covered' and Seth with that damned quick-draw holster . . ."

I wasn't one of Eva's fans and her mood didn't make me a convert. I headed for the door.

"Wait. I need a way to keep Vasiliev on ice while you're in Russia. Heidelberg used to be your town. Got any ideas?"

"There's a morgue at the U.S. Army hospital in Landstuhl. That's ninety minutes west of here. You could keep the body there if Langley gets clearance from the Pentagon. By the way, what happens if I get pulled aside for a palm print at Sheremetyevo Airport?"

"Got that covered," said Eva, with her old confidence. "Jill, get our cosmetic surgeon down here. We just may have to cut off Vasiliev's hand and let Max take it to Moscow."

I wasn't sure she was joking.

CHAPTER 9

THAT EVENING, I used Vasiliev's ID to catch his 10:25 Aeroflot flight to Moscow. I rode first class. Vasiliev must have had a friend in the GRU travel office. Once the cabin door was closed, I headed for the restroom. On the way, I casually surveyed my fellow passengers for anyone who looked like a Russian sky marshal. I didn't spot any obvious candidates. I guess you don't hijack planes flying *to* Russia. If Moscow is your destination, you've already been hijacked, like me.

The cabin was comfortable, but I was in pain and looked like I'd been in a wreck. My right arm was strapped to my body with a contraption that also held my wrist in a sling. My jaw was aching, swollen, and bandaged, courtesy of Eva's *cosmetic surgeon*. He wasn't really a surgeon; he was Jim, the CIA disguise specialist I met at Seth's initial briefing. After Eva stopped Vasiliev's escape attempt with two bullets, I went up to the second floor where Jim was waiting to give the final prep for my Moscow kamikaze mission.

Eva was observing and Jill Rucker had some props, a fashionable ski jacket and Vasiliev's carry-on, packed with his clothes and other articles that identified me as the Russian.

Eva came out of her post-shooting trauma to tell me, "Jim is going to fix your face."

Jim and I sat down at the table. He opened Vasiliev's passport to the picture page and laid it faceup on the table. Scanning it, Jim noted, "Vasiliev's face is fuller than yours. I'm going to alter your features a bit to reduce the probabilities that the Russian's facial recognition software will match the face you're going to be wearing with Maxwell Geller's face."

"That's a damn good idea." There might have been a hint of skepticism in that comment.

Jim opened a bag containing the tools of his deceptive trade. "I'm going to insert a prosthesis into either side of your mouth to fill your face out a bit." Jim invaded my mouth with rubber gloves and chunks of what felt like porcelain. That finished, he gave me a mirror to view his handywork. I thought I looked more like Don Corleone in *The Godfather* movie than Gregory Vasiliev, the GRU assassin. But after he cut my hair, lightened my eyebrows, and inserted contact lenses, the face I was wearing looked a lot like the face on Vasiliev's passport.

Jim wasn't satisfied. "I don't know how hard you want to play this, but it would help if your jaw was just a little larger."

"What's wrong?" I asked.

"Well, I'd like to break up your jawline just a bit."

"Okay."

"How do you want to go, soft or hard?"

"What is the difference?"

"Soft, I could just apply some makeup that looks like a bruise and bandage your jaw. If the Russians make you remove the bandage, which is a remote possibility, the makeup might not fool them. If you want to go hard, I could punch you just hard enough to raise a real bruise."

"You're kidding."

"Not really." He announced with pride, "I was a Golden Gloves champ in 1995."

I gave him a long, hard look. "When was the last time you threw a punch?"

"Five days ago, in the gym at Langley."

"Okay, go hard, but if you break my jaw, I'll shoot you."

Jim laughed and hit me with a lightning left jab before I even thought about bracing for it. That's how I got a real bruise, a bandage, and an aching jaw. *My country, 'tis of thee . . .*

Jim apologized. "Sorry about the sucker punch, but I didn't want you to tense up. It does less damage if you're relaxed. Now, we're going to prep you in case the Russians pull you aside for a random hand-print check. "Where's Vasiliev?"

"In the basement," said Eva. "He's dead."

Evidently, Vasiliev wasn't Jim's first corpse. Without missing a beat, he said, "Well, it's easier when they're not kicking and screaming. How long?"

"About an hour," replied Eva.

In the basement the three of us unwrapped enough of Vasiliev to get his right arm free of the plastic floor covering. He was not looking or smelling good. Jim opened his bag of magic and removed a metal box with the dimensions of a sheet of typing paper and four inches deep. We watched as he covered Vasiliev's thumb with a condom and carefully pressed the dead man's hand into the mold, making an impression of his palm and fingerprints.

"The thumb," explained Jim, "is a problem because it's not flat like the fingers. It's turned toward the index finger at an angle. So, you have to make a separate mold to get a good impression." He proceeded to do just that. The thumb mold was about the size of a thick cell phone. Jim opened it and pressed Vasiliev's thumb into the mold medium.

"There." He smiled with satisfaction. The mold held a perfect impression of Vasiliev's thumb. "What we're going to do now is give you a print of Vasiliev's right palm and fingerprints." Jim was obviously enjoying his tutorial.

He removed two spray paint cans from his case, one red, the other blue.

Jim laid his left hand on the table, palm up. To me he said, "I want you to do something, and you have to practice until I'm satisfied. Stand behind me and roll your right hand across my left, in one smooth motion. Start at my wrist and roll your hand over my palm and four fingers all the way to my fingertips. Forget my thumb. Pretend you are trying to impose your palm and finger images on mine. Be exceptionally careful when you get to my fingerprints. I want you to roll your fingertips forward over mine, not side to side. Your technique is very important. Do not allow your fingertips to slide over mine. Got it?"

"Got it."

I repeated the roll several times until Jim was satisfied. "Good. Now, I'm going to give you a copy of Vasiliev's fingerprints."

He sprayed my right hand with a heavy coat of the stuff in the blue can and said, "Carefully, I want you to roll your hand, from wrist to fingertips, in the mold of Vasiliev's hand just as we practiced—a steady forward motion and pressure. No slips."

I executed the procedure under Jim's worried gaze.

"That was good." There was relief in Jim's voice. "Now the thumb." He removed the condom from my thumb and sprayed it. "The thumb requires a different motion. I want you to roll your thumb from left to right in Vasiliev's thumb mold. Use the same motion you would if I were taking your thumbprint."

When I finished, Jim said, "Hold your hand up and look away from it."

He sprayed a liberal amount of aerosol on my hand and said, "Let it dry and do not use that hand for any purpose until you're through immigration and customs in Moscow."

Jim took what looked like a pair of ordinary ski mittens from his case. He gave one to Jill. She snapped it to the clip on my ski jacket.

Jim slipped the other one over my outstretched right hand. With a smirk, he said, "This is the one with the magic in it. It has a special insulation that will keep Vasiliev's prints on your hand for about six hours. That should be more than enough time for you to fly to Moscow and get through immigration."

"What happens if the flight is delayed and I don't make it to Moscow by hour six?"

"In that case, I recommend a variation of the advice General Mattis gave his Marines during the invasion of Afghanistan: be evasive, be creative, and have a plan to kill everyone you meet."

Jim held up a bar of soap. "This is special. Use this to remove Vasiliev's prints." He handed the soap to Jill. "Would you put this in his suitcase?"

Jim produced a medical harness and used it to strap my right arm to my body and put my wrist into the sling. "This will immobilize your hand and help protect those new prints while you travel. Don't use the hand and keep it away from extreme temperatures. Good luck."

Jim shut down his operation, said goodbye, and departed.

Jill held my new ski jacket. I shoved my left arm into the sleeve and she draped the jacket over my shoulders. She gave a playful tug to the worn ski pass tied to a pocket zipper. Looking me over, she enjoyed saying, "You've been in one hell of an accident. You really should stay away from those ski slopes, Mr. Vasiliev."

Jill tucked a dog-eared, Russian language paperback edition of *The Brothers Karamazov* into my jacket pocket, using the zipper to secure it at an angle that made the title visible. She stood back and admired her contributions to my disguise. "There," she said. "Go get yourself shot."

Old feuds die hard.

Eva drove me to the Frankfurt airport. On the way, she briefed me on the details of my skiing accident: who, where, when, and how. From then on, my fate was in my hands.

* * *

It was after 3 a.m., Monday, when my flight landed at Sheremetyevo Airport. A flight attendant helped me get my left arm into the ski jacket, draped it over my shoulders, and pulled my carry-on from the overhead.

In the terminal, lines were short at the few open immigration booths. I went to the nearest one and supplemented my swollen jaw and immobilized right arm with a pained grimace. The immigration booth was the size of two hall closets. A sour-faced, middle-aged blonde in a pale blue uniform shirt with epaulets and a black tie peered down at me from the high counter to my left. I surrendered my passport. She held it up for what seemed like minutes, her eyes darting between the passport and my face. Looking unsatisfied, she put the passport down on her side of the counter and asked, in Russian, "Why is your face bandaged."

"I tried to knock down a tree with it on the ski slope."

"Where were you skiing?"

"Garmisch, Germany."

She held up my passport again and compared it to my face. After consulting her computer, she prepared an immigration card for me. Good sign.

She must have pressed a button because a male uniformed immigration officer materialized on the far side of the booth. The sour blonde gave him my passport and immigration card. He examined my documents with a scowl and said, "Follow me." Bad sign.

CHAPTER 10

THE IMMIGRATION OFFICER led me away from the sour blonde to a three-sided enclosure with a handprint machine kiosk in the center of the far wall. He looked me up and down. "How did the fight start?"

"There was no fight. I was in a skiing accident."

He waited for details. I gave him the story Eva had me memorize on our drive to the airport.

I added, "Damned German crashed into me. I hope my grandfather killed his grandfather at Stalingrad."

He was not impressed by my knowledge of Russo-German military history.

"Did he target you because you're Russian?"

I sighed. "He couldn't ski and was showing off for his girlfriend."

He asked, "How bad is your hand injury?"

"Bruised and painful."

"Where are your skis?"

"At the bottom of the Zugspitze." Responding to his blank look, I added, "It's a mountain on the border between Germany and Austria. I was knocked out of my skis and they continued down the mountain."

The ski jacket was still draped over my right shoulder. The title on *The Brothers Karamazov* paperback was peeking out of my pocket, as Jill intended.

He asked, "Is this your first reading of *Karamazov*?"

I didn't know whether this guy was amusing himself on a slow night or if he was suspicious of me, but that was a trick question. The novel is required reading for Russian schoolchildren.

He repeated the question with a bit more force. "Is this your first reading of *Karamazov*?"

"No. This time I'm reading it for the humor."

He suppressed a smile. "Take off your mitten, put your right hand on the screen—" he gestured to the palmprint machine— "and look straight ahead." With a grimace of mock pain, I undid my wrist sling and placed my hand on the screen. He shoved my passport into the slot beneath. A light flashed, indicating that the Russians had my picture, passport, and handprint. Actually, they had my bandaged face and Vasiliev's passport and handprint. The computer was running those images through the immigration databases.

No alarms went off, but he was not satisfied. We stood staring at each other while he tapped my passport against his palm. "Maybe I should have the airport doctor examine your arm."

I said a firm, "Thank you, no." I looked at my watch. "In four hours, I have an appointment at the GRU clinic. I'm sure their facilities are more than adequate to my needs."

He stood straighter and gave me Vasiliev's passport. "Welcome home."

I breezed through customs and caught a cab to the Platnaya Parkovka parking lot outside of Leningradsky Train Station. My getaway car was there, as promised. I drove it to a quiet street and checked the trunk. Everything I asked for was there: food, rifles, ammunition, forged papers, license plates, and money. What I had forgotten to ask for was a pistol. Damn! That's what happens when you rush into an operation. I drove back to the train station, parked in a different spot, and took a cab to my favorite Moscow hospital. It was the one where

Dr. Zhukov had disguised Jill Rucker and me for our escape from Moscow two years ago.

The emergency room door was the only open entrance. I asked for Zhukov. The admitting clerk looked up at the wall clock—it was nearly 5 a.m.—and informed me, "Dr. Zhukov does not arrive until 7:30. She scrutinized my bandaged face and arm sling. "Would you like to be seen by the duty physician?"

"No. Dr. Zhukov treated me last time. Can I wait for him in the lobby?"

Reluctantly, she granted permission, but I didn't go to the lobby. I took the stairs to the second floor, picked the lock on Zhukov's office, and stretched out on his couch for a nap.

I was startled out of a sound sleep when Zhukov opened the door and flipped on the lights. He was surprised and disturbed by my presence. He quickly shut the door and, in a harsh whisper, asked, "What the hell are you doing back in Moscow!"

"I forgot something."

"Well, Moscow has not forgotten you. The security services are still looking for people who helped you escape. That means they're looking for me." He walked to his desk and threw down his keys. "And the FSB isn't your only worry. Arkady had many friends. They want to avenge his death." He spat out the rest in a harsh whisper. "And they want to know what you did with the documents Arkady gave you."

"I didn't kill Arkady."

"You may have difficulty explaining that, hanging upside down with a gag in your mouth. What do you want?"

"First, I want a scalpel, four tongue depressors, and a roll of adhesive tape."

Zhukov was sullen. "Are you in Moscow to open a medical practice?"

"No. I'm going to make a shank."

"A what?"

"A makeshift knife. Don't you watch American prison movies? I need a weapon."

Zhukov sighed, left the room, and returned ten minutes later with my shank components. He watched while I sandwiched the handle of the scalpel between the tongue depressors and wrapped the depressors in adhesive tape.

"What else can I contribute to your demise?" He was serious.

I laughed. "I need to see Pavel."

"Pavel is the last person who wants to see you. He brought you to Omega and you betrayed us. Omega is not happy with Pavel because of you."

"I did not betray Omega. I don't have time to explain. I have to meet someone. I'll explain everything to Pavel when I see him. Call and arrange a meeting for me. Tell him a man wants to sell him a Mercedes with a good heater. He'll know who I am. Get a time and place for us to discuss the sale. It has to be this afternoon. I'll call you for the details."

Zhukov was not happy when I left.

After grabbing a quick breakfast in the hospital cafeteria, I headed for another meeting with a man who didn't know I was coming, but first a detour. I took the Metro to Arabatskya Station and caught a cab to Maly Kislovsky Lane, the location of the Russian Institute of Theater Arts. I gave the cabbie fifty euros and told him to park. "Turn the motor off. I'm waiting for someone."

I wasn't sure who, but it didn't take long to pick him out of the stream of students headed for the Institute. My target was a skinny kid wearing a backpack and carrying a book on acting. He looked too young to be enrolled at the Institute, just what I needed.

I jumped out of the cab and fast-walked to catch him. In Russian, I said, "Excuse me. Are you a student at the Arts Institute?"

He stepped back and gave me a wary, "Yes?"

"I need to hire an actor for two hours this morning. Who should I speak to?"

He looked me up and down, probably assessing my respectability. "What's the job?"

"It's a non-speaking part. I need someone to sit on a bench at a school and pretend to be my son. I'm playing a birthday joke on a friend." That was convincing. Maybe I should have charged him for acting lessons.

The kid asked, "How much are you paying?"

"One hundred euros and a cab ride back here. If you're interested, I have the cab waiting." I gestured to the vehicle.

"No stops?" It was a question and a requirement.

"Directly to the school and back, same cab."

"I can do it. Show me the euros."

I gave him two twenties. "You get the other sixty when the job is done."

We got into the cab and I gave the driver instructions to our destination.

The kid said, "You want to tell me about the joke?"

"I told you this was not a speaking part. Why are you speaking?"

The kid shrugged and looked out the window for the rest of the trip.

I didn't need conversation. I needed time to think. We were headed for a surprise meeting with Sergei Golovkin. According to Rodney—who got his information from our military attaché in Moscow, who got it from RAMPART—Sergei had recommended me to bring RAMPART out of Russia. I wanted to hear Sergei confirm that recommendation.

I had to plan for two possibilities. The first was that RAMPART was a legitimate defector. If so, Sergei was my only source of firsthand information about him.

The other possibility was that RAMPART was bait to trap me. In that case, the Russians knew Sergei was spying for the CIA and were using him to sweeten the trap. The FSB would have Sergei and RAMPART under surveillance, waiting for me to make contact. Moscow Rule #4 states, *Everyone is potentially under opposition control.* In that eventuality, I would slit Sergei's throat, forget RAMPART, and make a run for the Finnish border.

CHAPTER 11

OUT OF PERSONAL inclination and professional necessity, Sergei Golovkin—FSB intelligence analyst and CIA asset—code name: CRYSTAL—was precise, punctual, and predictable. So, I could pinpoint, almost to the minute, when he would arrive at his daughter's school. I knew because that had often been our rendezvous when I ran him for the Agency. I was determined to get there first to ambush him . . . and kill him, if he had sold me out to the FSB.

As our cab neared the building, I said to the driver, "Slow down. Take us past the school and around the corner. I'm looking for my friend's car."

Actually, I was looking for indicators that the FSB was watching the school. If Sergei had betrayed me, this would be a logical place for an FSB trap.

The cabbie passed the school, went to the end of the block, and turned right. Half a block down, the kid and I got out. I gave the driver a fifty-euro note and told him to wait for us. With the kid in tow, I circled the block, checking the school's rear exit. As we approached the street where the school's front entrance was located, I saw a couple get out of a car and enter the corner café where Sergei habitually got his morning coffee. I watched through the window as they took separate tables. We turned the corner and joined the flow of students and parents as they walked to the school's front gate and across the cobblestone courtyard to the building.

The school had a T-shaped floorplan, the stem being a long hall that stretched from the entrance to the rear exit with classrooms and administrative offices on either side. At the building's entrance, we were at the intersection of the stem and the crossbar of the *T*, halls stretching out to our right and left. Classrooms were on the inside of the hall. The outside wall had large windows looking into the entrance courtyard.

I parked the kid just inside the door, walked two windows to the left, and took out my pocket camera. It had a powerful telescopic lens that let me see a lot farther than a normal camera of its size. I used it to scan the buildings across the street from the school.

When I had seen enough, I steered the kid to a scarred wooden bench outside of the admin office, reserved for students about to have a close encounter of the unpleasant kind with the headmaster.

I said, "Sit here. Keep your head down. If anyone asks who you are, tell them Boris Prosky and you're waiting for your father. Don't say anything else and don't go anywhere."

The kid nodded. I stood beside him, my back to the entrance. Minutes later, Sergei passed us holding his daughter's hand. He didn't notice me and continued down the hall to a classroom.

I told the kid, "I'm going to the men's room. Stay put."

I timed my walk to meet Sergei opposite the men's room as he walked back toward the front entrance.

He looked at me and went pale. I gave him a slight nod toward the men's room and entered with Sergei following. I pointed. He checked the stalls and gave me a thumbs-up. We were alone. I shoved a rubber wedge under the door to keep out intruders.

Sergei started to speak. I put a finger to my lips for silence and shoved him against the wall with Zhukov's scalpel against his throat.

I was angry. He was shocked, but didn't resist while I patted him down for a wire. He was clean. That was good for me, better for him.

In a harsh whisper, I snarled, "Why did you give me up to the FSB?"

"What are you talking about?"

"This school is crawling with surveillance. The car at the back gate. The yellow building directly across the street, second-floor window. There's a guy with a video camera on a tripod. Your café on the corner. I saw a couple walk in and sit at different tables so they could observe the entire room. What's going on, Sergei?"

"I swear, I don't know."

I tried to read his expression. I saw confusion, not fear. "You're FSB. Didn't they teach you how to spot surveillance?"

"Of course, but I'm an analyst. I don't worry about it. Russia is a surveillance society."

We looked at each other, anger growing in his eyes, doubt growing in my mind.

Sergei said, "Please take that blade away from my throat."

When I did, he asked, "What the hell are you doing back in Moscow?"

"You sent for me."

"What are you talking about? I didn't send for you. Even if I had, I wouldn't expect you to come. You're a wanted man in Russia and you're rich. It makes no sense for you to be here."

Not many people knew I was rich—my lawyer, a few at the CIA, and Russian intelligence. "How do you know that I'm rich, Sergei?" I tightened my grip on the makeshift knife.

"Everyone in our security services knows. The Kremlin put out a worldwide alert for you. It says that when you robbed the Allgemeine Volksbank two years ago, you stole codes that allowed you to hack into AVB and steal ten million dollars. The SVR"—Russian foreign intelligence agency—"has orders to look for you in wealthy enclaves around the globe. They're monitoring high-end property sales and bribing bankers to flag new clients who transfer more than five million dollars. You must have really pissed off somebody in the Kremlin." Sergei paused and asked, "Did you steal from AVB?"

"Of course not." Sergei had helped me. I owed him an explanation. "After the CIA fired me, I was hired to do the job that brought me here two years ago. I didn't know my employer was a front for the SVR. When I got the information they wanted, they stole five million dollars from me, half of my fee. I outsmarted them and got it back. The Kremlin's unhappy about it. This time, I'm here about the friend you referred."

He nodded, but looked surprised.

I said, "Tell me about him. Who mentioned my name first, you or him?"

Sergei pursed his lips and looked away, trying to remember. I didn't rush him. The answer might mean life or death . . . for me. If Petrov—a.k.a. RAMPART—was the first to mention my name, his defection story was probably designed to lure me back to Russia. The Justice Ministry wanted to try me for the bank job and the FSB wanted me for the names of my Russian contacts.

Sergei reviewed the circumstances, more to trigger his memory than for me. "Petrov wanted to defect. He came to me for the name of a Moscow CIA contact. I told him it wasn't safe to contact CIA locals. He asked about you. He saw us talking in my car during your last visit. He knew your name, face, and CIA connection from television accounts of the bank robbery."

Everybody in Moscow believed I had robbed the bank, everybody except the Kremlin chiefs and a few oligarchs. They knew I had stolen evidence of their money laundering operation.

Sergei said, "Petrov asked how to contact you. I didn't know. How did he contact you?"

"It doesn't matter. Why did he come to you?"

"We've been friends since childhood."

"Do you trust him?"

"With my life."

That was good enough for Sergei, but not for me. I was risking *my* life.

"Why does he want to defect?"

"He fought in three wars and has post-traumatic stress disorder. The army is going to promote him and send him back into combat. He won't last for a fourth tour."

"Where are they sending him, Syria?"

"No. The Defense Ministry is opening a new front."

"Where?"

"I don't know. That's what Petrov wants to trade for his ticket out of Russia."

"What's Petrov's job now?"

"War plans officer at the Ministry of Defense."

"Is he married?"

"Yes."

"Does his wife want to defect with him?"

"I think so."

In Heidelberg, Eva had given me Petrov's signal that he wanted a meeting. I like to make my own contact arrangements, especially when my life depends on it. With Sergei under surveillance, I couldn't risk using him as my courier to Petrov. There was one other option.

I cautioned him, "You should stay away from the Petrovs. Have your wife visit them and deliver these instructions to Petrov, not his wife." I gave Sergei the locations and schedule I wanted the Petrovs to follow. I added, "Tell him not to try to evade surveillance. I'll handle that."

Sergei was alarmed. "Why would Petrov be followed?"

"Because he talks to you, and you're being followed." I reminded him of the photographer across the street and the stakeouts in his café and at the school's back gate.

Sergei's expression registered concern followed by resignation.

To distract him from his darker thoughts, I said, "Describe Petrov."

Slowly, Sergei refocused. "Military bearing. Handsome. Thick black hair. Broken nose. He's about 175 centimeters, 84 kilos." Translation: five-eight, 185 pounds. I'm not a fan of the metric system.

"His wife?"

"Same height, blond, and very attractive. What else do you want to know?"

That was enough. His description matched the photographs Eva showed me in Heidelberg.

"Petrov needs to know that he and his wife must be at the Metro station on time and follow my instructions. If they deviate from the schedule, I won't try for a second meeting."

Sergei gave his watch a worried glance. "If I'm being followed, I've been here too long."

I had anticipated that. "Go to the headmaster's office and ask about your daughter's progress. That will account for your time, if the FSB wants to know why you were delayed."

As he started to leave, I said, "If the FSB is here for me, they're watching you. The CIA has exfiltration plans for assets. Do you want to be pulled out?"

Sergei said a prompt, "No."

"Don't be a hero. You're already one in the eyes of the CIA. If you change your mind, signal your handler. He'll get you out."

There was sadness in his voice. "This is my home, my country. I can't leave Russia, Max."

"In that case, don't contact anyone on our side . . . ever again. If the FSB only suspects you of espionage, but they don't have evidence, sooner or later they'll give up and back off."

Sergei sighed. "And if they do have evidence, sooner or later they will interrogate me."

"You have the pill?"

"Yes."

I hugged him. "Goodbye, Sergei."

He said, "Good luck, Max."

CHAPTER 12

Later that day
FSB Headquarters, Moscow

ZABLUDA WAS AT his desk reviewing surveillance reports when he got the call.

The man on the other end of the call said, "Colonel Zabluda, this is Kraskin. You wanted to know if the subject, Sergei Golovkin, deviated from his routine. This morning, he took his daughter to school and was in the building much longer than usual. When he left, he didn't make his usual coffee stop at the café. He went directly to his car and drove to work."

Such a small deviation from his usual routine, thought Zabluda, but that's how spies meet spies and load or clear message drops.

"Did you observe anything else out of the ordinary?" asked Zabluda.

"No, Colonel."

"Did anyone enter or leave by other than the front gate?"

"No, sir."

"Very well. Go to the school. Say you were supposed to meet Golovkin there and you're late for the appointment. See if you can find out why he went off schedule. Be discreet. You are a friend, not FSB. Oh, and email me the video you took of the school's entrance."

"I already have, Colonel. It should be in your computer's inbox now."

Zabluda booted up his laptop, downloaded the video footage, and began to view it. The coverage was initiated well before students and parents began to arrive. The camera frame covered a narrow segment of sidewalk in front of the school, the wrought iron entrance gate, and the segment of the cobblestone courtyard leading to the building's entrance. Zabluda filled his coffee cup and settled down to the boring job of watching for something out of place.

As students began to arrive, Zabluda was interrupted by a knock on his open door. His visitor was Major Ipatiev. Zabluda looked up and smiled broadly. "Ipatiev!" He paused the video and the two men met in the center of the room, hugging each other.

Before Ipatiev could speak, Zabluda said, "Sit down. What have they got you doing?"

"Riding a desk at GRU headquarters, reading field reports from Unit 29155."

"Sounds exciting." It didn't.

Ipatiev said, "I have bad news about Gregory Vasiliev, the spotter we used to take down Bogdanovich in England. German newspapers reported that he and his team were killed in Heidelberg during a wet work operation against a Chechen."

"Did they get the Chechen?"

"No, sir."

Gravely, Zabluda said, "Vasiliev was a good man, very imaginative in his approach."

Ipatiev shifted gears. "I came to thank you for protecting me during the inquiry. I appreciate you telling the investigators that I thought I was following Moscow's orders when we took the money from Geller. I don't think they believed you." With a laugh, he added, "I know I didn't. I still don't understand why they didn't shoot both of us."

"We have a benefactor in the Kremlin, Ipatiev."

"Who?"

"The president himself."

"You're joking," said Ipatiev in disbelief.

"No. He forgave us. He was pleased that we killed the defector Bogdanovich and his MI6 handlers under the noses of the British."

"When are we going back to the field?"

"When I can prove a certain person is a CIA mole. If not, the firing squad may still await us."

"In that case," said Ipatiev, "why not ensure that the necessary proof is found in his possession?"

"That won't work with General Orlov. He may be the last honest man in Moscow. The president relies on him for truthful assessments, even if he ignores them. I have to prove myself to the general with honest work to get out of here. I spend my days—and nights—reading surveillance reports and viewing dull surveillance footage, trying to prove or disprove that the subject is a CIA mole. I was viewing one when you knocked."

"In that case, I leave you to save us." Ipatiev moved to get up.

Zabluda stopped him with a gentle hand on the wrist. "Stay. View this one with me. I need fresh eyes. My surveillance subject altered his behavior pattern this morning." Zabluda rotated the laptop so both of them could see the screen, and started the video. Parents and students were entering the school's gate.

Ipatiev asked, "Which one is your subject?"

"I'll watch him. You watch for anything that doesn't fit."

It was a multi-grade school. Older students arrived alone. Parents arrived with younger ones, deposited them, and left for home or work. Sergei, hand in hand with little Natasha, entered the gate with a knot of other parents and students. However, he was one of the last to leave. Zabluda paused the video a moment, then watched Sergei walk out of the frame.

Ipatiev said, "That's your mole?"

"Suspected mole."

The video continued to run as parents trickled out of the school, until no one exited.

Zabluda turned to Ipatiev. "What did you see?"

Ipatiev bowed his head and closed his eyes to concentrate. "All of the parents left their children in the building and came out alone . . . except one man. He had an older boy with him. Let's see the video again."

Zabluda ran the video back to where parents began exiting the school and let it run.

"There," said Ipatiev, pointing at the screen.

On the computer screen, a man in a fur hat with ear flaps tied under his chin and a muffler covering his nose and mouth exited the school gate. He was accompanied by a boy in a hoodie, wearing a backpack. They turned right and walked out of camera range.

Ipatiev said, "Take the video back to where those two entered the school."

Zabluda obliged. They waited several frames before the man and boy came into view from the right. The pair walked to the gate, turned right, and entered the school courtyard. Zabluda fast-forwarded the video to catch them leaving.

Ipatiev noted, "They have their faces covered and they're looking down. That's camera-avoidance behavior."

Zabluda ran the video back to where the pair entered the courtyard and walked to the school building. He paused the video, zoomed in on a head-to-heels shot of the man, and stared at the screen. The two Russians watched the man walk across the courtyard to the school's front door,

Zabluda asked, "Where have we seen a man who walks like that?"

"London and Geneva, two years ago." Ipatiev turned to Zabluda in disbelief. "That can't be Maxwell Geller."

"That's Geller. He met Sergei Golovkin in the school. I'd bet my pension on it."

"Who's the boy with Geller?" asked Ipatiev.

"The boy doesn't matter. He's cover so Geller could blend with parents and students entering the school." Zabluda smelled blood. "If Maxwell Geller is in Moscow, I'm going to hunt him down and kill him. I'll alert every security service in this city."

Tentatively, Ipatiev said, "An observation and a suggestion, sir."

"Speak your mind."

"You—we—have had many opportunities to kill Geller, but he escaped. If you initiate a manhunt on this evidence and Geller escapes again, our superiors, especially our president, might not be as forgiving this time."

"What are you proposing, Ipatiev?"

"Maybe . . . we didn't see Geller in that video. We saw a man. Could be Geller, could be someone who looks like Geller. It might be better to wait until you have conclusive proof that this man is Geller—and you have him in a box he can't escape from."

Zabluda stared angrily at Ipatiev and considered the proposal. Then, his expression turned thoughtful. "I'm already tracking Sergei Golovkin and his associates. I could let them lead me to Geller and roll up the entire network."

Ipatiev suggested, "You could also forget about Geller. Let someone else discover that he's here, if he is . . . and if they can. If Geller escapes from Moscow undetected, well . . ."

After Ipatiev departed, Zabluda sat at his desk, thinking. He had no intention of forgetting about Maxwell Geller.

CHAPTER 13

IN THE SCHOOL men's room, Sergei and I parted for what I hoped would be the last time. I let him leave first so that the kid—my actor—wouldn't see us together.

A few minutes later, I joined the kid at the bench and gave him sixty euros. "Well done."

"I didn't do anything."

"You followed instructions, the mark of a good movie star. Directors are going to love you."

The kid beamed.

I said, "Let's go. Cover your face with your scarf. Pull your hood forward. Keep your eyes on the ground until we're in the cab."

We exited the school gate, walked down the block and around the corner. Our cab was waiting. In indifferent silence, we rode back to the Institute of Theater Arts where I dropped the kid. I had the cabbie take me to Arabatskya Metro Station. On the way, I gave him a twenty-euro note to use his cell phone and called Dr. Zhukov.

When he picked up, I said, "Thank you for the medical instruments. You'll be happy to hear that surgery was not required. Were you able to contact the gentleman we discussed in your office this morning?"

"Come to my building now," Zhukov instructed. "Someone will meet you in the lobby." Abruptly, he broke the connection.

That didn't sound like a red-carpet invitation, but I needed Pavel and his organization. Pavel owed me for telling him the identity of his biological father. On the other hand, I owed him and his Omega Group friends an explanation for why their comrade, Arkady, was killed during my alleged Moscow bank robbery. Worse still, I owed them an explanation for why the CIA, FBI, and Justice Department had buried evidence—that Arkady gave his life for—proving that the President of the United States was up to his armpits in laundered Russian money.

I took another cab to Zhukov's hospital. As I paid the cabbie, a man exited the hospital and walked casually toward me. He had a smile and carried a folded newspaper. I waited to see if he was my contact. Behind me, a car pulled into the space vacated by my cab. The man with the smile quickened his pace toward me. As we came face-to-face, he pulled a gun from the folded newspaper and jammed it into my stomach. Two men jumped out of the car, grabbed me, and dragged me into the back seat. We were gone before anyone noticed. Or, if you notice something like that in Moscow, you pretended you didn't. The U.S. State Department had Russia on a list of thirty-six countries—including Afghanistan and Yemen—where kidnapping and hostage-taking is a problem. Now, it was my problem.

I was wedged between the two heavies who had grabbed me. The man with the gun jumped in next to the driver. We sped away from the curb and headed for a secluded corner of the hospital parking lot, and stopped. The man who had pointed his gun at me turned in his seat and took a vicious swing at my head with a flat leather blackjack. I went down for the count.

I came to facedown on the back-seat floor. It smelled of dirt and engine oil. Two big Russians on the back seat had their shoes planted firmly on my back. One of them pulled my hands behind me and tied my wrists together and pulled a hood over my head. The other man bound my ankles with what felt like bungee cord. After a no-talking thirty minutes, the car turned into a driveway and stopped. I heard the familiar grinding of gears as the garage door cranked, and I knew where I was. It was not a place I wanted to be.

The Backseat Boys treaded heavily on me as they exited the car and pulled me out by my legs. They stood me up, freed my legs, and shoved me further into the building. I was standing in the familiar maintenance bay of a big garage. Just as I remembered, the back wall was adorned with a Russian Federation flag that had a black-and-white military-like patch sewn to its center. The patch contained an eagle claw holding a globe with an arrow imbedded in it. The banner beneath contained one word: Omega. It was the name of an anti-government underground cell.

During my previous visit, the symbology was explained by the group's angry ideologue. "Omega is the last letter in the Greek alphabet. For us, it signifies the time when the pillage of Mother Russia's resources ends." With fire in her green eyes and a quivering finger pointed at the wall, she said, "This is our flag, the Omega flag—the claw, globe, and arrow, superimposed on the flag of the Russian Federation. The arrow signifies pursuit—pursuit of the thieves who have stolen Mother Russia's wealth. The globe shows that they have hidden that stolen wealth around the world and we will follow it to those hiding places. The claw symbolizes our global reach and our intention to claw back that wealth, return it to Russia, and punish the thieves."

There was a long wooden table beneath the flag. Seated facing me, in tribunal formation, were some of the same people who had been there during my previous visit. Other faces were new. The studious-looking younger man and cell leader who sat at the center of the table had been replaced by an older fellow. His black hair was parted in the middle revealing a large forehead. He had burning dark eyes, a moustache, and goatee. Although his hair wasn't long, he reminded me of photographs of Rasputin, the Russian mystic.

The redhead female ideologue sat to his right. This time, there was no fire or quivering fingers from her, only a stillness and the menacing glare of intense anger.

The policeman I knew as Yuri sat to the leader's left. He had driven Jill Rucker and me to the airport for our daring escape after the bank job.

Among the missing were the cultured fellow from the Finance Ministry, and Arkady, who was dead. The seats of those former members were now filled by a couple of guys in coveralls and worn brown leather waistcoats over weightlifters' shoulders. They were the bookends for this group. I guessed this was the new Omega executive committee—maybe my execution committee.

The Backseat Boys marched me to a chair facing the tribunal and sat me down. Pavel, my primary contact and only Russian friend during my previous Moscow visit, didn't have a seat at the table. He stood to the side, an ominous sign he had fallen from favor with the group, probably because of me. This was not going to be a fun experience.

In heavily accented English, the leader said, "You must be insane, returning to Moscow."

"I agree."

"At the bank, why did you kill Arkady?"

"My partner killed him."

"There is no difference. We want to know why."

"A security camera caught Arkady passing thumb drives to me. Two guards barged into the room and had us at gunpoint. My partner shot the guards . . . and Arkady. I'm sorry. The other choice was to leave him to be interrogated by the FSB. He would have given up all of you."

"You don't know that. Arkady was brave. He wouldn't have risked his life to give you the thumb drives if he lacked courage."

"Arkady was brave," I agreed, "but he wouldn't have withstood torture by the FSB." I turned to Yuri, the policeman. "How about it? Would Arkady have stood up under harsh interrogation?"

The leader looked at Yuri, who shook his head.

"Where is this merciful partner of yours?" He was asking about Jill.

"I don't know. She was my partner just for the Moscow mission. She's CIA. I'm not."

"So you say. Arkady gave you documents proving that your president was laundering money for Russian oligarchs. There was no mention of the documents in the special prosecutor's report by your Justice Department or in your news media. What happened to those documents?"

"I took them to the DOJ—"

One of the Backseat Boys hit me on the side of my head hard enough to rattle my teeth. I fell to the side, but the other Boy shoved me back into the chair.

"You are a liar," said the leader. "Omega has spies, too. We know you were paid ten million dollars for Arkady's documents and the other incriminating information about your president."

"You didn't let me finish. I traded the documents for ten million, yes. Later, I got them back and took them to our special prosecutor in Washington. I was too late. The prosecutor had completed his investigation by the time I got to his office. I took the evidence to the CIA. At that point, I had kept my promise to you."

"Why didn't the CIA release the information?"

"I don't know." I did know, but I wasn't going to tell them. I had given my word to Rodney. I reminded them, "I didn't work for the CIA then, and I don't now."

"You keep telling us that. I don't believe you. Why did you come back to Russia?"

"I was forced to come back to do a job."

"Who forced you?"

"The CIA."

The bookends laughed.

"If you don't work for the CIA, how could they force you to come back to Moscow?"

"They threatened to put someone I care about in harm's way."

One of the bookends said, "Is the CIA now taking lessons from the FSB?"

The leader glared down the table at the speaker to let him know his humor wasn't appreciated. He turned back to me. "What is this job you came to Moscow to do?"

"I can't tell you that."

The other bookend gave me a grim smile and said, "He could tell us, but he would have to kill us." He laughed.

The leader shot a glance at the Backseat Boy standing next to me. Backseat hit me again, harder. I saw stars.

"Alright, I won't tell you." I braced for another head shot.

The leader waved off the blackjack. "Why should we believe you or trust you?"

"You know I'm wanted in Russia for bank robbery and murder. You also know I was paid millions for Arkady's documents. Why would I come back unless someone forced me to?"

That gave them pause. The leader, the redhead ideologue, and the cop, Yuri, conducted a conference in whispers. The bookends just stared at me like I was already dead meat.

The leader said, "This job you came to do, I understand that you want Pavel's help?"

"I do."

"Why should we help you?"

"The job will help your cause and mine."

"Our cause needs money."

Omega was pulling a shakedown. They knew I didn't have another option. Otherwise, I wouldn't have asked to see Pavel. I said, "I'll donate twenty thousand euros to your cause. Do you have a way to get it from the U.S. Embassy?"

"The Swiss Embassy would be better," said the leader. "Pavel will give you instructions."

One of the bookends spoke up. "And another fifty thousand for Arkady's widow."

Keeping my eyes on the leader, I said, "Arkady didn't have a widow. Do you think I would cause a man's death and not check to see if he had a family?"

The leader gave the bookend a disgusted glare and said to me, "Fifty thousand for our cause, and you have our support."

"Thirty," was my counteroffer.

"Forty."

"Thirty-two."

He said, "Thirty-five."

I nodded. I had to let him win so he could save face and I could get out of that den of thieves.

"What do you need from Omega?"

"Secrecy. I need you to limit the knowledge that I'm in Moscow to the people in this room. I want Pavel to be my only contact with Omega and only he will know what I'm doing. He can tell you what he knows about my operation after I've left Russia. Agreed?"

The leader looked both ways and got nods. "Agreed." He addressed Pavel. "See to the needs of our celebrity CIA visitor."

Pavel didn't speak. He just glared at me.

"What else?" asked the leader.

"I need a good gun with a silencer."

"Did you come back to assassinate someone?" asked Yuri.

"No. I'm a wanted man here. I don't intend to be taken alive."

Weapons must have been Yuri's department. He nodded to one of the Backseat Boys, who left, returned a few minutes later, and dropped a heavy cloth bag into my lap. Inside, I found a Russian PB automatic, silencer, a holster, and two eight-round ammunition clips.

"Is there a place where I can test-fire this?"

The fellow who had dropped the hardware in my lap got a nod from Yuri and led me to a windowless room. He took the lid off a 55-gallon oil drum filled with sandbags, and gestured for me to have at it. I shoved the clip into the gun and fired into the drum, one round with the silencer, one round without it. The gun worked perfectly. We went back to face the tribunal.

The leader asked, "Are you satisfied, Mr. Max?"

"I am. Thank you."

He looked at my rumpled clothes. "I understand you spent the night on Dr. Zhukov's couch. Do you need a place to stay?"

"For a few days, yes."

The leader turned to Pavel. "We're finished here. Find suitable accommodations for our visitor . . . something uncomfortable." Arkady's death had left a bitter aftertaste with this group.

Pavel started walking. I followed.

"A final request," said the leader. "Now that you are armed, try not to kill any of us this time."

Maybe I should start with you, was my first thought. Pavel took my arm and steered me to his car. A man in coveralls raised the door and Pavel drove us into the street.

I asked, "Where are you taking me?"

"To the farm where you hid on your last trip."

"I can't stay there."

"Why not?"

"The farm has been compromised. The Russian security services know about it."

For the first time, he looked directly at me and I saw anger. "How do you know that?"

I couldn't give Pavel a straight answer because I had given my word to Rodney that I would never disclose what I knew about a certain double agent, who—like me—had been forced to work for the CIA because someone he loved was being threatened. The CIA had compromised one of his adult sons, a captain in the Russian army.

My answer to Pavel was, "I can't tell you how I know the farm is compromised. You'll have to take my word."

Pavel pulled his car to the curb and sat there staring through the windshield for a time. Finally, he said, "I will take you to my father's— to General Grishin's—apartment."

"What about the general and good old Uncle Dimitri?" who wanted to kill me when I got caught in Grishin's apartment during my last visit.

"Uncle Dimitri and the general are hunting at the general's dacha on the Volga. They go there every year after Winter Festival. It reminds them of their childhood in the country."

I didn't object. Pavel made a U-turn and headed back to the city center.

We drove a while before I asked, "Why so quiet, Pavel?"

"You damaged my standing with Omega, Max. I introduced you to the group on your last visit and you betrayed us. Because of you, Arkady died for nothing. Worse, his death revealed that we had an informant in the Allgemeine Volksbank money laundering operation. Some council members wanted to turn you over to the security services, but they would have to explain how we came to know a former CIA officer."

"They could have killed me."

"They may. For now, they want your money."

"I'm really sorry about Arkady."

He said simply, "It is done."

We drove to a building in the Arbat District. The retired general's apartment was on the tenth floor. It was compact, but comfortable, with a small kitchen, expansive living room, master bedroom, and a smaller guest room with twin beds. Aside from the creature comforts, the location fit well with my plan to meet Petrov.

Pavel gave me the key and his phone number. "Do you need anything else?" His tone was indifferent, but I was paying his group thirty-five thousand euros of my own money to keep me satisfied . . . and alive. My needs were satisfied and Pavel departed. I propped a chair under the doorknob, raided the general's pantry, and cooked dinner. Afterwards, I slept.

For two days, I rested in the general's apartment, waiting for Thursday. With Sergei under surveillance, I couldn't risk contacting him to ask if his wife passed my instructions to Petrov for our meeting. I spent the time planning my approach, and gaming options for getting him and his wife to the pickup point for that diplomatic flight that would solve everyone's problems. I also considered how I would kill him, and maybe myself, if Petrov had led me into a trap.

CHAPTER 14

THE URGENT MESSAGE lay on Zabluda's desk when he returned from lunch: *Call Major Ipatiev at GRU headquarters.*

Zabluda dialed his former comrade in arms. Ipatiev came on the line and said, "When I visited your office, I told you that Gregory Vasiliev had been killed in Germany while trying to take out a Chechen. My section chief knew I had worked with Vasiliev and asked me to close out his operational files. One of my tasks was to delete his passport from the immigration database. I discovered a surprising fact. The day before the Germans reported Vasiliev dead, he used his passport to enter the Federation at Sheremetyevo Airport."

"Maybe Vasiliev left papers on a corpse to confuse the Germans while he escaped."

"He hasn't reported for duty, and Germans don't make those kinds of mistakes. Yet, an immigration officer handprinted Vasiliev and ran his passport."

"Then, it's a computer error, but why are you telling me?"

"I emailed you a copy of the immigration processing. Take a look. I'll stay on the line."

Impatiently, Zabluda booted up his computer and ran the video. He saw Vasiliev walking from the immigration booth to the handprint machine.

"Notice anything unusual?" asked Ipatiev

"Part of his face is bandaged and his arm is in a sling."

Ipatiev said, "I'm emailing you a close-up photograph of the man with Vasiliev's passport, taken at the handprint machine. Look at the photo and run the video again. See how he walks."

Zabluda examined the photo and replayed the video. He hissed, "That's Maxwell Geller! Damn him! How did he fake Vasiliev's fingerprints and get by facial recognition?"

"I put that question to a computer expert. He told me the algorithm first matches the fingerprints to the passport holder. If they agree, the algorithm overrides any facial recognition anomalies because it's less accurate than fingerprints. The problem is those fingerprints are definitely Vasiliev's, but the man is definitely Geller. What do you want to do?"

"Have you reported this?"

"No. I can delay for forty-eight hours. Other aspects of Vasiliev's demise need my attention. Since Geller is in Russia, technically his case falls under the FSB. I thought you might want a head start before the GRU gets involved."

"What I want is Geller's head on a platter."

CHAPTER 15

Thursday, 5:00 p.m.
Moscow

PETROV AND HIS wife were waiting on the platform at the Arbat Metro Station when I arrived. The instructions I sent them—using Sergei's wife as my courier—were to take the Blue Line to Parti-yanskaya Station, do some shopping at the nearby AST Mall, have dinner, and take a cab to the Kronwerk Cinema, where I would contact them. Provided they were not followed.

When the Blue Line train arrived, the Petrovs pushed their way into the last car along with other commuters. I entered and took an aisle seat next to a stout Russian lady. She tried to fold into herself so that no part of her body would touch mine. Even with that move, a quarter of me was hanging off the seat, but I had a decent view of the passengers. The car wasn't crowded, but no two empty seats were side by side. As the Petrovs moved to the next car to find seats together, I watched for anyone watching them.

There were lots of different uniforms on that car, as there always are in Moscow. Suddenly, I felt naked. Two years ago, a grainy photo of me was posted in every Moscow subway car and station. Then, I remembered I was still wearing the Vasiliev disguise, minus the arm sling. I relaxed and refocused.

We passed a couple of stations, and I was about to rate the Petrovs dry cleaned—free of surveillance—when I saw her. The woman wore a fur hat and coat. When she steadied herself against the lurching starts and stops of the train by holding onto a pole, her wrist was even with her lips, and she spoke into the sleeve of her coat. I watched her move forward until she could see into the Petrovs' car. After a while, it was clear that she was coordinating surveillance of the couple by directing tails on and off the train at successive stops. Through a window, I watched commuters waiting to board the Petrovs' car. The tails wore earpieces, probably taking directions from the woman in the fur coat. They would take a seat or stand near the Petrovs, ride for a few stops, get off, and be replaced by another loner or couple. I memorized their faces.

The Petrovs got off at Partiyanskaya Metro Station and walked up the broad staircase, past the huge sculpture of a woman and two men depicting World War II Russian partisans, for which the station was named.

The evening was cold to my Australian acclimatized blood, but it was unusually warm for that time of year in Moscow. My targets walked the few blocks to the AST mall. They split up, shopped, and met for dinner.

I had to get to our planned meeting point ahead of the Petrovs to see if it was safe to make contact. I took a cab to the Kronwerk Cinema, about a mile away. Ninety minutes later, I watched the Petrovs arrive and purchase tickets. She headed for the restroom; Petrov stood by, waiting for me to make contact. The fur coat lady from the Metro and some of the earpiece commuters were cruising the lobby. Their presence confirmed that Petrov was either bait in a Max Geller trap, or the FSB was suspicious of him. Although I had sent Petrov word that there wouldn't be a second attempt if the first meet was compromised, the challenge took hold of me. I was in the game again and determined to find a safe place to approach Petrov, one that didn't tip the FSB that I was in Moscow. Some perverse part of me wanted to prove that I still had the chops to outfox the Russians. I knew I had to control that impulse. What was the caution? *Discipline 007, discipline.*

It was almost midnight when I arrived at the Petrovs' residence, a nice apartment building in the Arbat District. It suggested that there was more money in the family coffers than a Russian lieutenant colonel's pay and his wife's salary as a secretary at the Defense Ministry.

I picked the lock on the outside door. Inside, I gave the basement door lock the same service and went down for a quick inspection. Satisfied, I went upstairs to the entrance hall, unscrewed the bulb, and waited in darkness.

Petrov and his wife arrived shortly after midnight. He commented on the light being out as they entered the elevator. I chose that moment to step out of the darkness and catch the elevator door before it closed.

Speaking Russian, I said, "Excuse me, Colonel." They were startled. I quickly added, "I'm Major Stasivich from the Defense Ministry. I have an urgent message for you."

Petrov could see my face clearly in the glow of the elevator's fluorescent ceiling light. I had removed the bandages and he recognized me. I glanced at his wife, then at him. "Sir, I was instructed to give you the message in private."

Petrov told his wife, "Go on, Olga. I'll be up in a few minutes."

Olga gave me a skeptical glance and pressed the *up* button as soon as her husband stepped out of the elevator, into the darkened hallway. I put a finger to my lips for silence and pointed my pistol at his head. He didn't flinch. I took him by the lapel of his heavy overcoat and led him down to the basement. The only illumination was moonlight reflected off the snow, coming through high basement windows. Petrov didn't object while I patted him down for a wire.

"Okay. Let's talk," I said.

He was angry. "First, you don't contact me at the filling station. Then, you send Sergei's wife to say you will contact me at the cinema, but you don't. What is going on?"

"You tell me. The FSB surveillance team was all over you this evening: on the Metro platform, in the train, at the shopping center, and waiting for you at the cinema."

He shrugged. "If anyone followed me, it was GRU counterintelligence. I have extensive access to Federation war plans. They follow me periodically to be sure I'm not peddling secrets to Western intelligence agents."

"You weren't followed by GRU agents. They were FSB . . . the same people who would like to get their hands on me."

"You think I betrayed you?"

"Did you?"

"No. How can you be so sure it was the FSB following me? Does your excellent CIA training help you identify who is FSB and who is GRU?"

"There was a woman coordinating your surveillance on the Metro this evening. Two days ago, she was staked out in the café where your friend Sergei has his morning coffee. That's not a coincidence. Sergei is FSB. So, if he's under suspicion, FSB counterintelligence people were following him, not GRU."

In the moonlight, I saw Petrov frown. "Why would the FSB be following Sergei?"

"Maybe they suspect him of spying for the CIA."

"Is he?"

"How should I know. I don't work for the CIA." Never give up your assets.

"Then, why are you here?"

"The CIA blackmailed me to bring you out because you asked for me. Why me?"

"Sergei warned me not to trust the local CIA agents to keep my identity secret from the wrong people in Washington. He trusts you, and I was impressed by your escape after you robbed the Allgemeine Volksbank. Now that you are here, what took you so long?"

"How did you think this would work?" I asked. "You slip our attaché a note one day and the next morning the Batmobile picks you up at your apartment and drives you out of Russia?"

The Batmobile reference didn't register. He said, "I expected you to act with urgency!"

"I didn't know you existed until a week ago, and here I am. That's pretty damned urgent in my book."

"Well, you have come too late. I have another way out of Russia."

"What! You had me come all this way for nothing? Why didn't you tell us?"

"There was no time. The arrangements were made three days ago."

"What arrangements?"

"Next week, my wife and I are going to Tallinn, Estonia, on holiday. I will be accompanied by another officer—an old friend—and his wife. While we are there, we will be under surveillance by the GRU and there could be a security detail to protect us. That is being discussed. So, I will need your assistance in Tallinn to get away from them."

"Why would you need a security detail on a holiday?"

"I told you, I have access to many state secrets."

I was mad as hell, but there was no point in taking it out on Petrov. Shit happens. You always hope it doesn't happen to you, but things do go wrong in the land of smoke and mirrors. Having a temper tantrum is rarely helpful. You can either shoot someone or get on with the mission. My old patriotic work ethic kicked in, along with my instinct for self-preservation. Langley needed to know if this guy was a legitimate defector and I needed to know if he was part of an FSB plot to lure me back to Moscow for trial and execution.

I asked, "Why do you want to defect?"

"I can't do this anymore."

"Can't do what anymore?"

A flash of anger. "You were sent here to be my guide, not my father confessor. The CIA knows why I want to defect and what I have to offer. If you don't help me, you—and your country—will be sorry."

"I'm sorry already, and I wasn't sent here. I was forced to come here at great personal risk. So, you need to tell me why it was worth risking my life to come back to Moscow."

"I have details of certain Federation activities of vital concern to the United States. That's all I will say."

"Let me say something to you. The easiest way out of this mess for me is to kill you and tell Langley you changed your mind about defecting. When—no, if—Langley hears that you've been shot, they'll assume your government found out you were trying to peddle secrets to the CIA. So, unless you want to die in this cellar, you had better answer my questions."

Petrov glared at me, and I saw something go wild in his eyes. He put his arms back and out from his sides like he was flying and leaned into my gun. "You want to shoot me? Shoot! I-don't-give-a-shit." He wasn't angry. He was calm. Resigned to his fate.

I believed him. He intended to defect or die, not caring which. I remembered Sergei telling me that Petrov suffered from post-traumatic stress. I recognized the desperation of a burned-out warrior. In that moment, he wanted me to shoot him.

As Petrov advanced against my gun, I backed up until he almost pinned me against the wall. I did a quick sidestep and he lunged forward, catching himself with his palms. There he was, braced against the wall, arms outstretched and straight, his head hanging down between his broad shoulders in utter defeat. His fur hat fell to the floor.

I gave him a moment to compose himself. When he turned to face me, I could see a film of sweat on his forehead. There was weariness in his voice. "Are you going to help me or not?"

At that moment, I wanted nothing to do with him. He was a threat. Not a physical one, but unstable. I didn't want to be driving through some checkpoint and have him flip out. Maybe I could persuade him to give me the information and stay in Russia if he focused on the repercussions of a defection. "When you defect, what happens to your children?" He had two.

"My children have committed to Putin's Russia. Both work for state security, not choices I wanted them to make." There was sadness in his voice. His veneer of confidence had evaporated. He was just a guy, talking to another guy . . . about subjects that could get us both killed.

"And your parents, what about them?"

"My parents are dead."

I knew that, but I kept checking for inconsistencies to tip me off if the man was not who he claimed to be.

"Does your wife know your plans?"

He paused. When he spoke, confidence had seeped back into his voice. "Not yet."

"Are your wife's parents living?" Rodney hadn't briefed me. "If so, life will be difficult for them when you defect."

"Don't worry about them. They enjoy all the luxuries available to corrupt servants of our corrupt state." He looked at the ceiling. "This building is one of their luxuries. It is time for me to make choices for my life."

Nothing goes according to plan. I asked, "What if the ministry cancels your trip to Tallinn?"

"It will not be canceled."

"How can you be sure?"

"Because it's not just a holiday."

"What is it?"

"It's the reason the CIA sent you to bring me over. That's all I'm going to tell you."

I believed him. "What's the name of your hotel in Tallinn?"

"The Radisson Blu Sky, but that could change for security reasons. If you're going to help me, you need to be at the airport when we arrive. Follow us to the hotel so you can be sure of my location. I will leave my schedule with the hotel concierge for Mr. Stasivich. That's you."

Petrov smoothed his hair into place and turned away to retrieve his hat from the floor. Looking me in the eye, he said, "Now, if you're not going to shoot me, I need to go upstairs before my wife gets worried and comes down to check." Before going up, he said, "Good night, Mr. Geller. Thank you for coming. I am aware of the risk you are taking, blackmail or not."

The thanks of a grateful defector weren't going to fix this. There was no way to spin it. I had failed on both elements of my mission. I wasn't going to get Petrov out and I hadn't been able to determine if he was really defecting or helping the FSB trap me. The fact that I didn't find a wire on him meant nothing. There are mics that look like coat buttons and transmit conversations through an antenna in your hat. The Russians—and the CIA—are always coming up with some new, almost undetectable, gizmo. And for all I knew, Petrov was upstairs calling an FSB goon squad to pounce on me as I left the building.

My getaway plan was to disable the alarm on the building's back door, step into the alley, and disappear. As I was about to have a go at the alarm, I stopped, cold. I remembered the FSB car blocking the back gate of the school where I met Sergei. They had anticipated that a runner might exit through the rear door. Part of that same FSB team was covering Petrov and, more than likely, they would have a car at his back door. Slipping out the back after midnight was guaranteed to result in an interrogation. I checked the gun in my overcoat pocket and walked out the front door into the cold Moscow night.

It had snowed some, the light fluffy stuff. The street was quiet, no foot or vehicle traffic. A few cars were parked at the curbs on both sides of the street. I was about thirty steps away from the door when I noticed it. Ahead of me, across the street, I saw a car that hadn't been there when I entered the building. Two men got out. The one on the passenger's side was tall and slim. The driver was tall and beefy. Their overcoats and fur hats were black against the snow and streetlight as they trudged toward me, their boots crunching on the fresh snow.

I was thinking of the Mattis doctrine: "Have a plan to kill everyone you meet." My gun was equipped with a silencer. I could drop these guys and keep walking. No question. But that wouldn't solve my problem. The FSB probably had a camera trained on Petrov's building, just as they did on Sergei's school, and probably more manpower in shouting distance. Killing these two might trigger a gun battle right there, and, if I got away, a manhunt, for sure. I would have difficulty getting out of Moscow. I needed a story that explained why I was there.

The two men stopped a few feet in front of me. The beefy driver held a blackjack at his side. I recognized him from the FSB stakeout in Sergei's coffee shop. The thin one held up his credentials and said two of the most feared and hated words a Russian can hear, "State security."

I said, "Good evening," and tried to look too stupid to be frightened. He asked, "You live in this building?"

"I was visiting a friend."

"What is your friend's name?"

"Please. She is a married lady."

They smiled at each other. The beefy one asked, "What did she do, use you and throw you out on the street after the neighbors were asleep?"

"Her husband returned to Moscow a day early. He just called from the airport. He's on his way home. He's my boss. I can't be here when he arrives. I'll lose my job."

The tall one said, "A clear case of adultery."

"If I have committed a crime, can I please pay you the fine and get away from his house?"

The tall one turned to his partner. "What do you think is the appropriate fine for adultery."

"Hard to say," replied The Beef. "Depends on how deeply he has penetrated this family."

They laughed.

I heard a subtle change in their tone. These hoods knew where they were. Apartments on that street go for six or seven figures and the arriving owner had the power to fire people. If you're nobodies who sit outside his building after midnight, in a cold car, you don't want to be caught interviewing the evidence that a man with that kind of juice has a condom in his caviar. But these guys couldn't just walk away. I had to give them a face-saver and end their bullshit.

"Maybe, if I could open my wallet, you could take the appropriate fine. May I . . . ?"

Slowly, I removed my wallet from the breast pocket of my overcoat and opened it. I learned on my tour in Moscow to keep enough cash in my wallet to make a bribe—a viable alternative to the paperwork involved in taking me in for some minor offense. Their greedy eyes focused on the contents. The beefy guy grabbed all the paper money and handed it to his boss. The boss ignored the rubles, took two hundred-euro notes, and shoved them into his overcoat pocket. Then, he carefully counted a selection of twenties and fifties, and shoved them into his other pocket. He handed what was left to The Beef, who stuffed the bills into his pocket.

The tall guy said, "Sasha, don't be greedy. Leave him Metro fare."

Sasha snorted, pocketed his blackjack, counted off a few rubles, and threw them at my feet. This guy was pushing the envelope. I kept an eye on him as I picked up the money. If he tried to blackjack me while I was bending over, I was going to shoot him and his boss.

When I stood, the beefy one nodded toward the end of the block. "Get your ass out of here and don't come back."

I moved away quickly and walked back to General Grishin's apartment.

Actually, that stakeout encounter ended well for me. They took a bribe. That guaranteed I wouldn't show up in their surveillance report. The reason the tall one selected a variety of bills from my stash was to distribute shares to his crew—other watchers on the street and maybe a cameraman recording the comings and goings at Petrov's building.

The short-term outcome was a success. I survived. Long-term might be a problem. Petrov knew I was in Moscow. I had no idea where his loyalties lay. None of my questions had answers. Why was Petrov defecting? Was he bait? Why was the FSB tailing Petrov? Was his wife ready to give up the comfort of her six- or seven-figure apartment and leave her parents to the tender mercies of the FSB? To make matters worse, Petrov had refused to leave Moscow with me. I had failed by every standard, Rodney's and my own.

Answers or not, one thing was clear: I had to get out of Moscow before the FSB knew I was there, and before the GRU started asking how Vasiliev could be dead in Germany and passing through airport customs in Moscow. In thirty-six hours, on Saturday, I had a prearranged exfil meeting with a Moscow Station rep. I was going to exfil myself the hell out of Russia on that diplomatic flight. After that, RAMPART was not my problem.

I went to bed. Sleep came quickly, but not rest. I had nightmares of an unhappy Vanessa in Australia, and visions of her in Moscow trying unsuccessfully to get away from the FSB shakedown I had experienced outside of Petrov's building.

CHAPTER 16

Friday morning
FSB Headquarters, Moscow

THE SURVEILLANCE REPORT told Zabluda nothing. He was about to file it when a young man in civilian clothes knocked and entered his office.

"Sir, I am Junior Sergeant Burkov. Are you the officer directing surveillance of the Petrovs?"

"Yes. I was just reading your report from last night's activities."

"May I close the door, sir? I need to speak to you in private."

"Of course."

Unlike many of the middle-grade officers at FSB headquarters, Zabluda had served in the field with Russian special forces where rank meant little, and relationships were everything. He was not indifferent to men who spent long hours on frigid streets and cold cars where heaters—if they existed—were turned off so as not to alert the target being spied upon.

"What's on your mind, Sergeant?"

"I'm here to inform you of an irregularity. May I see the report with my signature, sir?"

Zabluda handed him the document.

Burkov examined it. "I didn't write this report, sir, and this is not my signature."

"Who did write it?"

"I suspect my supervisor, Senior Sergeant Chernoff."

"Why would he do that?"

"To cover up an irregularity. My team took over surveillance of the Petrovs when they arrived home, about midnight. We had two men in a car covering the alley behind Colonel Petrov's building. Senior Sergeant Chernoff and Sergeant Korilovich were in a car, covering the front. My partner and I were in an apartment across the street observing the front entrance. He was spotting with binoculars. I was operating a camera with a telescopic lens.

"About twenty minutes after Colonel Petrov and his wife entered their apartment building, a man came out. I photographed him, checked my watch, and made a note for my report."

Zabluda checked the report. "There's no mention of that here. Go on."

"Senior Sergeant Chernoff and Sergeant Korilovich were parked on my side of the street. They left their car and intercepted the man who had exited the Petrovs' building. I photographed the encounter. The man took out his wallet. I thought they were checking his identification, but they took his money and let him go. Later, when Senior Sergeant Chernoff relieved me, he gave me seventy euros. I said, 'What is this for?' He said, 'It's for your new glasses. You didn't see what you think you saw.' Then, he took my camera and deleted photographs of the exchange."

Burkov handed Zabluda an envelope. "This contains the chip from my camera. I know a bit about photography. A good technician can restore the photographs. The seventy euros he gave me are also in this envelope. The bills look new. The lab may be able to lift fingerprints."

Zabluda was suspicious. "Are you accusing Senior Sergeant Chernoff of taking a bribe?"

"No, sir. I am not here to make accusations. I just came to report my observations and my conversation with Senior Sergeant Chernoff."

"And you didn't prepare this surveillance report?"

"No, sir. Senior Sergeant Chernoff told me he would take care of it."

Zabluda dismissed Burkov with a warning to keep his irregularities report confidential. After the sergeant had gone, he took the camera card to the photo lab and the money to the fingerprint lab.

His last stop was the personnel office where the deputy personnel officer, a major, brought him the files on Junior Sergeant Burkov and his supervisor, Senior Sergeant Chernoff. For half an hour, Zabluda sat in an interview room reviewing the sergeants' work histories.

The major stopped in the doorway and asked, "Sir, are you finding everything you need?"

"No. What I need is not in these files."

"Maybe I can help. I interviewed those men for a study."

"What kind of study?"

"The chief personnel officer had a theory that supervisors passed over for promotion tend to disapprove the promotion of their subordinates, especially much younger subordinates. My data supported his theory. Senior Sergeant Chernoff has been passed over enough times to be a Jew. He refuses to recommend Junior Sergeant Burkov for promotion."

"Why?"

"I don't know Chernoff's motivations, but those two men could not be more of a mismatch. Burkov is young, ambitious, and obeys the rules. Chernoff is old school, his paperwork is sloppy, and he bends rules to the breaking point. He's been offered jobs at headquarters, but turned them down. He prefers the streets."

"Where there is less supervision," noted Zabluda. "In your opinion, would Burkov take a bribe?"

"Never."

"Chernoff?"

"Chernoff would never refuse a bribe."

*　　*　　*

It was just after 2 p.m. Friday, when Senior Sergeant Chernoff responded to an urgent call requiring him to report to Colonel Zabluda, in his office.

"Senior Sergeant Chernoff, reporting, sir," said the tall man as he stood in front of Zabluda's desk and saluted.

Zabluda left him standing at attention and said, "I hope I didn't disrupt your sleep cycle. I know you're on the midnight-to-eight shift, but we are in a critical phase of the Petrov surveillance. I need your help."

"Whatever you need, sir."

"We had reason to believe that antisocial agents would attempt to contact Colonel Petrov during the past twenty-four hours." Zabluda handed Chernoff a sheet of paper. "This is the shift report from your surveillance last night, signed by Junior Sergeant Burkov. He reported no activity. As shift supervisor, can you verify its accuracy?"

Chernoff glanced at the document. "It was a quiet night, sir."

"Was it?" Zabluda showed Chernoff a head-and-shoulders photograph of Max Geller. "Do you recognize this man?"

Zabluda watched a fountain of crimson rise from Chernoff's collar to his cheeks.

Chernoff said, "He looks familiar. Who is he?" Another evasive answer.

Zabluda said, "Maybe these photographs will refresh your memory." It was a group photo of Chernoff and his partner, Sergeant Korilovich, confronting Max Geller. Geller was offering his wallet. The next one showed Chernoff with his hand in Geller's wallet. In the final shot, Chernoff was holding Geller's wallet and stuffing money into his coat pocket.

Zabluda took a plastic, see-through bag from his desk drawer and placed it in front of Chernoff. It contained euro notes. "This is the bribe money you gave Junior Sergeant Burkov. It has your fingerprints. Do you need to see more, Senior Sergeant. Because I have more."

Chernoff was ash-white and his voice was a whisper. "No, sir."

"Unless you want this to go up the chain of command, you belong to me, Chernoff. Do we understand each other?"

"Yes, sir. I would prefer that you handle this matter at your level."

"Good. In return for my discretion, I have a job for you. It's a confidential job. You answer to me alone." Zabluda tapped Geller's photograph. "I want you to find this man. Be quick, be thorough, and be discreet. I want nothing in writing, audio, or video form and no computer searches, just shoe leather."

"Who is this man, sir?"

"He is an American spy who apparently met with Petrov in his apartment building while you were sitting across the street in your car. Let's see if you can redeem yourself for that act of gross negligence, Senior Sergeant. Here's a list of the fifteen men for your detail." He handed the list to Chernoff. "It's your job to make sure they keep their mouths shut about this job."

Zabluda continued. "He could not have walked far in the cold. Check the cameras in every Metro station within walking distance of the Petrov residence. Look for arrivals between midnight and 1 a.m. Then, draw a circle thirty minutes' walking time from the point where you took your bribe." Zabluda emphasized the word bribe. "Check every traffic camera. Interview every cab driver who picked up a male passenger within that circle. If you don't find him after that, check the security camera on every building inside your circle."

Chernoff interrupted him. "With respect, sir. I know how to conduct a manhunt."

"You also know how to conduct surveillance. If you had used that knowledge last night, we wouldn't be here today. Find him or don't come back, Chernoff."

"Sir, may I speak bluntly in my defense."

"Not defense, mitigation. Go ahead."

"I know that Sergeant Burkov reported me. Burkov lives with his parents. He pays no rent. He buys no food. He has no girlfriends. Why? Because he is always spouting nonsense about how only the proper administration of justice can save Russia. What he says comes out of the mouth of inexperience. He thinks he's the only one who ever thought that justice was a good idea.

"In a few years," continued Chernoff, "Burkov will be living on the Outer Ring in one of those shitty little Khruschyovka apartments with cracks in the ceiling and bad plumbing. He'll have a wife and two children, and not enough money to feed them decent meals from one payday to the next. Then, he'll be wearing a sign around his neck that says, 'I take bribes. Pay here.' When I take a bribe, I share it with my men because they are living Burkov's future right now."

"So," said Zabluda, "should I view you as the Robin Hood of Moscow or just a bad sergeant? Your recent fitness reports say that you are barely competent and a borderline alcoholic."

Chernoff stiffened. "I can run an operation, Colonel, if there were any operations worth my talents. If you checked my file, you know I've earned my share of commendations. I was good enough at this job for the mafia to put a price on my head, before the mafia became part of the government. Now, when I run a good operation, I tell headquarters to give the credit and commendations to my men. They need promotions to survive."

"Do you give them credit for your vodka breath, too? I can smell it on you now."

"I will tell you a secret, Colonel. Every morning before I leave for work, I swish a little vodka around in my mouth and put a touch behind each ear. After a while, they stopped offering me desk jobs. They keep me on the street and that's good enough. It's my little rebellion, my way of not becoming part of the lie."

"What lie?"

"That everything is going well here."

CHAPTER 17

Saturday morning
Moscow

Two policemen stood on the pavement outside my restaurant. I was lingering over a late morning breakfast in the Arbat District, killing time until my afternoon rendezvous with the CIA rep and anticipating my diplomatic flight out of Moscow. I was at ease, but vigilant, when two events heightened my situational awareness. In plain English, that term means you are sufficiently attuned to what's going on around you to take advantage of unanticipated opportunities, and to make sure you're not caught at a disadvantage by unforeseen events. For example, you don't become so focused on your meal that you don't notice when some FSB goon comes through the back door and sticks a gun in your ear.

The first of the two events occurred when I glanced through the restaurant window and saw two men stop outside, look up, come in, and ask for the manager. They were in civilian clothes, but carried themselves with the swagger of Moscow heat. The manager went into obsequious mode and ushered them back to his office near the restrooms.

The second event occurred across the street from the restaurant. There were two clothing stores next to each other. A couple of men stopped in front of the stores and looked up. They conferred briefly, split up, and one entered each store. My awareness warning jumped to high alert. They had been looking up at security cameras covering the street and were the same FSB goons who took bribes from me at Petrov's apartment building the previous night.

I dropped enough rubles on the table to pay for my meal and headed for the restroom. Slowing as I passed the manager's office, I heard him tell the heat, "I can't help you. Each morning when we come in, we erase the digital images from the previous night, unless there has been trouble on the street."

These guys—and the ones across the street—were looking for someone on the street last night. I was the likely target. That meant they knew I had talked to Petrov—bad news—or they knew who I was—really bad news. I had to get out of the Arbat before they found the right security camera and me. There might even be footage of me going into General Grishin's apartment building. I called Pavel and told him—in clumsy code—to get my stuff from the apartment and bring it to the doctor's office. We had only one doctor in common, Zhukov.

It was clear that I needed to get out of Russia fast. Colonel Burke, our Army attaché in Moscow, was my official travel agent, and it was only justice for him to get me on that diplomatic flight. He got me into this mess when he delivered RAMPART's request for my services to the Agency. However, it would be foolhardy to contact Burke directly at the embassy.

Before I left Heidelberg, Eva, through Langley, set up a contact for me to get messages to Burke. That contact was Burke's wife. I was having breakfast, on my way to meet her, when the heat came looking at those building cameras.

As usual, traffic was awful in Moscow. I took a cab to kill time. I had the driver make unnecessary stops on the way to my destination, the Slavyansky Bulvar Metro Station, near the Oceana Shopping Mall. The mall is a modern, four-story affair built around a fountain. It's a monstrosity on the outside and gorgeous inside, with everything you ever wanted to buy—except a one-way ticket out of Moscow with no questions asked. My contact was there, shopping. At the appointed time, I was waiting for her on the Metro platform near a ticket machine.

The woman was petite and wore a heavy cloth coat and fur hat. She joined me on the Metro platform, taking care not to stand too close. When she got within hearing distance, I pretended to get a cell phone call while she pretended not to listen. For the benefit of anyone watching her and for the station cameras, I put my phone to one ear, a finger in the other, and turned slightly away from her, but I spoke loud enough for her to hear.

To my imaginary caller, I said, "I arrived from Vladivostok two days ago," the code sentence to confirm my identity.

In a low voice she asked, "Status?"

Into my phone, I said, "Listen, there's been a change in plan. My client decided to stay in Moscow. I'm leaving for St. Petersburg at 6 p.m."

Translation: RAMPART's not leaving. I need to leave Moscow. Pick me up at the rendezvous, code-named St. Petersburg, at 6 p.m. tonight. Working with Eva, I had arranged for several pickup points around Moscow with the names of other Russian cities. St. Petersburg was Dr. Zhukov's hospital.

She replied, "Package status?" She wanted a Petrov update.

Still with my back to her, I said, "The delivery schedule has been changed. That machinery is heavy, and they are going to have to break it into two packages. So, the shipping point and the delivery schedule have been adjusted."

"What's the new schedule and location?" for getting Petrov out, she asked.

"Tell you when I know." I added, "Can your man meet me at the train station before I leave for St. Petersburg?" Translation: "Can your husband pick me up at the St. Petersburg rendezvous tonight?"

She said, "Yes," just as the train pulled into the station.

We entered the car and took seats away from each other.

I needed a place to hole up until my evening meeting with Colonel Burke. Returning to the Arbat District was not a good idea, with the FSB doing a door-to-door, camera-to-camera search. I headed for the hospital and Dr. Zhukov's office.

CHAPTER 18

ZHUKOV WAS OFF on Saturdays. I picked his lock again, propped a chairback under the doorknob, and stretched out on the couch for a nap. Situational awareness is fine, but so is some G.I. wisdom from World War II: "A smart soldier never walks when he can ride, never stands when he can sit, never sits when he can lie down, and never stays awake when he can sleep." Save your strength for the coming battle.

My cell phone alarm awakened me in time to prepare for my exit meeting. I put on a white lab coat from Zhukov's closet, draped his stethoscope around my neck, and took up my vigil at a window overlooking the hospital parking lot. It was dark when the attaché's car arrived. Three people got out: Colonel Burke, in civvies, Mrs. Burke, and another woman.

The FSB car that tailed them from the embassy pulled onto the parking lot and stopped abruptly. A woman jumped out and followed the trio to the emergency entrance. The FSB driver parked his car in a space that gave him a view of Burke's vehicle.

Now, for the tricky part. I gave them time to in-process the sick woman and went down to the ER in my white coat, face mask, and surgical cap. Burke and his wife—my contact from the Metro platform—were holding hands and trying to look worried when I approached. In Russian, I asked, "Did you bring in the American woman?"

"English, please," requested Mrs. Burke.

"Sorry." I repeated the question in English. They told me they had.

I asked, "Would you come with me, please? We have matters to discuss."

I led them down a long corridor to the front lobby, deserted at that hour. As we passed the stairs up to Zhukov's floor, I whispered to Colonel Burke, "Up the stairs, past the elevator, second office on the right."

The FSB woman followed us, conspicuous in the empty corridor.

I sat the Burkes down and began an earnest conversation—in heavily accented English—about the patient. The FSB woman peeled off and went into the ladies' room on the near side of the lobby. As soon as she was out of sight, Burke made a dash for the stairway and disappeared. A few minutes later, his FSB shadow exited the ladies' room. She was puzzled to see me talking to Mrs. Burke and the colonel missing.

I looked at the men's room on the far side of the lobby and asked, loudly, for the benefit of the shadow, "Is your husband ill?"

"He has a slight stomach virus."

"You can wait for him here if you like," I suggested, "or go back to the emergency room."

Mrs. Burke opted for the ER. We headed back that way. Our FSB shadow looked confused. She decided to wait for the colonel to exit the restroom and pretended to inspect the window display of the closed gift shop.

I left Mrs. Burke in the ER and took the elevator up to Zhukov's floor. When I got to the office, Colonel Burke was waiting. He had a thick, squat body and Slavic features. The man could pass for a Russian. That was probably why he had been assigned to Moscow.

Burke had already scanned the office, including the desk name-plate. "Who is Dr. Zhukov?"

"Someone who forgot to lock his office." He didn't need to know Zhukov was helping me. "Who's playing the sick woman you brought in?"

"My niece. She's visiting and volunteered to help. The embassy doctor gave her something to elevate her blood pressure and pulse rate. She's faking abdominal pains. They'll have to scan her to rule out appendicitis. We have time."

He changed the subject abruptly, "Why didn't you bring RAMPART out last night? We had the diplomatic flight ready to go." His tone was disapproving.

"RAMPART changed his mind. He wants a later date."

"He doesn't get to change his damned mind. He goes when we say so."

"The time wasn't right for him. You're his guy in Moscow. You should have known."

"And you should have cold-cocked him and brought him out over your shoulder."

"The FSB had him under surveillance."

That surprised Burke, but he recovered, with suspicion. "How did you speak to him if he was being followed?"

"This isn't my first meeting with a Russian in Moscow, Burke. I spent a couple of years at Moscow Station, while you were eating sand in the Middle East."

Burke gave me a hard look. "So, what's RAMPART's new plan?"

"He wants to delay his defection until a later date."

"Until when?"

"Until he tells you he's ready." Burke had no need to know RAMPART's plan to defect in Estonia. I have gut feelings about who I can trust and I didn't trust Burke.

"Where will you be in the meantime?" Burke asked.

"Not in Moscow. What's the plan to get me on that diplomatic flight to Washington?"

"That's a problem. Not only did you fail to deliver RAMPART, you've become a liability. The FSB knows you're in Moscow. They came to the embassy this morning and demanded that the ambassador turn you over for trial."

"How do they know I'm here?"

"They had pictures of you from a street camera. The ambassador doesn't want an incident with the Russians. He disavowed you and canceled the diplomatic flight. There's no way to smuggle you out right now. The Russians are on full alert at air and rail terminals, and spot-checking vehicles on streets and highways."

There goes Murphy, again! "When's the next diplomatic flight?"

"To be determined."

"What am I supposed to do in the meantime?"

"Lay low."

"Where?"

"Wherever you stayed during your last visit . . . when you robbed the bank."

"That location is compromised."

"Then, you have a problem. Orders from Langley are that you can't leave Moscow without RAMPART. Tell him to stay put. I'll get word to you when it's safe to move."

My gut said Burke didn't know about my getaway car at the train station.

He gave me a cell phone, code instructions, and pickup points. I listened with one ear. The other ear listened to that internal voice saying, *Get the hell out of Moscow, now!*

Curiosity overcame good sense. I wanted to know what the CIA hadn't told me. I said, "I'm concerned about RAMPART. He was unstable. If he won't follow instructions, we could have a disaster when we try to move him. Tell me what you know about this guy and his wife."

Burke went bureaucratic on me. "Sorry. I can't give you any information that's not directly related to transporting you and RAMPART out of Russia. Weren't you briefed before you came to Moscow?"

"Nobody briefed me that he might change your well-oiled plan to get him out . . . or that he's suicidal! He leaned into my gun and dared me to shoot him. No, he *wanted* me to shoot him. If he's that unstable, I should have been warned."

"The RAMPART I know is not unstable."

"Well, what RAMPART do you know? What is so special about this guy?"

"What did your Langley handler tell you?"

"He told me a fairy tale. He said RAMPART proved his bona fides by delivering parts of the Russian war plan for Syria. That's a joke. Nobody in Washington cares about Russia's plans for Syria. That ship sailed when the last administration left town. Anyway, Putin doesn't care about Syria. He wants to reclaim the landmass of the old Soviet Union. He's going for Belarus, Ukraine, the Black Sea, and the Baltic. So, what's so special about a guy who brings us the war plan for Syria?"

"What makes you think he's special?"

"He demands, and gets, a specific guide—me—to bring him over. That triggers a worldwide search for a Russian whose identity I can steal. My old Agency boss blackmails me to come here, at the risk of my life, and puts all the resources of Moscow Station at my disposal, including a diplomatic flight. Again, I ask you, what is so special about RAMPART?"

"I-don't-know."

"You knew him in Egypt. Cairo Station would have had a file on him. What was in it?"

"Are you deaf? I can't tell you anything unless it relates to your transportation, period."

I pulled the gun from my waistband and held it at my side. "I'm running out of time and patience, Burke. This is a Russian gun. I can solve my Moscow problems by shooting you and RAMPART, and blaming the FSB. Are you going to answer my questions or not?"

Burke didn't blink. "Screw you. I've looked down gun barrels before. What else you got?"

"I've got your wife and I don't even have to shoot her."

All of a sudden, he wasn't so cocky. "What about my wife?"

"She's a CIA officer, working under State Department cover. Your homelife will get really miserable if I out her and she loses her career because you're being stubborn."

"You'll go to jail if you out her."

"I know this game way better than you. The Agency won't be able to trace the leak to me. Even if they do, I'm not subject to U.S. law. I renounced my citizenship when the CIA screwed up my life and fired me. Are you going to tell me about RAMPART or not?"

"They told me you were a son of a bitch."

"Then you know I'm not bluffing."

He leaned forward, maybe preparing to charge me.

"Don't be a dead hero. I've never shot a colonel, but I'd sure like to know if you bleed blood or bullshit."

Burke was angry. I stayed out of reach and let him cool off. When he finally spoke, he was sullen and deliberate, picking his words carefully. "Petrov's—RAMPART's—embassy file said he was a decorated officer in the Russian tank troops. A smart and careful planner. Something of a military academic. He's written articles on the use of tanks in urban warfare."

"Combat time?"

"Lots of it."

"What about his mental profile?"

"There was nothing to suggest he was unstable, just the opposite."

"Did he have a good relationship with his wife? Those Russian compounds are known for lots of trans-marriage hanky-panky."

"Olga was with him in Egypt. There were no known extramarital relationships for either of them. We looked for that. Based on what I saw, they were in love."

Maybe. "It would have been standard procedure for you to try to recruit him. What was the goal? Were you trying to cultivate a future asset or did you want something specific from him?"

He hesitated.

"Don't go need-to-know on me, Burke. I'm risking my life to bring this guy over."

"There were two goals. Immediately? Recruit a rising star to spy for us. The long game was using RAMPART to penetrate a Cyprus bank run by his father-in-law. It laundered money for Moscow and held accounts for the GRU and SVR. Their cash was used to finance covert operations in the Middle East and Africa."

"What was RAMPART's response?"

"Negative. He is—was—a patriot. Now, it looks like he's seen the light."

"Or the darkness. Tell me about your social interactions with him."

"I saw Petrov and his wife at official functions sponsored by the Egyptian government. We had drinks occasionally, just the two of us. We sparred. He tried to recruit me."

I gave Burke a nasty smile. "Was he successful?"

Burke didn't think that worthy of a response. He just stared bullets at me. "Are we done?"

We were. Burke went down to the ER to finish the charade.

I wasn't sure what useful information I'd gotten from him. In intelligence work, you never know until other pieces of the puzzle reveal themselves.

All my work evaluations described me as tenacious. That was a polite way of saying I was too stubborn for my own good. I don't like to come away from an operation empty-handed, even if I've been forced into it. When the primary objective is unattainable, I go for an alternate. I had one in mind, but I needed help and I wasn't going to get any from Moscow Station.

Those thoughts were interrupted when Pavel arrived with the suitcase I left at General Grishin's apartment and more bad news. "FSB agents are showing your picture to everyone in the Arbat. You should conclude your business and leave Moscow, now."

"I agree, but I need help from Omega. Do you have a motorway map in your car?"

While Pavel went to the parking lot to get it, I began working on a plan to evade Russian highway surveillance. Burke said the Russians were spot-checking traffic going out of the city.

Pavel returned with the map and we opened it on Dr. Zhukov's desk.

There are lots of highways out of Moscow—the center of the Russian Federation's universe. I had three selection criteria. The route had to get me out of Russia fast, take me to a friendly country, and through a border station where I could bluff, bribe, bypass, or blast my way to safety. The M9 Motorway to Latvia met those criteria. Unfortunately, it would be obvious to anyone pursuing me. The least likely route and the easiest crossing was at the Finnish border, especially on a weekend. People who don't know Russia have a Berlin Wall view of the country's borders. Russians do try to exercise strict border control, but easy exits do exist. There are about twenty regular and provisional crossing points into Finland. Nearly two million Russian tourists cross into Finland every year and spend about $250 million on vacations and consumer goods. A lot of that money is spent at the Zsar Outlet Village, a high-end shopping center on the Finnish side, near the Vaalimaa-Torfyanovka customs checkpoint. That was my target. I had the required forged credentials.

The downside? Finland was twelve hours and six hundred miles from Moscow. I would have to rest on the way. It was bone-chilling cold and sleeping in the car would be suicide by hypothermia. It also gave the FSB more time to find me. I needed some magic.

"Pavel, say I was driving a car on the M9 Motorway and I wanted it to disappear, but keep the car moving west. What are my options?"

Pavel had a quick and devious mind. "Two possibilities, one bad, one good. You could pretend to have a breakdown and call a vehicle transporter to load your car. That is not a good solution. You would have to ride beside the driver and risk being recognized, or stay out of sight in your car, where you would freeze. The other solution would be to drive your car into a large van. You would be concealed and could remain in your car, protected from the elements."

"Do you know someone with a van that can carry a four-door sedan?"

"Yes. It can be arranged. When and where do you need it?"

I pointed to a spot on the map. "Here, on the M9, just after the Rhzev exit, at midnight."

Pavel raised his eyebrows. "Tonight?" He consulted his watch. "We shouldn't use anyone from Moscow. It would be better if the traffic cameras don't record both of you leaving the city. We have such a van in Tver," a city northeast of the Rhzev exit. "If the driver is available, he would have to be paid." That was part notice and part how much.

"Five hundred euros, and fuel."

"A thousand euros, no fuel. Do you want to be driven to the Latvian border?"

"Maybe, but he needs to know the roads north from the V. Luki exit, if we have to detour." Veikiye Luki is an exit that provides accesses to good roads in all directions.

Pavel told me, "It will take an hour to arrange. I need to use a telephone where truck transports are normally scheduled. Otherwise, it would sound suspicious, if the FSB is listening, and they are always listening. I'll call you here."

After Pavel departed, I stretched out on the couch, but couldn't sleep right away. Murphy invaded my mind. What if the van didn't show? What if it broke down and I still had to drive a long way without rest? I needed a Murphy solution. I went to sleep before I came up with one.

An hour later, Pavel called me on Dr. Zhukov's phone. "I didn't have time to come in. I slipped the medical records under your door."

I got the envelope and tore it open. It contained instructions and a diagram of my rendezvous point with the van. "Got it. Thank you." He rang off without a word. That was odd.

I took a cab to Leningradsky Train Station and, checking for tails, walked to my getaway car. Sitting behind the wheel, I accepted the reality that had been lurking in my mind since Burke told me my flight out of Moscow had been canceled. The map told the story. Any route out of Russia was going to require a lot of driving and some sleep. I needed another driver so I wouldn't have to stop. I had one in mind.

Thinking of him resurrected an unpleasant truth about the spy business. Sometime during your training or field experience, you come to understand that you're in the people business: deceiving people, using people to achieve your ends, and destroying people, literally, or their credibility. To get out of Russia, I needed to use some people . . . and, maybe, help them.

Two years ago, they gave me evidence proving Ted Walldrum was a liar and—along with the other evidence I had collected—could have helped impeach him. I gave them hope that the CIA might help them defect and paid for their help by putting money in a Swiss account. They were never going to spend it unless they got out of Russia and, given what they knew about Walldrum, they were never going to get out. Maybe we could help each other again.

I drove to a Stalinesque apartment building in a lower-class section of Moscow, walked up four flights and down a long hall to a door that had seen better days. I knocked lightly.

Boris Kuzmick opened the door. He was as I remembered him from our first and only meeting in Gorky Park two years ago. He was a tall man with a large face that was covered with a five o'clock shadow and a scowl, made more menacing by heavy, dark eyebrows. His evening ensemble consisted of an undershirt, uniform pants held up by suspenders, and heavy socks. Saturday night on the poor side of town. His jaw dropped. He never expected to see me again, nor I him.

"May I come in?"

Boris recovered, put a finger to his lips for silence, and motioned for me to back up. He stepped into the hall, pulling the door closed. He whispered, "What are you doing here?"

Following his lead, we carried on the rest of our conversation in whispers. "I came to get you, Yulia, and the baby. It's time to go."

"Go where?"

"Out of Russia. Can we talk inside?"

"No." In an even lower whisper he said, "The apartment is bugged."

"Why?"

"Not now. What do you want me to do?"

"You have to leave right now. No delays, no phone calls, no good-byes to anyone. Dress in warm, comfortable clothes and wear boots in case we have to move on foot for a long period. Bring one suitcase. Pack what you need for the baby for two days. Tell Yulia to bring her makeup and her worst housedress. You pack a good suit, shirt, and tie, and your FSB uniform."

"I'll have to say something to mislead the microphones."

I gave that some thought. "Do you have any important relatives?"

"No, but Yulia has a cousin in the Duma. He's one of Putin's loudest supporters."

"Tell Yulia—and the microphones—that her cousin is having a party at his home tomorrow and sent a car for you."

For the first time, Boris smiled, as he nodded agreement.

I warned him, "In exactly fifteen minutes, I'm going to drive a black sedan to the front door. Be there. We're on a tight schedule."

Boris turned to enter the apartment. I put a hand on his shoulder and whispered, "Bring your album of *kompromat* photographs, your gun, handcuffs, and FSB credentials."

CHAPTER 19

Saturday, 11:30 p.m.
FSB Headquarters, Moscow

GELLER HAD BEEN spotted by an informant. That was the phone message. It ended Zabluda's promising evening with a lady and put him in an ugly mood when he entered the headquarters building. His weekend was being interrupted by bribe-taking Senior Sergeant Chernoff. He paused at the door to remove his fur hat and gloves, and threw open his overcoat with a flair that sent the light snow flying from its shoulders. Chernoff was waiting.

"Where is he?" demanded Zabluda.

"In interrogation with Sergeant Korilovich."

The other bribe-taker, thought Zabluda. He strode down the long corridor with Chernoff trying to keep up.

"Who is this sharp-eyed citizen you got me out of bed for?" asked Zabluda.

"He's a paid informant, sir."

"Paid to do what?"

"To observe and report on the antisocial activities of Yulia Kuzmickova."

They strode on in hostile silence, the clack of their bootheels echoing through the empty corridor until Zabluda stopped abruptly. "Well, Chernoff, am I supposed to guess who Yulia Kuzmickova is, or is she a state secret?"

In a low voice, Chernoff said, "With respect, sir, she is in the category of a state secret. Kuzmickova was a maid at the Riga-Ritz Hotel when alleged prostitutes allegedly performed the golden shower for the current president of the United States."

Zabluda sneered. "That, again. She should have been eliminated years ago."

"That solution was considered . . . and discarded."

"Why?"

"Yulia Kuzmickova is the cousin of an influential member of the Duma. He intervened on her behalf."

Zabluda grunted his dissatisfaction. "Everybody in Moscow has an influential cousin these days. You can't kill anyone except reporters and celebrity politicians without first climbing a family tree. Russia has changed a lot since Stalin's day."

"Those were the good old days," said Chernoff, with an uncharacteristic display of sarcasm and backbone. "Stalin killed all of my wife's relatives except her mother, and she died five years ago. So, if I wanted to murder my wife, I wouldn't have to consult anyone."

Eyes averted, Chernoff edged past Zabluda and led him downstairs to the interrogation room.

When Chernoff and Zabluda entered the room, Korilovich stood. "Good morning, sir."

Zabluda ignored him and focused on the informant, who was not the obsequious troll Zabluda had imagined. He was a grandfatherly-looking man with well-groomed white hair and the self-confident demeanor Zabluda had observed in good soldiers.

Zabluda pulled up a chair and sat facing the informant. "Where, exactly, did you see the man you identified for Sergeant Chernoff?"

"In the Voykovsky District. I live in an apartment building there. Yulia Kuzmickova is my neighbor and surveillance target. Our apartments are on the same floor. She is newly married and shares the apartment with her husband, Boris Kuzmick."

"Kuzmick is FSB," explained Chernoff.

The informant continued, "Their apartment is equipped with both recording and listening devices. I can hear what is said as it occurs. This evening at eight o'clock, the man I identified as Maxwell Geller rang the bell to the Kuzmick apartment. When their bell rings, one rings in my apartment. I went to the peephole in my door to observe. Boris came into the hall and talked to Geller. They spoke briefly. I couldn't hear what was said and the microphones were out of range."

"And you got a good look at this visitor during their conversation?"

"I saw him face-on as he left. He had to walk directly toward my apartment to reach the stairs. I observed him for several seconds through the peephole in my door."

"What happened next?"

"Boris went into the apartment and woke up Yulia. He said her cousin was having a party the next day and had sent a car for them. They had to pack for a one-night stay at her cousin's house and they had to hurry. The car was coming for them in fifteen minutes. It seemed odd that the driver would park somewhere else, walk to the apartment, and come back for them. Why didn't he park outside and wait?"

"Go on," Zabluda said, encouragingly.

"Yulia didn't believe him. She said her cousin would never invite a hotel maid to one of his parties, except to turn down the beds of his Kremlin guests he's always sucking up to. That also alerted me that something was not right.

"A few minutes later, the car arrived. The Kuzmicks got in. Because their conversation was suspicious, I took a picture of the car's license plate."

Chernoff handed an enlarged photograph of the plate to Zabluda, who showed it to the informer. "Is this the plate?"

"Yes, sir."

"Stolen from a car park last week," said Chernoff.

Zabluda asked the informant, "What did you do after you photographed the plate?"

"I entered their apartment. It was untidy. Drawers, closets, and cupboards were open. I called my supervisor. He took down the license plate information and told me to come in and bring my recordings and log. I gave them to Sergeant Chernoff."

"What time did the car leave with the Kuzmicks?"

"Eight thirty-seven p.m. It's in my log."

Chernoff interjected, "At nine o'clock, a traffic camera photographed the car turning off the Outer Ring onto Motorway 9, headed west." He handed Zabluda the photograph of a man. Zabluda showed it to the informant.

"Is this the man you saw at the door of the Kuzmicks' apartment?"

"Yes."

"No doubt?"

"No doubt, sir. I saw his face many times on the television after the bank robbery in 2018. That's the CIA agent they called Maxwell Geller."

"Why didn't you stop him?"

"He killed guards during the bank robbery. I assumed he was armed. I was not."

Zabluda didn't like that answer, but it was reasonable. "You've done good work. Go back to your apartment. Call your supervisor if Geller or the Kuzmicks return."

When the informant had gone, Zabluda turned to Chernoff. "Contact the GAI"—the General Administration for Traffic Safety. "Find someone who knows every kilometer of the motorway system west of Moscow and get him in here, now!"

Chernoff hesitated before saying, "Sir, it's almost one o'clock Saturday morning..."

"Sergeant, I know what day it is and I'm reasonably sure of the time. What I don't know is if you are going to live up to that—*I used to be really good at this job*—borscht you tried to serve me when I reprimanded you for letting Geller slip through your fingers. Or, are you just going to be a timekeeper for this operation?"

"I'll take care of it, sir."

"I'm happy to hear that, Senior Sergeant Chernoff. Now, go pull someone out of a bar, bed, or bordello who knows the Federation's road system. Do you need any further guidance?"

"Whose authority should I use when I contact GAI?"

"Mine. Tell our GAI colleagues we're hunting a man on the Federation's most wanted list. If this CIA spy gets away, I'll be happy to share the blame with them."

CHAPTER 20

Saturday, 8:37 p.m.
Escape from Moscow

EXACTLY FIFTEEN MINUTES after I left Boris in the hallway, Yulia, carrying a baby, and Boris slid into the back seat of my getaway car. They were dressed for arctic conditions.

Yulia, the sourball I remembered, greeted me with broken English and sarcasm. "Why you take two years to come back for us, Max? Guilty conscience?"

"You know what Moscow streets are like. I was caught in traffic."

"Two years? Musta been drug traffic," sneered Yulia.

Boris was embarrassed by Yulia's comment and tried to counter her bad mouth. "I knew you were coming back for us, Maxwell. No man left behind, right?"

Yulia would not be still. She came back with trash talk that she could have heard only on the internet. "Boris is bullshittin' you, homes. He don't believe you are coming back. He said you let us twist in the wind."

Boris let a slight smile escape. I hit the gas and headed for the Moscow Ring and the M9 Motorway.

There wasn't much talking for the first two hours. That was fine with me. I didn't need any more of Yulia's vitriol and no one wanted to wake the baby. Also, I suspected my passengers were holding their breaths until we escaped the threatening gravity of Moscow. When the time came for the baby's feeding, we stopped long enough for

Yulia and Boris to move to the front seats. Boris took the wheel. I napped on the back seat. The three of us kept that rough rotation for the rest of the trip: drive two hours, ride shotgun holding the baby for two hours, and the third person sleeping on the back seat for two.

It was a dark night. Traffic was light. The roads were mostly free of ice. Western Russia was having an unusually warm winter. We made good time.

I woke up in time to see a sign announcing we were ten kilometers from the Rzhev exit. I said, "We're changing our mode of transportation. The transfer point is a highway maintenance yard just after the Rzhev exit. Watch for it."

My thoughts turned to security. "Boris, keep your FSB ID and pistol handy. If we're stopped, I'm your driver, Sergeant Alek Pedorin," the name on my phony FSB ID.

Yulia interrupted to inform us, from her apparently vast store of useless information, "Alek means *defender of men*. You will defend us from here to the border?"

I ignored her and told Boris, "If we have to explain, Yulia is your prisoner. You're on a classified mission. We all speak Russian."

A kilometer past the Rzhev exit, I spotted a sign pointing to the maintenance yard. Boris slowed, cut the lights, and pulled off the highway onto a gravel road. The yard gates were secured with a heavy chain and padlock. Holding a small flashlight in my mouth, I picked the lock and guided Boris to the back of a large warehouse. That's where the van was supposed to be waiting. It wasn't. Boris and Yulia stayed in the car while I took a quick tour of the yard, gun in one hand, flashlight in the other. No van. Fucking Murphy!

I had three concerns. One, the weather. We needed to keep the car's motor and heater running to stay warm. Two, the van might not come. Three, while we were waiting for it, some conscientious highway patrolman might show up for a routine yard check.

As the minutes turned into half an hour, other worries took over. We were burning gas to keep the heater running. Stopping to fill up later might alert the authorities to our location. More important than gasoline, we were burning travel time. The Finnish border was ten hours away. If we didn't move soon, we wouldn't get there before sunup. Daylight would be a disadvantage. I decided to give the van driver another twenty minutes. After that, we would hit the road.

With the motor running and the windows cracked to keep from killing ourselves with carbon monoxide poisoning, the car was getting cold. We huddled together in the back seat to consolidate body heat. Yulia and the baby were sandwiched between me and Boris. I set the alarm on my cell phone in case we fell asleep.

Our wake-up call wasn't the alarm. It was two flashlight beams, one on either side of the car, and the harsh voice of a policeman saying, "All of you, keep your hands in sight! You men get out of the car."

Boris and I exited on opposite sides. The patrolman on my side shoved me over to join Boris. We stood there, hands in the air. The boss cop asked, "What are you doing here?"

Boris answered. "For the purposes of your shift report, we are not here. I'm with state security. We're waiting for the other members of my team. You don't want to be here when they arrive. My credentials are in my right-hand coat pocket."

"Turn around," ordered the patrolman.

Either this guy confused right with left when we turned, or he didn't want to shift his gun to his left hand. In any event, he patted Boris' left pocket.

"You're carrying a gun."

"Of course. Did you expect me to be out here with a bow and arrow?"

He took the gun and fished Boris' ID out of the other pocket. There was a pause before he said, "Turn around and put your hands down." He returned the ID, but kept the gun.

We all just stood there in the silence and the cold. I couldn't read the cop's mind, but I guessed this whole, woman-with-baby, with two guys behind a warehouse, in the middle of the night scenario was challenging his concept of a state security operation. He made a decision. "Run the license plate," he told his partner. "See if it's state security."

In the darkness, I couldn't see the patrol car, but wherever it was, the cop never got there. He was a few feet from us when I heard a couple of popping sounds. The cop and his flashlight fell to the ground. The boss cop covering us turned toward the sound. There were two more pops. He fell backwards into our arms. Someone in front of us turned on a flashlight. I could see two holes in the cop's green jacket and blood spurting from both. He had taken a double-tap to the heart by someone who knew where to tap.

Instinctively, Boris and I dropped the cop's body and went for guns.

A familiar voice came out of the darkness, speaking English with a heavy Russian accent. "Relax, Max. Your van is here." It was disturbingly casual considering what had just happened. The man came to us and shined a flashlight on his face. It was the leering mug of one of the bookends from the Omega group garage meeting.

With irritation, I said, "You're late."

"You're lucky. I considered not coming. Arkady Abramov was my friend." He added, "Do you know what will happen to me and my family if I get caught helping you?" He didn't wait for an answer. "Let's see your money."

I handed him the agreed-upon thousand euros in hundreds.

He shoved the bills into the pocket of his heavy jacket without counting them. "Put the policemen in their car and drive it into the woods behind the warehouse. Try not to leave blood trails. I'll be back." He melted into the blackness.

We left Yulia in the car, her mouth agape in disbelief. Boris and I found the patrol car and loaded the dead policemen into the trunk. Boris took the wheel. I guided him into the woods with my flashlight.

One of the deceased had a portable police radio on his equipment belt. Boris took it. "We can use this to monitor their operations."

Good thinking, Boris.

We rejoined Yulia and the baby. Soon, we heard a wheezing motor and saw a tractor trailer emerge from the darkness, parking lights on. The van backed up to the warehouse loading dock.

While his assistant opened the trailer's back doors, Mr. Bookends, our assassin-slash-driver, came over, looked into the back seat, and addressed me. "You stay in the car. They get out. The woman and baby can sit in the cab while we load." To Boris he said, "Watch the gate. If anyone comes, kill them."

Turning back to me, he said, "Drive your car to other end of the warehouse. Go up the concrete ramp onto the loading dock. I will guide you into the van."

Once the car was in the van, he used chains to anchor the wheels to metal eyes in the floor, and chocked the wheels with wooden wedges.

"It will get cold back here," he warned. "You want the woman and baby to ride up front?"

"Maybe at the next stop," I said. I wouldn't trust this guy with a woman or a baby. You get a feeling about people. My gut feeling about this guy was not good.

He shrugged. "Don't run your car heater with the motor on. In this weather, the tailpipe smoke will drift through the ceiling vents and be visible outside. There are two large panels at the front of this compartment. Remove them. They conceal electric heaters."

He led me to the front wall, and we pulled the panels from the electric heaters and turned them on full blast. Mr. Bookends also introduced me to his buzzer system. "I have buzzer in my cab. It rings back here. I buzz you when we get near rest stop or exit. Once for rest stop. Twice for exit." He pointed to a buzzer near the heaters. "You buzz me once if you want to stop, twice if you want me to exit."

Mr. Bookends faced me. My flashlight's red filter cast a satanic glow on his features. "If police are noticing us, I buzz three times. If they are stopping us, four times."

I nodded.

"Where are we going?" he asked.

"Direction Latvia." I laid my map on the car's hood, held the flashlight, and used my forefinger to trace our route west on M9. I stopped at the V. Luki—for Velikiye Luki—exit. "Let me know when we're twenty kilometers from this exit. If we need to avoid roadblocks, leave M9. Take the back roads north to M20, toward St. Petersburg."

I was deliberately vague. If things got hairy, I didn't want him to have our exact destination. Also, I wasn't sure we could make the Finnish border before sunup.

Boxes lined the sidewalls and were stacked high. Bookends said, "When I get out, stack boxes between your car and doors, three deep, wall-to-wall, ceiling high, in case we get stopped for inspection. If they go behind boxes, kill them. Do it quick and quiet. I help if I can."

He was going to help. That made me feel all better.

Bookends gave me a nasty grin and said, "Make yourself comfortable." He jumped out and locked us in. Minutes later we pulled onto the M9 and headed west.

We had lost time, but we were invisible to the highway police. We had heat and the van walls were insulated. I was impressed with the layout of the cargo compartment and the driver's skills. This was not the first time he had hauled contraband, human or vehicular.

My personal angst was that I had added two dead cops to my account of bad deeds in Russia. In the words of the playwright Ravenscroft, *In for a penny, in for a pound.*

As we began the three-hour drive to the V. Luki exit, we huddled in front of the electric heaters. Yulia stood with us, holding the baby in a kind of bandolier sling made of a blanket. She stayed with us until the heat forced her into the car. She put the baby in his bassinet on the driver's seat, covered him with the blanket, and cranked back the passenger seat for a nap.

I'd had a bad feeling about this family ever since they got into my car in Moscow—and put it to Boris as delicately as I could. "The last time we met, Yulia was pushing a baby carriage. I thought your son would be two years old by now . . ."

"Two years and four months . . . if he had lived." Boris stared straight ahead. "He died in his sleep, not long after you left Moscow. The doctor said the cause was something called 'sudden infant death syndrome.'"

"I'm very sorry, Boris."

He turned to me, his eyes glistening, and whispered, "Don't speak of this to Yulia. She grieved until she got pregnant last year. Now, she lives in fear that it could happen again. It has been two years of hell." He looked away and stared into the red glow of the electric heaters.

As a distraction, I showed Boris the contents of our car trunk. He pawed through the food and water. Impressed, he picked one of the AKs, worked the action, and put it back. With a nod of approval, he said, "I hope we don't have to use those."

I held up a set of spare license plates. "We *do* have to use these."

Boris helped me remove the old plates and mount new ones. Afterward, we leaned on the car hood and let the heaters toast us. He had a flask of vodka. We took a couple of swigs each.

Boris said, "You're wanted in Russia. You didn't come back for us. Why are you here?"

"I came back for love."

"I don't see your woman in the car. Or did you fall in love with my Yulia, last time?"

We shared a quiet laugh. Yulia was tough to love. I didn't even like her. I said, "The woman I love is in trouble in the States. I came so she wouldn't have to."

"So, you are still CIA?"

"I'm not CIA. I'm a contract hire, like those little green men Putin sends to Ukraine."

"Okay." Boris sounded unconvinced and changed the subject. "Your last visit, a few days after you left us in Gorky Park, your face was all over the television and newspapers. I don't believe everything I read or see, but did you and your girlfriend rob the Allgemeine Volksbank? They said you got away with several million rubles."

"We weren't there for rubles, we wanted gold—intelligence gold."

"I knew it! Oligarchs have accounts at AVB. It's the first link in the money laundering chain. You went there to get *kompromat*—evidence against your president."

"No comment."

I knew what was coming. He said it with a tinge of anger. "What happened to the pictures I gave you, the ones with your president watching prostitutes pee on a bed at the Riga-Ritz?"

"You didn't give me anything, you sold them to me. I gave them to the authorities. That's all I can tell you."

"You know, Max, I have no ideology. I don't hate my country or love yours. I just think yours is a better neighborhood. Basically, every country is the same. People steal as much as they can to live a comfortable life. The laws—the rules—they are there to be broken."

"Maybe," I said, "but in my country, when someone breaks the rules, there's usually a penalty. As for ideology, give me democracy every time."

Boris reminded me, "Winston Churchill said it's the worst form of government, except for all the others."

"If it's so bad, why do you want to come to the States?"

While he was chewing on that, I asked, "Why is your apartment bugged?"

Boris sighed. "Before you robbed the bank, you gave Yulia a lot of money to arrange our meeting in Gorky Park, more than she had ever seen. I took none for myself, but I warned her to be careful with her spending. She wasn't. Those hundred-dollar bills were noticed by the FSB."

"I'm sorry. I should have paid her in smaller denominations."

Boris shrugged. "That may not have mattered. Yulia is one of the few people outside the security services who witnessed the indiscretions of your president-to-be at the Ritz. For that reason, the FSB maintains an interest in her. Sudden wealth is always an indicator of antisocial activity. The FSB interrogated her. Yulia is smart. She told them she earned the money renting her body to guests at the hotel where she works." Boris grimaced as he spoke the words.

"But the FSB didn't buy it."

"No. She was in trouble. Her cousin—the one in the Duma—has influence and he intervened. He knew I loved Yulia. He got me reassigned from oblivion in Tula so we could get married." Proudly, Boris raised his hand to show me the ring. "I was told—ordered—to keep her out of trouble, but the FSB wanted insurance. They not-so-secretly bugged our apartment and I'm sure someone on our floor is spying on us. That's how we do it." Boris coaxed the vodka flask from his pocket and took a swig. I declined.

"Boris, do you think your spy saw us leave for this trip?"

"Yes. They look for pattern changes. It is not our pattern to visit Duma members on the weekend. Our departure has probably been reported."

CHAPTER 21

Sunday, 2 a.m.
FSB Operations Center, Moscow

SENIOR SERGEANT CHERNOFF was updating Colonel Zabluda on the hunt for Max Geller.

Chernoff introduced a lean, studious-looking man in aviator's glasses and a rumpled suit. "This is Captain Fedkin, a GAI operations officer. He's responsible for patrols on motorways and secondary roads west of Moscow. Together, we made certain assumptions about possible escape routes for the spy, Geller, and his accomplices.

"Our first assumption: Geller wants to get out of Russia as quickly as possible. Going east would not solve that problem. We are concentrating the search on the roads west of Moscow leading to countries bordering the Russian Federation."

Zabluda was skeptical. "Geller would have anticipated that. Why focus only on the west?"

Fedkin answered. "At nine o'clock last night, one of our traffic cameras photographed a car entering the M9 Motorway, heading west. Its rear license plate matched the one provided by your informant. If Geller is trying to get out of Russia, that direction offers him the fastest exit."

Chernoff added, "We faxed descriptions of the fugitives, their car, and the license plate to Roads and Traffic Police and the Border Service. Special alerts have been sent to all motorway patrols between

Moscow and Federation borders with Belarus, Latvia, Estonia, and Finland. Our checkpoints at crossings into those countries are also on alert, and some are being reinforced with additional staff."

Zabluda nodded his approval.

"Second assumption," continued Chernoff. "We do not have the element of surprise. Geller's passenger, Boris Kuzmick, is FSB. If he knew we had listening devices in his apartment, he will assume that the FSB knows he and his family are on the run. He would have told Geller.

"Third, if Geller knows we are hunting him, he may try to evade us by deception."

"What sort of deception?" asked Zabluda.

"Change cars, steal or hijack one."

"Maybe," mused Zabluda, "but he wouldn't get off the motorway. That would slow him down. He might steal one at a rest stop."

Fedkin spoke up. "A stolen car there would be detected quickly and reported. That would give you his location. It would be very risky for him."

Zabluda was dismissive. "Risk may not be a deterrent to a man who robbed a bank in Moscow and returns to the city two years later."

"He could kidnap someone with a car," suggested Chernoff.

"Possible," agreed Zabluda, "but that would mean another body to service: rest stops, food, escape attempts, and hostile ears to over-hear his plans. Unlikely," concluded Zabluda. "So, Geller increases his chances of being detected by staying with his car. What are the advantages?"

Chernoff answered, "He knows its mechanical condition. He won't lose time stealing another, and we won't know where he is unless he's spotted by a motorway patrol."

Zabluda asked, "If he stays with the car, is it possible he could alter its appearance?"

Chernoff shook his head doubtfully. "It's too cold to paint it in the open. He would need a warm enclosure, and it would take time. His best chance to throw the police off would be to steal a license plate at a rest stop. It's less likely to be missed there . . . or maybe he has a spare."

"Of course," said Zabluda, sitting up straight. "Fedkin, have your GAI contacts tell us if license plates have been stolen from black Zils in Moscow during the past two weeks."

Fedkin made a quick call and hurried back to brief Zabluda. "Based on the assumptions and your requirements, as relayed to me by Senior Sergeant Chernoff, I made a list of probable routes out of the Federation for your fugitives. Here they are." Fedkin used his computer to project a route chart on the wall screen.

ROUTE	ROUTE #	HOURS AWAY	KILOMETERS
Moscow to Belarus via Roslavl M3 to A101	1	5	300
Moscow to Belarus via Smolensk M3 to A101	2	5	500
Moscow to Belarus via Zlynka M3 to M13	3	7+	610
Moscow to Ukraine via Hulkhiv M2 to A142	4	6+	565
Moscow to Latvia via Sabezh M9	5	7	650
Moscow to Finland via Vyborg E105 to M10	6	12+	1000

Fedkin started to talk Zabluda through them, but the colonel stopped him with a raised palm. The room was quiet as Zabluda alternated his attention between the chart projection on the screen and a military map on the table in front of him.

Finally, Zabluda nodded and said, "Very well," and gave his attention exclusively to the route projections on the screen. "Eliminate routes 1, 2, and 3. Geller won't go to Belarus. He was stationed in Moscow. Assume he knows we've infiltrated Belarus security services. We will be notified if he crosses into that country. Chernoff, contact the SVR and tell them to notify the appropriate contacts in Belarus."

"I've already notified them, sir."

Zabluda gave the sergeant an appreciative nod and continued his route analysis. "Geller won't take Route 4. Eastern Ukraine is a war zone. He could run into our soldiers or a militia sympathetic to Moscow. All the same, alert the military headquarters there."

Zabluda continued his analysis. "Route 6 to Finland is very long, we will have many opportunities to intercept him. That leaves Route 5 to Latvia. That is his most likely route. It's short and direct. Do you agree, Chernoff?"

"Yes, Colonel, but Geller would know we know that. He might do something unexpected."

Zabluda peered at the map. "I think . . . if I were Geller, I would get on the M9 out of Moscow and drive as fast and as far as I could. Then, I would do something unexpected at . . . here." He pointed to the Velikiye Luki exit.

"Why there?" asked Chernoff.

"Look at the map. He can get off here and go north, or south, into Belarus. As I said, it's unfriendly, but he might risk it, if we were closing in on him."

"Or," said Chernoff, "he could go south, to make us think he's headed for Belarus, and double back to the north for another crossing point into Latvia."

Zabluda disagreed. "He won't double back. Time is not on his side." He paused. "On the other hand, if he exits north off of M9, he can take secondary roads to the Latvian border or go north on the M2 to

Pskov. From there, he has two routes into Estonia or he can go to Finland through St. Petersburg and Vyborg. We wouldn't be expecting that. So, he might try it. To foreclose those options, we have to stop him before he gets to the M9 Velikiye Luki exit."

Zabluda folded the map and shoved it into his jacket pocket. "Get me a helicopter. I want to observe traffic on M9."

Hesitantly, Fedkin said, "Colonel, there are enclosures where Geller could paint his car."

"Where?" demanded Zabluda.

"Maintenance yards. We have warehouses for storing snowplows and other equipment."

"Have your patrols check every one."

CHAPTER 22

BORIS REACHED BACK from the driver's seat and gently shook me awake. He spoke softly so as not to awaken Yulia dozing in the passenger's seat with the baby sleeping on her lap. "We've got problems, Max. I've been monitoring the police radio frequency. They are setting up a roadblock at the V. Luki exit."

"Anything else?"

"They found the two dead policemen at the maintenance yard."

"That was fast," and a big problem. "What are they saying?"

"It's what they are not saying that concerns me. They didn't say the radio I took is missing."

"Damn! They're using the signal to track us. Turn it off and take out the batteries."

"I turned the radio off, but I'm sure they have a fix on our signal. Besides, I can't remove the batteries. The battery compartment requires a special key and is constructed from heavy material. We would need a large hammer to break into it."

"Why would they make it hard to remove batteries?"

"A few years ago, there was a big accident in the fog on the M2 Motorway. The investigation found that some motorway patrolmen were working a second job when they should have been on patrol. They took the batteries out of their radios so they couldn't be contacted or tracked. Now, the batteries are just another part of our surveillance society."

"You knew that when you took the damn radio! Why did you take it?" My shout awakened Yulia and the baby stirred.

"I took a calculated risk. I didn't think they would find the dead policemen so soon."

"You don't get to take a calculated risk without my say-so! This is my show! I make those decisions!"

Yulia asked, "What's going on?"

"What's going on? Boris is trying to get us killed! That's what's going on!"

Yulia was going to ask more questions, but our van driver rang the buzzer, alerting me that we were twenty kilometers from the V. Luki exit. I buzzed back the signal for him to take it.

Boris was explaining his screwup to Yulia in harmless terms.

I interrupted him. "Where's the damned radio?"

"I covered it with tinfoil from one of your meal packets and put it in the toolbox in your trunk."

"Tinfoil won't stop it from sending our location."

"I know that, but maybe it will stress the battery and weaken the signal."

Maybe pigs will learn to fly before the FSB catches us. "How long will that take?"

"I don't know."

"Why didn't you throw it out one of the vents?"

"I thought of that. They are too small . . . and if I could throw it out, anyone driving near us would see radio parts bouncing along the highway. I'm sorry. I did the best I could."

A very uncomfortable silence was broken when Boris said, hopefully, "The radio said they were looking for a black sedan. They're not looking for a van."

Boris knew very well that if they had direction-finding equipment at the roadblock, we were toast. He voiced my thoughts. "This might be a good time to load the Kalashnikovs."

Or drink hemlock.

We got the AKs from the trunk and shoved a banana clip into each.

Her skepticism apparent, Yulia watched us for a while, then asked, "And what happens to Yulia and the baby while Butch Cassidy and the Sundance Kid are shooting it out with the Federales?"

This lady was annoying and thought herself way too hip to American culture for my tastes. I had to take her down a peg. "Federales are Mexican. Butch and Sundance died in Bolivia, killed by city officials of San Vincente and just three soldiers from the Ajaria Regiment."

She shot back, "The police will be happy to hear your version, or is it Bullivia-shit."

Boris gave her a reproving glare. "Yulia, don't be difficult. We must work together."

Yulia gave him a hateful look in return. Again, I wondered what he saw in her.

Boris sighed and offered Yulia his pistol. She gave him a long, hard look before taking it. None of us wanted to be taken alive by the FSB. I wondered if Yulia would shoot the baby.

I asked Boris, "Does Yulia know how to use your gun?"

"Yes. She made me teach her after the FSB interrogated her about the money. They showed her gruesome photographs of Russians who lied to them. She vowed to kill herself before allowing another interrogation."

We rode in silence as the van barreled toward the V. Luki exit. Yulia stared through the windshield, one hand on the baby, the other holding Boris' pistol. Boris and I leaned against the hood, me cradling the AK-47 in my arms, while he smoked what might be his last cigarette.

I asked, "Who's teaching Yulia American history and slang?"

Boris smiled. "The FSB put her in a program so she can converse with English-speaking guests at the hotel where she works . . . gather a little intelligence from them, maybe."

I had no polite comeback for that. I checked my watch. It was almost 4:00 a.m. Sunday morning. We were twelve hours from the Finnish border. We were not going to make it.

The van decelerated for the V. Luki exit roadblock. Yulia got out and put the baby in his bassinet on the floor behind the driver's seat. Weapons in hand, the three of us leaned against the car trunk, with only three stacks of boxes between us, the doors . . . and certain death.

At the roadblock, our van inched along. Then, it stopped, the motor cut off, and nothing happened for ten long minutes. It was nerve-wracking to stand there in the dark, blind to what was going on outside. Suddenly, there was shouting. Boris and I slid rounds into the chambers of our AK-47s just before the doors of the cargo compartment swung open. Someone climbed into the van and began rummaging through the ceiling-high stack of boxes a few feet in front of us.

Judging from the conversation, it was a highway patrolman who had entered the van. He was asking questions and Mr. Bookends' gravelly voice answered. Bookends explained that he was moving a family's belongings from Rhzev to the city of Velikiye Luki. I imagined him fingering the pistol in the pocket of his coveralls.

Abruptly, questions and answers stopped. We heard the cop scramble out of the van and the doors slam shut. We relaxed. Boris and I put our AKs on safe and stowed them in the car trunk.

The motor started and the van swung to the right. We were on the V. Luki off-ramp. Each of us exhaled in relief. When we were a safe distance from the roadblock, I pressed the buzzer once for the driver to stop.

Boris asked, "Is there a plan?"

"You mean one that you can't screw up?"

He didn't reply. All of us were on edge.

"First," I said, "we're going to get the car out of this van and ditch that damned radio."

"I know where we can do both," Boris offered.

The van slowed and stopped. Mr. Bookends opened one of the doors, climbed into the compartment, and moved a few boxes so he could see us. "What now?"

Boris asked, "Do you know the soccer field near the Amaris Hotel?"

"What about it?"

"We want to unload the car there."

Since I was paying for the trip, Bookends addressed me, in his so-so English. "Won't work. Takes time to unload. Is open space. Somebody see us . . . or we get another visit from the police. I take you to private place. Not far from here. Okay?"

Going to a private place with Mr. Bookends under any circumstances did not ring my happiness bell, but he made sense. He drove us to a warehouse in an industrial district. I'm sure it was a way station for whatever contraband Mr. Bookends usually smuggled.

Bookends parked the van at the warehouse loading platform. Boris and I helped him and his silent assistant unload the boxes that concealed our sedan.

When we finished, Bookends said, "Back your car into warehouse—you can drive it out front door. No drop-off there."

I drove the car out of the van and parked it next to a five-ton truck.

Bookends said, "Come to office. See map. I show you where you are, where you go."

Carrying the baby, Yulia made a move toward the sedan.

In Russian, Bookends told her, "You come to the office, too. It's warm there."

Yulia entered first, followed by Boris, then me. Bookends brought up the rear. Pavel was waiting for us. Good news. He was holding a pistol. Very bad news. When I hesitated, Bookends gave me a shove from behind.

The office was lit by a single desk lamp. Emerging from a shadowy corner like a ghost came the Rasputin character—and new Omega leader-apparent—from our Moscow garage meeting.

I asked, "What's going on?"

"Renegotiation," said Rasputin.

"What are we renegotiating?"

"The cost of getting you out of Russia."

Bookends emptied our pockets, took my pistol, and dumped everything on a worktable against the back wall. As he examined our documents, Bookends—switching to Russian—told Rasputin, "This one," nodding at Boris, "is FSB." Then, he smiled at me. "Max has also joined FSB. Good forgery." He threw our creds back onto the worktable. Meanwhile, Pavel removed weapons and supplies from my car trunk.

I asked Rasputin, "What do you want?"

"On your last visit to Moscow, you killed Arkady and robbed his bank of seven hundred thousand rubles. We are dedicated to reclaiming Russia's stolen wealth. We want those rubles."

"Your people know I went to that bank to get evidence from Arkady. I didn't steal any money. Why would you believe your news services? They lie all the time."

"Yes, but—as you in the West say—we Russians have been conditioned to believe the lies of our propaganda organs." His phony smile morphed into a deadly serious scowl. "We want that money or you are not going anywhere."

"Seven hundred thousand rubles is less than ten thousand dollars. I've already promised you thirty-five thousand. Don't you understand the conversion rate?"

"We rounded up . . . to two hundred thousand dollars. That leaves you short one hundred and sixty-five thousand."

"Where am I going to get that much money?"

"Call your CIA contact in Moscow." Bookends shoved a cell phone at me.

"I don't have a CIA contact in Moscow. I'm working directly for my handler at Langley."

"Call somebody in the States who can help you." Bookends offered a sat phone.

I looked at my watch. "It's after nine o'clock Saturday night in Washington. The people who could help me won't be able to get that much money until Monday morning."

"We'll wait." Rasputin told Mr. Bookends, "Leave the woman and baby in the office. Take these two to the truck and make them uncomfortable."

Bookends and his assistant prodded Boris and me into the bay with their guns and handcuffed us to the bumper of the five-ton truck, one arm inside the bumper, one arm outside. The beams connecting the bumper to the truck body kept us from escaping.

"You going to leave us like this until the money comes?" I asked Bookends.

"We get a room ready for you soon. Got to move the dead bodies out first." He gave us a nasty smile, then yelled to the office, "Pavel, bring a couple of stools for these assholes."

That, he got grammatically correct.

Bookends went back to the office. Pavel arrived with the stools.

I was more than angry. "Why did you sell me out, Pavel?"

"When you killed Arkady, you damaged my standing with Omega. I must do this to regain it."

"Is this how you repay me and honor your father?" During my last visit, I gave Pavel information about his biological father, who had defected to England.

"He made his decisions. I must make mine. I helped you before. You should not have come back."

"Are they going to kill us after they get the money?"

"I don't know."

A while later, our jailers were in the office, gathered around the desk, talking. Yulia sat in a corner holding the baby. Boris and I were adjusting to the awkward position of sitting on stools, while resting our heads on the truck's bumper. At the far end of the warehouse, two shots ripped the lock from the door. Bookends and his assistant driver ran out of the office, guns pointed in the direction of the shooting. Behind them, a uniformed policeman came in from the loading dock and mowed them down in a hail of AK-47 bullets.

In Russian, I yelled to him, "More in the office!" and nodded toward it.

Boris yelled, "Yulia, get down!"

The two cops converged on the office. The one from the loading dock fired a burst through the office window overlooking the maintenance bay. It caught Pavel and Rasputin, chest- and face-high. They went down. The shooter entered the office to check his kills. He came out shortly with a firm grip on Yulia's upper arm. She looked scared and was carrying her screaming baby in the makeshift blanket sling. The cop stood her against the wall and said, "Stay there. Don't move."

At that point, I was expecting the rest of the SWAT team to rush in. That didn't happen. The cops saw that we were handcuffed and moved on to clear the rest of the building. They had no backup. That struck me as odd. Both cops were tall and beefy, with moves and haircuts that screamed ex-military. Whatever their skills, two cops don't take down a warehouse with an unknown number of bad guys inside unless they've been watching too much Crockett and Tubbs, Riggs and Murtaugh, or Bosch and J. Edgar . . . or they're cowboys and wanted sole credit for the bust. That meant they were overconfident and reckless. Those traits and the two-to-two odds could work in our favor, if Boris and I could get out of the cuffs.

After the cops cleared the building, they came to us.

Boris took the initiative. "We're FSB. Our credentials are on the worktable in the office."

The cop with the pistol holstered it and went to the office. He returned holding our creds and the radio Boris had taken from the dead cop at the maintenance yard. To his partner, he said, "Looks like we've found the killers. I guess they didn't know this radio could be tracked." He shoved the radio into the pocket of his cargo pants and came to us, reading our FSB credentials.

His partner glanced at the documents and asked us, "What are you doing here?"

Boris answered. "We're investigating a gang of smugglers. We were waiting to meet an informant at the Rhzev maintenance yard on the M9 Motorway. Those men ambushed us. They were interrupted by the arrival of a patrol car doing a routine check. They killed the patrolmen and brought us here."

"Why would they do that?"

"To torture us for the name of the informant. You saved our lives."

They seemed to buy Boris' fairy tale, but didn't move to unlock our cuffs. The baby, who had been screaming since the shooting started, finally got their attention.

The cop asked Yulia, "What are you doing here?"

Yulia said, "I don't know," and delivered an Academy Award performance of a frightened woman, shoulders hunched, head down, eyes darting, but looking away, all the while clutching the crying baby to her chest.

Disgusted, the cop turned back to us. "Who's this woman?"

"I don't know," said Boris. "She was with them at the maintenance yard."

"You called her name when the shooting started."

"I heard one of the dead men say it."

The cops looked at each other and I knew this was not going to get better. The cop holding our creds asked his partner, "What do you want to do?"

"Call headquarters. Tell them we found the radio, and we have four bodies and three prisoners . . . and a baby. Let the supervisor sort this out when he gets here."

The other cop hesitated. "This is FSB business . . ."

"That's why we're not getting involved. Call headquarters."

The cop took his radio from his harness. That's when Yulia pulled the pistol Boris had given her at the V. Luki roadblock and shot him in the neck. Before the other cop could turn, Yulia shot him twice in the head. The baby's screams went off the decibel chart. Clutching him, Yulia got the handcuff keys from Bookends' pocket and freed us.

We reloaded my trunk with the things Pavel had taken. I kept out a map, sat phone, and cell phone. We piled into the car, Yulia and the baby in the back seat, Boris behind the wheel, and me riding shotgun. We sped away from the warehouse as fast as the secondary roads would allow.

Between our captivity at the warehouse and our delay at the Rhzev maintenance yard, we had lost hours. There was no way we could get to the Finnish border before daylight or before the police caught us. Time for a change of plan.

I checked the map and told Boris, "Go north. Get on M20 to Pskov." I turned on the cell.

"Who are you calling?" he asked.

"The cavalry."

Yulia, our Americana expert and perpetual cynic, said, "I hope it's not Custer."

It was Sherri. I texted her the coordinates for our probable destination.

CHAPTER 23

Sunday, well before sunrise.
Russian-Estonian Border Region

My ORIGINAL PLAN to make an hours-of-darkness crossing into Finland at the town of Vaalimaa was not going to work. We were eleven hours away from that crossing and fugitives in a cop-killer manhunt. Time to run, not walk, to the nearest Russia exit.

"Where are we going?" Boris asked.

Before I could answer, Yulia said, "Wherever it is, will we get there before spring? I got only one bottle left for the baby."

Boris nodded toward Yulia, gave me an eyeroll, and waited for my answer.

I asked him, "Do you know the villages around Lake Pskov?"

"Some, yes. My father used to take me ice fishing on the lake."

"Which village is close and the best place to steal a boat?"

Boris was surprised, but quickly recovered. "Balsovo, but the lake is probably frozen over."

Yulia asked, "Are we going to ice skate to freedom?"

"The lake's not frozen. I checked." Global warming had made it to Russia. "Can we make Balsovo before sunup?"

"Yes, but the Lake Pskov shoreline is a controlled area. We need special passes to get to the lakefront and they have a strict protocol for the movement of boats. You have to notify the control center when you plan to go out and must return by sundown."

"Returning won't be our problem."

"They have shore and water patrols to enforce the curfew, Max."

"In that case, we need a little deception. Yulia, slip into that old housedress I asked you to bring and let me have your makeup kit."

The border between Russia and Estonia runs down the middle of Lake Pskov. If we couldn't make it to the Finnish border, the lake was a good place to cross. When I worked at Moscow Station, we considered it one of the best routes to exfiltrate a burned agent or a high-value defector. The shoreline is dotted with small, dispersed fishing villages, home to an aging population. Not a lot of traffic. Not a lot of crime and cops, lots of boats. Also, I was sure we would have less of a hassle there with no ID papers for Yulia and the baby. As an added benefit, crossing the lake would give me a quick route to the Estonian capital city, Tallinn. It was there that RAMPART wanted me to spring him from his handlers. Sometimes an unexpected change of plans can work to your advantage. *Moscow Rule #20: Keep your options open.*

An hour or so after leaving the warehouse, we passed through the town of Pskov and arrived at one of the checkpoints controlling access to the lakeshore. We had stopped briefly and changed into our game clothes. I was in an FSB uniform and driving. Boris and Yulia were in the back seat. He wore his FSB uniform. Yulia was in a flimsy gray housedress with her coat draped over her shoulders. She was leaning forward, her forearms resting on her thighs. Boris' handcuffs were on her wrists and visible. She turned away from the harsh light of the guard shack so that most of her face was obscured. I had used the rouge in her makeup kit to paint fake bruises on her chin, throat, arms, and legs, and she had a couple of the baby's cotton balls in her cheeks. Yulia looked like the victim of a harsh interrogation.

The guard came to my window. I handed him Boris' FSB ID and my fake. I kept my right hand near the pistol jammed between my right thigh and the seat.

The guard examined our papers. "You need a special pass for the waterfront."

"We're not going to the waterfront," said Boris. "We're taking this road to the M20."

"I wasn't told that anyone without a permit would be transiting the lakefront sector."

In a dismissive tone, Boris said, "That's because we don't need local assistance."

The guard held our IDs while he digested that. "I need to see the woman's papers."

"The woman is my prisoner," said Boris. "She's being deported to Finland for anti-government activities. I have her passport and extradition paper." He held up—but didn't surrender—the fake Finnish passport I was given for RAMPART's wife.

The guard hesitated.

"Right now," Boris told him, "this woman does not exist in your world. If you inspect her papers, you will know her name, see her face, and she will exist. Should some . . . terrible accident befall her on the way to Finland, there could be an investigation. You might be summoned to Moscow and questioned. In that event, the knowledge of her existence could become an inconvenient burden for you."

The guard looked at Yulia's fake bruises. He handed me our credentials and waved us on. When we were well away from his post, I stopped the car. Yulia changed back into warm clothes. I took my infrared beacons from the trunk and taped one to each side mirror, pointing up. If Sherri had an eye in the sky, the IR beacons would let her track us.

Boris asked, "Are you expecting close air support?" He was starting to sound like Yulia.

"If we're lucky, yes. I'm hoping I have friends on the other side of the lake."

I texted Sherri two sets of eight-digit coordinates: one set for Balsovo, with our ETA, and a set for the village of Beresje, our destination on the Estonian side of the lake. Boris gave me a doubtful look, but said nothing. We drove on to find our boat.

Balsovo is a coastal village situated on the south side of a sparsely populated peninsula that separates one of the largest lakes in Europe into two bodies of water, Lake Peipus in the north and Lake Pskov in the south. The lakes are connected by a narrow strip of water flowing past the tip of the peninsula. On a map, it looks like two kidney-shaped lakes connected by a stream. The tip of that peninsula juts into that stream and is about a mile from Estonia.

The peninsula tip is also uninhabited and the logical place to cross. It's also the logical place for trip-wire alarms, motion sensors, and other trinkets designed to discourage illegal crossings. My plan was to steal a boat, go due west along the southern coast of the peninsula until I got within five kilometers of the Estonian coast, and make a run for it. Hopefully, Sherri—not the Estonian Border Patrol—would meet me there with transportation and we would scoot north to Tallinn and the sanctuary of the American embassy.

It was still dark when we got to Balsovo. Sunrise was not until 8:59. The village was small and the dock was easy to find. I parked on a gravel lot near the water. We sat in the car for a while to be sure no one was about.

"Are we just going to sit here?" grumbled Yulia.

"We're going to steal a boat and sail to Estonia . . . and freedom," I said.

"It's about time."

The baby was awake again. Yulia stayed with him in the car while Boris and I went to the small dock to check out the boats. The lake was covered in a cloak of fog, turned an eerie glowing gray by spotlights on both sides of the border.

Boris peered into the haze on the Estonian side. "Lots of lights over there, Max, and a radar station. You sure you want to cross here?"

"We don't have a choice. That guard reported us as soon as we left his post. Patrols are probably searching for us right now. Let's find a boat."

"There," said Boris. "That's the one."

The boat was a collection of rotting wood and rusting metal held together by a coat of peeling gray paint. Nobody would steal a boat like that. So, it was probably unlocked, and the controls would be simple enough for us to operate. I asked Boris if he knew how to drive it. He did.

As we got closer, we could see that the winches and fishing machinery on deck were well maintained. Maybe the motor was, too. Just what we needed. The boat was a sixty-footer. The superstructure, containing the wheelhouse and crew accommodations, was crammed into the forward half of the vessel, along with fishing nets, winches, and other equipment. The aft half was a flat deck for processing fish when the nets pulled them in. Boris and I stepped off the dock and onto the deck. Guns ready, we checked the superstructure. Nobody home and the ignition key was hanging on a wall hook. We went back to the car to get Yulia, the baby, the AKs and ammo, and what was left of the food and water.

When everyone was onboard, Boris studied the controls, checked the gas gauge, and started the motor. Suddenly, a high-intensity light swept the boat from dockside. I could make out the silhouettes of two policemen in the headlights of the patrol car behind them.

From their direction, a megaphone-amplified voice shouted, "Stop what you are doing! Turn the motor off. Get out of the boat with your hands up!"

Just then, a police launch emerged from the fog to block our escape across the lake.

Quickly, we agreed on a plan. Boris cuffed Yulia's wrists and ran his belt between the two cuffs to strap the chain to Yulia's belly. Then, the three of us filed out of the wheelhouse, Yulia in the middle position.

I whispered to Boris, "Take the one closest to us."

Three abreast, we walked toward the dock, positioning ourselves to keep the superstructure between us and the policemen on the launch blocking our escape. They didn't have line-of-sight or a shot at us. Boris held one of Yulia's arms above the elbow; I took the other. We held up our FSB credentials in our outboard hands.

Boris shouted, "FSB! This is a matter of state security! Not your business! Leave us!"

They didn't. One of the policemen stepped onto the deck and swept us with his flashlight.

When his beam found Yulia's handcuffed wrists, she shouted, "Help! They're going to kill me!" She threw herself at the policeman, knocking him off balance. As Yulia lunged forward, Boris and I snatched our pistols from the small of her back where they had been held in place by Boris' belt. Boris dropped into a crouch and shot the deck patrolman twice. The report of his gun rolled across the lake like cannon fire.

Off balance, Yulia fell on top of Boris' target, and out of my line of fire.

I was shooting left-handed. Normally, I don't. To compensate, I aimed center of mass and fired three shots at the dockside patrolman with the megaphone. He went down.

Boris and I grabbed Yulia by her arms and dragged her to cover behind the superstructure and machinery. Now, we had to deal with the launch blocking our boat.

From what I had observed before the shooting started, there were three patrolmen on the launch: one at the controls and two shooters on deck. Because our position denied them line-of-sight, the shooters raced to opposite ends of their launch to get a bead on us. I fired twice, leading the one racing aft. He ran right into my bullets and went down. The other shooter made it to the bow of the launch. We shifted to our left so he couldn't see us. Boris ducked into the superstructure and opened up on him with an AK-47. The patrolman was slammed backwards into the launch's superstructure and pitched forward into the lake. By that time, it was clear to everyone on both sides of the lake that a major firefight was in progress.

The launch driver realized his guys had lost the battle. Before he could pull away, I ran forward to the bow of our boat and leaped onto the launch. The driver heard me hit the deck. He let go of the controls, turned, and went for his sidearm. I fired twice. He slumped backwards against the wheel and fell to the deck. The launch began to weave erratically. I took the wheel and noticed a remote for the autopilot. An idea came to me. I guided the launch back to the boat we were going to steal and jumped aboard.

Suddenly, there was a tremendous explosion behind us. It was somewhere between Balsovo and the seashore guard post we had passed earlier.

Boris asked, "Is that your cavalry?"

"Joy cometh in the morning."

"What?"

Evidently, Boris had skipped Bible class. Before I could explain, another explosion boomed across the lake. This time, it was from the Estonian side. Their shore floodlights went out.

I said, "That's my cavalry."

Boris pointed to the Estonian shore. "Look."

Through the fog, we saw a red light, a green light, and a flashing white light between them.

"Those are my guys!" I told Boris. "Take the controls and aim the boat for that white light. I'm going to create a little diversion. Give me a direction for the Estonian radar station."

Boris pointed to a position southwest of the three-light set on the other side of the lake. I used the autopilot remote to set a course and speed for the patrol launch. With no one at the controls, she sped off on a west-southwest course that would cause her to make landfall well south of our destination. The launch wasn't going to fool them, but it would force them to make a choice. My reasoning: they would focus on a boat headed for the radar tower first. That could give us enough time to get away.

The baby, who had been in the bassinet during the shooting, was now in Yulia's arms and screaming. Yulia calmly rocked him and told us, "You know, five Russians tried this a couple of years ago. The Estonians caught them and sent them back to Russia."

I could have gone all day without that encouraging piece of news.

Boris hit the gas and our bucket of bolts chugged along the peninsula coast toward Estonia. As we pulled away from the dock, two patrol cars with flashing lights barreled into the parking area.

Bullets ripped through the boat's wooden superstructure and pinged off metal, but the fishing machinery behind the wheelhouse took most of the hits and protected us. Boris didn't turn on the running lights, and before long, we were just a bad memory to the Russian border patrol. That didn't stop them from firing into the fog, hoping for a lucky shot. They didn't get one. Our friends on the Estonian side were smart enough to turn off the light set. Before they did, I took an azimuth reading and told Boris to put the boat on that course.

The bucket of bolts had radar and sonar, antiquated, but serviceable. Boris used them to steer us away from the peninsula coast so we wouldn't run aground. There was a radio, too. I climbed up to the antenna and taped an IR beacon to it. If Sherri had an eye in the sky, she could track our progress and turn on the three lights when we got close enough.

We heard lots of vehicle traffic on both sides of the lake, but it was too late to worry about that. We had to worry about how to deal with the Estonians if they caught us.

The peninsula terminates in a boot toe formation. We had to be careful we didn't run smack into the instep. Somewhere behind us there was a Russian boat in the water. Boris put our boat into a ninety-degree left turn, followed later by ninety degrees right. That's when we saw the red, white, and green lights. Boris set warp speed and we hurtled toward the white light. On radar and sonar, the shore was coming at us fast. I grabbed a railing and gave Boris a skeptical look. He smiled, hit the brakes, rotated the boat, and we backed right up to the white beacon. There was a bloodcurdling grinding sound as the propeller blades tried to cut through rock. Boris killed the motor, and we ran to the back deck.

Sherri and Tony-D were waiting for us in black battledress and carrying short-barrel CAR-15 rifles with big suppressors.

"The cavalry," I said to Yulia and Boris.

Sherry yelled, "Welcome to Estonia! Get your asses out of that boat! Let's go!"

We scrambled off the boat and up the embankment to a road, Yulia carrying the baby, me carrying the backpack of baby accessories, and Boris lugging the one suitcase of belongings they had brought into their new lives.

An ambulance awaited us on the coast road, lights out, a driver at the wheel, motor running. Sherri and Tony-D pushed us into the back and joined us. Tony-D banged the panel behind the driver and the ambulance laid rubber, heading north.

The baby had become a mobile tinnitus generator. Yulia popped the last bottle of milk into his screaming, red face, saving us all from brain damage and child abuse charges.

Somewhere south of us, a hellacious explosion ripped through the night.

Sherri saw my worried look. "Relax, Max. We're not blowing up infrastructure. That's just an explosion to distract the border guards. We put C-4 on a drone, landed it in an open field, and pressed the boom button." Refocusing, she said, "Don't touch anything. Don't leave prints." She handed each of us new arrivals a set of latex gloves.

Tony-D gave Boris a suspicious once-over and turned to me. "You didn't tell us you were bringing family."

"I couldn't find a babysitter."

Tony-D grunted. "Why is this guy wearing an FSB uniform?"

"He's FSB . . . and a friend. Meet Boris. This is Mrs. Boris. That is Baby Boris." No need for real names. I introduced Tony-D and Sherri. "This is my brother. Address him as Brother Max. This is my sister. Call her Sister Max."

Yulia recognized Sherri from my bank robbing days in Moscow. She told Sherri, "You were a reporter when we met in Gorky Park two years ago. Now, you are what . . . SEAL Team 6 witch?" Yulia gave Sherri's tactical gear a pointedly disdainful up-and-down.

Sherri doesn't take crap from anybody. "The last time I saw you," she replied, "you were peddling dirty pictures of my president in Gorky Park." She cocked her head to one side and looked at the rouge bruise I painted on Yulia's cheek. "What's your new occupation, punching bag?"

I interrupted the bra measuring contest. "Ladies! We're on the same side."

Without a hint of embarrassment, Tony-D and Sherri peeled down to their skivvies and put on EMT uniforms. Boris watched shapely Sherri. Pissed Yulia watched bad Boris.

Sherri picked up on the bitchy vibe and explained, in Russian, "If we get stopped, we don't want to look like SEAL Team 6." She instructed Boris and me, "Get out of those FSB uniforms." To Boris, she said, "If you have civilian clothes in that suitcase, put them on."

To me, she said, "Max, you're our patient. Lie down on the stretcher."

Sherri and Tony-D rigged me to a phony transfusion bottle and covered me with a blood-splattered blanket. A couple of miles from Beresje, the driver turned on his red flashing light, but not the siren. No point in calling undue attention to us on a pre-dawn Sunday morning.

After a fifteen-minute drive northwest on Route 45, the ambulance pulled into the parking lot of a small regional hospital in Rapina. We abandoned the ambulance and transferred to a pre-positioned black minivan. With our ambulance driver behind the wheel, we returned to Route 45 and began the three-hour drive northwest to Tallinn. Destiny was moving me toward Petrov.

Sherri monitored the Estonian Border Patrol frequency. They were on full alert—or as alert as they get before dawn on Sunday—calling for roadblocks on our route as far north of us as Tartu, and as far south to the Saatse border crossing into Russia. There was also frantic Russian chatter on another frequency. They had found the bodies at the Balsovo dock. On a third frequency, we could hear the Russians talking to their liaison officer on the Estonian side. We all understood Russian. Boris translated the Estonian chatter. The rest of us sat quietly wondering if we were going to beat the Estonians to those roadblocks.

CHAPTER 24

THE AMBUSH WAS in place for General Orlov, Zabluda's boss, when he entered the ornate office. He arrived a few minutes early, but the three men in chairs clustered around the deputy minister's desk had been there long enough for cigarette butts to have collected in the ashtrays at their feet. Orlov noticed a magazine spread open over the deputy's phone console. He saw the red light that indicated the intercom was on reflected in the glass covering a photograph behind the deputy's desk. Someone not in the room was interested and listening.

Orlov greeted the deputy with a simple, "Minister," and sat in the empty chair. Of the other three men in the semicircle facing the deputy, two were generals and one was a civilian whom Orlov did not know and was not introduced. The generals represented the GRU—military intelligence—and the SVR—foreign intelligence.

Orlov, the FSB representative, smiled at his colleagues and observed, "GRU, SVR, and FSB. The organs of state security are assembled. Whose organs are we going after today?"

"Your humor is misplaced, General," replied the deputy. "Your Colonel Zabluda had quite a time last night, commandeering a helicopter, bullying the highway patrol and border guards to do his bidding. Roadblocks, border crossings reenforced or closed, to what end?

We have four dead highway patrolmen, five dead border guards, a patrol boat at the bottom of Lake Pskov, a border violation with the Estonians, and Maxwell Geller escaped. Tell us what happened."

Orlov replied, "With respect, Minister, everyone here"—he looked at the unknown civilian—"almost everyone here knows that Lieutenant Colonel Zabluda is not my Colonel Zabluda. He is a GRU assassin transferred to me at the FSB for rehabilitation after missteps in the field. I was ordered to give him meaningful work and evaluate his capabilities."

The deputy minister pressed his lips together in a gesture of impatience.

Orlov continued. "Zabluda was engaged in that meaningful work last night, as senior on-call officer. An informant observed CIA agent Maxwell Geller at an apartment in the Voykovsky District and reported the incident to FSB headquarters. Zabluda was notified and initiated those actions with the highway patrol and border guards, which were entirely appropriate."

"Except that Geller got away," observed the deputy minister, with a sneer.

"That is correct," replied Orlov. "This is the second time in two years that Geller has roamed Moscow and eluded Zabluda. It appears that the GRU's best assassin is no match for him."

"Which brings us to the next subject. Why is Colonel Zabluda asking questions about Colonel Alexi Petrov at the Ministry of Defense?"

"He's doing so at my direction. Colonel Petrov was frequently observed in the company of an FSB officer suspected of spying for the CIA. I directed my staff to follow up on everyone having repeated contacts with the suspect."

The GRU general said, "Petrov is a military officer. Why didn't you inform us?"

"There was no reason to inform the GRU," replied Orlov. "I have no evidence that Petrov is involved in espionage. Why cast a shadow on a decorated officer without evidence?"

The deputy minister interrupted the exchange. "How did you come by the information that your FSB officer was a suspected spy?"

"An anonymous tip."

"Was the subject of that tip Sergei Golovkin, an FSB analyst?"

When Orlov hesitated, the minister said, "Now is not the time for caution, General. I'm here to bring coordination to the operational chaos surrounding Geller and his contacts. Was the allegation that Golovkin was recruited by Maxwell Geller?"

"Yes. I had Golovkin under surveillance. He met with Colonel Petrov, I directed Zabluda to build a dossier on Petrov."

The deputy gave the GRU general a *There, you see?* look. The ambush had misfired. He said, "Well, gentlemen, my assessment is that everyone here has been operating in good faith, but at cross purposes. Let me bring you up to date and expand your perspectives.

"Two years ago, former CIA agent Maxwell Geller came to Russia to gather certain very sensitive intelligence. He roamed the country, from St. Petersburg to Moscow, collected that intelligence, robbed a bank, and escaped. His escapades embarrassed the security services and enraged our president. The SVR was given orders to track down Geller so that the GRU could kill him. As a wise man said, 'For every problem, there is a solution that is quick, easy, and wrong.' This was the wrong solution.

"Nevertheless, ten days ago, the GRU found Geller on a beach in Australia and tried to kill him . . . tried and failed." The deputy gave the GRU general a stern look. "Geller and persons unknown killed three GRU would-be assassins. So much for the shortsighted approach.

"Fortunately, we had strategic thinkers who saw the problem and the solution differently. For Geller to have survived in St. Petersburg and Moscow for days and escape the country, he had to have a network of people who hid him, fed him, transported him, and provided information. Elimination of that network should have been the focus of your efforts. Geller is the means to that end. Dead, he was—and is—of no value to us.

"So, our strategic thinkers formed a special cell to identify Geller's support network. The obvious interrogation target was Geller. So, while the SVR and the GRU were trying to locate and kill Geller, this cell devised a plan to lure Geller back to Moscow, where we could question him, roll up his network, and execute all of them."

"Who is in this special cell?" asked the GRU general.

The deputy shut off that inquiry with, "I did not hear that question, you did not ask it."

Addressing Orlov, the deputy said, "General, you were not the only one who received an anonymous tip that Sergei Golovkin might be a spy working with Geller."

It was Orlov's turn to be indignant. "Why wasn't I informed? Golovkin is my responsibility."

"I'm informing you now." To the group, the deputy announced, "The decision as to who was, and who was not, informed was made above the level of anyone in this room.

"As I was saying," continued the deputy, "while the manhunt for Geller was underway in Australia, the special cell devised a plan to lure Geller to Moscow. Reviewing Sergei Golovkin's background, they found that Petrov and Golovkin were longtime friends. We had Petrov approach Golovkin and set a trap for Geller. Petrov told Golovkin that he wanted to defect. His only demand was that Geller bring him out of Russia. Petrov was ideal bait, with war planning and policy experience at the Defense Ministry. That package was sure to attract the CIA."

The SVR general asked, "Petrov willingly betrayed his friend Golovkin?"

"Petrov is a patriot. His friend is a suspected spy," said the deputy. He looked at General Orlov. "You may not have caught Golovkin red-handed, but we have him on tape admitting that he talked to Geller during his Moscow visit two years ago. We have not moved on him because that would have alerted his CIA handler and whatever Moscow network they have.

"In any event," continued the deputy, "Golovkin told Petrov he didn't know how to contact Geller. So, Petrov approached the Army attaché at the American Embassy, a Colonel Burke, and gave him the defection request. We assume the attaché notified the CIA, but they took months to send Geller. He finally arrived in Moscow using the identity of Gregory Vasiliev, yet another failed GRU assassin." The deputy shot another glare of dissatisfaction at the GRU general.

"The special cell's plan," said the deputy minister, "would proceed in four steps. Geller would contact Petrov and arrange the defection. Petrov would notify us of the details. When the defection was underway, our security services would move in, capture Geller and his accomplices, interrogate them, and roll up the entire network.

"We knew Geller would suspect the defection was a trap. So as not to scare Geller off, we did not place Petrov under surveillance. However—" he looked over at General Orlov—"without our knowledge, you had Petrov under surveillance because of his association with Sergei Golovkin. We must assume that Geller detected your surveillance and suspected that Petrov's defection was a trap. So, he bolted for Estonia without ever contacting Petrov."

General Orlov saw the reflection of the red intercom button in the glass frame behind the deputy minister's desk and knew this was the moment for truth, no matter how unpleasant. He said, "Minister, there may be another explanation for Geller's actions."

"Please explain," said the skeptical deputy minister.

* * *

When Junior Sergeant Burkov heard nothing from Zabluda about the bribe he reported, Burkov took the matter to personnel. Personnel informed General Orlov. The general was now informing the deputy minister—and the person listening on the deputy's intercom line—that Geller was stopped outside of Petrov's apartment and bribed his way out of an arrest.

* * *

The GRU general demanded to know, "What have you done about the corrupt incompetents who let Geller escape!"

Orlov ignored the general and told the deputy minister, "I accept responsibility for their failure. They will be punished, but quality is an issue that cannot be resolved by punishment." He gazed at his peers one at a time. "The SVR and GRU get the pick of recruits, have quicker promotions and better working conditions. The FSB gets leftovers. Performance reflects quality."

The deputy leaned forward and fixed his gaze on Orlov. "Yes, but you are not a leftover, are you, General? You come with the endorsement of the Federation president."

"Putting an excellent rider on a sick horse does not change the outcome of the race, Minister," replied Orlov. Quickly, he added, "If I may get to my point, Minister, it is possible that Geller may have made contact with Petrov in Petrov's apartment building."

The deputy addressed the civilian. "Did Petrov inform you of a contact with Geller?"

"No, Deputy Minister."

The GRU general noted, "Geller is in Tallinn; Petrov is going to Tallin. That can't be a coincidence."

Orlov replied, "It may be. It is possible that Estonia was not Geller's first choice. He presented a Finnish passport for his female prisoner at the guard post, and we found counterfeit Finnish license plates in the trunk of the car he abandoned at the Balsovo waterfront."

"It's possible the Finnish artifacts were designed to mislead us," countered the GRU general.

"I don't think so," replied Orlov. "If Geller intended to cross into Estonia, why didn't he have counterfeit Estonian passports and license plates, and cross the border quietly without gunfire? I believe he was headed for Finland and, when the manhunt was closing in, he had to make a quick exit from the Federation."

The unidentified civilian joined the conversation. "There are two possibilities. One, the FSB surveillance scared Geller off and he never contacted Petrov. Two, Geller contacted Petrov, is planning to help him defect in Tallinn, and Petrov will contact us when he knows the plan."

General Orlov said, "There is a third possibility. Geller did contact Petrov in Moscow. Together, they are planning a real defection for Petrov in Tallinn. That is the CIA's goal."

Alarmed, the GRU general said, "That cannot be permitted! Petrov knows the details of OPERATION BEARCLAW."

Orlov asked, "What is OPERATION BEARCLAW?"

"It doesn't concern the FSB," said the deputy minister.

"It concerns the GRU," said the military intelligence general. "If there is any possibility that Petrov will defect, we must stop him now!"

In a decisive tone, the deputy minister said, "Here is what we will do."

After the deputy minister issued instructions, the intercom light on his desk went out.

CHAPTER 25

Sunday, 9 a.m.
U.S. Embassy, Tallinn, Estonia

THE SURPRISE CALL had come on my sat phone about two hours after we crossed Lake Pskov. We were on the road to Tallinn. The caller was Rodney. I didn't know what time zone he was in, but wherever he was, it wasn't business hours. It was Saturday in the States and Sunday in Australia. I assumed the call was important.

"Yeah?" I was tired and sounded like it.

Rodney must have been getting reports of my exploits from Moscow Station or he was watching on satellite, as Sherri's team and mine fired up the shores of Lake Pskov. He asked, "Max, how's World War III going?"

"We're winning. What do you want? Make it quick. I'm reloading."

"RAMPART sent a message to his friend, the colonel." He meant Burke. "The colonel relayed it to me. RAMPART wants you to meet him on Sunday evening by the sea. He said you'd know where."

Tallinn. "Anything else."

"He said to bring friends. It's going to be a big party." That meant a heavy Russian security detail was accompanying RAMPART. The job wasn't getting easier. Rodney added, "When you get to where I think you're going, send me an update."

I broke the connection.

*   *   *

The U.S. Embassy in Tallinn is a tall, gray rectangle of a building located at Kentmanni 20, a quiet street near the park. We arrived there
at 9 a.m. Sunday morning and parked as close to the embassy as security barriers would allow. Everyone else stayed in the van while I
walked to the entrance and showed my phony passport to the Marine
guard.

"I have an emergency. I need to speak to the duty officer. If he wants
to verify my identity, ask him to call this number at Langley." I gave
him Rodney's number. Langley would patch the call through to him,
wherever in the world he was.

I waited in the bulletproof, glass-enclosed entrance while the Marine made the call.

It was a long wait before a grumpy fellow showed up who looked to
be my age and sleepy. He introduced himself as Watkins and said,
"Follow me."

He led me to an interview room on the second floor. When we
were uncomfortably seated in the sparsely furnished, soundproofed
cubicle he said, "Sorry for your wait. The duty officer called me after
he talked to Langley. I'm the CIA station chief. I know you're not the
person named in your credentials. You're Max Geller. The Agency
fired you two years ago for bad-mouthing the president."

"Langley brought me back in just for this op."

"Why are you here?"

"I was in Moscow. The op went sideways. My primary exfil route
through Finland was blocked. I shifted to my secondary, through
Estonia."

"Okay, but why are you *here* . . . at the embassy?"

"I need help."

"Like what?"

"I've got people with me. Some have been up for eighteen hours. We need a safe place to rest and plan our next move."

"Did you create that kerfuffle down at Lake Pskov last night?"

"On the advice of counsel, I respectfully decline to answer that question."

"I don't see your counsel."

"I keep my own counsel. That works better for spies, don't you think? Can we get back to putting up my people?"

"You can't stay at a hotel. The Estonian authorities are looking for the people who crossed Lake Pskov last night. They'll check hotels first. So will the Russians. How many with you?"

"Three Americans on my team." They were probably freezing in the van by now. I added, "If I'm lucky, five more Americans will join me soon. My op has shifted to Tallinn."

Watkins took a card from his wallet and wrote an address and an entry code on it. "This is a safehouse. It'll be tight for you and eight people, but it's adequate."

"I also have a Russian family of three with me, a mother, father, and baby."

"What's their story?"

"I was in a bind. They helped me escape. They can't go back to Russia."

"I'm not sure that's sufficient grounds for asylum."

Watkins was going bureaucratic on me. So, I went nuclear. "The man of the family is an FSB officer with vital national security information, strictly need-to-know."

"What don't I need to know?"

"The name of a mole at Langley." That wasn't true, but it shut him down.

"How do you know they're not bullshitting you?"

"I've seen the compromising photos." That wasn't true either, but I had seen compromising photographs of someone in the White House. "The Russian family needs to stay here in the embassy, where it's safe, until I'm ready to take them to Langley."

"When are you leaving?"

"I need to send a message to Langley to find out."

"And I'll have to get guidance from Langley and talk to the ambassador."

"I expected you to."

Watkins took me to the SCIF—secure compartmented information facility. While he called Langley to get whatever he needed to cover his posterior, I drafted a message to Rodney.

MOSCOW RAMPART FESTIVAL CANCELED. STAR DID NOT LIKE VENUE. NEW LOCATION IS TALLINN. ESTONIA. SEND A PLATOON-SIZED ARMED SECURITY DETAIL IMMEDIATELY. SHOW STARTS THIS P.M. EXPECTING HOOLIGANS. LIMITED WINDOW OF OPPORTUNITY. SEND FAX PHOTO OF STAR FOR SECURITY TEAM BRIEFING. SEND AUTHORITY TO STATION CHIEF AND AMBASSADOR FOR USE OF LOCAL ASSETS, IF NEEDED. BREAK. EXFIL FLIGHT REQUIRED FOR TWELVE PASSENGERS. WHEN RAMPART FESTIVAL IS OVER.

I had to make sure that Boris, Yulia, and their baby got a chance at freedom, and security from Moscow's reprisals. I couldn't rely on Rodney for that. He was a coldhearted SOB. Once RAMPART was in my custody, he would abandon Boris and Yulia without a second thought. The only way they could get a fair shake was for me to box

Rodney in by going over his head. Before I gave the message to the code clerk, I added the following:

BREAK. I WAS ASSISTED IN RAMPART OPERATION BY
FAMILY OF THREE RUSSIAN NATIONALS SEEKING
ASYLUM. MAN WAS WITH FSB UNTIL LAST WEEK.
HAS KNOWLEDGE AND PHOTOS OF COMPROMISED
U.S. VISITORS TO RUSSIA. WOMAN WORKED IN
SITUATIONS WHERE WESTERN GOVERNMENT
OFFICIALS WERE COMPROMISED. REQUEST
AUTHORITY TO EVACUATE THEM WITH RAMPART.
OTHER OPTIONS FATAL.

To prevent Rodney from screwing Boris and his family, I addressed copies to the Director of Operations and to the CIA's mole hunters. As an added safeguard—and screw you, Rodney—I sent a copy to the FBI's Counterintelligence Division. Having touched all the bureaucratic bases, I gave the message to the code clerk.

Watkins arranged temporary housing in the embassy for Boris, Yulia, and the baby. Sherri and her guys drove across town to the safehouse. I napped on the embassy duty officer's bed, waiting for Rodney to answer my message. When it came in, Watkins awakened me. We returned to the SCIF, and he watched my face fall as I read the bad news in the decoded message.

RAMPART PHOTO COMING IMMEDIATELY BY
SECURE FAX. BREAK. SECURITY TEAM NOT
AVAILABLE WITHIN SPECIFIED TIME FRAME. THIS
IS YOUR AUTHORIZATION TO USE LOCAL
EMBASSY-CERTIFIED ASSETS FOR RAMPART
FESTIVAL. DISCLOSE ONLY NECESSARY INFO TO

LOCALS. BREAK. EXFIL PLANE ENROUTE FROM UK.
ETA 0100 HRS TOMORROW. PILOT WILL CONTACT
YOU VIA SAT PHONE SIXTY MINUTES FROM
TOUCHDOWN. BREAK. FLY RAMPART AND
ASYLUM-SEEKERS TO DC VIA RAMSTEIN AFB. SPEED
ESSENTIAL. RESPIRATORY VIRUS SPREADING FROM
CHINA. INTERNATIONAL BORDER CLOSINGS
IMMINENT.

I showed Watkins the message.

"Is there anything I can do?"

"I need manpower. I'm bringing over a defector. He arrives in Tallinn today by air with a Russian security escort. I need a surveillance team to follow them from the airport to their hotel. They may switch hotels as a security precaution."

"What about the crew you brought with you?"

"They're not official. They shouldn't be involved in this."

Testily, he asked, "Weren't they involved at Lake Pskov?"

"I don't know what you're talking about."

Watkins looked away in disgust. He appeared to be lost in thought before asking, "Is your defector coming in with the Russian Foreign Ministry group?"

"What Foreign Ministry group?"

"The Russians and Estonians have had a border dispute for years. A Russian delegation is flying in to negotiate a resolution. Their advance team is due in this evening. The main body arrives on Tuesday. Could your defector be with them?"

"That's possible."

"Maybe airport surveillance won't be necessary. I can get their arrival times, the names of the delegates, and their hotel reservations. What else do you need?"

"The defector is coming willingly, but I need a local team to snatch him and his wife from their security."

"How many people do you need?"

"That's guesswork until I see where my package is staying. For planning, let's say a driver, four security men, and four handlers for the package and his wife."

Watkins shook his head. "This is a small station. I don't have the manpower or skill sets."

"What are my options?"

"The Estonians won't help. You've already pissed them off at Lake Pskov, and they won't cross the Russians with a delegation here to resolve the border issue. Your only option is local contractors."

"Are they trustworthy and competent?"

"Trustworthy? Yes. Competent? They're not Tier 1 operators. On a job like this, they might turn out to be tears in your beer."

I felt my body downshift and gave Watkins a blank stare.

He said, "You're asleep on your feet. I'll drive you to the safehouse. Get some rest and let me work the problem. I'll get back to you when I have something."

At the safehouse, everyone was asleep on a bed, floor, or couch. I set my alarm for four hours. Fully clothed, I stretched out on the bed next to Sherri. She didn't stir.

CHAPTER 26

Sunday, late afternoon
CIA safehouse, Tallinn, Estonia

RUSSIANS HAD SURROUNDED the hotel where Petrov—a.k.a. RAMPART—and his wife were staying, according to Watkins, the CIA station chief in Tallinn.

Thirty minutes before I got that news, Watkins had come to the safehouse and awakened me. I got up without disturbing Sherri and followed him to the kitchen. I sat at the table trying to bring my brain online. He brewed coffee and updated me on Estonian and Russian efforts to find whoever made the Lake Pskov crossing the previous night.

When we were wrapped around cups of coffee, Watkins said, "I've got good news—"

"That coffee smells like good news," Sherri announced. She entered the kitchen dressed in black cargo pants and a black t-shirt, her hair in a ponytail, looking for all the world like Sara Connor in the second *Terminator* movie. Sherri filled a cup and sat with us. Before Watkins could spread the good news, Tony-D and Jack, our driver, entered the kitchen, filled up at the coffeepot, and joined us.

"So," I said, "what's the good news?"

"You won't need a surveillance team at the airport. The Russian delegation arrives at 10 p.m. tonight and I know which hotels they reserved."

"Hotels, plural?" I asked.

"Yeah. They booked a second hotel earlier today, but they're not changing hotels. They're splitting the delegation, which is unusual." Watkins handed me two computer-printed guest lists on hotel stationery, with room numbers. He explained, "The first list is from the hotel where most of the Russian delegates will be staying. The second list is the new booking for a much smaller group. Is your defector listed on either sheet?"

There he was, Alexi Petrov. "He's with the smaller group."

Watkins said, "That's interesting, because early this afternoon, a group of Russian tourists arrived from Moscow on a chartered flight. They got last-minute accommodations for hotels and bed-and-breakfast rentals surrounding the hotel where your defector is booked."

Watkins opened a city map and spread it across the table. One building was circled in green ink, surrounded by four red dots on nearby buildings. He explained, "The circle is where the small delegation is staying. These red dots are the rooms for those Moscow tourists. From their windows, the tourists can observe every entrance and exit from your defector's hotel."

Tony-D said, "That looks like one big Russian bear trap to me. Going into the hotel is like stepping on the pressure plate and those little red dots move in to disable you."

"Is that a trap for you?" Watkins asked me.

"Looks like it . . . or my Russian really wants to defect, and Moscow found out. In that case, it could be a trap for both of us."

"Or," mused Sherry, "there are snipers behind those red dots, waiting to kill you."

"I'm betting they want me alive."

"They didn't in Australia," Sherri reminded me. I had told her about Bondi Beach.

Tony-D suggested. "Maybe they wanted you alive and the hoods in Australia didn't get the word. The Russians love show trials that embarrass the CIA and impress their countrymen."

We were speculating and, at that point, it didn't matter. I had to go in after RAMPART or abandon the mission. I told Watkins, "You did a great job of finding my defector. Did you find a team to help me get him away from his security detail?"

Watkins responded with sympathy. "That's a problem. In light of the Lake Pskov incident, I had to brief the ambassador that I was helping you. He called the State Department who called the CIA, who called my division chief at Langley, who called me. The bad news is I've been ordered to cease all assistance to you and break contact. The concern is that if the Russians find out that U.S. Embassy personnel here helped one of their people defect, they might pull out of the border negotiations. That would damage our relationship with the Estonians."

Sherry spoke my thoughts. "The rest of the story being, if Max botches the defection and gets caught, Washington can deny their involvement because the CIA fired Max two years ago."

"I assume that's their reasoning," replied Watkins. "I'm sorry."

I was pissed and puzzled. "How the hell does Langley expect me to liberate this Russian without people?"

Watkins had the answer. "Rodney sent a message. He's recruiting a contract team for you. He wants you to stand down for forty-eight hours so they have time to get here."

I reminded everyone, "The full complement of Russian security hoods will be here tonight. The best time to spring this defector is right after he checks in. It's the period of maximum confusion. They're getting settled; they haven't exercised their security routines."

Sherri cautioned, "Max, this sounds like a good time to walk away."

I didn't want to ask, but I had no choice. "Sherri, can you and your team help me with this?"

"There's just me, Jack, and Tony-D. Those are bad odds for a head-to-head with Russians."

"When will your guys get here from Finland?"

"They're on a plane to the States. I released them when you texted me you were crossing at Lake Pskov."

"Damn!"

Watkins handed me two rolled documents. "You might need these." As I removed the rubber bands from each, he said, "That's the lobby floor plan for the hotel where your defector will be staying. The other one is the plan for his floor."

I asked Sherri, "How would you do this with just the four of us?"

"Jesus, Max . . ." Sherri examined the floor plans with Tony-D and Jack looking over her shoulders. After a while she said, "I can think of lots of ways to get into the hotel. The problem is getting out." She traced the red dots surrounding the hotel and looked at me. "There are four doors and the loading dock. The Russians have them all under observation. They might want you alive, but they might shoot the rest of us."

I know Sherri. That didn't sound like a definite *no can do*. I let her work the problem.

She turned to Watkins. "We'll need some equipment. Can you help with that?"

"I'll get you anything that doesn't go 'boom' and can't be traced to me."

We put our heads together and drew up a shopping list, and assigned Jack to go with the station chief and bring back our equipment.

Watkins read the list and said, "Walk me out, Max." At the door, he gave me more bad news. "The ambassador had me move your

Russian family out of the embassy. I got them a suite at this airport hotel." He gave me a card with the address, room number, and a password. "I paid a couple of retired Estonian cops to babysit them until they leave. The cops are reliable, but they'll just be a trip wire if the Russians try to take the Kuzmicks from you."

I was angry. "This is the second time in three days an ambassador has pulled support from my operation. What the hell is wrong with diplomats in this part of the world?"

"They serve at the pleasure of the president, and the president is not pleased by anything that might piss off the Russians. It's not just the ambassador, Max. My orders from the ambassador and Langley are to put Boris and his family on the plane Rodney told you was arriving from the UK. He's sending another plane in forty-eight hours with an extraction team to help you free up your defector."

"Rodney has my phone number. Why isn't he telling me this?"

"I think the Kuzmick family part of your op has been taken out of Rodney's hands. My orders are coming from my boss at Langley and the ambassador is getting traffic from Foggy Bottom. You kicked a hornet's nest when you copied that last message to the DO and the FBI." He smiled. "Isn't that what you intended?"

"Bet your ass," I answered, with a smile of my own.

"I hear some people back at the Agency are calling you Mad Max Geller."

"I am mad." I was remembering how Rodney had blackmailed me into this mess.

Watkins said, "Got some shopping to do. Good luck, Max."

We didn't have much time to prepare before RAMPART and his Russian escort arrived at Lennart Meri Tallinn Airport. Our plan had to be simple, surprise the Russians, and be perfectly executed.

CHAPTER 27

Late Sunday night
RAMPART's hotel, Tallinn, Estonia

THE RUSSIAN GUARD was waiting with a scowl and his hand on his hip holster when Sherri got off the hotel elevator on the fourth floor. She wore slacks and a hotel blazer, and was pushing a cart of welcome baskets loaded with bottles of vodka, tins of caviar, and other goodies.

Before the guard could speak, Sherri smiled and addressed him in Russian. "Good evening. We have gift baskets for your delegation, compliments of the Estonian Ministry of Foreign Affairs." She maneuvered the cart around him and headed for Petrov's suite.

Pulling a second cart of baskets, I backed off the elevator so the guard wouldn't see my face and maybe recognize me. Deliberately, I headed in the opposite direction, away from Sherri.

As we anticipated, the guard considered a male the greater threat. He turned away from Sherri and yelled at me, "Stop!" That's when Sherri clobbered him with her blackjack. He dropped like a sack of rocks.

While I taped his mouth, hands, and ankles, Sherri sent the elevator down and Tony-D came up to join us, carrying our weapons bag. We dragged the guard and my basket cart into the elevator and pressed the hold button. Then, with Tony-D covering our rear, and Sherri pushing the gift basket cart, the three of us headed for Petrov's suite.

When we got there, Tony-D and I stood out of sight on either side of the door. Sherri knocked and said a cheerful, "Room service. Gift baskets, compliments of the Estonian Ministry of Foreign Affairs."

An attractive blonde opened the door.

"Mrs. Petrov?" asked Sherri, in Russian.

"Yes?"

Sherri repeated the Ministry of Foreign Affairs greeting and pushed the cart into the suite. The woman stepped aside. When Sherri passed, the blonde pulled a gun.

I stepped into the room, tore the gun from the woman's hand, and pushed her to the floor.

Tony-D darted in and shut the door.

"What the hell . . . ?" said a surprised Sherri.

"This isn't Petrov's wife," I explained. "She's security. Check the suite."

While they did, I flex-cuffed the blonde's hands behind her back. Before I gagged her, she said, "You're trapped. The alarm went out when you took down the elevator guard. He was wearing a fall detector."

Sherri and Tony-D emerged seconds later with Alexi Petrov in tow.

I asked Petrov, "Are you okay?"

"Yes."

"Where's your wife?"

"She didn't come. At the last minute, the ministry replaced her with that woman." Petrov nodded to the one I had just gagged.

Someone banged on the door and shouted, in a Russian accent, "Maxwell Geller, you are trapped! There is no escape! Come out with your hands up!"

I said a quiet, urgent, "Let's go," to my team.

Sherri and Tony-D removed the gift basket and tablecloth from the cart and took off the tabletop. The compartment beneath contained more weapons, a coiled nylon rope, a linear shape charge, and pairs of work gloves. Sherri and Tony-D headed for the bedroom.

I told Petrov, "Turn the lights out."

I placed electrical tape over the door's peephole and around the bottom edge so that there was no space between the door and the carpet, in case they tried to insert a mic or camera underneath to find out what we were up to.

Bang! Bang! Bang! on the door. "Maxwell Geller, come out with your hands up!"

In a whisper I told Petrov, "Help me pile furniture in front of this door. They'll breach it when they get tired of talking."

We blocked the door with the couch and a couple of heavy chairs and went to the bedroom. Sherri was securing one end of the nylon rope to the metal bed frame. Tony-D had ripped down the curtains and was placing the shaped charge in a rectangle around the edges of the window.

Banging at the door continued. Someone said, "Come out now and no one will be hurt!"

Sure. I went to the living room and shouted, "I'll come out, but I want to surrender to the Estonian police! You have no authority here!"

I handed Petrov a pair of work gloves. "Put these on. Are you ready to go?"

"Where?"

"Rappelling."

Tony-D and Sherry joined us in the living room. We crouched behind the wet bar and Tony-D said—just loud enough for the four of us to hear—"Fire in the hole." He detonated the shaped charge with an ear-splitting boom, sending a spray of glass out from the building and raining down on the sidewalk. We rushed into the bedroom. Tony-D grabbed a blanket from the bed and threw it over jagged edges of glass on the windowsill. Sherri tossed the coil of nylon rope out the window and watched it snake down to the sidewalk.

At that moment, Jack turned the corner with our van, parked under Petrov's bedroom window, and tossed grenades. Billowing white smoke obscured the van and drifted up to mask our exit.

Sherri rappelled down the face of the building to the sidewalk and took up a position behind the van, covering the Russian observation post across the street—one of those red dots—with her CAR-15. Jack, our driver, just kept popping smoke.

In quick succession, Petrov and Tony-D followed Sherri down the rappelling rope. I tossed smoke and tear gas grenades into the living room and hit the rope. Before the first Russian breached the door of Petrov's suite, we were away from the hotel, with Jack at the wheel. No shots fired.

On the way to the airport, my sat phone rang. It was Rodney. He was not happy. "Did you get the movement plan for the asylum seekers?"

"Yes." I was deliberately short with him and I wasn't going to tell him we had RAMPART. If he was sending help, we might need it.

Rodney said, "We have a problem. Lakenheath is socked in. Bad weather. Transport for your family is on a twenty-four-hour delay. Hold them in place. I'll get back to you."

Great! We had blasted, smoked, and gassed a whole hotel floor and half a city block. Tallinn police and Russians were looking for us, the safehouse was off limits, and Rodney's guidance was, "Sit on your thumb for another day." But where?

CHAPTER 28

Sunday night and Monday morning
Lennart Meri Tallin Airport, Estonia

IT WASN'T SAFE to stay at the airport hotel where the Tallinn station chief had stashed the Kuzmicks, but we were out of options. Jack dropped us there and parked next to an adjacent hotel to throw off pursuers. Sherri used a fake ID and charm to get us two rooms adjoining the suite occupied by Boris Kuzmick, Yulia, and the baby. That simplified our security plan.

I split up the rent-a-cops Watkins had hired to guard the Kuzmicks. We worked out shifts so that one cop and one of Sherri's team would be in the hall at all times. Sherri bunked on the couch in the Kuzmicks' suite. Jack, Tony-D, and a cop shared a room. The other cop stayed with me and Petrov. Our cop slept on a pull-out-of-the-closet-and-unfold bed, shoved against the door. That made him our first line of room defense against invaders.

The cop's bed blocking the door also kept Petrov from changing his mind and sneaking out to rejoin his Russian friends. It happens. Ask Special Agent Michael Rochford. In 1985, he was the FBI's handler for a defecting KGB colonel, Vitali Yurchenko. After months of interrogation, Vitali walked away from his FBI guards in Georgetown. He was next seen at a Russian Embassy press conference in Washington and, later, flew back to Moscow. Either he was part of a

KGB deception, or he just changed his mind and went home. That wasn't going to happen to me.

I woke up at 3 a.m., as the cop who had been sleeping by the door left for his hall shift. The lights were off. Petrov stood at the window, peering out into the darkness, a forbidden cigarette in one hand and a pulled back curtain in the other.

"See something?" I asked.

"A bleak future."

"It will look brighter in Washington. Get some rest. You've got a long trip ahead."

"I don't sleep much anymore. Bad dreams. Combat." He let the curtain go and came over to sit on his bed, facing me.

"Were you in combat?" he asked.

"Yes, in the army."

"Nightmares?"

"Not for a while. Where did you see action?"

"Ukraine, Syria, and Chechnya." He was silent for a while. "Fucking Syria. Assad gasses children just so he doesn't have to open a dental practice. What kind of man is that?"

I got up, took a small bottle of pills from my go-bag, and shook it to get his attention. "Our army uses these to help soldiers sleep on long flights. Want one?"

"I don't usually take drugs. I've seen the bad results in my family." That didn't sound like a rejection. He relented. "Maybe a couple . . . for later."

I shook two pills into his palm and cautioned, "Only one at a time. They're potent."

For a while, we sat across from each other in silence. He stared at the carpet between our beds and smoked another cigarette.

I said, "We'll get unwanted attention if the smoke alarm goes off."

He nodded and stubbed out the butt in his palm. "What was your job in the army?"

"Killing people."

"Your nightmares, how did you get over them?"

"I stopped killing people."

Petrov grunted, maybe to stifle a laugh or to signal understanding.

What I told him was a lie. I was an intelligence analyst in the army, but this was a time for bullshit and bonding, not harsh truths.

Wistfully, he said, "My best tour was Cairo." At the mention of that city, his mood shifted out of the dark place. "I was attaché there, but you knew that." He warmed to the memory. "Clean sheets, lots of parties, good food . . . and some spying." For the first time, he smiled at me. "It was the best time for my marriage. My wife loved the diplomatic circuit and she was good at it. She even recruited an Egyptian diplomat to spy on his country." Petrov uttered a little laugh. "He thought he was going to sleep with her. Too much James Bond."

I needed information. "I'm sorry they dropped your wife from the trip. Do you know why?"

"I've thought of nothing else since it happened." He gave me an intense stare. "When we met in my basement, you said the FSB had me under surveillance. They must have seen you leave."

That was exactly what happened, but I told him, "That's possible. We'll try to get her out."

"How?"

"There's always a jailed Russian spy to trade with Moscow."

Petrov uttered a doubtful grunt. "That sounds very time-consuming." With passion, he added, "My marriage is the only good thing left in my life, Geller."

"You didn't come to Tallinn to negotiate a border dispute. Why are you here?"

"The answer will cost you a plane ride to Washington. It's part of my deal to defect."

We sat in near-darkness, illuminated only by the reflection of parking lot lights slipping between the parted curtains. Petrov wanted to talk about his career. I let him, hoping for a clue as to what made him so valuable to Langley. I didn't hear one. When the nightstand clock showed 4 a.m., he asked, "What time do they begin serving breakfast?"

"We're eating combat rations in our rooms so people don't notice us." He understood. I tossed him a meal package from my go-bag.

Petrov left it on the bed and went to the coffeemaker. He held up a packet. "We have coffee without caffeine. I may try to get some sleep after I eat. He poured bottled water into the machine. "Want a cup?"

"Sure. Make mine diesel."

He gave me a quizzical look.

"With caffeine," I explained.

The machine gurgled. Petrov filled our cups and brought the brew over. He touched his cup to mine. "To an uneventful flight." We took big swallows and tore open our ration packets.

I thought we had exhausted conversational topics, but midway through the meal, Petrov said, "You have an excellent team. They conducted a very professional operation to get me out of the hotel last night. Thank you." After a pause, he told me, "I read that you robbed a bank during your last visit to Moscow. Is that true?"

"You know better than to believe what you read in Moscow papers."

He smiled. "I also saw it on television. Better?"

"Worse. On Russian television, you get lies and pictures of lies."

That got a big laugh. Then, he got serious. "How long are we here?"

"As long as it takes."

* * *

It was later Monday morning when a shoulder shake forced me out of a sound sleep.

Sherri was saying an urgent, "Max, wake up!"

I was groggy and irritated. My brain tried to engage. "What!"

"Your defector is gone!"

"Gone where?" Quickly, I realized that was a question for later. The immediate question was, "Is RAMPART bait or a defector?"

If RAMPART was a defector, my only problem was finding him. On the other hand, if RAMPART was bait, he deserted us to get out of the kill zone before the Russians arrived. That last thought was bringing me out of my brain fog fast, but I was wobbly. I stood and had to grab the nightstand for support. The digital clock read 7:08 a.m. The second thing I saw was my coffee cup and I knew. Petrov had drugged me with the sleeping pills I gave him.

Our predicament distracted me from my murderous thoughts. "Sherri, this location has been compromised! Send Jack to get the van. Get everybody up and packed. We're leaving."

Sherri said a cool, "I figured as much when we couldn't find him. The van is downstairs, and everyone is ready to leave except you. I couldn't wake you up. Where are we going?"

"The safehouse."

"Watkins said it was off-limits and he's probably changed the lock combination."

"Then blow the damn lock or climb in the window. Just get everyone off the streets. Now!" I was dressing as fast as I could. Sherri hesitated. I yelled, "Now! Move!"

"Are you coming with us?"

"No. I'm going to go find that son-of-a-bitch defector and put a bullet in his kneecap."

"You might be spotted, Max. If the Russians know we're here, they'll be all over the airport. It's you they want."

"After the hotel caper in Tallinn, we're all wanted. I want you to get Boris and his family away from here." I was fully awake and angry. "Who was on hall duty when the defector left?" Whoever it was, I wanted to shoot him.

"Tony-D and Udo, the rent-a-cop. Tony-D was taking a bathroom break. So, Udo was the one who saw the defector leave."

"Tell both of the rent-a-cops to meet me in the lobby in five minutes. Go!"

Sherri gave me tight lips and a curt nod. "See you when I see you."

I grabbed my go-bag. and went down to question the rent-a-cops. The only thing of value Udo told me was that Petrov took his bag down to the lobby about 5:30, claiming he was going to fill it with snacks for his trip. He never came back. I gave the cops a big tip and told them to get away from the airport fast.

There was a woman at the reception desk. I asked, "How long have you been here?"

"Since midnight. I'm working a twelve-hour shift. One of my colleagues is sick."

"Have you seen my father this morning?" I described Petrov and his clothes.

"Yes, sir. He came down about five thirty and asked me to turn on the computers. He wanted to check his flight."

"Flight to where?"

"He didn't say."

The two computers were visible from the reception desk. "Which computer did he use?"

"That one." She pointed to it.

"Has anyone used it since he did?"

"I don't believe so, sir."

I went to the computer and pulled down the history menu. Petrov had been on a popular travel website. I printed out all twelve pages of the screen he had been viewing. There were eleven possible flights on the listing. He wouldn't have made it to the terminal in time to get the first two. They left shortly after 5 a.m. Eight of the flights were hours long, with stops. Petrov would have wanted to get to his destination quickly. Lufthansa had the shortest flight, nine-plus hours, with one stop in Frankfurt. That's the one I would have taken.

The hotel shuttle dropped me at the terminal, and I studied the staff at the Lufthansa ticket counter. There were two women, one mature and a younger one. My bet was that the mature one wouldn't bend the rules. The young one might, with the proper incentive. I took an empty ticket sleeve from the trash and inserted a five-hundred-euro note. I put another one beneath the sleeve and approached the young one when she wasn't busy.

I put on a worried look and said, "Excuse me, I'm looking for my father. He has Alzheimer's and he wandered away from our hotel this morning, while the family was sleeping. We're traveling to Cyprus. Can you tell me if he came to your counter?" I showed her the photograph Rodney faxed me. I thought I saw recognition in her eyes, but she said, "I'm very sorry, sir. I can't discuss passengers and their flights."

"Oh, I understand. I just want to know if you saw him in the terminal this morning." I put the ticket sleeve on the counter and raised a corner so she could see the euro note inside.

She hesitated before saying, "I . . . I did see him in the airport at about 5:45 this morning."

"Thank you so much." I put one of the printout pages on the counter and rotated it so she could read. "Would you look at this flight routing." It was the 6:20 a.m. Lufthansa flight, arriving at Larnaca Airport at 4:10 p.m.

"Sir, I cannot discuss flights."

"I wouldn't ask you to. Just look at this routing, please." I patted the ticket sleeve.

She stole a glance at the older woman who was busy with a passenger.

"No flight information," I assured her. "Just answer one question." I raised the ticket sleeve and showed her the other five-hundred-euro note beneath it. "If I stood at the international arrivals gate in Larnaca Airport at about 4:10 p.m. this evening, would you say that it's very likely that I would see my father or is it unlikely."

"Very likely, I think."

"You've been so kind. Would you dispose of this ticket sleeve for me? I hate litter."

"Of course." She smiled. I smiled and walked away.

Then, my sat phone rang. It was the pilot from Lakenheath Air Force Base.

"RAMPART DADDY, this is your flight home. We are six-zero minutes from Tallinn. Have your passengers at the military terminal, ready to fly. Diplomatic clearance is required. I hear your situation is delicate. Therefore, we will have zero loiter time on the ground. Copy?"

I copied and called Sherri to bring everyone back to the airport. Luckily, she hadn't blown the safehouse lock. My second call was to Watkins, asking him to meet us and grease the diplomatic machinery for our departure.

What I hadn't told our pilot—or anyone else—was that we weren't going home. We were going to follow Petrov to Larnaca International Airport on the island of Cyprus. According to the good Colonel Burke, that's where Petrov's father-in-law ran a Russian bank and money-laundering machine, as well as a depository for SVR/GRU covert ops money.

Whether defector or bait, Petrov was running away from me and the Russians. So, why would he go to a place where the Russians and the CIA were sure to look for him?

CHAPTER 29

A CRISIS MEETING, the subject being Lieutenant Colonel Alexi Petrov, was convened for the second time in three days. This time, there was no ambush. The bureaucratic explosions had already gone off elsewhere in the Kremlin. General Orlov, the civilian from the mysterious planning cell, and the GRU and SVR generals were again seated before the deputy minister's desk. There was one new addition, an army general from the Defense Ministry staff.

The deputy minister was in a bad mood as he addressed his first remarks to the GRU general. "It was a simple task. Set a trap. Wait for Geller to take the bait. Grab him. Bring him to Moscow for interrogation and trial. Is that correct, General, or did I miss some tactical nuance, some arcane bit of entrapment science that would render such a simple plan unworkable?"

The chastened GRU general said, "The plan was workable, Deputy Minister."

"Then, why didn't it work?" The question was rhetorical. "It didn't work," continued the deputy minister, "because the officers charged with the duty of capturing Maxwell Geller didn't do their research! If they had, they would have realized that the only possible way for him to escape was to go out the window and walk down the outside wall of the hotel to the street, which is what he did. He got into a waiting van and disappeared in a cloud of smoke, literally."

The deputy minister shifted his focus from the embarrassed general to the group. "For any of you who spent the last three days on the space station, Maxwell Geller got away, along with his entire team . . . and Lieutenant Colonel Alexi Petrov."

"Petrov defected to the Americans?" asked the worried army general.

"Yes." Fixing a stern glare on the GRU general again, the deputy minister said, "It seems we are unable to capture our enemies or keep our friends."

The army general said, "Petrov knows about OPERATION BEAR-CLAW."

The deputy minister announced, "There will be no mention of OPERATION BEARCLAW in this room or outside of it. What you need to know is that Petrov has escaped from Geller. He's in Cyprus."

The army general looked a bit less worried. "Is that good news?"

"I think not," said the deputy minister.

"I don't understand."

The deputy minister explained. "Petrov flew to Cyprus to escape from Geller and from us. It seems he has deceived both sides. First, he pretended to help us trap Geller here in Moscow. When he contacted Geller, he pretended to defect. After Geller freed him in Tallinn, he double-crossed Geller and flew to Cyprus."

General Orlov asked, "What was Petrov doing in Tallinn?"

"That is not open for discussion," replied the GRU general.

Irritated, Orlov said, "All right. What is he doing in Cyprus? Is that open for discussion?"

The SVR representative answered, "His father-in-law manages one of our banks there. Petrov had him convey demands to the ministry.

Petrov wants three million euros and his wife delivered to him in Cyprus."

"In return for what?" asked Orlov.

The deputy minister answered. "Not divulging certain Federation secrets to the Americans."

"What secrets?"

"They are secrets," replied the testy deputy minister, "because not everyone is supposed to know them." He continued. "So, we have a major cockup on our hands. We must salvage as much as possible from it. However, I don't think we or the Americans know Petrov's true intentions. Therefore, we shouldn't believe anything he says."

The deputy minister addressed the GRU general. "Petrov is in Cyprus. Assume that Geller will soon be there, too. The man is resourceful . . . and a human wrecking ball. Four dead highway patrolmen, five dead border guards, two boats sunk on Lake Pskov, and the floor of a hotel ruined in Tallinn. All in less than a week. That is enough! Find Geller and kill him."

Calmer, the deputy minister said, "Petrov is the greater problem. He will be in hiding. Use whatever resources are necessary to locate him and keep him under surveillance. Be invisible, but do not allow him to contact the CIA or any other Western intelligence service. If you cannot prevent a contact, eliminate whoever Petrov talks to, immediately. Petrov cannot be allowed to convey what he knows and what he has to the West.

"Your third mission is of equal importance. Petrov said he has documents to make good on his threat to expose Federation secrets, if we do not comply with his demands. Those documents may be in paper or digital form. Find them quickly. When you have done that, either bring Petrov and his wife back to Moscow or kill them."

The GRU general spoke up. "Finding those documents could take time. Aside from searching the obvious places, are there any suggestions to guide our efforts?"

"The special unit has devised a plan. We will use Petrov's wife to pry the location of the documents out of him and tell you where they are."

The deputy minister turned to General Orlov. "I'm sure you have been wondering about the role of the FSB in this operation."

"I have."

"Your job is to convince Petrov's wife to betray him and help the GRU find those documents. You have thirty hours to prepare Olga Petrovna for that task. When she is ready to cooperate, you will notify me. I will notify the GRU, and they will see to it that she joins her husband in Cyprus."

"With respect, Minister, I've examined the histories of the Petrovs. They are a devoted and loving couple. I don't think Petrov's wife would betray him."

"Any betrayal is possible with the proper incentives, General." The deputy minister raised his chin to the civilian, who had been mute to that point.

The civilian handed General Orlov a file and said, "We, too, have examined the Petrovs' relationship. This contains the incentive you need, including a script to guide the preparation of Petrov's wife."

Orlov opened the file and examined the contents with growing concern, followed by anger.

The deputy minister said, "That will be all. You have work to do. Keep me informed." As chairs scraped and boots shuffled, he added, "General Orlov, stay for a minute."

As Orlov returned to his chair, the deputy minister said, "No need to sit. This won't take long. I've thought a lot about why we are here, in this office, at this time, with these problems. It's because of Colonel Zabluda. He could have—and should have—killed Geller two years ago, but greed got the better of him, and he chose stealing money over his duty to the Federation. We both know Zabluda should be rotting

in prison, but he is a presidential favorite. Give him the job of subvert-
ing Petrov's wife. When he's finished, send him back to the GRU so
he can go to Cyprus and kill Maxwell Geller."

"Is that what the Federation president wants?"

The deputy banged his desk. "The Federation president wants this
mess cleaned up! Now! You think because you drink vodka occasionally with the president and reminisce about the good old days in Berlin, he shares all of his ideas about spies and defectors with you? He
didn't discuss this with you because he knows your opinion about
pursuing enemies of the state into safe havens. You don't approve."

The deputy minister stood and sneered at Orlov. "You're nothing
but a policeman, a technocrat without imagination. You observe, you
find spies and the disloyal, you bug them, surveil them, collect the
evidence of their betrayal, and lock them up. And if, for some reason,
the traitors are geographically out of reach, you are willing to write
them off as the cost of doing business. You don't understand the value
of fear of pursuit as a deterrent to actions against the state."

"I understand the theory of its value, Minister. I have not observed
successful application of that theory. If the theory were sound, there
would be no Alexi Petrovs in this world."

The deputy minister became very still and spoke in an even voice.
"The task before you is not theoretical. It requires practical skill, your
specialty. You are to personally supervise Zabluda in the preparation
of Petrov's wife for her duties to the state."

Orlov lifted the file in both hands. "What if she doesn't believe this
or won't betray him?"

"In that case, tell her that the continued well-being of her children
and parents depends on her cooperation."

CHAPTER 30

ZABLUDA WAS ABOUT to destroy a marriage. Olga Petrovna—Alexi Petrov's wife—worked in the building as a secretary. He invited her to a conference room for the interview. The ambience was less intimidating than an interview room. Intimidation would come later.

When he was seated across the conference table from Olga, Zabluda introduced himself as an FSB officer. He asked, "Do you know where your husband is?"

"In Tallinn on state business."

"You were scheduled to accompany Alexi to Tallinn until the ministry decided not to send both of you. Did Alexi tell you why you were going to Tallinn?"

"We were going on holiday, but he had state business to conduct while we were there."

"What state business?"

"Alexi never discusses his work with me."

"Tell me about the man you talked to when you got home from the cinema last Saturday."

Olga was surprised that he knew about the incident. "He was waiting for Alexi in the hall when we arrived. He said he was Major Stasivich from the ministry, with an urgent message for my husband. I went up to the apartment. He and Alexi talked downstairs."

"How long did they talk?"

"About twenty-five minutes."

"Had you seen this man before Saturday?"

"No." Olga was annoyed. "Can you tell me why you are asking these questions?"

"In time. How is your marriage? I need an honest answer."

"Alexi and I are very happy. We could not ask for a better relationship."

Methodically, Zabluda began to destroy that relationship. "I'm embarrassed to ask, but are you and your husband on good terms, intimately?"

Olga bristled and said a frosty, "I don't think either of us have complaints in that regard."

There was a folder in front of Zabluda. In the moments before he opened it, disturbing thoughts came to mind. He had killed men without mercy or remorse, but they knew the game. Until now, he had never destroyed a spirit. This woman was an innocent. What he was about to do reminded him that, in the city, there were men with sick minds and empty souls who would corrupt anything, anyone, any relationship to bend it to their will. He was about to become the instrument and victim of their evil.

Zabluda opened the file and removed a head-and-shoulders photograph of a stunningly beautiful brunette and placed it in front of her. Olga was a blonde.

"Do you know this woman?"

"No." There was a question in Olga's eyes and a wrinkle in her brow.

Zabluda continued his march to the cliff. "Does your husband know her?"

"I don't know everyone Alexi knows."

Zabluda passed another photo across the table. It was a full-length shot of the brunette striding toward the camera. She was shapely in jeans tucked into thigh-high boots. Her long coat was open and flowed behind her in the breeze. There was a sexy, radiant smile on her face. The woman exuded the vitality of youth.

Olga squirmed and said a testy, "I don't know her."

Zabluda place a third photo beside the first two. It was a doctored shot of the brunette—in the same outfit—and Alexi Petrov having coffee at a tall café table, smiling at each other.

Olga was silent.

"She's an executive with an American company here in Moscow. She really works for the CIA. Her job is to get state secrets from officers like your Alexi."

Olga gave the photo a dismissive glance. "Alexi has never discussed state secrets with me. I'm sure he wouldn't discuss them with her, with anyone."

Zabluda placed the fourth photo in front of Olga. It was taken from above, by a camera in a ceiling light fixture or an FSB photographer standing on a ladder. The brunette was on her back in bed, her head thrown back, eyes closed tight, mouth agape in a silent scream of ecstasy. There was a naked man on top of her. Olga's eyes went immediately to the familiar dark birthmark on the man's back, partially obscured by the woman's clawing hand. The FSB had taken the staged photo in black-and-white so that Olga couldn't detect coloration differences between her husband's actual birthmark and the phony birthmark tattooed on the man in bed with the brunette. A color comparison would have given away the game.

Olga sucked in a breath. Her lower lip quivered and she looked away from the photograph. Tears formed in her eyes. "How long? How long have they been . . . ?"

"The relationship began two months after he returned from Syria."

"Relationship!" There were tears and fire in Olga's eyes.

Zabluda laid a packet of tissues on the table. "Take a few minutes to compose yourself."

He left her alone and joined General Orlov at the one-way window looking into the room. They watched and waited. When Olga recovered, she did what they anticipated she would. She inspected the photo carefully, looking for some clue that the man in the photo was not her Alexi. Then, she noticed what they wanted her to see. It was an army uniform laid out neatly on a chair near the bed, Petrov's name tag clearly visible above the pocket. Olga shoved the photo away.

Orlov said, "Well done, Zabluda."

"Thank you, sir. I'm sure Mother Russia and my mother are proud of me today."

The general didn't look at Zabluda as he spoke. His arms were folded across his chest, and he stared through the window at Olga. There was a wistful quality in his voice. "When an officer is good at his job, his superiors might tolerate sarcasm and other minor acts of insubordination. On the other hand, when an officer has allowed a CIA spy to roam the streets of Moscow unhindered . . . twice . . . the bar of tolerance is very low. You should look down occasionally, Colonel, and be careful you don't trip on it." The general turned his back to Zabluda and walked away.

Zabluda gave Olga a few more minutes before he returned to the room. There was a water carafe and glasses on the table. Zabluda filled a glass and set it in front of her.

Olga glanced at it, then at him. "Do you have anything stronger, Colonel?"

Zabluda took another glass from the tray and poured her a drink from the flask he carried in his attaché case. Olga drank, clutching the glass like a life preserver, as he gathered up the damning photographs. When she finished the vodka, he began again, this time with an edge.

"The man you know as Major Stasivich is a CIA spy and the colleague of this woman. His name is Maxwell Geller. Your husband has been consorting with these two spies to acquire state secrets. In fact, he has threatened to give the Americans secret documents unless we give him three million euros and send you to Cyprus to join him."

Olga's face registered shock.

Zabluda continued. "If your husband gives those documents to the Americans, your family will naturally fall under suspicion. You and your children enjoy a good life here in Moscow, as do your parents, in Cyprus. That will change. I can assure you that your children's careers in the security services would be terminated. Adjustments would be made to your father's employment and position in society. These changes would affect your mother. Their property could be confiscated. The authorities are already wondering why your husband chose your father to deliver his blackmail demands."

Olga knew where this was going and how to stop it. "How can I help you?"

"Your husband is asking for you. We want you to go to him. The bank will give him the money. Go with him wherever he asks, but you must do two things for us. Find out where he keeps the documents he stole from the Defense Ministry and tell us where they are."

"What will happen to Alexi when you have the documents?"

"Alexi is a traitor. I suggest you focus on what will happen to you and the rest of your family if those documents fall into the wrong hands.

"Now," continued Zabluda, "it is possible that your husband will attempt to defect to the United States, even after we meet his demands. So, if you see Geller or discover where your husband has hidden the documents, you must signal us immediately. I will tell you how."

"What if Alexi keeps his intentions hidden from me?"

"You will demand to be informed, in advance, of his every move. Tell him that he has endangered you, your children, and your parents and, unless he is completely transparent with you, you will take drastic action. Let him guess what that action might be. He will imagine the worst. Can you do that for Mother Russia?"

She looked at him for several seconds before saying, "I can do that for the state."

"Good. Go home. Pack as if you are leaving for good, two or three bags at most."

Olga recoiled. "Three bags! My life is in that apartment."

"Your life—Olga Petrovna—is in the hands of the state. Pack your bags and wait at home. A man will come to take you to the airport. He will give you a headscarf, red on one side, blue on the other. Keep it with you at all times. When you know where Alexi has hidden the documents, wear the red side out. If you see Maxwell Geller or know his whereabouts, wear the blue side out. Someone will contact you. You will be under constant surveillance.

"When you arrive in Cyprus, you will rush into your husband's loving arms. You will be nervous, but he will expect that. He will know that we talked to you. Don't deny it. However, it would be best if you don't confront him about the woman in these photographs. If you do, he will deny knowing her. Arguing with him about her, or even raising the subject, will cause him to mistrust you and make it impossible for you to discover the location of the documents and his future plans."

Zabluda released Olga Petrovna and sat at the conference table considering what and who he would need to find and kill Maxwell Geller in Cyprus. When he had compiled a mental list, he gathered up his papers and photographs, and returned to FSB headquarters to clear his office.

CHAPTER 31

Ramstein U.S. Air Force Base, Germany

BAD NEWS DOESN'T get better with age. As soon as our flight out of Tallinn was airborne, I found a quiet space on the plane and used my sat phone to tell Rodney that Petrov had slipped away from me and fled to Cyprus. I wanted to go after him.

Rodney let me simmer in an uncomfortable silence before he said, "You need help. I'll have people meet you at Ramstein and we'll talk when you get there. On the way, be thinking of an excuse for why you have your own private army with you. I know about Sherri and her crew."

Of course, he knew. The Tallinn station chief had to clear us to board the flight. He reported the passenger list to Langley. Coming up with an explanation for Sherri and her crew could wait. I stretched out across four canvas seats hanging from the fuselage and slept without worry for the first time in weeks.

* * *

Three hours and forty minutes after our Tallinn departure, we landed at Ramstein. When the Kuzmick family, Sherri and her crew, and I entered the VIP arrivals lounge, Jill Rucker and Eva Soriano were waiting for me in a back corner. Jill gave me a sarcastic smile. Eva had a scowl.

I peeled off from the group and went to greet my Heidelberg co-conspirators. Jill said, "Leave it to Mad Max Geller to screw up the only time off we've had in months. You're lucky we took our vacation in Europe."

Eva was not amused. "What the hell happened, Max?"

I gave them the CliffsNotes version of my odyssey from Moscow to Tallinn.

Eva grunted. I couldn't tell if it meant *you did your best*, or *you really screwed that up*. She asked, "Did you see the Gulfstream 550 on the apron?"

"I did."

"That's your transport to Cyprus. Rodney wants us to go along and babysit you so you don't lose RAMPART again." She dialed Rodney on her sat phone and handed the instrument to me. "Your master's voice."

Rodney got right to business. "I'm told you know RAMPART has a relative at a certain financial institution in Cyprus. We've been monitoring communications to and from that institution. RAMPART has contacted the relative twice. He asked the relative to relay financial demands to Moscow. In return, RAMPART has promised Moscow to void his commitment to us. You cannot let that happen, Max. What the hell is going on?"

"I'll tell you when I know."

"Know this. In addition to his financial demands, RAMPART wants his wife sent to him in Cyprus. Sounds like a potential disappearing act to me. And one more thing. RAMPART is moving around the island. His calls to his relative have come from two different locations. I'm sending a drone with a SIGINT"—signals intelligence—"package to help you pinpoint his location. What else do you need?"

"I need a mission contract for Sherri and her guys, starting ten days ago. I wouldn't be alive without them."

"We'll discuss that when you have RAMPART."

"I'm not leaving Ramstein until Sherri has a signed contract for herself and two assistants at the usual rate."

"If you won't go to Cyprus, I'll send Jill and Eva without you."

"No, you won't."

"Why won't I?"

"You don't want Agency employees on the front end of this operation, because if it goes sour, you want to blame me, a disgruntled, ex-CIA employee, trying to pull off something to repair his tattered reputation. The Russians might not believe that story, but if you can sell it at the White House, nobody at the Agency gets fired."

"You're pushing the envelope, Max."

"The envelope had better have some cash in it for Sherri, if you want RAMPART."

"Maybe I should send Vanessa to Cyprus for RAMPART."

"Don't fuck with me anymore than you already have. Send Sherri a contract or forget RAMPART." I broke the connection.

The contract was faxed to the Gulfstream 550 an hour later. I said farewell to Boris, Yulia, and the baby, and watched them re-board our Tallinn aircraft for the States. Minutes later, Eva, Jill, Sherri, Tony-D, me, along with Jack, the driver, and two drone operators, Thompson and Riggins, climbed aboard the executive jet. All of us dressed in borrowed Air Force flight suits for comfort during the four-hour flight to Cyprus.

CHAPTER 32

ZABLUDA WAS LEAVING his office for what he hoped was the last time, happy at the prospect of rejoining his former colleagues in the GRU. Before he got to the door, the phone rang with a summons from General Orlov. Zabluda assumed it would be an obligatory going-away lecture. He entered Orlov's office with a jaunty stride and saluted.

In a less gruff voice than usual, the general said, "Sit down, Zabluda." It was the first time Orlov had offered him a chair.

Orlov came from behind his desk and stood close to Zabluda. "I have bad news. There's no easy way to say it. I am sorry. Your son, Mikhail, was killed in Syria."

Zabluda slumped back in the chair, speechless for seconds. Composing himself, he asked, "When? How?"

"He was shot by a sniper three days ago."

"Why . . . why am I just being told?"

"The men in his unit—your old Spetsnaz unit—knew you would want them to find the shooter. They delayed notification until they could."

"Did they find him?"

"Unfortunately, no. We do have reliable information that an American sniper fired the shot."

"In Syria?"

"Small teams of American special forces are helping the resistance."

"How do you know it was an American? The insurgents have snipers, too."

"The shot was made from over 2200 meters. Even on their lucky days, insurgents don't shoot like that . . . and a Syrian informant reported that an American sniper team was operating in the area where the shot originated."

An awkward silence followed. It was broken when the general said, "Of course, you're not going to Cyprus, now. You'll remain here at the FSB until further notice. Take some time off to settle your son's affairs." Zabluda was divorced.

"I would like a few days, sir." There were definitely affairs to settle. One of them was his own. It was not consensual and carried the death penalty.

* * *

That evening
The Bolshoy Kamenny Bridge over the Moscow River

Zabluda's secret contact joined the pedestrian traffic headed south over the bridge. Zabluda was smoking a cigarette and strolling at a leisurely pace so the contact—known as Source Ivan at the CIA—could catch up. Night had fallen. The floodlit Kremlin was in the background, over their left shoulders.

When they were side by side, the contact, an older man with silver hair peeking from beneath his ushanka fur hat, spoke to Zabluda. "Your message said urgent. Is there a problem?"

"I'm no longer of use to you. I can't travel. I've been indefinitely assigned to the FSB."

"Why the change?"

"Rehabilitation. The president forgave me for stealing five million dollars from Max Geller."

"That wasn't Geller's money. It belonged to the state."

"And from whom did the state steal it?"

"A moot point. You're lucky. Why would the president forgive you?"

With forced jocularity, Zabluda said, "He's a fan of Kosty's greatest hits."

"Yes. It is hard to find a good assassin these days." Sarcasm. "Did you hear about the cockups in Australia and Germany? Your GRU colleagues are slipping."

They continued to walk, freezing their conversation when others passed close by.

The silver-haired man said, "Maybe you will get your passport back after you've done your penance."

Zabluda was somber. "That doesn't matter. I won't carry anymore messages to the CIA for you. An American sniper killed my son Mikhail three days ago, in Syria."

The contact stopped and looked pained. "I'm so sorry, Konstantine."

"Mikhail," said Zabluda, "was the only reason I agreed to work for you. The CIA used him to blackmail me. They had a pillow talk recording of Mikhail and a woman. He told her something he shouldn't have. It was no great secret, just enough to ruin his career. They threatened to leak it, if I didn't act as your courier on my trips abroad. Now, that Mikhail is . . . gone, they have no hold on me. I'm through."

"Where does that leave us?" asked the older man.

"I won't turn you in, if that's what you're asking, but I won't help. I don't want you to contact me again, ever, socially or professionally."

They walked in silence. Zabluda stopped, drew a last puff on the cigarette, and ground it out. They faced each other.

Source Ivan said, "They won't let you walk away, Konstantine. You took money. There are receipts. They could expose you."

"If they do, I will expose you. You're far more valuable to them than I am. They prefer your information to retaliating against me. They will release me. You convince them."

It was dark and they were nearing the south end of the bridge.

Zabluda asked, "Did you know they were using Mikhail to force me to work for you?"

"No."

"I think you did. You needed someone you knew and could trust to deliver your camera cartridges to the Americans. I think you identified me to the CIA as someone who met those qualifications and they stalked both of my sons until they got leverage. When they entrapped Mikhail, they had me. I had no choice but to do your bidding or destroy my son."

"I'm sorry, Konstantine."

"Don't apologize for betraying me. Espionage is a harsh game. I know the rules better than most. You did it because you have a passion for the ideological fight. I have no such passion. All I ever wanted was to be a good soldier for a cause I believed in."

"Do you still believe in the cause you're fighting for?"

"I'm not fighting. I'm sitting at a desk, directing corrupt policemen as they chase ants who carry bits of information to other ants, who make them into a mosaic that no one cares about. I won't be at the FSB forever. When they release me, I will have my revenge."

"What will you do?"

"Max Geller was my only professional failure. Sparing him was my only professional mistake. I will find a way to kill him."

CHAPTER 33

Flying to the Island of Cyprus

SOMETHING WAS WRONG! That realization awakened me from a sound sleep. I lunged forward against the seat belt, eyeballs bulging, thoughts racing—backwards to the facts, forward to where they might lead. My movement awakened Jill, facing me across the table we shared.

"Are you okay, Max?"

"Yeah." My rapid heartbeat had a different answer. To distract both of us, I looked out of the plane's window at the fluffy cloud cover moving sluggishly beneath us.

"Something's wrong," I said.

"With what?"

"RAMPART drugs me and he's into the wind, being chased by the CIA and the Russians. For a few hours, he's free. He can go anywhere. In a world of possibilities, why does he choose Cyprus? It's a small island with restricted travel between the Greek and Turkish sections, and lots of Russians."

Jill's view was, "He wants money. That's where the bank is. He knows the Russians have funds stashed there for black ops."

"What's his expectation, that he's going to walk out of his father-in-law's bank with suitcases full of euros? He wouldn't get to the front door. How would you handle the money?"

"I would have gone to Zurich, opened an account, and told the Russians to wire the money there. He could have accessed the account from anywhere in the world."

"RAMPART didn't go to Cyprus for the money. That leaves his wife. Why have her delivered to Cyprus?"

Jill mused, "What if the wife is just a decoy? In that case, when RAMPART gets the three million euros, he leaves his wife to the GRU and he's off to the far side of the world with a trophy bimbo, half his age."

"That's not how I read him. The Petrovs have a solid relationship."

"The divorce courts are full of solid relationships gone bad, Max. A middle-aged man with new freedom and three million euros is a ticking time bomb of hormones. I wouldn't trust him around the corner."

"I've got more than three million euros. You wanted to run away with me, even after I put stitches in your forehead." Immediately, I regretted reminding her of that episode.

Jill was unruffled. "That was different. We've been through fire together."

"Well, I don't see Petrov with a trophy bimbo. Olga Petrovna is a babe."

"Why is her husband sending her to the Russian wolves in Cyprus?"

Again, I looked out the window, hoping the answers would come to me. Almost to myself, I asked, "What the hell is so special about Cyprus?"

From across the aisle, Eva said, "Well, for one thing, it's got hotel rooms and that's the only place we're going to get any sleep, if you two keep going on with the Sherlock Holmes–Dr. Watson dialogue. Shut up, think about it, and wake me when you figure it out."

I said, "Maybe you can help, and all of us could get some sleep. The attaché in Moscow told me that the Agency was keeping an eye on the father-in-law's bank and wanted to recruit RAMPART to penetrate it. Call Rodney on your sat phone and ask him to get us a history of RAMPART's visits to Cyprus—his wife's visits, too. Get surveillance reports, if they're available. I want to know what they did on Cyprus and who they did it with."

Eva heaved a sigh and got her phone from a bag in the overhead.

When she finished relaying my request to Rodney, we were an hour from touchdown. I woke up the team and assigned surveillance tasks.

Sherri and I would pick up Olga Petrovna when she landed at the airport and stay on her.

Tony-D and Jack had the dicey task of bugging the father-in-law's house and setting up a static observation post nearby to watch the house and monitor the bugs. NSA was monitoring communications to and from father-in-law's bank. Rodney would call with anything important.

Since Rodney wanted Jill and Eva to be invisible, they were to pose as tourists and roam the streets near father-in-law's bank, looking for Petrov and spotting the Russian opposition. They also had to serve as our mobile reserve in the event we got a RAMPART sighting that no one else could cover.

The two operators for the SIGINT drone would work out of our plane in shifts and call me if they triangulated Petrov's location.

We didn't have nearly enough people for the operation, but we had what we had. And, as some apologist for a lack of preparation once said, "You don't go to war with what you want, you go with what you have."

We tested our communications, checked our weapons, and waited for final approach. Rodney had arranged for us to avoid the commercial airport at Larnaca and land across the bay at Royal Air Force Base

Akrotiri. The Brits wouldn't ask questions about our weapons and surveillance equipment. Customs officials at Larnaca would not have been amused.

As we landed, a voice in my head was asking, "Why Cyprus, Petrov? Why Cyprus?"

CHAPTER 34

The Island of Cyprus, Greek Cypriot Republic
Day 1

RUSSIAN AGENTS FOLLOWED Olga Petrovna from the arrival hall at Larnaca Airport.

Sherri whispered, "Max," and nodded in their direction.

We followed and watched another Russian team take over Olga's surveillance as she exited the terminal, even though Alexi Petrov had sent explicit instructions that she was not to be followed. He had to know those instructions would not be obeyed. My guess? RAMPART was miles from the airport when his wife landed. The terminal was crawling with Russians. I was concerned that one of them might recognize me or Sherri from my infamous bank-robbing days in Moscow, but it was too late to worry about that. Anyway, I began growing a deliberately scraggly moustache in Tallinn, hoping the Russians wouldn't expect that from a usually clean-cut guy like me.

At the terminal entrance, Olga's mother, Martina, ran to her daughter. They embraced and clung desperately to each other. Weeping, Martina took Olga's hand and led her to a chauffeured car. They headed for home in upscale Larnaca, a short drive from the bank managed by Olga's father. Jack, our driver, had rented a villa close enough to the home so that he and Tony-D could monitor Olga's comings and goings. Being careful not to disturb the GRU bugs already in place, Tony-D had bugged Martina's house as soon as she left for the airport to meet her daughter.

As the day wore on, we heard—via Tony-D's bugs—Olga refusing to leave the house and her mother protesting the amount of vodka her daughter was drinking. At that point, Sherri and I left and returned to the plane for a status check of the SIGINT drone.

Riggins, our chief drone operator, handed me a map of Cyprus. "This came by secure fax from Langley. Blue dots show the origins of RAMPART's two calls to his father-in-law."

The first dot and date/time tag showed the call was made the day after RAMPART arrived from Tallinn. It originated in Limassol, a city forty-five miles west of Larnaca. The second dot was tagged a day later in Paphros, eighty-five miles from Larnaca. RAMPART was moving away from us and the Russians. Smart man . . . but what was his destination?

I asked, "When will the drone be airborne?"

"We launch after dark. Once the bird is up, I'll give you RAMPART's location in real time."

That might be helpful or not. Obviously, RAMPART intended to be a moving target.

At midnight, I got a call at the Brit visitors' quarters where we were staying. The caller was Thompson, the duty drone driver. "RAMPART just called his father-in-law from Patmos tou Kampou, a little village on the northwest coast."

I got the Cyprus map from my go-bag. "I don't see it on my map."

"That's how small it is. You probably want to know that the village is on the other side of the Green Line in Turkish territory. To travel there, you need to hire a driver and get a special pass."

"RAMPART has a helper," I said, thinking out loud. "What was his message?"

"He wanted his father-in-law to tell Moscow that the three million euros must be deposited by international transfer to a bank of his choice at exactly 3:35 local time, Friday. He'll call at 3:30, Friday, with the account information. RAMPART wants his father-in-law to transfer the funds on his personal computer, from home, and he has to be alone in the house during the transfer. Once RAMPART verifies that the money has been deposited, he'll give his father-in-law instructions for swapping the documents for Olga. I have a recording if you want the word-for-word."

"Thanks, Thompson. Wake me if RAMPART makes another call."

I dialed Eva's room. She was grumpy. "Are you trying to break me by sleep deprivation?"

"RAMPART just made a call to his father-in-law."

"What did he say?" I could almost see her sitting up in bed, the brain fog vanishing.

"Tell you later. He's on the move and he has help. Did Rodney get back to you about those surveillance reports covering RAMPART's visits to Cyprus?"

"Not yet."

"Call him, now. I need to know who's helping RAMPART move around and where he's going. Who are his friends? What taxi services did he use? Did he have a favorite? Did he stay at a particular hotel? Get anything that would give us a clue to his hideout, especially locations on the island's north coast."

"I'm on it."

It was night in Washington. Rodney was about to get his own taste of sleep deprivation. Couldn't happen to a nicer guy.

Day 2

Early the next morning, Tony-D called to give me feed from his bug. Olga Petrovna was staying home for the day. She had a hangover. Her mother was worried and hovering.

I showered, shaved, and got breakfast at a Greek vendor's shop on what is known as the Brits Sovereign Base Area. That includes RAF Base Akrotiri, where we landed. As I ate, I mulled over what Thompson told me and what I knew about Cyprus. The base was a mixture of traditional military air operations, top secret electronic spying, and local civilian life. Its unique sovereignty status was a provision of the treaty that granted Cyprus independence from Britain after World War II. After years of violent clashes between the Greek-Catholic and Turkish-Muslim inhabitants, the UN stepped in and separated the island into two sections at the Green Line, Turkish-controlled in the north, Greek-controlled in the south. What was RAMPART doing north of the Green Line and how did he get there?

I gave up on those questions and focused on Sherri. She had slept in. I took her breakfast and waited for her in my room. When she was ready, we drove our rented car to the hangar where our plane was housed. The drone jockey gave Sherri the short version of RAMPART's midnight message before Riggins, his relief, came on shift. I checked the new blue dot on the SIGINT map where the last transmission was plotted. Sure enough, it was the other side of the Green Line.

Olga was staying home under the watchful eyes of Tony-D and Jack. Sherri and I discussed how to spend our day. Before we reached a decision, Eva came in, looking sleep deprived.

She plopped into a seat and announced, "Rodney gave me access to the RAMPART surveillance reports through a secure link at GCHQ here." GCHQ is the electronic spy ear that targets Africa, the Mediterranean, and the Middle East. Think of it as Brit NSA in the Med.

"The reports are nothingburgers," Eva told us. "RAMPART comes here once or twice a year on leave, never on official business, as far as Langley knows. He does the things a soldier normally does on R-and-R.

"Olga is usually here when he arrives. They stay with the in-laws. He doesn't go out for a day or two, probably decompressing. On the third or fourth day, his father-in-law gives the couple a party. The guests are local bankers and businessmen-clients of the bank. No Russians, tourists, spies, or diplomats are invited. That keeps the in-laws' cover legit.

"After party day," continued Eva, "the Petrovs make the tourist rounds, shopping, beaches, restaurants, and sailing. In the evenings, they're at high-end bars and dance venues. Petrov spends one day fishing alone with his father-in-law. Olga spends that day with her mother."

"Any unusual contacts?"

"Just the usual unusual ones you'd expect. An MI6 couple, posing as tourists, tried to befriend them on the beach. Petrov wasn't having any, thank you. Another time, a Russian catches Petrov alone at the bar and invites him to an orgy with some ripe, young sparrows. It's obviously a honey trap to see if Petrov is a security risk. Petrov wasn't partaking. Then, there's the usual GRU covert surveillance. They gave up after a few days because Petrov appears to be a solid citizen of the Russian Federation."

"Except he's extorting that Federation for three million and threatening to spill its secrets," said Sherri.

"There is that," admitted Eva. "I'm going back to bed. Don't call if you need me."

Sherri and I went to the rented villa and relieved Tony-D and Jack for a few hours. When they returned, we hit the beach. The weather was mild. We got in some R-and-R of our own.

I didn't see Jill all day. No problem. Everybody needed a rest. Things would get hot soon.

That night, RAMPART called his father-in-law, gave him an internet address, and told him to post a picture of Olga holding the local newspaper with the date visible. Olga's photo had to be posted every day until the exchange was completed. The drone operator called to notify me. I filed it, forgot it, and went back to sleep.

Day 3

Tony-D called my room early. "Your target has cabin fever. She's going to Nissi Beach today. Dad is sending a car for her at 10:00 a.m. Recess is over."

I alerted Sherri, Eva, and Jill. Then, I went through my morning exercise routine, ate, and the three of us drove to the hangar. The plane had the capability for us to listen to the feed from the bug in the home of Olga's parents. I fast-forwarded to the passage Tony-D had mentioned.

At a tense breakfast with her parents, Olga announced, "I have been penned up in this house for two days. I can't stand it any longer. I'm going to Nissi Beach."

"Olga, it's too cold to swim," her father protested.

"I'm Russian, Papa. I can swim in the Arctic, if I want."

Papa lost that argument but insisted on having a car take Olga to the beach at ten, as Tony-D said. It was 7:30 a.m. We had time to plan. Tony-D would follow Olga from home to the beach, try to ID her Russian tails for us, and guide Jill and Eva to Olga. They would set up a cabana behind her position. Sherri and I would also set up a cabana and stroll the beach pretending to be lovers, keeping one eye on Olga and the other on the lookout for RAMPART. Since the beach fun wouldn't begin for two hours, we sat in those plush cabin seats, drinking coffee and trying to wake up.

My thoughts of Olga going out on her third day in Cyprus triggered thoughts of those three million euros her husband wanted in hush money.

I said, "Eva, did I hear you were a hostage negotiator before you joined the Agency?"

"Yeah. My company insured executives and skilled workers in the Middle East and South America."

"What was the asking prices for hostages, low to high?"

"At the low end, twenty-five or fifty thousand. The mid-range was a hundred thousand or five hundred thousand. If they had an executive or a worker with critical skills, they'd asked for a million or two. For senior executives, five or ten million. The highest demand I ever got was from this ex-FARC wannabe drug lord. He kidnapped the CEO of a construction company to finance his first big kilo buy. He wanted fifty million for the CEO. I told him for half that price, I could bribe the defense minister to send the whole army to hunt him down, and his gang." Eva smiled. "He settled for a million. The scumbag knew I was right about his defense minister."

"Did kidnappers ever ask for a multiple of three, three hundred thousand or three million?"

"Not that I recall."

"So, why is RAMPART asking for three million euros?"

"Maybe three is his lucky number. Maybe he learned to count in threes. Why are you getting wrapped around the axle about some Russian's math skills?"

"You said I was 'wrapped around the axle.' You meant I was 'distracted.'"

"Yes, Professor. Are you translating the *Urban Dictionary* into preppie-speak?"

"No. I'm remembering something Sherri said on the flight about distraction."

Eva turned to Sherri. "What did you say, dear?"

Reluctantly, Sherri allowed herself to be drawn into the conversation. "I said, maybe RAMPART sent his wife to Cyprus to distract the Russians. When he gets the three million euros, he'll leave her here and head for parts unknown with a young trophy bimbo."

My brain was on fire. "What if it's the other way around? What if RAMPART's goal is to get his wife away from the GRU and his demand for three million euros is the distraction? If we find three million an odd number, maybe the Russians do, too. That's where RAMPART wants their heads. Why three million and a call for it at exactly 3:30 on Friday. RAMPART wants all of us trying to solve the puzzle of the threes and forget what's important to RAMPART, Olga."

Eva was skeptical. "That's a theory without finance, Max. How will RAMPART survive without money to run and hide? You always follow the money."

"Not this time. When I talked to RAMPART in Moscow, he said his wife would be with him in Tallinn. The ministry pulled her off the trip and sent a GRU officer in her place. So, if the Petrovs were going to defect in Tallinn, they had to come up with another plan. That's why he came to Cyprus."

Eva disagreed. "Max, his plan was to lead you into a trap in that Tallinn hotel room."

"I'm not so sure. RAMPART could have turned me in to the FSB in Moscow or the GRU in Tallinn. He didn't. What he's doing is not logical to us, but we don't know *his* plan."

Sherri joined in. "I agree that something's not right. If RAMPART was being logical, he'd get Olga out first and stash her someplace safe. Then, he'd negotiate for transfer of the money and documents. How about it, Eva?"

Reluctantly, Eva admitted, "That's right. His negotiating strategy is ass-backwards. Besides, RAMPART must know that once he gives up those documents, he and his wife are dead. I'll be dead, too, if I don't get some sleep. I'm going to my room."

Thompson, the off-duty drone operator, entered the plane. "Max, I showed the coordinates of RAMPART's last transmission to a sergeant in the Brit operations center and asked him what was at that location. He said, 'Mate, there's nothing there.' No villages, no hotels, no beaches. At that location, the mountain drops into the sea. I asked him if someone could have placed a repeater there to mask the origin of the call. He said, 'Not unless he's a mountain goat.'"

As I looked at the map and the blue dot marking RAMPART's last transmission, it hit me. "Petrov is on a boat! That's how he gets around the island. The surveillance reports from Langley said RAMPART sails when he comes to Cyprus. He's on a boat! He docks, goes ashore, makes his calls, goes back to the boat, and moves on. This time, he called from the boat."

"Why did he call from such a remote area?" asked Sherri.

"He wants us—and the Russians—to think he's hiding out in the mountains, a long way from Olga." The second *a-ha* hit. "The boat! That's how he's going to grab Olga."

I checked my watch. It was 8:42. I called Tony-D on the separate secure channel we had for him. "Tony, turn the beach surveillance trip over to Jack. Meet me at the air base boat rental shop now! We've got to get to Nissi Beach before ten hundred hours."

"What's going on?"

"RAMPART may try to grab his wife this morning. Come heavy. From now on, all communications go over the secure team net."

When I signed off, Sherri was on the team net alerting Eva and Jill. "RAMPART's on a boat. Max thinks he's going to take Olga off the beach this morning. The Russians might play rough if they have both

Petrovs in their gunsights. Make sure they don't get off any rounds. You watch Olga's back. Jack and I will cover yours. Max and Tony-D will be boating off Nissi Beach."

As Sherri listened, her expression hardened. "I'm not giving you orders. I'm relaying orders from Max." Actually, she was giving orders—good ones. She told the listener, "Last time I checked, he was in charge of this operation. You got a problem with that, talk to him, and he's going to be busy for the rest of your life." Sherri ended the transmission with a terse, "Out." She must have been talking to Eva, who had an advanced case of *who's-in-charge-here?* which I discovered in Heidelberg. That happens when you sit at the right hand of Rodney too long.

Sherri went to her room to dress for the beach.

I checked my pistol and got my rifle and ammo mags from the plane's locker. I disassembled the rifle and put everything into a canvas carry-on bag. Ten minutes later, I was at the base boat rental shop looking for something fast, with a low profile. Tony-D, the only expert sailor on our team, arrived thirty minutes later and selected the closest thing they had to a cigarette boat.

As we loaded our gear aboard, Jack's voice came up on the team net and into our earpieces with an announcement. "Lady RAMPART is on her way to the beach."

"Does she have company?" I asked.

"I make Russians in two cars. Man and woman in the lead car. Two women and a man in the trail car. They're trying to make it look real." Jack described the cars. "You got a time frame for RAMPART's arrival?"

"All I have is a hunch."

After Jack signed off, Tony-D asked, "What's the plan?"

"If RAMPART gets Olga and keeps to the coast, we follow. If he heads for the open sea, we disable his boat and board her."

Tony-D opened a big canvas bag and showed me the thirty-six-inch tube—a Light Anti-tank Weapon. That was a for-sure disabler . . . and overkill.

Tony-D saw my reaction and reminded me, "You said to come heavy. This is heavy."

CHAPTER 35

Nissi Beach, Cyprus

THE BIG YAMAHA VX jet ski, a blue-and-white streak, came in fast from the east, turned right, and headed directly for the beach or, if you were paying attention, directly for Olga Petrovna. She was treading crystal blue water a hundred yards from shore. The scooter driver was hunched low with a life preserver dangling awkwardly from his right forearm and tethered to his waist by a rope.

As Tony-D and I watched through binoculars from the deck of our boat, the scooter zipped past Olga, made a sharp U-turn, and went directly at her. Olga faced the oncoming scooter, her arms outstretched to her front. The scooter driver slowed and looped the life preserver over her left arm. Olga locked her fingers together and the scooter took off, dragging her to deep water. The driver stopped, momentarily, pulled Olga onto the seat behind him, and headed west for the tip of Cape Pyla. I scanned the beach and saw a man in swim trunks running toward the water, pistol in his hand, but the Petrovs were out of range. He didn't have a shot.

Someone did. I saw Olga pitch forward as the scooter rounded the cape and disappeared.

Our boat was gaining on RAMPART. He slowed the scooter, driving with one hand and reaching back with the other to hold Olga on the seat behind him. He made for a forty-footer anchored in a coastal notch near the Sandy Bay Watersports concession. Olga was slumped against his back, her bathing suit soaked in blood. Petrov couldn't get her aboard without help.

Tony-D slowed our boat and pulled alongside the scooter, sandwiching it between us and the forty-footer. RAMPART wasn't going anywhere. He had been waiting for us to catch up.

I yelled, "Let us help you, Alexi!"

He nodded his okay and held on to Olga with both arms stretched behind him. In Petrov's eyes, I saw a man who cared more about his wife than three million euros.

Tony-D had our boat's first aid kit out and open. He had cross-trained as a medic during his years with U.S. Army Special Forces teams.

I told Alexi, "This man has medical training! Let's bring Olga aboard our boat. It's easier."

The three of us wrestled Olga aboard and laid her in the well deck where Tony-D went to work on her wounds. She had three. One was in her upper arm. Tony-D applied a tourniquet. The other was in her side about even with her right breast. After bandaging it expertly, Tony-D took Alexi's hand and placed it over the wound. "Apply pressure here. You will slow the bleeding."

The third was a head wound. It didn't look bad, but she was losing blood from it.

Tony-D looked at me. "We need to get her to a hospital, now!"

"No!" Alexi protested. "They will look there first."

"Not where we're going," said Tony-D. He turned the boat about and headed back for the UK Sovereign Base and its military hospital.

We had been sitting outside of the emergency room a couple of hours. The Brit doctor had shooed us out of the treatment suite so he, an anesthetist, and a pair of nurses could close Olga's wounds. We flooded back in as soon as Olga was bandaged.

The doc told us that a single bullet had passed between Olga's upper arm and rib cage, damaging both. The injuries were not life-threatening. Olga had a blood transfusion and lots of stitches, and she was unconscious. The head wound had stopped bleeding, but required evaluation by a neurosurgeon. I asked the doc to prep Olga for travel. We had to get out of Cyprus.

Without warning, a brigadier general arrived with a group captain and lieutenant in his slipstream.

"Who is the leader of this mob?" he demanded.

"I am, sir. Maxwell Geller."

"I'm Brigadier Simpson, the base commander. Be kind enough to tell me what the devil is going on?"

"This woman and her husband are Russian citizens. They have requested asylum in the United States."

"Is that so? I was called away from lunch with the notice that there is a Russian diplomat in my office. He told my aide that you and your blokes abducted two Russian citizens and shot one of them. I presume this patient is the lady you shot?"

I started to protest. He quickly amended it to, "Allegedly shot?"

The brigadier reached back and his senior aide placed a photo in his hand. He showed it to me. "The Russian provided this photo of you and informed my aide that you are wanted for bank robbery and murder in his country. He demanded that I place the lot of you under arrest and hold you incommunicado, until his security people arrive to take you into custody. Umm?"

While the brigadier reviewed my life of crime, Jill and Eva had been in a huddle, whispering. At that moment, Eva slipped out of the room.

To my surprise, Jill spoke up. "Brigadier, I'm a U.S. Marshal. These people are in my custody. Mr. Geller has been helping me with technical advice." Jill showed him the phony credentials that got her gun onto my flight from Australia.

Hands clasped behind his back, the brigadier leaned forward at the waist and examined Jill's ID with skepticism and without touching it. "Marshal Lori Sheen. Irish, is it?"

"Yes, sir," lied Jill, sticking with her cover.

"I'm surprised our American cousins allow the Irish to carry firearms. In England, we've had a rather bad experience with that. Are you from Texas, Marshal Sheen?"

"I beg your pardon, sir?"

"There is just one of you for this rather sizeable band of desperados. I wondered if you were from Texas. I understand that Texans send only one law enforcement officer if there is just one mob. Do I have that ratio correct?"

"There are two of us, sir," said Eva, reentering the room, phony credentials in one hand, sat phone in the other.

"Two of you? *Really*? That certainly alleviates my concern." He didn't bother to examine Eva's credentials.

She offered the brigadier her phone. "My supervisor in the States would like a word, sir."

The general pressed his lips together and put the instrument to his ear. "Brigadier Simpson here." He listened and scanned us with renewed interest. "How may I contribute to our Anglo-American partnership, sir? . . . *Really*?" He really enjoyed that word. "I see . . . Very well. Thank you for that clarification, General."

The brigadier returned Eva's phone. "That was the Chairman of the Joint Chiefs of Staff, your . . . supervisor? I may not be up to snuff on my organizational charts, but it was my impression that U.S. Marshals were under the jurisdiction of your Justice Department."

"We're part of a joint task force," Eva explained.

"Yes. I'm sure there's something out of joint here that requires task force–level attention and I want it off of my base e-*meed*-jut-ly."

He asked Olga's doctor, "How long before this woman can be travel-worthy and on the . . . marshals'. . . aeroplane?"

"Thirty minutes, sir."

The brigadier turned to his junior aide, "Call the tower. Clear their plane for departure in exactly"—he checked his watch—"sixty minutes. See to it that all of these liars are on board, along with their drone—" he gave me a harsh glance—"which is operating out of my base without authorization."

The aide shouted a wall-vibrating, "Sir!" and scooted out of the room.

Turning to his senior aide, the brigadier announced, "I'm going to finish my lunch. Go to my office. Entertain that Sov diplomat for exactly sixty-five minutes. Then, call a security detail and escort him on a tour of this hospital. Let's see if he can find his kidnapped Sov citizens and that fugitive from Moscow's merciful justice."

The senior aide, having protocol responsibilities, said, "Sir, with respect, the Russians don't like to be referred to as Soviets these days. They prefer 'citizens of the Russian Federation.'"

"Do they?" said the brigadier, with feigned surprise. "Well, Brown, a Sov diplomat by any other name is still KGB. Shakespeare said that. You'd do well to remember it."

He cautioned Jill, "Marshal Sheen, do be careful on your flight to wherever. I wouldn't turn my back on any of these blackguards." He addressed Eva, "And I wouldn't turn my back on Marshal Sheen, were I you." With a thin smile, the brigadier departed. Soon after, we got into vehicles and followed Olga's ambulance to the airfield for our flight to Ramstein, Germany.

As we lifted off, I stared out the window, wondering how the Russians found us so soon after the Nissi Beach shooting.

CHAPTER 36

Ramstein and Landstuhl, Germany

THE INTERROGATORS WERE waiting when our plane landed at Ramstein Air Force Base. Thanks to Eva's ever ready sat phone, Rodney had called ahead for RAMPART's debriefing to begin as soon as he was under U.S. control, and he was certainly being controlled. In addition to the interrogators, a sunglasses-and-submachine-gun crew formed a protective ring around him, as the chief-of-sunglasses hustled RAMPART into a Mercedes SUV that would whisk him to parts unknown. The Petrovs had entered a ring of twenty-four-seven protection to keep their GRU/SVR pursuers from ending their lives. That protection also came with an around-the-clock schedule of prison guards to keep RAMPART from changing his mind about delivering Russian secrets and just walking away, as Vitali Yurchenko did in Georgetown.

To no avail, RAMPART left protesting separation from his wife. The doctor in Cyprus told us that Olga needed an operation, maybe two. He sent along X-rays to prove it. Washington had wisely authorized Olga's medical care at the Army's general hospital in Landstuhl, a short ambulance ride from the air base. As RAMPART was being pushed into the Mercedes, medics loaded Olga into an ambulance and took her to a waiting surgery table.

There was another Langley team waiting to debrief me, Jill, Eva, and Sherri's team. They split us up so we couldn't coordinate our stories, took us to separate rooms, and turned on digital recorders. I don't know what anyone else told our inquisitors. I gave them the truth, except the part where Rodney blackmailed me into going to Moscow, because Rodney still had some control over Vanessa. Also, I didn't admit to shooting Russians. I'm not proud that I gave Boris and Yulia credit for those kills and hoped they would understand, if asked. I knew my lies wouldn't hold up over the long run, but as John Keynes said, "In the long run, we are all dead."

After my session was over, an Air Force sergeant took me to a private room in a barracks. I slept until Sherri and her guys woke me up hours later. We exchanged thanks and goodbyes.

Sherri gave me a wan smile. "See you when I see you, Max."

They left to catch a train to Frankfurt and a flight to the States. I went back to sleep.

I was awakened that evening by the chief-of-sunglasses, who had spirited RAMPART away earlier. No sunglasses, now. He wore a snugly fitting suit and, up close, looked like he lifted anvils for his morning workouts. His message: "RAMPART is at the hospital with his wife. He wants to see you."

We went out to the Mercedes. He opened the back door for me and there was Rodney.

"Surprised to see me?" he asked.

"Disappointed."

I slid onto the seat beside him. The chief-of-sunglasses drove us to the hospital grounds.

"You didn't waste any time getting here," I observed.

"There's no time to waste, but RAMPART is wasting it anyway."

"Didn't he give you the Russian crown jewels?"

"No. He refuses to discuss his treasures until he's in the States."

"He's one smart Russian."

"He wants to see you. You must have his trust. Convince him to tell us what he knows."

"You want me to vouch for your trustworthiness? One of us is in the wrong Mercedes."

"There's more at stake here than our personal relationship."

"That's exactly what's at stake. I won't do it. My job was to bring him out. Your job is to wring him out. I did my job. Do yours. Put RAMPART on a plane to Washington. Drive him by the Capitol. Twelve hours from now, he'll be in a safehouse spilling his guts."

"That's not what I had in mind."

"What you had in mind was to hear what RAMPART had to say before anyone in Washington hears it. That's why you came all this way so quickly."

When Rodney didn't respond, I asked, "How is Vanessa?"

"Not happy with either of us. She floated her résumé to other agencies."

I wanted to know if Vanessa had asked about me, but I couldn't give Rodney the satisfaction.

They dropped me at the Fisher House, where relatives stay while a family member is recuperating in the nearby hospital. There were two guards outside RAMPART's room. One seated, one standing. They knew I was coming. I entered without much scrutiny.

It was a pleasant but austere room. Petrov was sitting in one of two easy chairs by the window, a bottle of vodka and two glasses on the table beside him. He came and hugged me for a little longer than I was comfortable. When we decoupled, I joined him at the vodka bottle.

He poured me a shot and we spoke Russian. "Thank you for coming."

"My American friends suggested it, but I would have come anyway."

"Where is Tony? I need to thank him, too."

"On his way to the States. He knows you're grateful. How is Olga?"

"She's not awake. The doctors are cautious in their prognosis."

We spent the next hour or so drinking the neck and shoulders off the vodka bottle. Sometimes talking, sometimes not. I let him lead.

After one of our silences, he asked, "Who shot Olga?"

"I don't know. Five Russians in two cars followed Olga to Nissi Beach. When the shot was fired, we could account for four. I think the fifth man took the shots from someplace high up, a rooftop, maybe. At that range, it had to be a rifle."

I wasn't going to tell RAMPART the Russian who fired the shot was dead. Jack shot him as he came from a condo roof and left him in the stairwell.

I asked, "What was your plan after you and Olga got to your boat?"

"I would have contacted the American Embassy on Cyprus and asked for asylum."

There was no way to know if he was telling the truth. "What about the three million euros?"

"A deception. If they suspected I planned to defect no matter what, they would have killed Olga and me at their first opportunity. I wanted them to think they could salvage the operation."

"What operation?" My antenna was up.

Petrov smiled, but said nothing. I had crossed into forbidden territory.

"Why did you come to Moscow for me? It was dangerous for you."

In heavily redacted terms, I told him the Vanessa hostage story.

He downed a shot and observed, "We do foolish things for those we love. Have you talked to your woman since we arrived?"

"No. She doesn't return my calls."

"I'm sorry, but I'm glad it was you who came to Moscow. I don't think Olga and I would have gotten out if the CIA had sent someone else."

RAMPART poured another hefty shot of vodka and knocked it back. "I have a confession. I betrayed my best friend, Sergei, to get out. When I saw you with him during your last visit, I knew he was spying for the CIA. I knew how badly my government wanted you. I went to GRU counterintelligence and reported Sergei. I suggested that I be the bait to lure you back to Moscow. I knew they would agree. The GRU always wants to show they are the professionals and the FSB are amateurs."

"How did you know I wouldn't get caught if I returned to Moscow?"

"I had to take that chance. I knew you would suspect a trap. I believed that if you did come, you would have a plan that had a reasonable chance of success."

I grabbed the vodka bottle and poured myself a stiff one to keep from killing him. Sergei had been a valuable asset. I had recruited him and doomed him for helping me with the Ironside Dossier. Spying is a game of using people. Nobody escapes, not even the puppet masters.

I tried to stay focused. "So, when the ministry decided to send you to Tallinn, you thought it would be easier for you and Olga to defect there than in Moscow?"

"Yes, but I had to change my plan when the ministry removed Olga from the trip. They must have suspected something they couldn't prove, or they would have pulled me, too."

"Why was the ministry sending you to Tallinn when we first met? It wasn't for a vacation, and it wasn't to trap me."

"I will tell you that when I am in the United States."

Forbidden territory, again. I let it go, but kept my anger and curiosity.

"So, you changed your plan to defect in Tallinn, when Olga couldn't go. What then?"

"Olga and I planned her Nissi Beach escape before I left for Tallinn. We knew Cyprus and we didn't think the GRU would be prepared to pursue us by boat. How did you know I would try to take Olga from Nissi Beach?"

"Tell you when we get to the States." *You bastard.* I could barely contain my anger at his betrayal of Sergei. Time to go. I faked a polite "Goodnight" and left.

One of the guards outside RAMPART's room called the Mercedes chariot to pick me up. Which was what it almost had to do after all that vodka.

Again, the chief-of-sunglasses was driving. Rodney was in the back seat. I got into the front.

"Any success?" asked Rodney.

"I didn't try. He said we get no secrets until he's on U.S. soil."

Rodney changed subjects. "In Cyprus, who knew you were coming to Ramstein?"

"The pilot, copilot, and me. Why?"

"What was the destination on your flight plan filed in Cyprus?"

"Lakenheath. We diverted to Ramstein to get Olga to a hospital ASAP. I didn't tell anyone else until we were airborne." His questions were burning off the vodka and forcing me to focus.

"In that case," said Rodney, "can you explain how the Russian consul general in Frankfurt knows enough about your movements to tell the U.S. consul general in Frankfurt that kidnapped Russian citizens and fugitives are being sheltered at Ramstein and Landstuhl?"

CHAPTER 37

THREE HOURS AFTER Rodney asked that question, we were on a C-130 medical evacuation flight to Andrews Air Force Base in Maryland.

C-130 med evac planes carry a nursing staff and are outfitted with special oxygen and electrical systems to support movement of up to seventy-four patients, with all their tubes, tanks, and monitors. Olga Petrovna was attached to several, and the only patient on our flight. Her neurosurgeon was along for the ride. The remaining passengers were Petrov, Rodney, Jill, Eva, me, the interrogators, and the sunglasses-and-submachinegun crew.

I had no desire to go to the States, but with Russians on my trail, I took the fastest route to safety. The Bondi Beach shootout was a fresh memory, and I was sure Vanessa wouldn't be at the airport to greet me with a flower lei or the promise of a bloomin' lay. My plan was to find a nice hotel, get into the tub with a fifth of scotch, and stay there until my mind changed.

Rodney had a different plan. He plopped into the seat beside me. "When we get to Washington, the director would like you to stay in the area until RAMPART adjusts to his new circumstances. With Olga hospitalized, you're the only one he knows. You could be a friend, if he needs one."

"Bring in Colonel Burke from Moscow."

"RAMPART knows Burke, but he trusts you."

* * *

It was 5:00 a.m. when we touched down at Andrews Air Force Base. The sunglasses-and-submachine-gun boys took RAMPART to a safehouse in a caravan of black Chevy Suburbans. A med evac helicopter flew Olga and her neurosurgeon to Bethesda Naval Medical Center north of Washington, D.C.

The rest of us were helicoptered to CIA headquarters at Langley. We'd been traveling for more hours than I could remember. It would have been kind to let us get some sleep. Instead, we were going to be questioned, again, while we were tired and irritated enough to blurt out the truth.

Each defector gets a case officer. Petrov's was Albert—not his real name, of course. Albert hadn't made the trip to Ramstein. He was fresh; I was tired. It was an effective pairing, like fish and a cold Pinot Noir.

In a small, quiet room, with the recorder running, Albert began, "Mad Max Geller," and opened his leather-bound notepad.

"Just Max."

"Well, Max, what motive did RAMPART give for offering his services to the CIA?"

"He said he was sick of killing. He told me he had nightmares about combat."

"Did he?"

"Not with me. We weren't together long, but he didn't sleep much and smoked a lot."

Albert made a note with his gold pen. RAMPART's first stop was going to be a psychiatrist, who would give Albert a judgment about the defector's PTSD and state of mind.

"What did RAMPART tell you about the information he was offering us?"

"Nothing."

"You didn't ask?" Albert was trying to determine if I had heard something I shouldn't have.

"I'm not inquisitive."

"Rodney told me you are very inquisitive, poking your nose into the Ironside Dossier."

"I was being paid—a lot—to ask questions on that trip."

Albert penned another note. "Don't you want to know why you were tasked to bring RAMPART over?"

"RAMPART asked for me. What I want to know is when this bullshit interview will end."

Albert made another note. Maybe *my* next stop would be the psychiatrist. He shifted gears and asked me the same questions I had answered in Germany. We parted on hostile terms.

Albert's "Don't-you-want-to-know-what-Petrov-has-to-trade?" questions were asked to find out how much I knew about RAMPART's intel. I no longer had a security clearance or a need to know. Albert and Rodney may have considered detaining me if I knew Petrov's secrets.

I called Vanessa. She didn't pick up. That message didn't require an interpreter.

It was past noon. I was beyond exhausted and hungry. I went to the CIA cafeteria for lunch. As I sat alone eating and wondering if I had the strength to make it to a hotel, Jill joined me.

"Are you as tired as I am?" she asked.

"More."

"What's next for you, Max? Back to Australia?"

"The director wants me to stay here while RAMPART gets used to new friends on the rubber hose squad." Jill laughed. I added, "Anyway, Australia is not the draw it once was."

Jill said, "I hear Vanessa might leave the Agency. She's not happy that you were sent to Moscow in her place. I'm sorry."

"Are you?"

"I never hid my opinion that Vanessa was wrong for you, but, like everyone else, you deserve your chance at unhappiness." She enjoyed saying that. "It makes real happiness all the sweeter, when you find it. By the way, where are you staying?"

"I'll find a hotel nearby." As an afterthought, I added, "And a rental car."

"Stay at my condo. My roommate left for an overseas assignment. Her suite is empty. You'll have a private room, bath, workspace, and kitchen privileges. You can ride to work with me or drop me off and use my car—" she smiled—"when the rubber hose squad doesn't need you."

Jill studied me. "Don't give me that look. This is not a sanctuary-for-sex offer. It's a business proposal so I can pay my mortgage. Give me half of the hotel rate and buy your own groceries."

"Let me think about it."

"Don't think too long. I've posted the vacancy on Agency bulletin boards."

I didn't think long. I removed the bulletin board posting and called her cell. I slept while she drove us to her condo in Sterling, Virginia.

Jill welcomed me with a home-cooked meal and scotch by the fireplace, afterwards.

"What's going to happen to RAMPART?" she asked.

"The counterintelligence team will vet him. They want to be sure he's not a disinformation artist or Russian troll. Their number one question is, 'Why is RAMPART betraying his country?' Le Carré wrote, 'If we trust the motive, we trust the man.' Is he being coerced or doing it for money, ideology, or ego needs? Those are the usual motives for treason. They'll also run RAMPART by the psychiatrist to see if he has PTSD or is faking."

"When will they polygraph him?"

"Probably after his sessions have been transcribed, so they can use the transcript to cross-examine him on the machine. Once they get enough of his statement on paper and whatever documents he brought over, they'll start checking against signals intercepts and human source intel at DIA, NSA, and FBI—any other agency or overseas allies that might have info that can confirm or refute RAMPART's story. If RAMPART's info is verifiable and valuable, the analysts will distill it and send the assessments to the intel community and our allies that have a need-to-know."

"After that?"

"They'll turn RAMPART inside out. His history, his contacts, everything he's ever done, knows, thought, or heard. That could take months or a year, or more. Then, a repeat of the verification process with the intel community."

Jill offered, "I hear RAMPART knows a lot about the workings of the Russian Defense Ministry. What if he tells the interrogators something that Ted Walldrum needs to know, as our president, but can't be trusted with because of his Russian connections?"

"If that happens, the Deep State is in deep do-do. Someone will have to make the decision to tell Walldrum or not tell him. No matter what they decide, it'll be wrong."

CHAPTER 38

A LOT HAD gone on in the weeks after we delivered RAMPART to the States. COVID-19 became a pandemic, and thousands were dying across the globe. One day, alone at Jill's condo, I got a call from the CIA personnel office. The man on the phone gave a name I didn't recognize. He also apologized. "Normally I would ask you to come in for a call of this nature, but the pandemic has caused us to modify procedures. I hope you understand. Vanessa Blake listed you in her file as the person to be notified in case of an emergency."

A chill ran down my spine. "I assume this is an emergency?"

"I'm sorry to inform you that it is. Ms. Blake is in intensive care at Prince of Wales Hospital in Sydney, Australia. She's being treated for the COVID-19 virus. The prognosis is not good." He said a lot more. I don't remember any of it, except his promise to keep me informed of any change in Vanessa's condition.

Direct flights between the States and the Pacific were becoming problematic. I reserved a flight to Sydney via Frankfurt, Germany, packed a bag, and took a cab to Dulles Airport. A ticket kiosk message directed me to the airline's counter.

The attendant took my passport and checked the computer. Something happened to her face—confusion, horror, pity? "I'm sorry, sir. You're on the no-fly list." She looked over my shoulder and nodded.

Suddenly, there was a masked man on either side of me. The one on my left flashed his credentials. "Mr. Geller, would you come with us, please?" His vice grip on my arm was not a request. The man on my right took my passport from the attendant and gripped my other arm.

"What the f—"

"Please don't make a scene, Mr. Geller. We have orders to take you to headquarters."

"My girlfriend is dying in a Sydney hospital! I need to get on that flight!"

"I'm sorry for your loss, Mr. Geller. We've been told she passed away."

My knees turned to jelly. "I need to sit down."

"You can sit in the car, sir."

I masked up and they took me to Rodney and his guard. "Max, my condolences. I am sorry about Vanessa. Her status was provided to you as a courtesy. Keep it to yourself until the formal notifications are made. We'll arrange a memorial for Vanessa soon."

Rodney didn't dwell on his sorrow. "Surrender your phone."

"Surrender? I don't like the sound of that. What's going on?"

"The Russian Ambassador has asked the State Department to turn over the kidnapped Petrovs."

"So . . . ?"

"So, the Russians know the Petrovs are in the States. That means they tracked you from Tallinn to Cyprus to Ramstein to Washington. How is that possible?"

"You think I was calling the Russians to tell them where to find Petrov? What's my motive? Oh, I get it. You think I wanted RAMPART taken out to sabotage your operation."

"Think?" Rodney sneered. "I'll tell you what I know. According to people who've been traveling with you, you were the only one slipping off into corners making calls."

"It's called privacy. I think it's mentioned in the Constitution."

"I don't give a shit what it's called. Give me your phone or I'll have it taken from you."

I put my cell phone on his desk.

"Eva had a sat phone. Are you checking her calls, too?"

"I already have." He nodded to the armed guard, who pulled on a pair of latex gloves, picked up my phone, and dropped it into a Faraday bag that prevents tracking.

Rodney opened the transcript of my Ramstein debriefing. "You told us you shared a room with RAMPART at the Tallinn airport, before he escaped. Did he have access to your phone?"

"No."

"You said you woke up and he was at the window. Could he have accessed your phone while you were asleep?"

"That's possible. My phone was on the nightstand between our beds."

"And there was an Estonian guard in the room with you, sleeping in a bed that blocked the door, you said. Could he have had access to your phone while you were asleep?"

"Possibly."

Rodney slammed the transcript shut. "I sent you to Moscow for one man; you came back with him and a family of three, the Kuzmicks. Did they have access to your phone, too?"

"They did not."

"I don't know if I should believe any of your statements about the Kuzmicks."

"They had no motive and no access. Why would you doubt me?"

"Because I doubt you were truthful about their actions when you crossed the Russian-Estonian border. You said they shot all five guards. They say you shot three of the guards. The FBI checked your gun. It had been fired."

"Well, you're never going to know the truth unless you dig the bullets out of those dead Russians, and we both know that's not going to happen."

"Do you want to amend your statement about the border shootings or not?"

"Not! What are you gonna do? Fire me? Oh, that's right, I don't work for the Agency. I'm just blackmail help."

"Is there anyone else who might have had access to your cell phone?"

"Jill. Eva. Sherri and her guys. As Chief Inspector Renko said, 'I suspect everyone.'"

"Who is Chief Inspector Renko?"

"A fictional character, just like the person you think bugged my phone."

"We'll see if he's fiction or he's you. In the meantime, I'm holding your passport. Keep yourself available. If I have to look for you, I'll put you in an ankle bracelet."

"I asked you to bring Vanessa back to the States so we could patch up our relationship. You refused; she's dead. You ought to be concerned that I might come looking for you."

My two masked escorts from the airport drove me back to Jill's condo, where I gave her an update. She commiserated. I dropped out.

* * *

During the weeks that followed, I was out of the Agency loop and glad. My anger at Rodney and Petrov was simmering without a release valve. I kept mostly to my rooms for a couple of weeks. Jill gave me space and was kind enough to keep me in food and on a restricted scotch diet. I was surprised that I didn't get condolences from people at the Agency who knew Vanessa and I were a couple, but many of them were busy grieving for their own COVID-19 dead. The world was shutting down. I got bored and tired of bad news. I ventured into Jill's space. We watched TV movies and played lots of word and board games. No sex games.

Finally, someone at the Agency wanted me. It was Albert, Petrov's case officer. Looking back, I suspect he asked Rodney to bring me in. Rodney thought I would be more cooperative if Albert asked.

Calling on Jill's landline, he said, "I'd like you to talk to RAMPART. He's a bit down. I'll send a car for you. Wear a face mask."

The car came at night, with a driver and two guards. They took me to a safehouse in Virginia farm country. Inside, a guard led me to a comfortable, first-floor living room. The lights were out. The room was illuminated by moonlight and the glow of Petrov's cigarette. He was standing at the window smoking and looking out into the darkness, as he had in Tallinn.

"Welcome to my new home, Max." He beckoned me to the window. "They won't let me look out until after dark, with the lights off."

"A wise precaution. How are you?"

"I am well. They told me you visited Olga."

"Before the pandemic took hold, yes. Now, entry to the hospital is restricted."

"They let me see her over a computer link."

"How is she?"

"Still unconscious. The head injury was worse than they thought. Her doctor said she is stable. Not getting worse or better. How is your woman? You didn't tell me her name."

"She was in the hospital with the virus. She's not getting worse, either." Petrov had enough pain of his own. He didn't need mine.

As we stood there, the reflection of a red laser hit the window and I dove at Petrov, knocking him to the floor. There was no weapon report, but the bullets turned the windowpane into a spiderweb and slammed into the opposite wall.

Hell broke loose outside the room. Guards were yelling and shoot-ing, but it sounded one-sided. The attackers must have been using weapons with sound suppressors. The door flew open, and one of the guards backed in, shooting at someone. Bullets turned the doorjamb to splinters and he fell backwards into the room, bleeding. His pistol slid across the floor. I grabbed it, but when I turned to face the door, a man in black had me covered with an Uzi submachine gun. I was dead.

Petrov leapt in front of me as the man pulled the trigger. I couldn't see body armor on the shooter, but I was sure he was wearing it. As Petrov dropped, I fired two shots at the gunman, neck and head. He fell backwards into the hall.

Petrov was alive with multiple torso wounds. Calling 9-1-1 wasn't an option. He was going to bleed out if I didn't get him to a hospital fast. The Suburban's GPS would locate the nearest one, and I'd have an ambulance meet me halfway. I stood Petrov up to carry him out over my shoulder. That's when the world exploded.

*   *   *

A masked nurse leaned into my field of vision. "How are you feeling, Mr. Geller?"

I had to think about it. "Like every part of my body is burning, stinging, or aching."

She disappeared and I heard her say, "Dr. Carter, Mr. Geller is awake." The nurse reentered my field of vision. "How many fingers do you see?"

"Enough for you to reach into a pill bottle and get me something for this freakin' headache."

She went mother superior on me. "Are you going to be a difficult patient, Mr. Geller?"

A masked doctor appeared. His picture was pinned to his white coat, with "Dr. Carter" printed across the bottom in black marker.

"How many fingers was the nurse holding up, Mr. Geller?" he asked.

"You two are in this together, aren't you?"

He was not amused. "The three of us are in this together to get you back on your feet. Try to cooperate." He softened his tone a bit and explained. "You've had a concussion. Double vision is one of the possible effects. So, how many fingers did you see?"

I wanted to show him one of mine. Instead, I said, "Three. I hope she wasn't holding up one-and-a-half just to screw with me."

The doctor sighed. The nurse pressed her lips together and turned away. Dr. Carter put on his bedside face and said, "Three is correct. That's good news."

"What's the bad news and will you please give me something for this headache!"

"We already have, but your brain is swollen, and you are going to be in pain until it returns to normal. That will take a while. You have a nasty bump on your head. I'm told you tried to put it through a wall."

"Feels like the wall won. How long have I been down?"

"Four days."

That was a shocker. "Am I in one piece?"

"Yes, but not out of the woods. Your concussion isn't life-threatening, but it can disturb brain functions like concentration, memory, and problem-solving. In addition to your headache, you may experience other symptoms: blurred or double vision, confusion, vomiting, dizziness, drowsiness, and weakness in your limbs." He sounded like a TV commercial for a new acne pill.

Dr. Carter continued, "You could also have emotional episodes and irritability, which you have already demonstrated for us. So, during your stay, we will determine if you have any of those other symptoms and treat them and the causes. However, rest is the best treatment for a concussion like yours. Give your brain time to repair itself. If you don't, you're asking for future trouble."

The doctor was not finished. "As for the rest of your body, you have lots of burns, bruises, and shrapnel wounds. You were in a room where two grenades went off, one concussion and one fragmentation. You really need to find more pleasant playmates, Mr. Geller."

Everybody wants to be a comedian. I'm the patient. I'll do the damned jokes.

"How serious are the frag wounds?" I asked.

"Luckily—and miraculously—none of your vital organs were penetrated, but some fragments are very close to vital organs. Surgery will be required, and complications are possible. We will do everything possible to put you back together. Do you have any other questions?"

"What hospital is this?"

"You are in a private hospital. We provide medical care for your agency. We'll begin your assessment and repair tomorrow. In the meantime, relax. Ask the nurse for anything you need." As Dr. Carter left, he said, "You have a visitor."

Jill Rucker came to the bed and stroked my cheek with the backs of her fingers. "I'm glad you're awake. I was worried."

"Did RAMPART make it?"

Jill shook her head slowly. "Sorry."

"Did Rodney get what he wanted from RAMPART?"

"I can't discuss that, Max."

"What about the guards?"

"Two dead at the safehouse. Two died at the hospital. You're the only survivor."

"I shot the guy who killed Petrov. What's the story on him?"

"All we found was a blood trail leading out of Petrov's room. The attackers policed up their dead, wounded, and weapons. They didn't leave anything behind but shell casings." A pause. "Can you answer some questions?"

"Not for Rodney."

"The DO sent me."

The Director of Operations! Rodney had to admit he struck out with me. That's satisfying.

She placed the little digital recorder on the pillow next to my head. I told Jill and the recorder everything I could remember about the safehouse attack. "What I don't understand is how they found us."

Jill told me. "They had a tracker in Olga's watch. It must have been there when she left Moscow for Cyprus. The day of the attack, one of the guards picked up Olga's belongings at the hospital and took them to Petrov at the safehouse."

I understood. "The Russians wanted to kill him before he could tell us anything, but they didn't know where he was, until he had the watch."

"Right. Did you hear any Russian being spoken during the attack?"

"All I heard was shooting and the guards yelling." Suddenly I was tired. "Jill, I can't talk anymore. I need to rest."

Days and weeks came and went. Meals came and went, some eaten, some not. Doctors and nurses entered, took vital signs, checked monitors, exchanged grave looks, and departed. Wheelchairs came and went, taking me to and from CAT scans and MRIs and X-rays and operating rooms. Therapists massaged my aching neck, back, and legs; taught me exercises; and forced me to take painful walks down polished hallways, with the tail flap of my hospital gown waving in the breeze. On TV, COVID-19 victims went and news of their departure came. Dreams of Vanessa and Claudia—an old flame that burned me—floated in and out of my brain. Through it all, the morphine drip dripped, until the day it stopped. The pain came and wouldn't leave.

The parade of doctors and nurses to check me and my monitors continued. Gradually, their grave looks became cheery smiles. Meanwhile, I began to walk the halls with no assistance and terminal boredom.

Jill kept up her visits. One day, after weeks of medical smiles, Jill asked, "How are you?"

"Addicted." The doctor had been right about irritability as a concussion side effect.

"Well, cold turkey starts soon. You're being discharged today. I came to drive you home. You need to get your thoughts together." She didn't say *thoughts*. "You have an audience with the director next Monday."

"About what?"

"RAMPART, I think. Whatever he told his inquisitors caused a real stir after he was killed. There's more than the usual activity at the Agency."

"What's happening?"

"Lots of meetings and visiting heavyweights from sister intelligence agencies and the Pentagon. I saw the Chairman of the Joint Chiefs, General McClure, slinking around the Seventh Floor in slacks and a polo shirt. This is the guy who wears a four-star tie clip when he's in civies, just so you know who you're talking to."

"What were you doing on the Seventh Floor?"

"Minding my business. Try it. A couple of days later, I saw the commanding general of the 18th Airborne Corps walking the hall in civvies. What do you make of it?"

"If your guess is right, RAMPART gave up some intel so sensitive that the director won't let it leave the building. The brass have to come to Langley to be briefed. Have you seen anyone from the White House?"

"No."

That was a good sign . . . and a bad one.

CHAPTER 39

May 2020
CIA Director's Office, Langley, Virginia

"Vanessa is alive," was the CIA Director's shocking revelation.

My Monday afternoon command performance in her seventh-floor office didn't begin with that shocker. When I arrived, the director shook my hand and offered me the chair. Her desk was bare except for a tray containing a bottle of my favorite scotch and two glasses.

She sat in her captain's chair and smiled at me, sparks dancing in her gray-green eyes. "Your doctor said a finger of scotch won't interfere with your medications. Join me." She poured while my brain searched for an appropriate response.

"Concussion can slow mental processes," the neurologist had told me. By the time the scotch was poured, I had managed only a thank-you smile.

The director handed me the whiskey. "To a speedy recovery."

We downed the shots. She poured another just for me. "Leave that one for later. You're going to need it."

She scooted her captain's chair back and crossed her legs. Over the desktop, I could see a little above her knee. A nice leg. Any leg probably looked nice, given my long hospital stay.

"I apologize for your treatment by the Agency two years ago. Had I been in this position at the time of your firing, there might have been a different outcome."

That was said by the woman who let Rodney use Vanessa to blackmail me into going to Russia, but who's keeping score? I just fell off the farmer's market truck on the way to Georgetown. Tell me more.

She did. "In spite of obstacles, you have performed beyond expectations, both with the Ironside Dossier and the RAMPART operation. You deserve the gratitude of this Agency and the country. In that vein, I have good news. Now would be the time to take that drink and brace yourself."

I did, and waited for the news.

"Vanessa is alive."

"What!" was all I could think to say, as my head spun, and the bottom fell out of my stomach.

"Vanessa was hospitalized for a short time. It had nothing to do with COVID-19. She's back at work, now. Prescott—" Rodney's real name—"concocted a cruel lie to deceive you."

"Why?"

"He wouldn't say. I suspect his motive was revenge. It is a documented fact that Prescott blamed you for killing those men on his yacht two years ago and trying to frame him for it." Dismissing the episode, she said, "Anyway, he's been disciplined and reassigned."

"To where?" I was steaming angry.

"Let it go, Max. Don't turn this hiccup into a major case of organizational indigestion."

I'm going to give this organization an enema when I get my hands on Prescott. "How did you find out about his lie?"

"Eva Soriano and Jill Rucker discovered it and brought the issue to me through complaint channels. They gave me permission to tell you their names, if you asked."

The director admitted, "The Agency has treated you badly more than once. Because of the current political climate, I can't make you whole. I can help Vanessa. I will see that she gets a mentor to groom her for leadership, provided she has the aptitude for it. She certainly has the desire. I hope you—and she—will consider that adequate recompense for all you've endured."

I answered by pouring myself a shot strong enough to interfere with my meds and swallowed it in one gulp. Nothing could adequately compensate me. I suspected Vanessa felt the same. She was Irish and had what the late Frank McCourt called Irish Alzheimer's: they forget everything but the grudges. Maybe I had it, too.

The director leaned forward, giving me a serious look. "You've sacrificed a great deal, but I need you to perform one more service for your country."

"My country is Australia."

"By pique, not by preference. This Agency wronged you, and you cut off your nose to spite your face. I understand. If the election falls right, you might be offered dual citizenship."

She was right about the nose-face thing, but I just didn't care. "What do you want, Director?"

"The information RAMPART gave us about Russian intentions—Russian military plans, actually—is frightening. Much of it cannot be corroborated by other sources. Sides have been taken in the intel community. Some believe what RAMPART gave us is Russian disinformation. Others believe the Russians have evil intentions and have done an excellent job of concealing their preparations . . . until RAMPART defected. I'm in the latter camp.

"In spite of any misgivings, a meeting has been scheduled to decide what to do about RAMPART's information. Most of the people attending know you or your work on the Ironside Dossier, or they have heard of your accomplishments. You bring to the table unique knowledge and credibility about the RAMPART defection. Questions may be asked that only you can answer. Max, I want you in that room."

"What did RAMPART tell you that's so important?"

She hesitated.

"It would be nice to know what I'm talking about, if someone asks me a question."

She committed. "For your ears only." The director took a pen and non-disclosure statement from her desk drawer and handed them to me. I signed and she briefed me.

"As you know, the presidential election is a few months away. No matter who wins, Russia intends to attack and occupy its former satellites on the Baltic Sea: Lithuania, Latvia, and Estonia. RAMPART was a member of the planning staff for that attack. He was to be promoted and given command of the brigade that would invade Estonia.

"His vacation to Estonia was a cover for him to conduct a reconnaissance of key facilities his forces would occupy. He and his wife planned to defect to you there. You know the rest of the story, you lived it. The code name for Russia's attack on the Baltic states is OPERATION BEARCLAW. We have to devise a plan to prevent it."

That was her priority and her problem, not mine. As soon as I could leave Langley, I purchased a burner cell phone and called Sherri.

When she heard my voice, she said, "Hello, Savior of the Western World. What can we mortals do for you today?" There was a smile in her voice.

"I need you to find Rodney for me."

"Where'd you lose him?"

"Be serious, Sherri. He gave me a false report that Vanessa was dead."

"Is Vanessa okay?"

"Yeah, but Rodney won't be when I get my hands on him. I need you to go find him, keep an eye on him, and give me his schedule."

"Why not find him yourself? You delivered the package, didn't you?" She was asking about Petrov.

"It was booby-trapped. I'm trying to defuse it."

"Max, I've already granted your annual death wish by going to Estonia. I'm not a foot soldier anymore. I have a consulting business to run. Try Tony-D. He's between jobs."

I thanked Sherri, called Tony-D, and gave him the mission.

"Okay, Max. What deliverables do you want?"

"Find Rodney. Get me his schedule, and track him until I say stop."

"What's the budget?"

"Whatever it takes."

My friend Tony-D sighed. "It's your money, Max, but the way you spend it, you're going to be broke before you're fifty."

"I've been broke before. This is the first time I've been a millionaire. Find his ass. Don't call me. I'll call you."

CHAPTER 40

The following day
Fort Detrick, Maryland, fifty miles north of Washington, D.C.

THE SECRET MEETING was held in a soundproof conference room, with negative air pressure. Negative pressure was achieved by having exhaust vents near the floor that remove air and toxins, like COVID-19, from the room faster than blowers in the ceiling can supply clean air. The participants had tested negative for the virus and masks were not in use.

Fort Detrick had been chosen because it was far from the prying eyes of the Washington press corps. They would have guessed something newsworthy was afoot when they saw all those black Chevy Suburbans converging on one location, followed by chase cars of bodyguards with their sunglasses and their heads on swivels.

Now, the attendees were huddled around the conference table. All were sub-cabinet senior executives because the people at cabinet-level—or above—couldn't be trusted not to fumble the ball or give the game away to the enemy. They had received the RAMPART briefing and were there to develop a coordinated strategy to deal with the planned Russian attack.

I was the only attendee not seated at the conference table. I took one of the wall chairs usually occupied by horse holders and straphangers, the D.C. pejoratives for the entourages of their powerful bosses. The discussions in that room were way too sensitive for entourage staffers.

That made me wonder why the director had insisted on my presence. Although I was no longer an Agency employee, she had given me an order I couldn't refuse. Vanessa did work for the Agency, and she was still a *de facto* hostage to secure my cooperation. Intelligence is about using people.

Still, I wasn't sure why the director wanted me there. I didn't think it was to answer questions. I sat where we had eye contact, watching her and listening for some clue as to my role. She must have checked me out before allowing me—a disgruntled former employee—to be involved in something this sensitive. I was just as sure the director knew I hated meetings. I had a reputation for disrupting them by shutting down recreational talkers and forcing attention on unpleasant essentials.

The discussions were contentious. A long, difficult workday slogged into evening, with meals catered in. Suit coats and military tunics were off and hanging on chair backs. Sleeves were rolled up. Ties were loosened. I could see a pair of empty, overturned high heels under the table. Tension had crept into the discussions. Some attendees were looking at their watches.

As the meeting ground to a deadlock, the director rolled her eyes, looked at me, and said, in a voice for all to hear, "Do you have something to add, Mr. Geller?"

Suddenly, I realized why she wanted me there. It was my job to give voice to what all of them were thinking, but none dare say, on pain of treason. The principals craned their necks or twisted in their chairs to see me.

Not even trying to conceal the post-concussion irritation Dr. Carter had warned me about, I said, "You're ignoring the five-hundred-pound gorilla in the room. Whatever you decide here doesn't matter, unless you get White House approval. We all know that's not going to happen. The only way to deal with the threat is to remove the president and the vice president from the decision-making process."

There were no gasps, no cries of outrage. They all knew I had told the dreaded truth. Apparently, that tore it for the FBI Director. He stood and removed his coat from the chairback and put it on. "I will not take part in this conversation." He headed for the door.

General McClure, Chairman of the Joint Chiefs of Staff, stopped him with a single word. "Brad!" It was part command, part caution, part question.

The FBI Director turned back and played his eyes over the group. "Don't worry. I didn't hear Mr. Geller's comment . . . but if it comes to the Bureau through any other channel, I'll notify the Secret Service and there will be an investigation."

They knew the political-military war game was over. I had hit them in the gut with reality. They had to make decisions that would change their worlds, and they were not ready. That was the time to go home, hold their loved ones, and assess the potential costs and benefits. Those costs could be high: destroyed careers, jail, and loss of lives. In the end, it didn't matter if they committed or sat on the sidelines. Just being in that room made them all conspirators. There were no good options. Decisions had to be made and submitted to the harsh judgement of history.

General McClure understood that the group was not ready to commit. He gave them a reprieve. "Why don't we adjourn and take some more time to work the problem." That suggestion ended the meeting.

As the attendees departed, the director gestured for me to stay put. When the only ones left in the room were me, the director, and McClure, she said, "Max, I've been working on a plan to deal with this problem if that group won't. It requires an operator with no connection to the Agency . . . or the government."

"Why is that?"

"Because if anyone inside the government is involved, it's going to look like what it is, a bunch of sub-cabinet officials trying to pull off a coup. The Deep State strikes back. That will be a bad precedent and not good for our democracy. I consulted with other people in government who I trust. They don't see any other way. We need to go outside the guardrails. For that, I need your help. Are you up for it?"

"How far outside the rails?"

"Wherever we must go to reach our destination. As you said, we have to take out the president and vice president, before the Russians execute OPERATION BEARCLAW."

That was as far outside the rails as you could go in a democracy. Why would I do it? To save Vanessa . . . from what . . . for what? Does she even want me? Does it matter, compared to this? There was a lot at stake, and I had already put myself in harm's way, killed Russians so she didn't have to, and so that the people sitting across this table could have the goodies. *Calm down, Max. Listen to their pitch.*

I didn't like the fact that McClure was in on this little secret. I was thinking military junta and I didn't like that thought. "If I help you take them out, then what?"

The director answered. "The Speaker of the House becomes president. She has the grit to handle the Russians."

McClure must have been reading my dark thoughts about his presence. He chimed in. "I think it would be good if the Speaker was in on this from the start. We could brief her on the problem. You worked for her before coming to the CIA. What do you think?"

I thought, *I have the feeling that I was handpicked for this a long time before I saw it coming and these two are way ahead of me and around the corner. I lived this scenario when I recruited spies. This time, I'm on the wrong side of the table.*

I told them, "Bringing the Speaker in now is a bad idea. She'll support the Constitution, not a coup in the planning stage. A better strategy would be to create conditions where she would normally have to be briefed on the RAMPART intel. Say, if she were number two in the line of succession to the presidency."

The director didn't shrink from the idea. "That would mean removing the vice president."

"I'm not killing anybody for you. Do you have anything that might make him bow out?"

"I may just have what you need."

CHAPTER 41

THE MANSION OVERLOOKED a lake twenty miles west of D.C. in Burke, Virginia. I rang the bell. A tall brunette wearing a black, floor-length, casual dress and way too much gold jewelry opened the door. She gave me a smile and a warm greeting.

"Thank you for coming... Mr. Brown." That was the name we had agreed on for this meeting. "She's waiting for you."

The hostess led me through a stop-and-frisk conducted by Secret Service agents before we entered a sunroom through French doors. My hostess departed and closed them behind her.

Gloria Pierce, the vice president's wife, sat on the edge of a chair, her arms folded and her ankles crossed. She wore a blue dress, pearls, and a frown, and didn't get up to greet me.

"I suppose you want to sit down," she said, glancing at the chair facing hers. I sat and laid my briefcase on the floor.

She said, "I dislike intrigue, Mr. Brown, or whatever your name is. I agreed to see you because you were recommended by someone I trust. What do you have that requires secrecy?"

"My intent was to honor your privacy and that of your husband. I couldn't approach him directly, nor do I think he would want me to. That's why I asked to see you... and because I know you were opposed to him running for vice president."

"I was opposed to him running for anything on a ticket with Ted Walldrum."

"Your husband will have to make some career decisions in the very near future. I came to provide information that may help."

"And why are you concerned about my husband's future?"

"I'm not concerned about his future. I'm concerned about the future of his country, as are you. If you'll permit me . . . ?"

I removed the digital recorder from my briefcase and set it on the table beside my chair. "I have a recording. It's a long one, but I'll play the segment of most interest to you and the vice president. Two people are speaking, President Walldrum and Ambassador Delores Garrison. I'm sure you'll recognize their voices." I pressed the PLAY button.

Walldrum: "I want you on my ticket. What do you want?"

Garrison: "If I join your campaign, I want your written pledge that I'll handle the defense and diplomatic portfolios. Frankly, Mr. President, you're a disaster in those areas. Your strength is on the domestic side. I'm proposing that when it comes to things international, you get the media events; you give me the credit for orchestrating things behind the scenes."

Walldrum (laughing): "You want to be my Dick Cheney?"

Garrison: "I want all those good 'ol boys who won't vote for a woman to be president to know that I can handle the job when my time comes."

Walldrum: "You'll have to take my word. I wouldn't put a promise like that on paper."

Garrison (coolly): "Maybe you've forgotten. You've issued a mountain of paper promises—contracts to pay companies who worked for you. Then, you reneged and took your IOU-holders to court and bled them with attorney fees until they gave up. I won't sign on, deliver the suburban, white, female vote for you and end up after the election on the sidelines with your broken promise and an empty portfolio."

Walldrum: "That won't happen. You will have plenty of visibility?"

Garrison: "Pierce has visibility. I want clout. Frankly, I don't need the VP's job. I'm sitting on a war chest of ten million in cash. I have promises of another thirty if I run. I can wait four years and run under my own banner."

Walldrum: "Will you feel comfortable working under me?"

Garrison: "I don't work *under* anyone. I work for voters. I've been a governor. Men are usually comfortable working under and with me."

Walldrum: "I want you on the ticket. You can't say 'no' to your president."

Garrison: "Then put your promise on paper and announce it frequently during the campaign. (Pause) What happens to Vice President Pierce? He knows where your bodies are buried. Will he go quietly when you announce I'm the pick for your second-term VP?"

Walldrum: "He's got no guts. He'll slink away like a dog, with his tail between his legs. I hate that little shit. He just stands behind me, smirking. I know what he's thinking. He's hoping I drop dead or get impeached and he'll just waltz into the Oval Office. The only reason I put him on my ticket in the first place was because he's a poster boy for evangelicals: God-fearing, clean, thrifty . . . all that bullshit. Well, fuck him! He's out. You're in, if you want to be with a winner."

When I stopped the recorder, Mrs. Pierce glared at it, then, at me. "Where did you get that?"

"Does it matter? You know it's authentic."

She gave the recorder another hateful look. "What do you want in return for . . . that?"

"What do you want for your husband? What legacy does he want for himself? He didn't come to Washington to play second fiddle to the likes of Ted Walldrum, only to get dumped. I think his best option is to take the moral high ground and resign from a corrupt administration. He can leave the White House on his own terms, or he can stay and get thrown under the bus like so many other 'good and faithful servants' who've labored at 1600 Pennsylvania Avenue."

She gave me a thoughtful look. "You didn't bring that recording here because you're concerned about my husband's reputation. It's already been tarnished. What's your game?"

"I'm an investigator of sorts. This past December, I was lying on a beach half a world away. The woman I love was beside me and I had enough money to last for the rest of my life. A man asked me to look into some concerns he had. During my investigation, I discovered that a very bad thing is about to happen to this country, and it involves the White House.

"What I discovered caused me to join a group that wants to prevent that bad thing from happening. It would be better for the country's defense if the vice president left the administration."

Mrs. Pierce looked at me. Her hostility had melted a little.

"Frankly, I—we—have no position for or against your husband or his politics. It's just that, in this particular instance, our interests in protecting the country and the vice president's well-being intersect. I'm here to persuade him to leave with dignity so we can do what we must. That's the truth. If you have a Bible handy, I'll take an oath on it."

"Oaths don't mean very much in Washington these days."

"We're not in Washington and I'm not from there. I'm a messenger from another world."

"You're not going to tell me what the bad thing is, are you?"

"I think you've heard enough from me and those on the recording."

"Will you leave the recording with me?"

"Of course not. It's proof that someone bugged the Oval Office."

"I could have the Secret Service agents detain you and confiscate it."

"If I thought you were that person, I would never have come. Good-bye, Mrs. Pierce."

*　*　*

General McClure and I sat behind tinted windows in the CIA direc-tor's SUV outside the general's home at Fort Myer, Virginia. It had been several weeks since I shared the recording with the vice presi-dent's wife.

The CIA Director told us, "Tomorrow, Walldrum will announce his pick for vice presidential running mate. It's going to be Pierce." She eyed me. "Apparently, the recording didn't do the trick."

"What recording?" asked McClure.

She was quick to say, "You don't want to know the details, General. Mr. Geller had a recording we hoped would motivate Vice President Pierce to resign. He didn't. We can't approach the president. So, we have no choice but to go to the Speaker." The director looked at me, again. "She knows you, Max. We need her guidance. We have no op-tions left without her."

"I'm not asking the Speaker of the House if she'd like to plan a coup. I know the answer. There may be another way. It's a very long shot."

CHAPTER 42

The Pentagon, Washington, D.C.

COUP D'ÉTAT, THAT's what we were planning. You couldn't spin it or make it pretty. General McClure and I were waiting in the Pentagon's famous and secure Tank when his aide, a colonel, ushered in Harold Whittaker, chief of staff for the Speaker of the U.S. House of Representatives. The aide departed, closing the door as McClure greeted Whittaker with a smile and a firm handshake.

"I'm sure it's been a busy day on Capitol Hill. Thank you for coming in, Harold."

"How could I resist? You sent a car for me and you said it wouldn't take long." Whittaker surveyed the room with a smile and fake awe. "So, this is the Pentagon's sanctum sanctorum. Is this where the joint chiefs make plans to destroy the world?"

"Or save it." The general was not amused. "You know Max Geller."

Whittaker was surprised to see me. "Hello, Max, I heard you were in Australia."

Before I could answer, McClure said, "Max brought me a proposal for a new war game and he's providing the CIA perspective for it."

Whittaker gave me a suspicious glance and addressed McClure. "Don't you have a current CIA employee as liaison for those things."

"Of course, but an outside perspective never hurts. Our regular liaison gives us the Agency line. For war games, we need an outside-the-box perspective. That's what Max brings. Take a seat, Harold."

We settled into comfortable chairs at the conference table, Whittaker on one side, facing me and the general.

Still a bit awed, Whittaker said, "I assume this room is soundproof."

"It is," replied McClure. "What's said in this room stays in this room."

"Why all the secrecy and security?"

"I need your insight to help me solve a delicate problem. Every time the president picks up a phone and calls overseas, the geopolitical and military ground shifts under my feet. The Pentagon can end up three steps, three weeks, or three years behind a new political reality."

Whittaker nodded, knowingly.

"I need a wargame model that incorporates new political assumptions to improve military responsiveness to civilian authority, especially in unusual situations involving national security emergencies. One reason the Pentagon is always behind the curve is that our current military exercises are based on political assumptions that have been discarded by the current president. Max has suggested a wargame model that incorporates a new and expanded set of political assumptions."

"That's quite a challenge, with this president," Whittaker acknowledged.

"Nevertheless, we must try. I want to game our capability to meet that challenge."

"I'm not sure how I can help, General."

"The Speaker of the House is third in line of succession to the Oval Office, after the vice president. As her chief of staff, I can use your insights to shape a game I'm considering."

Whittaker's eyebrows arched.

"You've participated in these games as a stand-in for the Speaker. You know that all of our scenarios for the military reinforcement of our European NATO allies are based on one key assumption, that Article 5 of the NATO Charter—an attack on one is an attack on all—will be invoked.

"Let me give you a hypothetical, Harold. Suppose the Pentagon has reliable intelligence that Russia plans to invade its former Soviet satellite nations on the Baltic Sea: Lithuania, Latvia, and Estonia . . . and Russia plans to attack when we are most vulnerable, during the transfer of presidential power, between the November election and the January inauguration."

Whittaker frowned. "The part about a Russian invasion, that's a hypothetical, right?"

McClure ignored him. "Our current president has made negative comments about NATO and even threatened to pull the U.S. out of the alliance. Suppose one or all of those Baltic states asks for military assistance under Article 5 of the Charter and the president refuses. Consider another assumption. What if the president and vice president were taken out of the chain of command simultaneously, their whereabouts known or unknown?

"Given your years with the current Speaker, tell me if she would be comfortable stepping into the Oval Office and giving the order for our forces to prevent or repel a Russian attack?"

Whittaker looked puzzled. "Short of a nuclear war, I can't think of a scenario where the president and vice president would be out of the chain of command at the same time."

The general leaned across the table, his voice urgent. "Think harder, Harold."

Whittaker's mouth fell open as comprehension registered. He sat back in the chair. His eyes widened as he looked at the general and me in disbelief. Then, the curtain came down, his features expressionless, his voice steady and firm. "In those circumstances, I don't think the Speaker would willingly walk into the Oval Office without a popular mandate. She defends constitutional processes at all costs."

McClure insisted, "The Constitution has already given her a mandate. Would she delay and abandon allies we're honor-bound to protect? Haven't we seen enough of that already in Ukraine and the Middle East?"

"You asked for my insight, General, not my agreement."

Whittaker stood. "Let me give both of you some advice. Avoid any military war games that assume the president and vice president are simultaneously out of the picture. Honest men and conspiracy nuts might misinterpret your intentions."

"But not you?"

Whittaker glanced around the room again. The ends of his mouth turned down. "Soundproof. That's good. What's said in the Tank stays in the Tank."

The general rose and went to the door. "Thank you for coming, Harold. I'll have my driver take you home." He offered a handshake that Whittaker ignored.

"No thank you. I'll take the Metro. I wouldn't want to disappear . . . like the president and vice president in one of your war games."

For a while, I sat with McClure. He was lost in thought. When the silence got heavy, I said, "General, I think we have to go with the plan I suggested earlier, the nuclear option."

"That is a very long shot, Geller."

"Do you have a better idea?"

"No. Contact the senator. If she agrees, we'll run with it, but it'll take time to put the people and hardware together. The FBI director has to be onboard for this. He has information we need to pull it off."

CHAPTER 43

Fall 2020
FBI Headquarters, Washington, D.C.

"GELLER, THAT'S CRAZY." The FBI Director didn't like my idea and he didn't like discussing it in his office.

General McClure came to my defense. "Geller is thinking outside the box, Brad."

"He's thinking outside the fucking ozone layer!"

"You wanted a peaceful solution to the problem. That's what Geller is proposing."

"Why did you bring it to me?" asked the director, making a point of ignoring yours truly.

I answered. "Your counterintelligence people know who's who inside the Russian Embassy. I need the name of someone who can get a message directly to the ambassador and won't run it by Russian intelligence first. We don't want Moscow to know what we're doing before General McClure talks to the ambassador."

Again, the director addressed McClure. "No. The Bureau is not getting involved in Geller's harebrained scheme. My business is law enforcement. You have a military problem. Find a military solution that doesn't involve the Bureau. And don't bring this issue to me again."

McClure made an unhappy face. "Let's go, Geller. We're done here."

"No, we're not done, not yet." I was angry. "Director, two years ago, I brought you evidence of corruption in the White House. You buried—"

"Don't say another word, Geller!"

"How about if I say it on the Sunday talk shows?"

"That's classified information. You'll go to jail."

"I don't think so. I collected that information as a private citizen, and it wasn't classified when I gave it to you. The Bureau classified it to protect an informant. Anyway, I didn't sign a non-disclosure statement. You want to keep that story off television, give me the name of someone with direct access to the Russian ambassador."

*   *   *

The name was Nadia. On Friday, I followed her into one of the upscale COVID-19 speakeasies that sprang up around D.C. for the beautiful—and stupid—people who had taken their disinfectant injection and believed they couldn't be touched by the virus. A "closed" sign was displayed on the door of the multi-story restaurant and bar. There were a few dim lights and no customers on the entry level. The action was upstairs, out of sight. Admittance was limited to VIP regulars.

I rang the newly installed bell for speakeasy clientele. By pressing two hundred-dollar bills against the crystal door pane and speaking Russian, the door guard let me in.

Upstairs, there was beverage service only. Tables and barstools were socially distanced, except for those who had found a companion with whom they didn't mind swapping potentially toxic air. No one wore a mask, except me.

The motif was imperial Russia. Walls were crimson and decorated with gold-framed versions of the double-headed eagle coat of arms, lighted paintings of tsars and tsarinas, and huge mirrors to make the rooms appear larger. The furniture was dark, plush leather, and there were some booths. Tables were covered with white cloths. The carpets picked up the red and brown accents from the walls and furniture, with flecks of yellow reflecting the framed wall hangings. The message was: bring money when you come.

It was early. The bar wasn't crowded, and my target was sitting there alone.

"Excuse me," I said in Russian. "Are you Nadia Mirov?"

Nadia turned away from the vodka martini she was stirring and gave me a seductive up-and-down. In a husky voice, she asked, "Who wants to know?"

I leaned into her perfume cloud and whispered, "Someone who wants to prevent nuclear war between Russia and the United States. I'm told you can get a message to the ambassador without going through your security services."

Nadia leaned away from me, rested her arm on the mink coat hanging on the back of her stool. She gave me a wry smile with full, red lips. "How do you know I'm not with security services?"

"If you were, I would feel more secure than I do right now."

She smiled, rich, dark hair flowing over one eye. I could understand why she had direct access to the Russian ambassador and why he would want direct access to her.

"Will you convey my message to the ambassador?"

The smile faded. "Who are you?"

"I'm not important. Give your ambassador the envelope I slipped into your coat pocket. It's an invitation to meet our top Pentagon general. The topic is OPERATION BEARCLAW. General McClure has not notified anyone in our government. He believes it would be mutually beneficial if the ambassador didn't discuss this with anyone in your government—or ours—until after the meeting."

* * *

One week later, the meeting was held at the ambassador's favorite Russian restaurant and bar. By coincidence—or not—it was the same one where I met Nadia. We wanted him on familiar ground and comfortable.

By the evening of our meeting, the speakeasy crowd had gotten the message from a sign on the front door: "Closed Indefinitely due to COVID-19." I paid the owner to give the place a good disinfecting, including our second-floor meeting room. No other services were required.

After the security hoods for each side checked the room for bombs, cameras, and hidden microphones, our team entered and sat down at a long, polished dinner table. Present were General McClure, the CIA Director, a Mr. Green from the NSA, and me. Oh, and we parked the surprise guest in the next room to wait for her cue.

The ambassador joined us a short time later. General McClure greeted him at the door, sat him at the head of the table, and introduced us, except that he just called me "Max."

"Why am I here, General?" asked the ambassador.

"To discuss war and peace."

The ambassador rolled his eyes. I think he had heard that one before.

McClure informed him, "We're here to discuss Russia's planned attack on the Baltic states of Estonia, Latvia, and Lithuania. Your Defense Ministry calls it OPERATION BEARCLAW."

The ambassador was dismissive. "I don't know what you are talking about. Where did you get such information, from one of your American conspiracy radio programs?"

The CIA director answered. "We got the information from a Russian army officer, Lieutenant Colonel Alexi Petrov. Do you know him?"

"Oh, yes. I know Petrov. He is an extortionist and purveyor of disinformation, a criminal wanted by the Russian Federation."

"Our government received three requests from yours to deliver Petrov and his wife," said the director. "Those requests stated the Petrovs had been kidnapped by CIA agents."

"Obviously, that was a mistake. Petrov is a fugitive." With a slight smile, the ambassador asked, "Is he in your custody now?"

"He was assassinated several weeks ago by persons unknown."

"Then justice has been done."

"Mr. Ambassador," said the director, "what matters is that we believe Petrov's statements and the documents he gave us to back them up."

"What disinformation did Petrov peddle to you in return for a soft life in the States?"

General McClure answered that one. "Colonel Petrov informed us that during our upcoming presidential election, Russia intends to engage in a bit of electronic mischief to create doubt regarding the winner. That would be annoying, but your follow-on plans might result in nuclear war. According to Petrov, during the period of transition between our November election and the January inauguration, Russia plans to invade our NATO allies on the Baltic Sea. He brought us your Defense Ministry's plan documenting that intention."

"Forgeries," declared the ambassador. "I told you the man is a disinformation artist."

The CIA director disagreed. "We believe them to be authentic." She handed the ambassador two documents. "Here is a photocopy of your war plan. This one is our English translation of it. Feel free to correct any errors."

The ambassador flipped through the documents and pushed them back to the CIA Director. "Those are just pieces of paper."

"We polygraphed and videotaped Petrov several times. He verified that war plan."

McClure chimed in. "For the third time, Ambassador, everyone at this table believes him. That is the first message we want you to take to your president."

"I don't take messages from sub-cabinet apparatchiks to my president. If there are messages, I take them from your State Department or your president."

"Since this is a military and intelligence matter, the State Department and White House are not involved. The second message we want you to convey to your president is that we have a plan of action to counter his attack on the Baltic states. We thought you would want to hear it so that you can inform him. Miscalculations lead to war."

I was thinking, *an innocent man would walk out now.* The ambassador didn't.

McClure said, "The gentleman seated to your right, Mr. Green, works in our National Security Agency. He has a Ph.D. in electrical engineering and master's degrees in both computer science and cryptology. His team develops codes and hardware that allow our president to launch nuclear missiles. He has something to show you."

Green hefted a 44-pound black leather satchel from the floor and placed it on the table in front of the ambassador. He removed an aluminum alloy attaché case from the satchel and unlocked it with a key on his long neck chain. Green raised the lid. It was the screen for a computer-like device. The words TOP SECRET appeared at the top of the screen, the U.S. presidential seal below. The bottom of the case contained an integrated black keyboard with an array of lights and switches near the base of the screen, surrounding a large red button inscribed with the word EXECUTE.

Mr. Green removed three black books from the case, describing them as he did. "Nuclear strike options. Safe locations for the president. Communication procedures."

"What you're looking at, Ambassador," said McClure, "is the football—everything needed to launch our nuclear weapons. The president has one just like it, with one exception. His doesn't work. This one does, and I control it. The president is far too unpredictable to be trusted with our nuclear arsenal."

McClure continued. "If your country launches an attack on the Baltic states and they invoke Article 5 of the NATO Charter, our president, being a good friend of the Russian Federation, may not respond. We will."

"This . . . is a coup," declared the ambassador. "You would go to jail, all of you."

"Mr. Ambassador, every one of us in this room has been in a combat zone as a soldier or civilian. Long ago we took an oath committing us to sacrifice our lives for this country. A few years in jail to save its honor is a small price to pay.

"Now," continued McClure, "you must be thinking that all you have to do to put an end to our plans is pick up the phone, call Ted Walldrum at the White House, and tell him about this meeting. He'll have us arrested and tried for sedition. I am equally sure that would happen. If it does, arrangements have been made to release your war plan and Colonel Petrov's videotaped statements to the world's major newspapers and to our NATO allies. I would remind you that England and France are also NATO members and have nuclear arsenals."

The ambassador sneered. "So, in the final analysis, the United States is just like those banana republics you disparage in your propaganda. The military steps in when they disapprove of decisions taken by their civilian leaders."

McClure disagreed. "On the contrary, Mr. Ambassador. We believe in civilian leadership. Max, please bring in our civilian leader. She will make the nuclear weapons release decision."

I went into the next room and returned with retired Senator Iris Dodson, a middle-aged blond woman of medium height. She wore a black satin shirt, pearls, and a black pantsuit to disguise her weight gain. Dodson greeted the ambassador with a cheery, "Hello, Dimitry. How's dirty tricks? Rigged any elections lately?" She sat at the end of the table opposite him.

The ambassador recoiled in surprise, but recovered quickly. His expression exuded contempt. "You," he hissed. "You are the leader of this coup?"

"*Coup* is a bit harsh, Dimitry. Consider us caretakers. We intend to guide our government through the period of uncertainty that your country has planned to create for us." She turned to McClure. "Show him the picture, General."

The ambassador examined the satellite photograph McClure gave him. "What is this?"

Senator Dodson explained. "That's a satellite shot of your president's favorite dacha on the Black Sea. When the first Russian tank crosses into a Baltic state, I'm going to put a Tomahawk missile right down the chimney of that house and turn it into a rock pile."

McClure cleared his throat.

"Yes, General?" said Dodson.

"Make that, two Tomahawks. The second one will turn the rock pile into talcum powder. Then, we'll start at your border with the Baltic states and walk nukes east to Moscow."

Dodson gave the ambassador a hard look.

He fumed, "This coup violates your precious Constitution, doesn't it?"

"A constitution," replied Dodson, "is just a worthless piece of paper—much like your own—unless citizens are willing to protect it—even die for it, as we are willing to do. Tell Vladimir Vladimirovich that if he thinks we're going to show up at a tank battle with a piece of paper, he has misjudged the American character. And he knows damned well he has misjudged mine."

Dodson stood. "That's all we have for you, Dimitry. Go tell your master that we know what he's up to and I mean to stop him. He fucked me during the election. It's his turn. Tell him to imagine how much pleasure it would give me to nuke his KGB ass into oblivion. Tell him I said that. Tell him word for word."

The ambassador gave Dodson an angry glare and departed without a word.

Dodson gave McClure a big smile. "Now, that's what I call shock and awe."

After Senator Dodson and her Secret Service detail departed, Mc-Clure asked no one in particular, "Do you think she was pissed that Russia screwed her in the last election?"

"'Hell hath no fury like a woman scorned,'" said the CIA director. "Well done, Max."

I wasn't ready to break out the champagne. "I'm not celebrating until I see what happens when the ambassador tells his president about this meeting."

CHAPTER 44

November 1, 2020
Office of the Russian Defense Minister, Moscow

"THE PRESIDENT'S AIDE is here to see you, sir," announced the voice on the intercom.

"Send him in," ordered the defense minister.

The aide, a colonel, entered the office and saluted. "Good afternoon, sir."

"Have you brought me good news, Colonel?"

"I have a message from the president. I leave the assessment of it to your good judgment."

"Spoken like a true diplomat." It wasn't a compliment.

The colonel unlocked a small briefcase attached to his left wrist, removed a single sheet of paper, and handed it to the minister.

The minister read it with growing concern. "I need to know the reason for this order. Is the president in his office?"

"Sir, this may not be a good time. The president was angry when I left him."

"With the ministry?" He meant, "With the minister?"

The colonel didn't respond.

"Tell me what you can without violating the president's confidence."

"The traitor Colonel Alexi Petrov gave the CIA your plan for OPERATION BEARCLAW. The Americans have undertaken countermeasures. The president is angry that the ministry staff did not detect

Colonel Petrov's treasonous tendencies before he defected. He also feels that the GRU exercised poor judgement by using Petrov, a man with so many of our secrets, as bait for Maxwell Geller."

"Thank you, Colonel. Tell the president I will issue the order to cancel OPERATION BEARCLAW immediately."

"Sir, the president wants you to call him after all units are stood down."

* * *

November 3, 2020
CIA Director's Office, Langley, Virginia

"Well done, Geller. Your idea worked." Those were the words of the CIA director with General McClure listening. She added, "NSA picked up lots of message traffic between the Russian Defense Ministry, its major headquarters, and subordinate field units. Satellite feeds show Russian military units being withdrawn from Baltic states' borders. Moscow called off OPERATION BEARCLAW."

General McClure cautioned the director, "Keep an eye on those units. Be sure they don't turn back and make a dash for the borders. Now that they're withdrawing, do you have any word on the Russians' next move?"

"Nothing on that in the ether or from human sources, so far."

CHAPTER 45

Saturday, Mid-November 2020
An indoor rifle range, Moscow

A BULLET TORE into Zabluda's target before he could pull the trigger on his rifle. He was irritated. This was a place for marksmen, not blind men who couldn't hit their own targets. He frowned to his right and left down the firing line to identify the idiot who had fired on his target. There, two shooters to his left, he saw the man known informally at the CIA as Source Ivan. Ivan smiled, raised his hand, and gave Zabluda a nod, indicating they meet behind the firing line.

Zabluda turned back to his rifle, adjusted the scope, and put three quick shots into the center ring of Ivan's target, as fast as he could operate the bolt and pull the trigger. His frustration somewhat relieved, he ejected the magazine from his rifle, cleared the chamber, and moved behind the line of masked and socially distanced shooters.

Ivan greeted him with, "Your father and I used to come here together to practice. You're a better shot than he ever was . . . and he was very good. I'm glad to see you've maintained your shooting skills. I think you could win the army sniper's trophy again."

"I won it twice. What would be the point?" Impatiently, Zabluda asked, "Are you here to tell me that your friends in Washington released me from their service?"

"They did, and there will be no repercussions. They understand your situation."

"That's nice of them," said Zabluda, with heavy sarcasm.

Ivan was unfazed. He said a pleasant, "You were correct. They value my services more highly than any action they could take against you."

"I knew they would. You didn't have to ruin my only pleasure by telling me in person. I asked you to never come near me again. I meant *never*."

"I would have honored your request, but, unfortunately, neither of us have a choice about this meeting. I'm here on official business."

"What business?"

"Business that can only be discussed between the two of us and in person." Quicky, Ivan added, "I bring you greetings from your benefactor in the Kremlin."

"Pu—"

"Don't say that name," Ivan cautioned, as he looked about to see if anyone was paying attention. "Your benefactor, who shall remain nameless, instructed me to convey his profound condolences on the loss of Mikhail. He wanted to know if you need anything."

"He's a little late, but give him my thanks. What I need is time. They say it heals the pain of loss. I doubt that."

"Have you spoken to your son Nikolai recently?"

"I wrote him when Mikhail was killed. He didn't answer. We're not on good terms."

"Your benefactor will be sorry to hear that, but I have news that may give you some comfort. The army will manage Nikolai's career to keep him from life-threatening assignments. He won't be told, of course. Brave young men gravitate to danger. Your benefactor said that you and your family have already made terrible sacrifices for Russia. He's grateful."

Zabluda asked, "What do you want?"

"To stay alive. Your benefactor is obsessed with finding the spy in his inner circle. He's giving each of us a task. I think he did it to see which tasks are leaked to the Americans."

"That's your problem. It doesn't concern me any longer."

"I'm afraid it does. My task is to give you a most secret assignment. Your benefactor wants you to assassinate this man." Ivan wouldn't say the name. He showed Zabluda a slip of paper containing a written acronym for the man's title: POTUS. President of the United States.

Zabluda laughed. "Of course. I'll leave immediately."

"I'm serious, Konstantine, as is your benefactor."

"Does my benefactor have any idea how difficult that would be?" Of course, he did. Zabluda was mentally treading water while he processed what was being asked of him.

"The level of difficulty is the reason you were chosen. You did well in London."

A Russian traitor and seven MI6 officers, thought Zabluda, *but . . .* "I wasn't trying to assassinate the queen or the prime minister in London."

"Consider this assignment a vote of confidence in your abilities."

Zabluda looked downrange as shots rang out from the firing line. In a distracted voice, he said, "In the advance sniper course, we studied that target's security arrangements. They are almost foolproof. Killing him would require nothing less than a suicide bomber, an infantry brigade, or a well-placed cruise missile."

Ivan disagreed. "In normal circumstances, your analysis would be correct. However, we have special intelligence about an event the target will attend and a vulnerability you can exploit."

"This makes no sense. The target has been a friend of Russia. My benefactor wants him killed because he lost an election?"

"The target can perform one final service for the Federation by dying," explained Ivan. "To his followers, he will die a hero, the victim of a Deep State conspiracy. With a little social media help from us, they will wreak havoc in the United States, maybe even bring down the government. That is your benefactor's ultimate goal. If you are the instrument that brings that about, I am authorized to tell you that you will get a promotion, maybe even skip a rank. I know you've always wanted to be a general. This is your opportunity."

"Do you find it ironic that my benefactor picked you to deliver this message? Are you going to tell the CIA?"

"It is ironic, and no, I will not inform the CIA. That would blow my cover."

"If you're serious, the order would have to come directly from my benefactor."

Ivan smiled. "You're a veteran of clandestine operations. Do you think you would be summoned to the highest level of our government to receive such an order in person?"

Zabluda knew that plausible denial was essential in such an operation. If he failed, he would be disavowed and branded a rogue with a personal agenda. If he succeeded, any direct link between him and the Kremlin might mean war with the United States. The last time a head of state gave a direct order to assassinate the U.S. president, it had ended badly. Saddam Hussein could attest to that, if one could schedule a séance.

Zabluda knew he didn't have a choice, and there was the dangle that his son Nikolai would be protected. Like his dead son, his remaining son was being used as hostage to bend him to a government's will. These bastards are all alike, American or Russian.

Zabluda asked, "Who else knows about this, other than you and my benefactor?"

"You will have a small support team in Washington. They won't know your name."

Zabluda made a disgusted face. "How is this supposed to work? There's a pandemic in progress."

"You will apply for leave immediately. Say you need to get away to deal with your grief."

Zabluda gave him a hateful stare.

"I'm sorry. It was just a suggestion. Say what you must. Tell your old shooting partner, Ipatiev, to do the same. There is a bag in my locker here." Ivan gave Zabluda the key. "It contains money, false identification papers, and instructions. You and Ipatiev must leave Russia as soon as possible, by whatever means you can. Make your way to the safehouse in Mexico City. You will rehearse the mission there. When you're ready, you will be smuggled into the United States at the Arizona border. Travel east to a safehouse in the state of Virginia, across the river from Washington, D.C. Your support team will be waiting to give you a final target briefing and take you to your shooting location. You have maximum flexibility as to how and when you travel, but you must arrive at the Virginia safehouse by New Year's Day."

"And what am I to do after I take the shot, kill myself?"

"I think you'll like what your benefactor has in mind for your escape. The shooting will be blamed on Maxwell Geller. You are to kill him yourself, at the site. Planning has already begun for that outcome."

CHAPTER 46

December 2020
Mexico

To AVOID RADAR detection, Zabluda's chartered jet flew low, skirting the western edge of Mexico City's sprawl, and landed at an apparently deserted airstrip. Before the steward could unload their bags, a camouflaged tanker emerged from the woods and began refueling the jet. No one spoke. This was a practiced routine.

At the far end of the airstrip, an aging Sikorsky Black Hawk helicopter waited, its rotor blades slicing through the air with a monotonous whop-whop-whop. The copilot and crew chief, in flight suits with no insignia or name tags, approached Zabluda and Ipatiev. The copilot asked Zabluda, "Are you here to see someone, *señor?*"

"Garcia," replied Zabluda.

"Follow me."

The helicopter took off to the east. After an hour's ride, the pilot banked into a hard left turn over a lake—Laguna de Zumpango—and landed on an empty soccer field not far from the water's edge. The chief unloaded their bags and sat them down a safe distance from the spinning helicopter blades. The helicopter lifted off and disappeared over the lake.

At the edge of the field, a dusty Land Rover waited in front of two small buildings. A teenager, tattooed from neck to wrists, ran to them. Without a word, he grabbed their bags and lugged them to the Land Rover, the two Russians following. The teenager stacked their luggage on the back seat, leaving room for Ipatiev. Zabluda rode next to the teenager who drove them to the Miguel Hidalgo neighborhood north of the city center. The drive ended in the courtyard of an unremarkable middle-class home. The teenager dismounted and motioned for the Russians to follow him. He rapped twice and returned to the Land Rover for their bags.

A mustachioed man in his forties, wearing a white shirt and khaki trousers, opened the door. He said a neutral, "Can I help you?"

"Garcia?" asked Zabluda.

"*Si, señor.* Welcome to Mexico. Please come in."

The teenager scooted around them, placed the Russians' bags in the hall, and disappeared into the house.

Zabluda asked, "Do you have a Christian name, Garcia?"

"*Si, señor.* I am Garcia."

"'Garcia' is your first and last name?"

"That is correct, *señor.*" It was also a lie.

Zabluda and Ipatiev exchanged glances and smiles.

Zabluda asked, "What is my name, Garcia?"

"I was told you are *El Jefe*, the boss. Your companion is to be called *El Segundo*, Number Two."

Garcia showed them to an austere room with two beds.

"It is not necessary to unpack, *señores,*" Garcia told them. "We leave for the mountains early tomorrow. In the meantime—" Garcia extended a hand to the dining room where the table was set—"I have food for you. After, I suggest a refreshing shower and rest."

Before dawn the next morning, Garcia and his two Russian guests loaded their weapons, bags, and rucksacks into the Land Rover. Garcia drove them back to the soccer field at the edge of Laguna de

Zumpango. The helicopter from the previous day landed, keeping its blades rotating. Again, the crew chief and copilot loaded their luggage. Garcia and the Russians climbed aboard.

The helicopter lifted off and headed southwest. After thirty minutes, cities and villages below them were replaced by mountains dotted with a few small villages. Two hours later, they were over tree-covered mountains. The chopper set down on a small grassy landing zone on the humpback of a ridge surrounded by other ridges. Again, the rotor blades never stopped turning. Zabluda, Ipatiev, and Garcia dismounted, and the crew chief helped them off-load their gear and several cartons of supplies. Minutes later, the helicopter vanished over the next ridge.

Zabluda looked at the mountains and woods around him and took a deep, satisfied breath. Once again, he and Ipatiev were a shooting team in the element they loved, doing what, long ago, they had been trained to do: kill men from a long way off with a good rifle.

Their roomy cabin was two hundred yards down the mountain, nestled in an elbow where the ridge twisted to the southwest. The threesome ferried the luggage and supplies from the landing zone to the cabin. Someone had been there recently to prep the place. The generator in the shack next to the cabin was humming. Lights and appliances were operating.

The cabin had a small entry hall and was laid out in the shape of a horseshoe. Five bedrooms formed the outside of the horseshoe. Inside the horseshoe, from right to left, were three rooms: a kitchen, a dining room just beyond the entry hall, and a recreation room.

Garcia said, "*Señores*, before we get settled, a few words of caution. We are in wild country, as you saw from the helicopter. In these mountains there are spiders, scorpions, snakes, and big cats: jaguar, puma, bobcat, margay, and ocelot. Never leave the immediate area of the cabin without your rifle. Here, we go locked and loaded at all times, except inside the cabin."

Zabluda asked, "Are we likely to get any surprise visitors?"

"No, *señor*. The nearest village is Pascala. It is small and a long, difficult walk over the mountains."

"What about hunters? You said there were big cats here. Suppose they find us shooting at simulated human targets and ask questions."

"In that case, it will be our job to see that those who ask them do not leave this place." Garcia added, "One more thing. If you have cell phones, no calls, *por favor*—otherwise, hunters may come and they won't be looking for wildlife."

Ipatiev asked, "Is female companionship available?"

Garcia was quick with, "Regrettably, no, *señor*."

"Vodka?" asked Ipatiev.

"No, *señor*."

Ipatiev turned to Zabluda. "*Señor* Garcia is the Abominable No-man." With irritation, he asked his host, "Are you running a monastery here, Garcia?"

"You will be here for just a short time, *El Segundo*. This is a business camp, not a recreational one. Only businesspeople are brought here to conduct business in private. Guests have an interest in keeping this place and what goes on here secret. We don't allow distractions."

Garcia shifted topics. "Meals. I will cook one of your choice, each day, breakfast or supper. If you desire other meals, there are combat rations and you have use of the kitchen. We begin practice at 7:30. See you in the morning, *señores*."

At 7:30 a.m. Zabluda, Ipatiev, and Garcia gathered on a flat expanse of cleared ground in front of the cabin. Zabluda lay on a tarp behind his rifle, pointed at a target one hundred yards away. The rifle was of American manufacture. It wouldn't do to leave a Russian rifle behind after shooting an American president. Ipatiev had set up a tripod-mounted spotter scope and range finder. Using the scope, Ipatiev observed the strike of the bullets on the target and called adjustments to Zabluda. Garcia stood to the side, observing, as the Russians went about checking the accuracy of the rifle they hoped would kill the President of the United States.

The process of zeroing—setting the rifle's sights so that the point of aim was the same as the point of impact on the target—went quickly. When two of Zabluda's hits were overlapping holes and the third below and almost touching the other two, he shifted to a second target. He drilled three shots into a triangular Venn diagram and pronounced the weapon zeroed. That ended the short-range practice, and it wasn't nine o'clock. However, that particular zero told Zabluda his rifle and scope were working properly at one hundred yards. Now, he had to zero the rifle for the actual distance over which he would be shooting in Washington.

Garcia looked through the spotter scope at Zabluda's shot group on each target. "*Bueno, señores.* Now, we go to practice at a place that is similar to conditions at your actual target."

They packed their gear in rucksacks, slung their rifles across their backs, and trekked for ninety minutes to the place Garcia had described. From the top of the next ridge, they picked their way down to an outcropping overlooking a flat valley floor about a thousand yards wide.

Garcia announced, "This is the place, *Jefe*." He handed Zabluda binoculars and pointed to four crude wooden head-and-shoulders silhouettes on the valley floor. "There are your targets. Ground distance, the actual target will be 670 meters, or 733 yards, if you prefer. The elevation when you actually shoot will be 154 meters, or 505 feet, about where we are now."

Zabluda said, "I will be shooting from a building, then?"

"*Si*, that is what I was told."

Zabluda took a tarp from his rucksack and laid it on the ground near the rim of the outcropping and got into the prone position, steadying his rifle on a filled sandbag. Behind Zabluda and to his left, Ipatiev set up the tripod-mounted spotting scope with built-in laser range finder and an additional piece of equipment that resembled a cell phone.

Garcia asked, "What is that cell phone device, *El Segundo*?"

"It's not a cell phone. It's a weather monitor with a self-contained ballistic computer."

"What is its purpose?"

"Have you done any long-range shooting?"

"No, *señor*. My shooting has been at close range with a pistol."

Ipatiev gave him a quizzical look but didn't question the close-range statement. "When you shoot at close range on a relatively flat surface—as we did at the cabin—not much affects the path of the bullet. At longer ranges—like for those targets in the valley—many factors affect where the bullet hits the target: wind speed and direction, temperature, muzzle velocity, bullet length, barometric pressure, even the distance of the scope above the bore. This device collects that information, analyzes it, and tells *El Jefe* where to aim so he can hit the target with his first shot. Sometimes, you don't get a second."

Zabluda growled, "Can we start before we need night vision goggles to see the targets?"

With that, the two Russians began a sequence of commands—in their native language—to engage the first target.

As spotter, Ipatiev started the sequence by identifying the target. "Target 1, to your right, head-and-shoulders, white tie." Garcia had painted ties of different colors on the black silhouettes.

Zabluda repeated the description to verify he was shooting at the target Ipatiev designated.

Ipatiev: "Check parallax and mil."

Zabluda checked that his eye and scope optics were aligned and on target, and announced the mil reading on his scope. Ipatiev consulted the ballistics computer to verify that Zabluda was aimed at the proper angle to hit the target, given environmental conditions.

Ipatiev: "Check level."

Zabluda checked to be sure his crosshairs were level on the target.

Ipatiev: "Holdover 3.4." That was the number of inches Zabluda had to position his crosshairs above the target to counter the effects of gravity on the bullet.

Zabluda adjusted his scope nob and took up the trigger slack. "Ready."

Ipatiev: "Left 4," was the windage adjustment.

Zabluda made the adjustment and fired. Bullet away.

Methodically, they engaged one target after another. Garcia watched as Zabluda drilled tight shot groups into the neckties of the first two targets. When Zabluda shifted his position to engage the third target, Garcia said, "*Jefe*, I am told you will be taking a head shot. I suggest you raise your aim point."

Zabluda's first shots went over the target's head. He made adjustments. After the head-shot misses became hits, he rolled away from his rifle. "That's enough for today."

The three men packed their gear and trekked back over the ridge to the cabin.

After their meal, Garcia cleaned the kitchen. Zabluda and Ipatiev remained at the table.

Ipatiev observed, "You were irritated today, my friend. What's wrong?"

Zabluda drew a breath before saying, "Every time I looked through that scope, I saw Mikhail's face on the target."

Ipatiev had also lost a son. "Do you want me to take the shot?"

"No. It's my responsibility. If anything goes wrong, I don't want them blaming you."

"If anything goes wrong, Moscow will throw *both* of us to the wolves."

Zabluda grunted. "If everything goes *right*, Moscow will throw us to the wolves."

Garcia joined them and Ipatiev asked, "*Señor* Garcia, have you always been a host for shooting parties?"

"This is a first for me. I am a materials engineer."

Ipatiev laughed. "Were you sent here as punishment?"

"No, *señor*. I was sent because you have need of my knowledge."

The statement distracted Zabluda from thoughts of Mikhail. Sarcastically, he asked, "Are you going to teach us to be better marksmen, *Señor* Garcia?"

"If I can, *Jefe*. Come to the recreation room. I will show you."

They followed Garcia to the rec room and joined him at a poker table. On it were two boxes, each holding twenty-five rounds of rifle ammunition, and a file card. Lying flat next to the boxes was what appeared to be a thick chunk of glass, the size of a computer keyboard.

Garcia stood the glass rectangle on its edge. "This appears to be a thick pane of glass. You can see through it with almost no distortion. Actually, it is a sandwich made of two panes of an acrylic alloy with a liquid center, a marvel of chemistry and engineering. It is designed to slow and deflect a bullet passing through. You can have a perfect aim, but a bullet passing through this material will be slowed and deflected from its intended aim point. The thickness of the front and back panes and the liquid center will either stop a bullet or slow it so that even if it hits a target not wearing body armor, the wound will most likely not be fatal."

Zabluda examined the pane and passed it to Ipatiev.

Garcia said, "Your target will be protected by a shield of this material. You need a head shot to take him out. To complicate matters, the shield will extend several inches above the target's head. I'm told you must aim above the shield and let gravity take your bullet to the target." Garcia slid the two boxes and a file card over to Zabluda. "The load and aerodynamic characteristics of these bullets have been modified to improve your chances of hitting your target. This card contains bullet data I'm told you need for your shooting calculations. We practice with these data tomorrow."

"Did you modify the ammunition?"

Garcia took his time answering and addressing both Russians. "You are guests here. So, I say this with respect and concern for your … comfort. Our organization values privacy. One who asks too many questions, himself, becomes a question mark. That is a dangerous mark to carry."

Zabluda bristled. "Are you threatening me, Garcia?"

"No, *Jefe*. A threat is something to be carried out in the future. I am acquainting you with history. Good night, *señores*."

The next morning found them at the outcropping from which Zabluda fired his practice rounds the previous day. Looking down into the valley through binoculars, Zabluda examined his new targets. The head-and-shoulders silhouettes had been replaced by three life-size silhouettes of standing men. Garcia had pulled them from their hiding place among the rocks. The targets were in a row, three feet apart. Earlier, Zabluda had watched with interest as Garcia drew a line in the sand three feet in front of the new targets and extending it a foot beyond the end targets. From his rucksack, Garcia took several sections of metal pole and threaded them together to form two poles, each eight feet high. He forced them into holes at either end of his sand line and stabilized them with sandbags. Finally, he connected the poles with a taut length of clothesline. Garcia had constructed a clothesline three feet in front of the silhouette targets and a foot above them.

When he climbed back up to the outcropping, Zabluda asked, "What is the purpose of the clothesline?"

"The standing silhouettes are your targets. They are six feet three inches tall, the height of your actual target. The clothesline represents the acrylic shield that will be protecting your target. It is a foot above your target's head. You must adjust your sights and firing angle so that the bullet goes above the clothesline and let gravity guide your bullet to the target for a head shot. Remember, the shield will deflect your bullet. A head shot, above the shield, is your only opportunity to take out your target. Use the modified rounds for this practice."

Zabluda ignored Garcia and loaded conventional rounds. For the next thirty minutes, with Ipatiev spotting, operating the ballistics computer, and calling adjustments, Zabluda tried to put rounds over the clothesline and into the target's head. The bullets went over the clothesline and headed for Earth orbit.

Without a word, Garcia went to Zabluda and placed a box of modified rounds on the tarp beside him.

When the modified rounds shredded the head of the first target, Zabluda shifted his aim to the second, his rounds cleared the clothesline and landed in a tight group on the target. He gave Garcia a look that might have been admiration or thanks. Zabluda chambered a round, took aim on the third target, and put a round over the clothesline through the forehead of the silhouette.

He did it twice more and said, "Let's go to the cabin." He didn't sound satisfied; he sounded angry. Maybe he had seen Mikhail again.

The next day, the helicopter touched down on the landing zone, where it had dropped them three days earlier. Garcia, Zabluda, and Ipatiev loaded their baggage and climbed aboard. Instead of returning to Mexico City, the chopper headed north and dropped them at Nogales International Airport. They took a hotel room in Garcia's name and rested. At nightfall, Garcia loaded them and their baggage into an air-conditioned VW van and drove into the desert. The compass on the dashboard told Zabluda they were headed north-northwest. Near midnight, Garcia stopped the van and they had a meal of combat rations and bottled water. A little after midnight, four men came out of the desert like ghosts and surrounded the van. Garcia got out and spoke to the leader. Minutes later, he returned to the van with a wiry, weathered man. He had piercing black eyes and wore camouflage fatigues. A MAC-10 machine pistol with silencer was slung across his chest.

"I leave you now, *señores*," said Garcia. "This is Juan. He has been paid to guide you across the border. His helpers will carry your luggage. There is a truck waiting for you south of Tucson. It will take you to the house of a friend. Rest until you are ready to travel. Then, you are on your own. A word of advice. It is impolite to ask questions from here on, unless they concern your travel arrangements. *Buena suerte, mis amigos.* Good luck." He drove off in the van.

Juan said, "There are patrols on both sides of the border. No talking. No smoking. No light. No noise. Follow me. Do what I do. If there is shooting, I do it. We go through a tunnel. It comes out on the U.S. side. Then we walk, maybe ninety minutes, to the pickup point. The truck will be waiting. If not, we wait. Let's go. *Vamos.*"

CHAPTER 47

December 2020
Jill Rucker's Condo, Sterling, Virginia

"WHAT'S WRONG, MAX?" Jill asked, as we were finishing a late dinner.

"Nothing." I tried to make it sound true, but it fell flat.

"That nothing is giving you nightmares. You've been yelling in your sleep. I heard you all the way into my bedroom. And you look worried. The Max Geller I know sleeps like a dead man and worries about nothing. Are you worried about Vanessa?"

"Yeah, but that's not it."

"Work?"

"You could call it that. I can't talk about it."

"Sure, you can. I know more about the RAMPART operation than you do, and my security clearance is higher than yours. In fact, you don't even have a clearance."

"Clearance is not the problem. If I tell you, you can't unhear it. You'll be a co-conspirator."

"Two years ago, I tried to shoot you. You could have destroyed my career. You didn't. Before that, we shot our way out of Moscow. We're blood family. You can tell me anything."

I was worried and made the leap. "The RAMPART operation didn't feel right from the start. Rodney told me RAMPART—Petrov—got his attention by giving up part of the Russian war plan for Syria. You don't give some Russian walk-in with low-value intel on Syria a seat on a diplomatic flight out of Moscow. That's too much risk for too little payoff."

"I agree. So, what was the bait that hooked Rodney?"

"You don't know everything about RAMPART. This is the part where you cover your ears."

"Oh, for God's sake, Max . . ."

"Okay. Forget Syria. Petrov knew Russia planned to attack and re-occupy her former satellite states on the Baltic: Estonia, Lithuania, and Latvia. The op was scheduled to kick off between our November presidential election and Inauguration Day in January."

Jill's jaw dropped.

"The CIA and the Pentagon are afraid that the current occupants of the White House won't come to the aid of NATO when Russia attacks. I've been helping with a plan to cut the president and vice president out of the chain of command and let the Speaker of the House—or someone else—stop the attacks."

With quiet awe, Jill said, "That's a coup, Max."

"Yeah, and I may be the fall guy when it goes down. As far back as Australia, I've had the feeling that I'm a couple of laps behind Rodney on the RAMPART op. Long before I went to Moscow, I think Rodney, the CIA director, General McClure, and the rest of the conspirators had gamed out this coup, with me as the fall guy."

"That sounds a bit paranoid, Max. Do you have any evidence?"

I briefed Jill on the meetings with General McClure, the CIA director, FBI director, the vice president's wife, the Speaker's chief of staff, the senator, everything. I told her, "What's worrying me is that in all of those meetings, I'm being sold as the face of the conspiracy.

'Max is our consultant.' 'What do you think of Max's idea?' 'Max, take this tape to the VP's wife.' It feels and sounds like a setup."

"Jesus, Max, that does sound bad." After some thought, Jill said, "With the exception of your visit to the vice president's wife, you weren't alone in those planning meetings. General McClure and the director were with you. When this is over, it won't matter if they say they were duped, and you were the brain and hand behind the coup. Everyone knows they were with you. Blaming you only works if—Oh, hell!"

"It only works if I'm dead."

That plunged us into silence until Jill asked, "How can I help?"

"Can you take some time off, just until after the inauguration? I'll pay your mortgage."

"That should be easy, with the virus lockdown and Rodney away. How would it help?"

"I need you to watch my back."

* * *

A week after Jill took leave, the Agency called her into the Langley campus for a day. She explained when she returned to the condo. "The counterintelligence staff had questions about that Mexico City wild goose chase you sent me on two years ago." Her tone told me she was still angry about the Mexico loyalty test I gave her, after we shot our way out of Moscow, and before I knew she was with the CIA. That was her problem. I had moved on.

I asked, "What did they want to know?"

"They asked me about one of the two Russians who were waiting for me at the airport. When I came out of the arrival hall, I heard one of them say, 'Ipatiev, here she comes.' I put that in my after-action report and that was the end of it."

"And . . . ?"

"Three days ago, Ipatiev was back on the radar. A border patrolman was tracking a small group of illegals, crossing from around Nogales into Arizona. He stumbled into one of them taking a pee. Somebody yelled, 'Ipatiev, look out!' Ipatiev hit the ground. The patrolman took three rounds, but told his story on the way to surgery, and he captured Ipatiev on his body cam."

"Are you sure about that name?"

"The patrolman was sure. He said the man who shouted had a Russian or Eastern European accent. Homeland Security ran Ipatiev's name and photo past the Five Eyes and got a hit from the Aussies. Two weeks ago, Ipatiev was caught on CCTV near a crime scene. He's wanted for questioning about a murder in Sydney. Do you know him, Max?"

"No." Hell, yes, I knew him. He walked out of a villa in Geneva with 2.5 million dollars of mine in a suitcase, but I got my revenge.

The Sydney-murder-Ipatiev connections gave me a sinking feeling. I didn't want the rest of the story, but I had to ask. "Who was the victim?"

"I'm sorry, Max. It was Vanessa."

That was a gut punch. My knees went weak. I sat down. Jill came over and put a hand on my shoulder. My response was a flash of anger. "Two weeks ago! Why am I just being told?"

"They were found in a burned-out car. It took dental records and time to ID them."

"They! Who the hell are *they*!"

"Vanessa was . . . with a date, according to a friend of hers in Sydney." A second gut punch. I was speechless.

Jill squeezed my shoulder gently and held it.

The anger wouldn't leave. "You said it took a few days to ID Vanessa. Why didn't the Agency tell me right away? I'm on her emergency notification list!"

"Max . . . Vanessa removed you from her list the same week you left for Moscow to bring out RAMPART. I guess she was really pissed that Rodney sent you instead of her."

The anger gave way to a hollowed-out feeling. Vanessa was gone. There was no space for denial and bargaining, only acceptance, grief, and guilt. "She wasn't trained! I went to Moscow so she wouldn't get herself killed or screw the op!"

Suddenly, the sense of loss was overwhelming. I sat, staring at nothing, Jill standing over me, her hand gentle on my shoulder.

She said, "There's one more thing. The Agency found a postcard addressed to you in Vanessa's mailbox. It didn't come in the mail. Someone put it there. It had a return address, but no stamp or postmark. The Agency traced the return address to a house outside Geneva, Switzerland. It was a dead end." Jill took a folded photocopy from the pocket of her slacks and handed it to me.

I read the neat penmanship: *Did money buy you happiness?*

"Other than what it says, does it have a hidden meaning?"

"It means Zabluda or Ipatiev killed Vanessa to get even with me."

"I don't understand. Zabluda's an Agency asset. What's his beef with you?"

"Two years ago, he stole five million dollars from me at that Geneva address. I got it back and probably ruined his career."

"With the Russians or the CIA?"

"Both, I hope." Inside, the rage returned to fight depression. Rage was winning.

CHAPTER 48

December 30, 2020
Alexandria, Virginia

THE ASSASSINS WERE gathered in a row house minutes from the 14th Street Bridge, a major route over the Potomac River into downtown Washington, D.C.

Zabluda and Ipatiev had arrived two nights earlier in the wee hours to avoid prying eyes. They were tired after the 2,300-mile drive from Tucson to Alexandria. Their Mexican friends on the U.S. side of the border had provided another VW van so they wouldn't have to use motels. They took turns sleeping and driving, stopping only for bathroom breaks and the occasional hot meal, preferring combat rations as they rode to avoid losing travel time. After Juan shot the patrolman at the border, they wanted to get as far away from Arizona as fast as possible. In Alexandria, they rested for a night and a day before getting their mission briefing.

The briefer was a short, stocky man with slick black hair and glasses. He had military bearing, wore an expensive suit, and exuded an air of superiority. Zabluda suspected he was SVR from the Russian embassy in Washington.

A second-floor bedroom had been converted to an austere briefing room. The bed had been removed and replaced by a tall cork bulletin board that leaned against the wall, with photographs thumbtacked to it. An assortment of chairs, folding and otherwise, were filled by Zabluda, Ipatiev, and eight strangers.

The briefer opened with, "Introductions? There are only a few things you need to know about each other. Everyone in this room is an experienced professional." He pointed to Zabluda. "This man goes by the name his Mexican friends gave him, *El Jefe*. He is your leader. His second in command—" he pointed to Ipatiev— "is *El Segundo*. The rest of you will be assigned code names for the purpose of radio and all other communications. You will not exchange names or other personal data."

Addressing Zabluda and pointing to a photograph on the cork board, the briefer said, "You will establish your shooting platform on the top-floor observation deck of this building. It's closed because of the COVID virus. When you arrive, it will be occupied by eight men: two security guards at the entrance, a three-man observation team on the top-floor observation deck, and a three-man team on the exhibit floor below them, resting. These teams alternate every ninety minutes to keep fresh eyes on the rally from the observation deck. You must take out the teams on the exhibit deck and the observation deck simultaneously, before they raise the alarm."

The briefer directed their attention to the next photograph. "He is your target, Ted Walldrum, President of the United States. That was the last time his name or position will be used. From now on, you will refer to him by the code name CROSSFIRE. Speak English only. The Secret Service can monitor your radio communications. Unfortunately, we cannot hack theirs. So, once you are in control of the observation deck, take a radio from one of the dead agents and monitor the Secret Service net for threats to your position."

"Transportation?" asked Ipatiev.

"Two vehicles." The briefer pointed to their photos. "*El Jefe, El Segundo*, and four men will be concealed in the rear compartment of the first vehicle. A driver and assistant will ride in the cab and take down the lobby guards. As soon as the lobby guards have been neutralized, the two men in the second vehicle will dismount and secure the lobby to keep any curious rally-goers away. Then, everyone from the first vehicle will enter the building, form two teams, take out the Secret Service observers on the exhibit and observation decks, and prepare the shooting platform."

Ipatiev looked up from a blueprint he had been studying. "The agents on both floors must be taken out at the same time. There's only one elevator. How do we accomplish that?"

"One team has to climb the stairs to the exhibit deck. The second team takes the elevator to the observation deck. Your attacks must be coordinated. When the elevator doors open on the observation deck, the other team must take out the agents on the exhibit deck below."

Ipatiev shot a skeptical glance at Zabluda.

Zabluda had another concern. "Once we are in control, everyone will be inside. How will we get atmospheric data—wind speed and so forth—to calculate a firing solution?"

"I was coming to that. We will have an agent in the rally crowd collecting data and transmitting it electronically to your ballistic computer. His instrument will be disguised as a camera."

The briefer moved on. "Once CROSSFIRE is in your sights, you have time to get off one shot—maybe two—before your location is known. When the Secret Service realizes that shots have been fired, three things will happen. The president will be surrounded and pulled from the stage, alive or not. Most Secret Service agents will look up, because a shot from the ground would have hit the president's protective shield. That will not happen if you do your job. Lastly, the Secret Service will contact their overwatch stations—your building being one—to see if they spotted the shooter. When your station doesn't answer, the quick reaction force will be deployed to surround your building. Therefore, you must leave immediately after taking the shot. If you delay, you will be trapped."

"Exit arrangements?" asked Zabluda.

"As soon as the Secret Service agents are dead and your shooting platform is prepared, the ambulance driver and one of the entrance guards will leave the building and prepare to drive you away from the site. After you take the shot at CROSSFIRE, leave the building immediately. Go to the ambulance. Your driver will take you to a safehouse in the district. Stay there until you get a message from me that it's safe to move."

"I don't like being in Washington. I might be recognized. Why can't we return to this house?"

"News of the president's death will go out immediately. The police will block bridges over the Potomac River, major roads, and public transportation. Thousands will have come to Washington just for the day to attend the rally. Within hours, exit avenues will have to reopen to let them leave. When they do, there will be a heavy police presence, with identification checks in effect."

"How long before we can leave Washington?" asked Zabluda.

"I will let you know. You have provisions for several days at the safehouse."

"Have you forgotten Maxwell Geller?"

"I'll get to him in a moment. You and Geller have history. I didn't want you distracted by it. First, you must be an established presence in the city before the rally attendees arrive. Tonight, you and *El Segundo* will be driven to a hotel near the rally location. Your cover is that you are in Washington to celebrate the New Year's holiday and to see the sights. The two mission vehicles are in your hotel garage and will remain there until shooting day. Your weapons, equipment, and communications gear will be kept in those vehicles until that day. Nothing incriminating will be kept in your hotel room. Hotel staffs throughout the area have been told to report any suspicious items, such as guns, ammunition, and bomb-making materials.

"Maxwell Geller will be delivered to your hotel prior to your departure for the shooting site. When the observation floor is secured, bring Geller up and make sure his fingerprints are on the rifle before you shoot. You won't have time afterwards. When you have taken your shot at CROSSFIRE, kill Geller with a Secret Service agent's pistol. Be sure to shoot him in the back from a low angle. Make it appear that Geller was holding the rifle when he was shot by the courageous Secret Service agent. Be sure to place the rifle near Geller before you leave the observation floor."

CHAPTER 49

January 5, 2021
Jill Rucker's Condo, Sterling, Virginia

"MR. GELLER, ARE you there?" His voice came over the intercom with an unpleasant metallic sound, as he pressed the doorbell again. I held the remote that controlled the door intercom and camera, and watched the persistent doorbell ringer on the TV screen.

Jill was out shopping. I was alone in the condo and disinclined to respond to external stimuli. The scotch-induced pain in my head did not need a doorbell accompaniment. I had spent the previous evening—make that the previous evenings—drowning thoughts of Vanessa and what might have been in a pool that had no bottom. The only beneficial aspect of the scotch was that it put the brakes on my impulse to rush into the COVID-19-infected streets and hunt down Zabluda and his sidekick, Ipatiev. The part of my brain that wasn't shedding dead cells reminded me that I had no idea where to look for Zabluda. Besides, I figured he would come looking for me, sooner or later. Anyone who burned Vanessa alive would want to see how much pain her death had inflicted. So, I was not inclined to answer the door, but the damned bell would not stop ringing.

The doorbell ringer on Jill's TV screen was in his thirties and wore a cap with a shiny black visor, and a tan uniform with a logo on the pocket. It matched the logo on his panel truck at the curb: Condor Legal Delivery Service.

As I watched this guy lean on the bell again, I thought of the sign that hung on the door of Frank Sinatra's Palm Springs home: "If you haven't been invited, you'd better have a damn good reason for ringing this bell."

I sighed and pressed the remote's mic symbol. "What do you want?"

The guy looked into the camera and said, "I have a letter for Mr. Maxwell Geller."

"Who gave you this address?"

"My dispatcher."

"Where did he get it?"

"Probably from one of the lawyers we deliver for. Is Mr. Geller here or not?"

"Leave the letter. I'll get it to him."

"I can't do that, sir. Gotta have a signature. This is an IEMD letter."

"What's 'IEMD'?"

"In Event of My Death. I guess Mr. Geller lost a friend or family member." Impatiently, he added, "Look, I gotta make a run to Hamilton. Will Mr. Geller be home later? I can swing by on my way back to D.C."

"Who's the letter from?"

He made a face and read the envelope. "A Vanessa Blake in Sydney, Australia."

"What's the date on the postmark?"

"Are you Geller or a postal inspector? There ain't no postmark. I'm delivering for the lawyer."

"I'm Geller. Hang on. Be down in a sec."

"Yeah. Well, bring some ID. You just spent a lotta time telling me Geller wasn't here."

I slipped the Glock into the back of my belt, went downstairs, and opened the door.

The messenger said, "I'm sorry for your loss, Mr. Geller. Sign here." He shoved the electronic signature pad at me. When I reached for it, he hit me with the stun gun.

CHAPTER 50

January 6, 2021, 10:15 a.m.
Washington, D. C.

THE AMBULANCE STOPPED in front of the building and parked to block the glass entry doors from the view of casual observers. Not far away, 30,000 not-so-casual observers had gathered on The Ellipse, eight hundred feet from the White House's South Lawn, to hear warm-up speakers and await the arrival of President Ted Walldrum. Two emergency medical technicians hopped out of the ambulance cab, grabbed resuscitation equipment from a side compartment, and quick-stepped to the building's entrance.

A uniformed Secret Service officer opened the door and stepped outside. He held up his palm, signaling them to stop, and said an unfriendly, "What do you want?"

"We got a call there was a possible heart attack victim here," explained one of the EMTs.

"You got the wrong address, pal."

The EMT driver laughed and looked up. "This is the Washington Monument, ain't it?"

Disgusted, the other EMT said, "Come on, Larry, let's go. It's just another crank call." He told the Secret Service officer, "The 9-1-1 line's been gettin' thirty crank calls a day since this rally mob came to town. What kind of people do that?"

"The wrong kind," replied the officer. A second officer came to the door and stood inside, hand near his gun. The outside officer said, "Thanks for coming, but you need to move on."

The EMTs turned away, dropped their equipment, and turned back with guns blazing. Silencers on the EMTs' pistols kept the noise down as bullets dropped the guards. Two rounds penetrated the glass door and killed the inside officer. The outside officer fell to the pavement with a head wound. Both were dead when they dropped.

On cue, a National Park Service vehicle drove up. Two uniformed rangers—men from the safehouse briefing—jumped out and dragged the downed officer into the monument's security screening facility and took up security positions. Outside, the EMTs pasted two large Kennedy Center posters over spiderweb patterns of bullet holes and concentric cracks in the glass door.

The lead EMT took a quick look at the mob on The Ellipse and spoke into the mic clipped to his jacket. "All clear. Bring him in."

The back doors of the ambulance slammed open. Zabluda, Ipatiev, and four EMT-clad gunmen scurried out carrying large canvas bags of equipment. Two of the gunmen pulled out a collapsible gurney with Max Geller strapped to it. There was a gag in his mouth. He was covered with a blanket, neck to feet. The gunmen pushed the gurney through the security screening facility, into the monument's lobby, and parked it near the elevator. One of the fake National Park Service officers watched over Geller. The second fake NPS officer replaced the security guards behind the shattered glass doors in the screening facility. The other six men in EMT uniforms formed into two teams of three. The team led by Ipatiev would take down the Secret Service spotters on the observation deck. The other three-man team, led by Zabluda, would climb the stairs and take down the spotters resting on the exhibit deck.

There are 896 steps to the monument's observation deck. The speed record for climbing them is twenty-one minutes. Zabluda and his men had to walk up only 881 to the exhibit deck.

Zabluda told Ipatiev, "Give me thirty minutes to get into position below the exhibit deck. I'll text you when I'm ready. That's your signal to come up on the elevator. Don't load until you get my signal. Once you open the elevator doors, both decks will know someone is coming up.

"The monument elevator takes a minute and forty seconds to reach the observation deck. Text me just before the elevator doors open. We will hit both decks at the same time."

To his team, Zabluda said, "Let's take a walk." They headed for the stairs.

Ipatiev returned to the security screening facility where he took a radio from one of the dead Secret Service guards, clipped it to his belt, and fitted the earpiece into his own ear. He rejoined his team in the lobby, where they checked their weapons and waited.

Half an hour later, Zabluda's team was ten steps below the exhibit deck entrance and out of sight. He sent a text to Ipatiev.

In the lobby, Ipatiev's team entered the elevator, and he pushed the button for the observation deck. As soon as they began their ascent, a Secret Service spotter on the observation deck radioed the dead lobby guards.

In his earpiece, Ipatiev heard, "I hear the elevator. What's going on?"

"Just coming up to get a quick photo of the crowd. Okay?" replied Ipatiev in his best American accent.

There was a pause. "Come on. There are thousands out there."

As the elevator approached the observation deck at the top of the monument, Ipatiev texted Zabluda.

The Exhibit Deck

Three Secret Service spotters were on break. One was seated on a bench just inside, and to the left of, the deck entrance. A thermos bottle and a silent portable radio sat on the bench beside him. He had been listening to speeches broadcast from The Ellipse. A second spotter stood facing him, his back to a large exhibit that concealed one wall of the elevator shaft.

The standing spotter asked, "Why'd you turn the radio off, man?"

"Did you hear that shit, 'trial by combat'? How much time you think that corner-office draft dodger spent outside the wire?"

The standing spotter smiled. "Do you count the time he stood outside a federal prison wire, watching the mobsters he put away being marched in?"

The smile disappeared as he glimpsed Zabluda entering and turned to face him. His eyes dropped to Zabluda's gun. He reached for his own. Zabluda shot him twice in the chest. The seated spotter dropped his coffee cup. That was as far as he got. The gunman behind Zabluda entered the room and shot him. The spotter slumped back against the wall and slid to the floor.

The third gunman came in behind Zabluda and the second shooter. He turned right and came face-to-face with the third spotter, who had been viewing an alcove display recounting the 2005 lightning strike on the monument. The spotter drew his gun while backing into the alcove for cover. Unfortunately, his legs were exposed due to the inward-sloping wall of the pyramid atop the monument. The gunman fired and hit both of the Secret Service spotter's legs. When he dropped to his knees, howling in pain, Zabluda finished him with a head shot.

"Check them," ordered Zabluda. He turned and dashed up the steps to the observation deck.

The Observation Deck

The Secret Service spotters on the observation deck were focused primarily on the two windows facing north. They provided a view of the crowd, the speakers' platform, and, farther in the distance, the South Lawn of the White House. A few minutes earlier, while Zabluda's team was still trudging upstairs to the exhibit deck, the Secret Service spotters saw a group of men break away from the rally at The Ellipse and head up the Mall toward the Capitol. One of the spotters moved to the two east-facing windows to follow the breakaways with his binoculars. At that moment, two things happened. Officers on the observation deck heard the unmistakable sound of suppressed shots being fired on the exhibit deck below. Also, they heard the doors open as the elevator reached their deck.

The elevator doors opened to the east, putting the officer watching the group moving toward the Capitol directly in Ipatiev's line of fire. He turned toward the elevator and Ipatiev shot him twice in the chest and once in the head. One gunman charged past Ipatiev and turned left toward the north-facing windows where they expected most of the spotters to be. He was killed by three bullets from the second spotter's gun. Ipatiev shot the spotter and shifted his gun toward the last one, who dodged toward the west windows, putting the elevator shaft between him and Ipatiev. Unfortunately, he had maneuvered himself into the gunsights of Ipatiev's third gunman who had gone to the right toward the west windows when he exited the elevator. The gunman fired four times and the last spotter fell. The fight was over before Zabluda could charge up the steps from the exhibit deck.

Zabluda surveyed the carnage and radioed the lobby. "I'm sending the elevator down with our casualty. Send up the equipment and bring Geller."

CHAPTER 51

January 6, 2021, 11:00 a.m.
Washington Monument Observation Deck

THE DRUG THEY shot into my arm was wearing off. I heard my name.

"He wants Geller on the observation deck," someone said.

I was lying faceup and strapped to an ambulance cot. I call it a gurney. It was one of those adjustable-level contraptions that allows the attendant to vary the height from about a foot off the floor to belt high on the average man. I was at the one-foot level. My wrists were flex-cuffed, as were my ankles. I pretended to be unconscious, watching the action through barely open eyelids. Glancing up, I saw a giant relief of George Washington's profile above elevator doors. Immediately, I knew I was in the Washington Monument. *What the hell am I doing here?*

Two men in dark blue jackets with EMT patches raised my gurney to waist level and pushed it—with me—into the elevator. They had unusual medical instruments, belt-holstered Glocks. Maybe they ministered only to terminal patients. They abandoned me momentarily to load equipment: a portable generator, a huge plastic container of water, an oversized attaché case, gun case, and canvas bags that went clunk when they hit the floor. Up we went.

The elevator doors opened on to the observation deck. I had been there in 2011, just before an earthquake damaged the monument.

A voice I recognized said, "Put him over there." It was Konstantine Zabluda, Russian assassin. Years ago, Rodney told me he was a double agent, working for the CIA. My curiosity and my stress hit new highs.

The observation deck is a cramped, hollow cube with an elevator shaft in the middle. Exiting the elevator puts you just a few steps from the nearest two windows. There are eight—four on each side—in cramped, U-shaped cubbyholes. There wasn't much space for me. The EMTs parked my gurney and me outside a corner storage room between the north and west walls, facing north, and lowered my gurney back to floor level.

I could see into the cubbyholes for the two windows facing north, overlooking the rally on The Ellipse. The center of activity on the deck was the north-facing window farthest from me. That's where they dropped most of the equipment that had come up on the elevator with me.

EMT-1—I gave them numbers because they weren't using names, just snapping fingers to get attention—EMT-1 opened a canvas bag and removed a big handheld, electric-powered saw, minus the blade.

Zabluda glanced at one of the north-facing windows marked with a big red "x" and gave the saw a skeptical look. "The window is made of four-inch ballistic glass. Are you sure that saw can do the job?"

EMT-2 opened the oversized attaché case. From the padded interior, he lifted a flat circular disc the size of a large skillet. "This is a diamond blade. It's used for rescue operations. We can cut a hole in this stone wall, if you want one."

"That won't be necessary. Just do the window and quickly." Zabluda glanced at his watch. "CROSSFIRE will begin his speech soon."

Until then, I had lost track of time, but that's when I knew I was attending Ted Walldrum's rally. It was not a good feeling. I didn't think those guys had kidnapped, drugged, and brought me up there to drop water balloons on the president's supporters.

EMT-1 attached the blade to the saw, connected a water hose to the nozzle on top of the blade housing, and ran the hose to the water container. Then, he donned protective clothing consisting of a Kevlar jacket and pants, heavy gloves, rubber boots, a face shield, and helmet.

EMT-2 removed large pads from two bags and laid them on the floor in front of the window. He told Zabluda, "The saw is water-cooled. These pads absorb the runoff, but it might get messy and dangerous when he starts the cut. You want to go down to the exhibit deck until he's finished?"

"I'll stay," said Zabluda, putting on a face shield. I didn't get one.

Before the cutting began, Zabluda pulled me off the gurney and dragged me by my shirt collar to the northeast corner of the deck. He sat on a folding cloth stool next to me where he could watch the window removal operation. I was still gagged, and my hands and ankles were flex-cuffed.

Zabluda looked angry. I thought he might throw a punch. Finally, he said, "Two years ago, I warned you we would find you. A prudent man would have gotten off the grid after you almost ruined my career and got your five million back. Why didn't you?"

He took the gag out of my mouth. "I did."

"Antarctica is off the grid. Anybody could find you in Sydney, Australia." Zabluda glanced at the EMTs and turned back to me. "What happened to the evidence you collected on Ted Walldrum's ties to the Kremlin?"

"It went into a Washington black hole."

Zabluda grunted. "Washington gets more like Moscow every day. What did you expect?"

"Justice."

"You wanted Walldrum destroyed, but you couldn't get it done. Now, I'm here to do it for you. Life is irony, don't you think?"

I was thinking, I might kill somebody today, but it won't be Walldrum. I said, "I thought Walldrum was Moscow's friend. Why are you here to kill him?"

"In geopolitics, there are no friends, only mutual interests. Walldrum lost the election. Moscow's interest in him has changed."

"Why am I here?"

"You tried so hard to collect evidence that would destroy Walldrum, it's only fitting that you should get the credit for killing him."

EMT-2 fired up the generator and plugged the saw cord into the outlet. EMT-1 flipped the on switch and proceeded to cut the rectangular window almost completely out of its frame, while the nozzle mounted on the blade guard kept a steady stream of cooling water on the glass. The water ran down the window, flowed across the stone wall below the window, and was absorbed into the floor pads. The saw made a hell of a noise, and I was hoping someone in the rally crowd below would hear it and tell a cop. That didn't happen.

When the window was cut on three sides, EMT-2, the saw operator's assistant, attached two barbell-looking devices to the glass. Each one had a suction cup at either end, joined by a handle. While the saw operator completed the final cut, the assistant held onto the suction cup devices to keep the glass from falling five hundred feet to the ground below. After the cut was completed, EMT-1 put the saw on the floor and grabbed the handle of one of the suction cup sets and helped his assistant remove the slab of glass from the frame. They carried it to one of the east-facing windows and placed it on the floor.

As soon as the glass was removed, our ears were assaulted by the din of the rally rising from The Ellipse. That was accompanied by a blast of cold air that dropped the deck's temperature to frigid. I was still wearing the shirt and pants I had on when the fake messenger hit me with the stun gun. That outfit was not designed for Washington's

January weather, five hundred feet above ground level. I was instantly chilled to the bone.

There wasn't much time left for explanations. I shouted to Zabluda, "Why did you kill Vanessa? She was a bystander."

Zabluda ignored me and told the EMTs, "It's almost time. Get those pads out of the way, dry the floor, and move the gurney to the window."

The EMTs dried the floor with leaf blowers and pushed my gurney to the window. Ipatiev came into my field of vision. I recognized him from my two-years-ago encounter with Zabluda. He supervised the EMTs as they cranked the gurney up until it was slightly above the windowsill. They locked the wheels and blocked them with rubber wedges. The gurney was about two feet wide and took up most of the space in the window's cubbyhole. I realized it was going to be Zabluda's shooting platform.

Ipatiev was monitoring a radio. He removed the earpiece, put the radio on the floor, and turned up the volume to hear the chatter. There wasn't much, but I could tell it came from Secret Service agents. Ipatiev greeted me with a nasty smile as he pulled on surgical gloves. He opened the gun case and removed a rifle with a mounted scope and sound suppressor, wiped it down, and laid it carefully on the gurney, next to a handheld ballistic computer.

Zabluda joined him in the cramped window alcove and said, "Bring Geller over here." The EMTs, now out of their protective gear, lifted me by my arms, dragged me across the floor, and pushed me into a sitting position, back against the elevator wall, near the gurney.

"Cut his hands loose and hold him," ordered Zabluda.

One of the EMTs cut the flex-cuffs from my wrists and twisted my left arm up behind my back to a painful angle. Ipatiev sat on my right shoulder and pulled my right arm between his legs. Zabluda donned surgical gloves, grabbed the rifle, and came to me. While Ipatiev held my wrist in a tight grip, Zabluda wrapped my fingers around the rifle so that my prints were on the trigger, stock, scope, and sound suppressor. He returned the rifle to the cot, brought three bullets to me, and forced my fingerprints onto those. Zabluda loaded the bullets into the rifle's magazine and got my prints on that, too.

One of the EMTs began packing equipment and moving it into the elevator.

Zabluda said, "Get Geller's fingerprints on the saw and leave it."

The EMT and Ipatiev gave me another fingerprint hand job.

Time was running out for me. Again, I asked, "Why did you kill Vanessa, Zabluda?"

He came over and squatted down to look into my face. "Did you feel pain when you heard of her death?"

"Of course."

"Then you felt what I felt when I was told an American sniper had killed my son in Syria."

"Your son was a soldier. Vanessa was—"

"A spy! There is no difference."

"Nobody is going to believe I pulled off this operation by myself."

"In time, you are correct, but they are going to find your dead body slumped over the rifle that fired the shot. You will have been shot by a courageous Secret Service officer, as his last act of patriotism. By the time your government finishes all the forensics and the diagrams, you will be who the public remembers. Americans love a lone gunman theory. Maybe your CIA colleagues helped you pull it off." He stood and looked down at me. "Now, shut up or I'll have you gagged."

My anger was boiling, but I was helpless.

Zabluda told the EMTs, "Cuff him and radio the rest of the team to leave the building, except the guards at the front door."

The EMT driver asked, "You want us to wait in the ambulance?"

"No. Go down to the exhibit deck and make sure all of the Secret Service spotters are dead. We leave no living witnesses. Then, come back up here."

As the EMTs left, President Ted Walldrum was introduced and a deafening roar went up from The Ellipse. The mob began chanting.

Zabluda climbed onto the gurney and flattened himself behind the rifle, barrel pointed down and resting on a partially filled sandbag. He peered through the scope. To Ipatiev, he said, "This height gives me a better angle than I had in Mexico. It should be an easy head shot."

Standing in a corner next to the gurney, Ipatiev surveyed the target with his spotter scope and began the drill. "Lock and load."

Zabluda inserted the magazine into his rifle and chambered a round.

Ipatiev: "Go to target."

Zabluda: "Man on platform, behind the podium, in black coat and gloves, facing south."

Ipatiev: "That's your target. Distance: 658 meters," 720 yards. "Check parallax and mills."

Zabluda adjusted his parallax knob and began milling. When his crosshairs were on the target, he announced the mills.

Ipatiev confirmed: "On target. Check level."

Zabluda checked the anti-cant device on his rifle to be sure it was level and his crosshairs were on the target.

Ipatiev gave Zabluda the holdover calculations from the ballistic computer, telling him how far above the target to aim his shot to counter the pull of gravity on the bullet.

Zabluda exhaled and took up the slack in his trigger and announced, "Ready."

With as much power as I could summon, I rammed the ambulance gurney with both feet. The rifle discharged as it kicked up and to the left.

Instantly, the Secret Service radio Ipatiev had been monitoring came alive. An agent called his operations center. "This is Station Fourteen. I think I've got a WINCHESTER."

Given that Zabluda had just fired a shot, I guessed WINCHESTER was code for, "Someone just took a shot at the president."

The operations center controller was not pleased. He shouted, "All stations, stand down! We do *not* have a confirmed WINCHESTER. Break. Station Fourteen, what do you mean, you *think* you have a WINCHESTER?"

"Something kicked up a divot on the South Lawn twenty yards from the White House. It could have been a bullet."

"It could have been a fucking gopher. POTUS will go apeshit if we pull him off the stage for a gopher sighting! Get your ass down there with a metal detector. If you find a bullet, call me. If you don't, stay the hell off the net."

As the shot went wild, I rolled closer to the left side of the gurney and kicked it again with all my strength. The rifle fell on my side of the gurney. Zabluda fell to the other, crashing into Ipatiev, taking them both to the floor. I heard a whack as his head hit the stone wall. Zabluda yelled and went silent. I saw him go limp on top of Ipatiev.

The rifle was in reach, but I couldn't operate it in cuffs. The power saw was on the floor behind me. I rolled to it, switched it on, and let the blade cut through the flex-cuffs. I grabbed the saw and freed my legs.

Ipatiev was untangling himself from a groggy Zabluda, but his right arm was pinned. Ipatiev reached across his body with his left hand and pulled his gun from its holster. He was going to get a shot before I could drop the saw and grab the rifle. As his left hand came free with the gun, I lunged at him with the saw. He shrieked as the 16-inch diamond blade cut through his forearm. Blood spurted everywhere. His gun hand—still holding the gun—slid across the floor, out of reach. He screamed curses in Russian, freed his right hand, and squeezed his left forearm, trying to stop the blood flow.

The screams must have revived Zabluda. Pinned in the corner, he struggled to his feet and used the gurney as a barrier to keep me and the saw away. Using the gurney as a battering ram, he tried to shove me backwards, past the generator, so he could cut power to the saw. I dropped the saw and pushed the gurney at him, forcing him back into the corner with Ipatiev.

Ipatiev was still screaming and cursing. He had torn off his belt to make a tourniquet for his arm, but his blood was everywhere. Zabluda slipped in it, trying to get a foothold. The rifle was on my side of the gurney. If I could let go of the gurney and grab the rifle, I might be able to kill them both.

Pinned in the corner, Zabluda saw my eyes dart toward the rifle. Without warning, he did a Bruce Lee, jumping straight up and landing, feet apart, on the gurney. Instinctively, I swung both arms, fingers locked, in a sweeping motion, like I was swinging a bat, knocking his feet from under him. He slid toward the open window, clawing at the gurney, his hands sliding over the bloody footprints he had just made. In desperation, he grabbed the stone sill, his body dangling out of the window.

As his bloody fingers slowly lost their grip, he yelled, "Geller, help me!"

"You killed Vanessa."

"I saved you in Moscow, two years ago!"

"You saved me so you could steal my money and put a target on my back, but you did save me. Here's some wisdom to take with you to hell, 'No good deed goes unpunished.'"

I watched, as his bloody fingers slid over the windowsill, and he fell five hundred feet to the pavement.

The commotion on the observation deck, especially Ipatiev's screams, had not gone unnoticed on the exhibit deck below. I heard feet rushing up the steps. A voice behind me yelled, "Geller, freeze!" It was one of the EMTs.

I thought of lunging for Ipatiev's gun, still in his severed hand. Too far away.

The EMT said, "Pick up the rifle and go to the window."

They wanted to make it look like I was at the window, with the rifle, when the Secret Service spotter shot me.

I reached down to get the rifle and I heard four muted shots behind me. I turned. There stood Tony-D and Jill Rucker with smoke curling out of their silencers. The EMTs were on the floor.

Tony-D said, "Explanations later! Let's get the hell out of here!"

"Unfinished business first. Give me your gun." He did.

I turned to Ipatiev and said, "This is for Vanessa." I shot him in the gut and the forehead.

CHAPTER 52

January 6, 2021, 1:30 p.m.

WITH A BIT too much satisfaction, Tony-D reminded me, "Max, I saved your ass twice this year. I'd ask for a raise, if I wasn't already overcharging you." We were headed east on Route 50, out of Washington, D.C. He took his eyes off the road briefly to give me a friendly smile.

I didn't smile back. The observation deck adrenaline was wearing off and I was sinking fast into depression. "How did you find me, Tony?"

"By following Rodney, as you requested. Two days ago, he leaves Fort Meade and stops at a filling station outside the gate. The guy at the next pump is topping off a delivery van. He and Rodney have a conversation. Then, the van follows Rodney all the way out to a condo near Dulles Airport. Rodney slows but keeps going. The van guy honks and pulls to the curb. He goes to a condo, rings the bell, and who answers the door? Maxwell Geller. The delivery guy pops you with the stun gun. Two hoods jump out of the van, throw you in the back, and they are into the wind, before I can say, 'kidnapping in progress.'

"I followed the van to a house in Alexandria. While I'm watching the place, I look up the condo where you were snatched. It belongs to Jill Rucker. Are you two . . . ?"

"No. I'm just renting a couple of rooms till the end of the month."

Tony-D continued. "Anyway, I'm sitting there watching and trying to decide if I should call the cops, when a platoon of muscle leaves. No sign of you, but one of the guys leaving is our old enemy, Zabluda. So, this is definitely not a job for cops. This is a big boys' game. I'm thinking, if I can get another gun or two, I can take the house early the next morning, catch them with their socks off, and spring you. My usual crew is out of town, so I called Jill and Sherri. Sherri comes but is not thrilled. Jill is pissed, pumped, and freaked. I think she's got a thing for you, man."

"Tony . . ."

"Okay. So, next morning, the three of us are minutes from taking down this Alexandria house and up comes an ambulance. The EMTs take you out on a stretcher and drive to a D.C. hotel garage, near the monument. They are joined by a National Park Service truck with two more guns. No opportunity to rescue you there. We followed the ambulance to the monument and waited 'til some of the muscle left. Then, we took down the phony National Park guys in the lobby and got up to the observation deck in time to see you doing the Texas chainsaw thing."

"That was a lot of trouble. Thank you."

"'Ain't nuthin' but a party,' a friend used to say."

"Where are Jill and Sherri?"

"You don't need to know."

"What I do need is a place to hide out for a while."

"I figured. I'm taking you to my place in Annapolis. Stay 'til you're ready to leave. No charge."

"Where is Rodney?"

"As of yesterday, out of town on business for three weeks, according to his office. I guess he wanted to have an alibi for that caper at the Washington Monument. He has an office in Reston, but he's all over the map, the Pentagon, NSA, FBI headquarters. Why am I following this roving ambassador of ill-will? Is Rodney hiding from somebody?"

"Me."

"Why?"

"He played a nasty trick on me. The director exiled him to keep us apart, but I owe him. Is he sleeping in his Georgetown house?"

"Sometimes. Sometimes not. Depends on where he's working for the day or if he gets lucky at the Mayflower bar."

"Any pattern?"

"You don't need one. I put a tracker on his car."

"What about the EMTs and the lobby guards . . . their bodies?"

"What bodies." Tony-D winked.

That told me all I needed to know about what Jill and Sherri were up to.

CHAPTER 53

January 20, 2021, 6 p.m.
The Reichsbruecke Bridge, Vienna, Austria

THE DOUBLE AGENT who had sent Zabluda to Washington from the Moscow rifle range walked slowly across the bridge. He passed Rodney with a glance and asked, "Am I clean?"

"Yes. You have no tails. My men have been watching your back since you left the hotel." Rodney joined him and they walked together. "How are you?"

"I'm well," said the agent. "I have a name for you, a potential replacement for Zabluda as my courier to you." The agent gave Rodney a slip of paper. "He's a diplomat with a weakness for too-young girls, I'm told. That weakness could be exploited."

"I'll look into it. Is this why you came to Vienna?"

"I'm attending a conference."

"Cover still intact with the Kremlin crowd, then?"

"They wouldn't let me travel on my own if they had doubts, but I'm sure they have bugged my hotel room and phone for insurance. And there is the occasional SVR thug skulking about."

The subject was irritating. He moved on. "What happened in Washington? I've heard no news of an attempt on the president's life."

"It didn't go well. Geller had help. They took out the entire assassination team and left Zabluda and Ipatiev to be found. The vehicles and the rest of the unit—EMTs and fake National Park Service guides—are missing. Luckily, the men were hard-core mercenaries. We concealed their employer. So, there have been no family inquiries."

"What about the Secret Service officers?"

"The White House cover story is that they were killed in an undercover operation against a counterfeiting ring. The president doesn't want to go to war with Russia during his last days in office."

"The Secret Service is going along with that?"

"They don't want a war either, not over a lame duck president who doesn't want to pursue the issue. Also, there's the potential for negative publicity. How could eight Secret Service officers have been killed less than a mile from the White House and no one held accountable?"

"In a way, this news is a relief," admitted the agent. "I thought Zabluda had abandoned the mission because he discovered the order to assassinate Walldrum came from the CIA, not the Kremlin."

"No. He went to his death believing what you told him, that he was doing his part for Mother Russia. Promising him a promotion and care for his son's career was a nice touch. By the way, the director sends her congratulations on that masterful bit of misdirection."

The agent enjoyed a satisfied smile. "I assume the rifle with Geller's fingerprints was not recovered?"

"It was not. Geller was thorough. Investigators found no evidence that he was ever in the Washington Monument on January 6."

"Maybe you should rehire him. He's a clever fellow."

"He's a pain in my ass. Anyway, he doesn't need a job and the frayed condition of our relationship wouldn't permit that." Rodney changed the subject. "Any idea when you want us to bring you out?"

"Maybe in a year or two. We'll see how your new president fares. He may need my help."

"Thank you. Those who are allowed speak highly of your product and your courage."

"Really? What do they call me at Langley?"

"Affectionately, Source Ivan."

Source Ivan smiled. "Until next time, then." He left Rodney standing at the end of the bridge.

CHAPTER 54

February 2021
Washington, D.C., Capital Yacht Club Dock, Aboard the Yacht Envy

THE GUN GREW heavy in my hand as I waited. Rodney came aboard after work on a Friday.

He entered by the aft door and descended the few steps into the lounge-galley where I was sitting. It was dark. He didn't notice me until he flipped the light switch.

"What the hell are you doing here! And in a wetsuit, dripping water on my upholstery?" He answered his question before I could. "You swam to my boat. Couldn't you pick the dock lock?"

I said, "Take off your coats and show me that you're not armed."

Rodney removed his overcoat and suit coat and laid them neatly on a bench. He raised his arms and made a full turn for me.

"Now, the ankles."

He pulled up each trouser leg. No ankle holster.

"Sit down, over there."

Rodney eased into the table nook across the cabin from me and clasped his hands together on the tabletop.

I scanned the cabin. "I like what you've done with the boat. Bullet holes plugged, blood cleaned up, bodies removed. Ni-i-ice."

"Maybe you should've cleaned it after you killed those men."

"I heard the FBI liked you for that hit, your fingerprints being all over their belongings."

"You tricked me, and I was cleared. What do you want?"

"I'd like something else cleared up about you, Petrov, and the RAMPART operation. Let me run the RAMPART scenario by you. Tell me if I have it right. Petrov goes to his old Cairo drinking buddy, Colonel Burke, our army attaché in Moscow. He says, 'I'm a war plans officer at the Russian Defense Ministry. The army is sending me back into combat. I have post-traumatic stress. I'd rather go to hell than go to war again. I want to defect. Help me and I'll give you Russia's war plan for Syria.'

"To prove he could deliver, Petrov gave Burke a thumb drive of secret documents. 'But,' he says, 'I want Max Geller to bring me out. He's the best. I don't trust the CIA guys in Moscow.' Burke sends the message and documents to you at Langley. Is that how it went down?"

"Essentially, yes." Rodney examined his fingernails.

"Then, you sent Petrov a message. 'Great! We'll get you out as soon as we find Geller. He doesn't work for the CIA anymore.'"

"I did."

"I don't believe you. Know what I would have told Petrov?"

"I'm sure you're going to tell me."

"I would have said, 'Thank you, Colonel Petrov. Your knowledge and experience would be invaluable to the CIA, but . . . we don't give a shit about Syria. Our politicians and the Pentagon have written Syria off. Go back to your ministry and bring me something juicy that makes snatching you off a Moscow street worth the risk and the diplomatic blowback. Bring me Russia's plans for attacking NATO or Ukraine. How about the cyberwar plan for attacking the U.S. homeland?' That's what I—or any CIA officer who wasn't sleepwalking—would have told him, but not you, not the master spy. You pulled him out to get a worthless war plan for Syria."

Rodney pressed his lips together and looked away.

"I have an alternate theory of how the RAMPART operation kicked off."

"You have the floor . . . and the gun."

"Here's what I think really happened. You didn't send Petrov back for something juicy, because he gave you the juice in his first message. Petrov was smart. He knew what would get Langley salivating. He told you the Russians were planning a big military operation against NATO. I'm guessing he told you it would be in the fall, but if you wanted to know the details of where and when, you had to get him out. Yet, you waited months before sending me to Moscow. Why? I think it was because you needed time to plan something."

"Plan what?"

"A coup, because getting the White House out of the decision loop was the only way the CIA and the Pentagon could be sure the United States would back NATO against the Russians."

Rodney gave me a derisive chuckle. "You are out of your mind."

"Am I? When Petrov sent you word of the attack, you knew he was offering you a gift dipped in poison. You had the intelligence scoop of a lifetime, advance warning of a Russian attack on NATO. The problem was if you accepted the gift too soon, the Agency and the Pentagon would have to tell Walldrum, and nobody wanted to take that intel to our Russia-friendly president. There's no telling what he would have done with it.

"So, the Agency and the Pentagon needed a plan to cut the White House out of the chain of command before the attack. You needed time to set that up. How? When? Who to read in? Who to leave out? Who did you need to make the plan work? Who would cooperate? Who wouldn't? You, the CIA director, General McClure, and whoever gamed it. That's why months went by before you sent me to bring Petrov out."

I knew I had it right. Rodney's dismissive attitude was melting. He was paying attention.

I continued to press it. "During the planning, it dawned on somebody in your group that Americans wouldn't tolerate a coup, well-intentioned or not. When Congress and the newspapers and the public discovered what you had done, they'd want someone's head. You needed a fall guy to take the blame. I'm pretty sure that's when you offered me up."

"You're delusional. Have you forgotten the Heidelberg operation? We needed time to get a face and prints that would get you into Russia. And we had to find you."

"You could have snatched any Russian hood off the streets who resembled me. Europe is crawling with GRU and SVR agents. I think Heidelberg just fell into your lap and you included it in your scheme at the last minute. That's why you rushed me from Australia to Germany.

"As for me being hard to find, even a junior officer like Jill said, 'Max, you were predictable. With money in the bank and no job, anybody with a brain knew you would go to Vanessa.'"

Rodney shook his head slowly in denial or annoyance. "You've got it all wrong. I didn't pick you, Petrov picked you. We planned around that."

"I'll never know who picked me. Petrov's dead and you're an incurable liar. What I do know—and what you knew—is that Max Geller had the perfect profile to take the fall when the coup was exposed. I'm a disgruntled former CIA employee, fired for criticizing President Walldrum. No one would be surprised that I was plotting against the White House or to find me dead and my prints on a rifle that fired shots at the president. Revenge was my motive. Case closed. As a bonus, I knew some of the key people you needed to pull off your coup. So, my name goes to the top of the fall guy list. I become the face and name of your conspiracy."

Rodney was indignant. "Nobody tricked you into participating. After you delivered Petrov, you were free. You could've walked away when the director asked you to go to Fort Detrick, but you didn't. You wanted to be a player again, just like you used to be at the Agency."

"I went to that meeting because the director promised to mentor Vanessa."

Rodney scoffed. "Tell yourself that, if that's what you need to hear. You went to pump your ego. What were you thinking? The director of the CIA needed you—and only you—to babysit her in a meeting with some of the best minds in Washington? Max Geller, the only one who can tell all those smart people that they had to cut the White House out of the action in order to deal with the Russian attack. You can't be that naïve."

Rodney became energized. "You weren't the victim of a conspiracy; you were a willing participant. You participated because you're a patriot. Everyone knows that about you, even people who don't like you. Two years ago, you followed up the leads in the Ironside Dossier and nailed Walldrum for what he was, a Russian puppet. So, you knew, better than anyone, that Walldrum had to be removed from the chain of command. If he had turned his back on NATO when Russia attacked, that would have destroyed our international security alliances, built up since World War II! It would have destroyed our system of government, too. You know that!"

It was rare for Rodney to become so animated. He smoothed his hair and composed himself. "On Fridays, I normally have a drink and a cigar to celebrate surviving the week. Do you mind?" He glanced at my gun. "Or am I being premature?"

I nodded. Rodney went to the cabinet above the sink, took out a brandy snifter, and poured himself a stiff Cognac. He inhaled the aroma and set it aside. Out came the cigar box. Rodney opened it. I enjoyed watching his self-satisfied expression dissolve into disappointment.

He looked up at me. "You took my gun. It seems I made a habit of underestimating you."

"It's not a habit. It's a mistake. I found the other one, too. Enjoy the brandy . . . while you can."

Rodney returned to the table with brandy and sat down heavily. He said, "There's something you should know. Our group was out of options when we couldn't get the vice president to resign or involve the Speaker. Your suggestion to use Senator Dodson and the football saved us. It was a stroke of pure genius. You'll go down in the Agency's secret history for it."

That was a history I would never read, thanks to him.

Rodney looked sad. "You're disappointed in us—me. Yet, you volunteered for the CIA, just as you volunteered for the coup. What did you expect from us, thrift, cleanliness, and fair play? The Agency was created for dirty tricks and deniability. You joined to partake of that culture and you did. You just didn't expect to be on the receiving end of the trickery. So, what do you want? Revenge? Absolution . . . for what had to be done? Forget it. Forgive yourself. Forgive others. Move on."

He took a long pull on the Cognac. I let him drink and talk to lower his guard.

"Tell me, Max, what would you have done in my shoes, put Petrov's intel in the PDB?" He was referring to the president's daily briefing.

"I don't fault you for what you did, Rodney. In your shoes, I would have tried to circumvent the White House, too. I fault you for not having the guts to stand up afterwards and say, 'Yes. I did it because it had to be done. The president is a Russian lackey.' If you're so keen on saving the system, trust that system to judge what you did."

Rodney smiled. "And spend the rest of my life in prison for sedition? No thank you. The system is good, but it's flawed and often unforgiving."

I was tired of political philosophy. "Did you have Vanessa killed?"

He looked surprised by the question. "Absolutely not. I had no quarrel with her. I suspect killing her was Zabluda's way of making you pay for ruining his career or exacting some misdirected revenge for the death of his son at the hands of one of our snipers. He went a little crazy after that."

"You wanted Zabluda to kill the president and frame me. Why?"

"Wherever did you get an idea like that?"

I took the waterproof bag from my wetsuit and tossed it to him. It contained photographs of him, at the gas station, talking to the man who kidnapped me at Jill's condo. Rodney examined the photos and let them fall to the floor. He was deflated and out of lies. It was a tired voice that asked, "How?"

"Tony-D has been following you since the director reassigned you from the Langley campus. The Russians didn't attack. So, again, I ask you: Why did you want Walldrum killed and me framed for his death?"

Rodney made a face. "Ted Walldrum was a cancer on the body politic. He needed to be removed."

"He needed removal two years ago. Why three weeks before he was due to leave office?"

"It was more complicated than that. Killing Walldrum was a way to tie up many loose ends. Zabluda was our courier for Source Ivan and wanted to terminate his relationship with us after his son was killed. We worried that, one day, Zabluda might reveal Ivan's identity. To prevent that, we were going to kill him, after he killed you and Walldrum. Two birds, one stone."

Rodney exhaled heavily and said, "Then, there's you, the third bird. Let us count the ways your very existence is troubling. You're the only person outside of government who knows that Source Ivan exists. Like Zabluda, you might—for some reason—disclose that to . . . your newspaper friend, Stan, for instance. You're also the only non-government person who knows what happened to the incriminating material on Walldrum. A few highly placed Washington officials don't sleep well, knowing you are privy to those secrets.

"Finally, there is this boat." Venom dripped from his words. "You killed men here and framed me for their deaths. Before that, I was on the fast track for top leadership in the Agency. The investigation cleared my name, but not the air. That shooting surfaced every time I was considered for promotion . . . and not selected. Your stunt derailed my career. Since you framed me, I thought it poetic justice that you should get the blame for assassinating Walldrum."

At that moment, I realized the depth of Rodney's hate for me. I couldn't believe he was not involved in Vanessa's murder. Her death was the thing that hurt me most . . . and Rodney wanted badly to hurt me. That knowledge was disorienting, but I tried to focus on the specifics of the boat incident.

"You sent those men here to kill me! I shot them in self-defense."

"Before I sent them, I warned you. I asked you for the evidence linking Walldrum to Moscow. Jill begged and even tried to kill you for it. You were determined to sell to the highest bidder. You were a mercenary who could expose one of the most valuable assets the Agency's ever had. What did you expect me to do, play nice? You became—and remain—an annoying inconvenience."

"What about the Secret Service agents who died in the Washington Monument, thanks to your assassination scheme? Were they an inconvenience, too?"

"They were paid to take a bullet for the president, and they took it." Rodney shrugged. "On the day in question, they were lookouts. They should have looked out."

His indifference made me angry and nauseated. "Any scotch in that cabinet?"

Rodney stared at me for a time, before he went to the liquor cabinet. I left my gun on the sofa and followed him. As he reached up to open the door, I took his cigar box gun from my pocket and fired a bullet into his right temple. He fell to the floor and looked up at me briefly, before his eyes rolled back. I used a dishtowel to wipe my prints from the gun and wrapped his fingers around the .32 automatic he loved.

That was the first time I had killed with premeditation for revenge. Revenge is not sweet. It is a bitter end at a void that can never be filled. It doesn't bring back a lost love, or repair a reputation, or reclaim a life trajectory that could have been. The purpose of revenge is to restore the cosmic balance so that the scales of justice are not forever tilted in favor of evildoers, and the counterweight borne for eternity by the hearts and souls of victims.

I went out into the darkness, eased over the side, and swam away.

AUTHOR'S NOTE

THE FIRST MAX Geller novel was *The President's Dossier*. Some readers viewed the book (or the author) as having a political agenda. That is simply not true. However, I don't let news or politics keep me from writing an intriguing story that would interest readers. For me, the best spy thrillers are plausible, based on known facts or suspicions. While I love a good conspiracy theory, the trick is not to abandon reality to follow it down a rabbit hole where a tub of Jim Jones political Kool-Aid awaits. It's just entertainment, folks.

I wrote *The Blood of Patriots and Traitors* as a Max Geller story because readers asked for more of what they liked in *The President's Dossier*. Some wanted to know if Max and Vanessa got together. Others asked about the fate of Zabluda, the villain, and his promise to track Max down and kill him. Many just liked Max and his crew as characters and wanted more of them. In such circumstances, the author's task is to give the reader more of the same, but make it different (the dream of all agents and publishers, and no easy task). More of the same was easy. Max joins Vanessa, goes back to Moscow, deals with the Omega group, gets chased by the FSB, puts his *Dossier* crew to work, and dramatically ends the Max-Zabluda conflict.

The hard part was answering two questions: (1) Why would Max—a man wanted in Russia—risk his life by returning to Moscow? and

(2) How do I make this story a continuation of *The President's Dossier*, using the same political context? The answers don't come while you're listening to Slash play the guitar cameo with Le Freak at Budokan. They come before dawn, when your pen is poised above a blank legal pad and a warm NASA coffee mug is nearby, its logo a stern reminder that, "Failure is not an option." That's when the Muse comes.

Please enjoy her gift.

ACKNOWLEDGMENTS

Many people made this book possible. Some are recognized here. All have my thanks.

Nelson DeMille and James Grady are thriller writers whose work first inspired me. Steve Berry and Jon Land gave me invaluable advice and their endorsements for the first Max Geller novel and for this one. Special thanks to James Grady—creator of the Condor character—who took a leap of faith. Cathy Palmer, the sole survivor of the book-in-a-box club, has supported me from the very first book. The Gross and Gardner families have always been in my corner with friendship, encouragement, and material support. On her deathbed, Ophelia made me promise to write through my grief. Barbara, my "cell mate" during two years of COVID lockdown, remains my cheerleader, advisor, politics junkie, and all-around special person. Her encouragement and advice were invaluable, as again, Max Geller and I descended into the shadowy worlds of spy fiction and harsh reality.

Kelly Gross (Lady Courage) is my friend and advisor on things Russian and German. Jay and Hannah Harris, Rebecca Shivvers, Betsy, Empress Jo, and Fred caught many of my mistakes, and provided encouragement and suggestions. I ignored some of their advice in pursuit of artistic expression. Hence, errors of commission and omission in this work are my responsibility. Maddie and Bef deserve my thanks for their artistry. I am most indebted to Pat and Bob Gussin and the Oceanview staff who made my dream of being a published writer come true. Finally, my thanks to the readers who purchased my books, posted reviews on the Amazon and Goodreads websites, and sent emails. Please continue posting your reviews and sign up for contests and my infrequent newsletter at https://jamesscottnovels.com (my website). Follow me on Facebook (James Scott Author) or Twitter (@scotty_jamesscott).

Best wishes to you all for good health and lots of good reading.

PUBLISHER'S NOTE

We hope that you enjoyed *THE BLOOD OF PATRIOTS AND TRAITORS,* the second in the Max Geller Spy Thriller Series.

The first in the series is *THE PRESIDENT'S DOSSIER.* The two novels stand on their own and can be read in any order. Here's more about *THE PRESIDENT'S DOSSIER*:

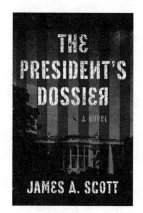

Is the U.S. president working for the Russians? Spy Max Geller is sent out to find evidence.

His assignment takes him on a dangerous covert-ops trip to Russia, tangled in the messy, incomprehensible world of Putin's regime. When he completes the mission, no one wants him back in. No one wants revealed what he knows about the U.S. President. Not the Russians. Not the CIA.

"Brimming with history, reality, intensity, and passion, James Scott draws the reader deep into his carefully crafted web. You're going to enjoy the pulse-pounding escapades."

—Steve Berry, *New York Times* best-selling author

We hope that you will enjoy reading *THE PRESIDENT'S DOS-SIER*, James A. Scott's prior novel, and that you will look forward to more to come.

For more information,
please visit https://jamesscottnovels.com.

If you liked *THE BLOOD OF PATRIOTS AND TRAITORS,* the author would be very appreciative if you would consider leaving a review. As you probably already know, book reviews are important to authors and they are very grateful when a reader makes the special effort to write a review, however brief.

Happy Reading,
Oceanview Publishing